NO LIMITS

NO SHAME SERIES BOOK 2

NORA PHOENIX

No Limits (No Shame Series Book 2) by Nora Phoenix

www.noraphoenix.com

PUBLISHER'S NOTE

1

The house was blissfully quiet, and Josh released a slow exhale. He'd curled up on the couch with a gay romance, snuggling under a velvety soft fleece blanket. December in New York, what a fucking nightmare. Wind cutting straight through your clothes to creep into your bones, flurries whipping around the house, with the forecast predicting more snow to come in the next few days —and winter hadn't even started yet. Couldn't Noah have found a hospital in, say, Florida to work at? Josh pulled the blanket up high, sighing as he dove back into his book.

The doorbell rang, and Josh almost jumped up. He took a deep, steadying breath before getting up to the hallway. He recognized him through the glass in the door, and his hand froze on the doorknob.

Connor.

The cop was not in uniform this time but sported olive-green cargo pants underneath his snow-dusted black winter jacket, a grey beanie protecting his head. Connor raised his hand in an awkward wave when he noticed Josh behind the door. What did he want now?

Josh opened the door. "Officer O'Connor," he said, his tone formal even though his pulse was speeding up.

The man was so fucking gorgeous, but Josh wasn't making a fool out of himself by assuming anything. Even if Noah and Indy were convinced the cop was gay and into him, Josh wasn't buying it. It had been three months since the robbery. If he'd been interested in Josh, Connor would've stopped by sooner. Josh couldn't blame the cop. No one would want to date a fuck-up like Josh, let alone a man as perfect as Connor.

"Call me Connor," the cop said. "Can I come in?"

Out of habit, Josh opened the door wide and let the man step inside. With Connor's massive body next to him, the hallway seemed small and crowded. Connor stomped his black boots to get rid of the snow, then took off his beanie and zipped his jacket open.

"How are you?" Josh asked, not quite able to keep the concern out of his voice. "Noah said you got hit by shards of concrete two months ago. Are you fully recovered?"

Connor blinked a few times. "I'm fine. They were minor cuts that healed quickly."

"Oh," Josh said. "That's good. And your partner?"

Something flashed in Connor's eyes. "Thanks to Noah, he's alive. It'll be a spell before he's back on the job, but that's not important."

A silence followed. Josh sighed inwardly. Was he supposed to say something? God, he sucked at social interactions like this. "Erm, Noah and Indy aren't home," he offered. *Connor thinks Indy is a woman,* he reminded himself. He'd better not fuck that up.

Connor jammed his hands into his pockets. Was he nervous as well? "That's okay. Actually, I wanted to talk to you."

"To me?"

"Could we maybe sit down?"

The confidence the cop had displayed on the previous two meetings had vanished. It was disconcerting, somehow. What was going on? Still, Josh nodded.

Connor took his jacket off and hung it on a coat hanger. *Stupid, you should have taken his jacket,* Josh berated himself. He was always too slow. Connor unlaced his boots, leaving them on the doormat, which Josh appreciated as it kept his floor clean.

Wordlessly, Josh gestured to the living room and followed Connor as he walked in. He was wearing a tight, black long sleeve shirt that accentuated every one of his powerful muscles. Josh couldn't deny himself a quick look at the guy's ass. Damn, the cop was packing a perfect, firm butt in those cargo pants. Well, everything about the cop was muscular and toned. Was he indeed gay, or had Noah and Indy been yanking his chain?

"Can I get you something to drink?" he asked, more out of politeness than expectations. "I have homemade lemonade?"

"You make your own lemonade?"

Josh shrugged. "Sure. Beats the overly sweet store-bought stuff."

"I'd like to try it."

Josh frowned as he poured two glasses of lemonade in the kitchen. The cop was off-duty, so what the hell was he doing here, and what did he want to talk to him about?

He put one glass on the coffee table in front of O'Connor who had found a spot on the sofa. Josh sat in one of the reading chairs and waited, clutching his own glass.

"Did Noah say anything?" Connor finally asked.

"About what?"

"About me, or what he and I talked about in the hospital?"

"No. He only told me you were hurt but that it wasn't serious, and that your partner needed surgery. Noah is serious about the privacy of his patients."

"Oh, okay." Connor dragged a hand through his hair, avoiding Josh's look. His hair was high and tight, though a tad longer than he would have worn it as a Marine. "I'd hoped he'd talked to you."

Josh's stomach was doing twists that were acutely uncomfortable, and his palms were getting sweaty. "You wanna maybe get to the point? You're making me nervous, and that's not a good thing for a guy with PTSD. Spit it out."

O'Connor looked as if he was in front of a firing squad. What the hell was bothering him? "I wanted to ask you out," he finally managed.

Josh barely avoided dropping his glass of lemonade, instead plunking it down on the table. Good thing they had thick, solid glassware. "You want to ask me out," he repeated stupidly.

"Yeah. Noah said it would be okay."

"You want to ask me out," Josh said again, his slow-as-shit brain unable to come up with anything else.

Connor got up from the couch, stuffed his hands back in his pockets. "Look, I get it, okay? Apparently, your boyfriend has a nasty sense of humor. He told me you guys weren't really together, and that he wouldn't mind me asking you out. Joke's on me, okay? Very funny, haha. I'll leave now."

Josh's brain was frozen, unable to react. Connor wanted to ask him out? What the fuck? Why?

When his brain had rebooted, Connor was gone, closing the front door with an angry bang.

He'd fucked it up. This gorgeous man was interested in

him, though heaven knew why, and he'd fucked it up because his brain had been uncooperative again. And what was worse, Josh didn't even have his number.

Josh sagged backward in the chair. Why on earth would a man like Connor be interested in him? The guy knew he had PTSD, that he was basically a fuck-up, right? And what the hell had Noah been thinking, talking about him to Connor, telling him they weren't really together. Couldn't he at least have given Josh a heads-up?

He buried his head in his hands. He'd never find anyone. Not like Noah loved Indy. God, the two of them were amazing, if equally sickening at times. He wanted that, too.

Noah had changed—he was less angry, happier. And witnessing Indy's transformation from a frightened, skittish guy into a more relaxed, confident person was nothing short of amazing. Josh loved Indy with all his heart—how could anyone not love this sweet man? Noah and Indy made every effort to include him, let him still sleep with them, and Noah had fucked him a few times even after he was together with Indy. When Noah was tired or in pain and his control was thin, he chose Josh over Indy. Indy couldn't handle rough sex, and Josh, well, he got off on it. Which was embarrassing as fuck if he thought about it, but between the three of them there was no judgment. They each came with emotional scars.

Josh wanted that for himself, someone he could love and who loved him. Someone who would accept him being fucked up and would be okay with it. Someone who wouldn't judge his sexual desires...maybe even satisfy them?

He'd done research into the whole Dom/sub thing after what Indy had said, and boy, had that blown his mind. Most of it was too kinky to even consider or downright freaky. But some videos he'd watched had exhilarated him. He'd been completely turned on, had jacked himself off hard. Afterward, he'd felt like crap. His chances of finding someone who would do that with him, within a loving relationship, were practically zero. How the fuck would he ever find someone, sitting at home, scared as he was of going out? And who the hell would love a damaged fuck-up like him?

Connor is interested. Was. There was no way he'd still be, not after Josh had gone all awkward and weirdo on him with his silent treatment. Maybe if he explained that it wasn't intentional? But how the fuck could he manage that if he didn't even have his phone number?

BEING a cop had definite positive sides, but damn, Connor hated the shitload of paperwork involved. He sighed as he filled out an arrest report on his computer. He and his partner had caught a guy driving with at least three times the legal amount of alcohol in his system, plus some other as of yet undetermined substances. It had been a fucking miracle the guy had even been able to put his keys in the ignition. Thank God he'd hit a tree before crashing into another car, or worse, killing someone.

"O'Connor, visitor," Lucky shouted.

Connor looked up from his screen. Who would come and visit him here? He debated asking Lucky for a name, then shrugged. He might as well go see who it was. He rose from his chair, stretched his back and cracked his neck, before making his way to the front waiting room.

Lucky, the station's receptionist, indicated his visitor with a jerk of her chin, and Connor followed her gesture.

Josh.

His faded Pats cap hid most of his face, but Connor

would recognize him anywhere. He was sitting ramrod straight in one of the chairs, his eyes trained on the ground, a crumpled magazine in his hands.

Connor's heart skipped a beat. What was Josh doing here? Was he upset about the way Connor had left four days ago? It had been wicked rude, Connor admitted to himself, but he'd been so fucking humiliated. Disappointed, too, in Noah Flint. He'd thought the guy had morals, but apparently not.

He jammed his hands into the pockets of his uniform pants. "Josh," he said simply.

Josh's head shot up. He fumbled with the magazine in his lap, almost dropping it before putting it on the chair next to him. Avoiding Connor's eyes, he rose. "I was wondering if we could maybe talk somewhere? In private?"

"Yah. Sure. Lucky, is there a room free?"

Lucky checked her list. "Room 3, for about half an hour."

Connor nodded. They'd be done way before that, was his guess. After all, what was there left to say? "Thanks."

"Follow me," he said to Josh. Damn, he sounded way too professional, too emotionally closed off. Like Josh was a citizen who came to file a complaint. What else could he do? He refused to let Josh break him again.

Josh had been so shy and flustered, yet so adorable in that store. Connor had barely been able to do his job, too shaken to concentrate. All he could think of was please, let this guy be gay. He'd thought Josh was, but the dynamic between Josh and Indy had thrown him off. And when Indy confessed to kissing Josh, and he hadn't seemed like he minded, Connor had been convinced he'd been wrong. Josh had to be straight.

But even after that, he had to see him again, had to know for certain. And when he'd come to his house and Noah had claimed him as his boyfriend, Connor had been sure everyone would have been able to hear something break inside of him. Still, he'd tried again, had stupidly believed Noah when he'd told him Josh was available. How Josh had gotten under his skin that fast, he had no idea, but he was done. His heart was too damn fragile to handle another rejection from this man.

He led the way to the interrogation room, which was a fancy word for a small room with a table and four chairs. Out of habit, he made sure the recording equipment was turned off.

"Grab a seat," he said. "Do you want coffee?"

Fuck, he hoped not. His stomach swirled uncomfortably even thinking about the smell.

Josh lowered himself in one of the chairs. "No. I don't drink coffee."

Connor mentally shook his head. Why did Josh have to be so damn perfect? He took a seat across from him, let out a long breath. "What can I do for you?"

Josh winced. Was Connor's professionalism bothering him? Connor's heart softened. He had to take it easy on the guy. It wasn't his fault, and besides, he had PTSD. Not something to trifle with.

"What's wrong, Josh?" he asked more friendly.

For the first time, Josh looked up to meet his eyes. "You left," he said, sounding shocked, then jerked his head as if to shake himself out of something. His eyes cast down again.

"Are you okay?" Connor asked, his voice even warmer.

Josh clenched his fists, then released again. "Yeah. Sorta. I wanted to know why you walked out."

Connor sighed. He should not have left like that. It was rude, cowardly, and considering his issues a nasty thing to do to Josh. He should've had the balls to face him, talk it out.

"I'm sorry," he said. "I was mad, but I shoulda given you a chance to say something."

Josh raised his stunning blue eyes to meet Connor's, and it took Connor's breath away. Damn, the guy was so beautiful. Handsome, would be the manlier word, but it didn't fit Josh. He truly was beautiful, pushing all kinds of protective buttons inside Connor he hadn't even been aware of possessing.

"Because of either the PTSD or the meds I take, my brain is slow sometimes, especially when I'm surprised or shocked. It takes me a while to respond," Josh said, his eyes all but pleading with Connor to understand.

Connor winced. Damn, he should have known. He'd been a complete asshole. God, what a Charlie Foxtrot. "I'm so sorry. I should've given you the opportunity to respond. I thought you were making fun of me or trying to find a way to let me down gently."

Those blue eyes never left his. "I wasn't. I was shocked."

"Why?"

Josh was quiet for a bit, but Connor gave him time. "You're gay," Josh said. It wasn't a question, so much as a statement.

"Yes." Connor's tone was defensive. Did Josh realize how momentous this occasion was? He'd never admitted this to anyone, ever.

"Is that why you came to the house when you were looking for Indy, instead of calling? Because you liked me?"

What, were they playing twenty questions now? Wasn't it obvious? "I wasn't sure if you were gay."

Josh snorted. "Dude, your gaydar is worse than mine."

Connor relaxed, a smile tugging at his lips. "That's what Noah said."

"Nothing wrong with Noah's gaydar."

"Is he gay?" Connor asked, daring to broach the topic they kept avoiding. "Are you together or not?"

"He's with Indy now."

Connor managed to keep the shock off his face. Noah and Indy were together? Was Noah bisexual? Interestingly enough, Josh didn't seem upset about it. He'd said it factually, with love, even. "And you're okay with that."

"Mostly."

Connor needed to know. "But you are gay, though?"

"I am."

"That's good," Connor said, then cleared his throat. So much for playing it cool. Oh, fuck it, that ship sailed long ago. He might as well go all in. "Look, before we continue this conversation, can you at least say something?"

Josh tilted his head to the side, his nose crumpling, making him look adorably cute. "About what?"

Connor threw his hands up in the air. "About whether you like me back. You still haven't said a damn thing on how you feel about me, if you like me or not."

This time, Josh's answer came wicked fast. "You're hot and damn sexy, but I don't know you well enough yet to decide if I like you."

Connor's mouth dropped open slightly. "You think I'm sexy?"

Josh rolled his eyes. "Dude, you're built like a tank, you're as masculine as they come, you have the whole uniform thing going with a healthy dose of dominant macho and 'don't fuck with me' thrown in. You're, like, the wet dream of every bottom, including me."

This brutally honest confession was not what Connor had expected from sweet, shy Josh. To be fair, the guy seemed a little flustered once the words were out, as if he'd said more than he'd wanted to. But holy fuck, those words had lit a fire inside of Connor.

"I've never done this before," Connor said. "I've never been in a relationship, haven't even dated, so I have no idea what I'm doing here or how to do this."

Understanding dawned in Josh's eyes, taking away his previous embarrassment, which was exactly what Connor had intended. He had this baffling urge to make Josh feel better. "You're not out," Josh said.

"No."

"But you've had..." Josh's voice trailed off, but Connor had no trouble filling in the blanks. Sex. Josh was asking him to share the most humiliating thing in his life. Hell, no. He'd rather go through hell week all over again.

"That's a little personal, don't you think?" he said.

Josh shook his head. "No, that's not how this works. I don't do secrets. You wanna get to know me, you need to talk. I watched through my telescope as Noah got blown up by that fucking IED, and I spent two weeks in a closed ward afterward because I couldn't process my feelings, couldn't talk about it. Still can't. Talking is hard for me, but that's why Noah and I have made it a rule. I know we're saps, discussing our feelings and shit, but it has helped me slowly get better. You need to get down with the program, or this thing will be over before it even starts."

Wow. That was the most Josh had ever spoken to him, and every word had reached deep inside Connor. It took guts to lay himself bare like this, to talk about what had traumatized him. It made Connor want to protect this sweet man all the more.

"Not here," he said, indicating the room they were in.

Josh nodded that he understood. "Can you come by tonight? Noah and Indy won't be home."

"Yah. It's a date."

Josh shook his head but smiled a little. "No. It's a talk to determine whether we'll have a date."

Connor couldn't help grinning. "No pressure, huh?"

Josh's gorgeous blue eyes fixed on him. "You're a fucking Marine. You got this."

2

Josh's stomach was twisted in dozens of knots, and his palms were sweaty. Noah had noticed his nervousness, unfortunately. Before he and Indy had left, he'd asked Josh what was wrong. Josh had denied it, not wanting to spill the beans about meeting Connor. It was none of Noah's business, not until Josh knew for sure it was a thing. If he told Noah, the man would get all protective and shit, which Josh appreciated to a certain degree, but not where it concerned Connor.

He'd cleaned the house vigorously, needing a distraction to keep him from counting down the hours, the fucking minutes until Connor would arrive. The living room was dusted and vacuumed, the kitchen sparkling and smelling of lemon-scented cleaning spray. He'd even scrubbed the toilet, putting fresh towels and new scented candles in the guest bathroom. Another sign Noah hadn't missed, judging by his raised eyebrows and pointed looks, but he'd refrained from commenting. Probably because Josh had blown off his previous question.

By the time the doorbell rang, Josh was a nervous wreck. "Hi," he said stupidly as he opened the door.

Connor smiled. "Hi."

"Come in."

Connor wore cargo pants again, navy blue ones this time, with a white long-sleeve shirt. Josh liked him most in his police uniform when his whole demeanor broadcasted masculinity and authority. He liked Connor all male dominant.

Connor followed him into the living room. "Lemonade?" Josh asked.

"Please."

He fixed them both a glass, then made his way back. They sat down across from each other, staring. Shit, this was awkward as fuck.

"I don't have experience with this either," Josh confessed. "So I don't know how we do this."

Connor relaxed at his words, his shoulders coming down and his face softening. "You said you needed to know things from me. Maybe you could start by sharing what you think I should know about you?"

Josh smiled. Smart move, letting him share first. That way, Connor got to keep up his defenses a little longer, could decide whether he was willing to lay himself bare. Considering how fucked up Josh was, he couldn't blame Connor for being careful. He had a right to know what he was getting into. He couldn't know how much he was asking from Josh, though. Josh had thought about it all day, ever since leaving the station. If he wanted this to happen, to even have a chance in hell of succeeding, he needed to be brutally honest. No matter what it cost him, Connor should know, if only to prevent them from getting their wires crossed.

He took a fortifying breath. "First, as you know, I have PTSD, and since you're a Marine, I assume you're familiar with it."

Connor nodded.

"My two known triggers are violence and being startled."

"Okay, that's good to know."

"I also have a sexual trauma."

Connor's face tightened, his nostrils flaring. He was angry, not disgusted, Josh noted, and let out the breath he'd been holding.

"Do you want to talk about it?" Connor offered.

Josh shook his head, appreciating the offer it more than he could express. "I can't. I wanted you to know, because I may give off mixed signals with sex, but I'm asking you to not take me up on anything you may interpret as an offer until I come out and say so."

"All right. You can trust me, Josh."

Josh stared at him for a long time before making up his mind. "I hope so. I haven't been with anyone since, except for Noah. And Indy."

He added Indy's name as an afterthought, not even realizing what he gave away. Connor's eyebrows raised all the way. Damn, he'd forgotten for a second Connor thought Indy was a woman.

Josh blushed fiercely. "It's not like that with Indy," he said, sounding defensive. "Once I trust you, I'll explain."

He needed to clarify more to Connor anyway, about his relationship with Noah for instance, but that could wait. That was on a need to know, and right now, the cop didn't need to know. Yet.

"It's okay, Josh. I don't understand, but I don't judge either. I appreciate you being honest with me."

"Your turn," Josh said, leaning back in his chair.

Connor swallowed. "What do you wanna know?"

"You. But let's start with the most obvious: why aren't you out and fucking everyone who offers himself to you? Because seriously, if you came out, there would be a line out the door."

Josh wasn't exaggerating. It was the question that had been on his mind since that morning. What was holding Connor back from coming out? And more importantly, why would he have no experience with relationships when he looked like that? He'd have no trouble finding someone, multiple someones, if even for one-night stands.

Connor was quiet for a long time, his eyes cast downward and avoiding Josh. What was he about to say that had him so hesitant?

Finally, the guy decided to talk. "I've jacked off with guys in my unit a couple of times—all hush, hush and all of us denying up and down we were gay. After I got back, I went to a gay bar a few times where I tried to hook up. I didn't like it, so I stopped going. That enough detail for you?"

"Those were the broad strokes, but we'll get to the details. Let's start with why you didn't like the hookups."

Connor was sweating. Actually sweating. Pearls of moisture beaded on his forehead, and he wiped them off with his hand. Josh had gotten used to talking about sex, to having sex, to watching it even. Damn, he'd witnessed Noah and Indy a week ago when they seemed to have forgotten he was in the room and had made love. He'd been turned on as fuck, but it hadn't weirded him out or made him even embarrassed in the slightest. Obviously, that was not the case with Connor. What made him so nervous about this?

"First, I guess I'm old-fashioned in the sense that I want to at least know somebody before I have sex. Since I'm not out, it's a big trust issue for me."

"I can respect that," Josh commented. "But there's more."

Connor looked down at the floor again, cracked his knuckles. "I don't like bottoming. Physically, it's okay, but I don't like being dominated by someone else."

Interesting choice of words, dominating. Did that mean he wanted to be the dominating one? *You're reading too much into this*, Josh scolded himself.

"So, you're a top. Big deal. All you have to do is find a bottom."

"Yeah, in theory."

There was something in Connor's voice that alerted Josh he still didn't have the full picture. Why would Connor have an issue finding someone to bottom for him? Even if he had little to no experience, there had to be a line of guys willing to show him the ropes. Damn, the guy was sexy as fuck. Any twink would bend over and tell him to have at it. Including Josh and he wasn't even a twink.

"So you've never fucked a guy," he concluded, frowning. "Did your hookups at least suck you or jack you off?"

"Oh, they gave me a hand job."

Dammit, he was still missing something. "Why? Most gay men love sucking cock, me included by the way." He blushed when he said it but ignored his embarrassment. Connor was laying himself bare, so this wasn't the time to get prudish. "I have a hard time believing nobody would want to bottom for you."

Connor's jaw clenched, and his head was shaking so subtly, Josh almost missed it. "Come on, out with it," Josh said. "What was the problem?"

Suddenly, Connor got up, unbuttoned his pants and dragged them and his boxers down in one harsh move. The erect cock that sprung free was fucking huge and bulging. It had a perfect upward curve, with thick veins pulsating on both sides. The cop's balls were equally big, and Josh's mouth watered, his cock straining against his underwear. He almost whimpered with pleasure. Oh, holy fuck, it would hurt so good to take that impossibly fat cock up his ass.

"Apparently," Connor said, his voice thick with emotion, "Nobody wants this in their mouth. And the two times I tried to fuck someone else, I couldn't even get it in half way before they called it off." Before Josh could say anything, Connor stuffed that gorgeous dick back in his pants with angry moves, yanking his shirt back down. "Forget it. This isn't working."

He was halfway to the door when Josh sprung up, hurried past him and stopped in front of Connor. Dammit, he was not letting Connor storm out a second time, and luckily, this time his brain cooperated. "Where the fuck do you think you're going?"

Josh was taller than Connor, but his lean body would have been no match for the guy had he decided to push his way through. Their faces were inches away from each other until Connor stepped back, casting his eyes downward, his shoulders sagging.

"Home. Come on, Josh, admit it. This is never gonna work."

The defeat in his posture and voice cut deep into Josh. There was something inherently wrong about seeing this proud man so down and rejected.

"If you think nobody wants you because your cock is too big, you haven't met the right men yet." Josh's words were harsh, but his tone was warm.

Connor grimaced. "Oh, you mean like the guy who offered me a grand if I was willing to shoot a porn video with him? Yeah, I've met men who liked my cock. Just not for the right reasons."

"Oh, fuck off. You're not even out. You've barely tried."

Connor's head shot up, fire blazing from his eyes. Josh preferred that ten times over him being all fatalistic. "I'm here, aren't I, trying? But you're as turned off by the idea as all the others."

Without thinking, Josh shoved him back with both hands, surprised he even managed it. "Ask me."

Connor's eyes flashed, but he didn't touch Josh, which earned him major points in Josh's book. "Ask you what?"

"Ask me if I'm turned off before assuming I am."

Connor let out a dismissive, bitter laugh. "Sure, because I love being humiliated some more. No thanks."

Josh grabbed Connor's hand and put it on his rock-hard dick. "Ask me."

The cop's eyes grew big. His face was a palette of emotions as he stared down at his hand covering Josh's groin. He swallowed. "Does it turn you off?" The words were barely audible.

"No, you fucking idiot, it makes me so hard I'm about to come in my pants." Josh pushed back against Connor's hand, grinding his erection against him. "Your cock is the most beautiful, impressive, mouth-watering, and fucking masculine dick I've ever seen."

Connor licked his lips, an undoubtedly unconscious gesture that shot straight to Josh's balls. "Can I kiss you?"

"No." Josh's answer was swift and definitive. "I like you, but I don't trust you, yet. But I might if we keep talking."

The cop's face, which had fallen at Josh's rejection, lit up. "What do you want to know?"

∼

CONNOR COULDN'T BELIEVE he'd dropped his pants like that. Fuck, it could have gone horribly wrong considering Josh's earlier confession of sexual trauma. What the hell had he been thinking?

He hadn't been. Thinking, that was. Not at all. Josh had kept asking questions until Connor had felt against a wall. It was an uncomfortable dichotomy, because on one hand, he wanted nothing more than to protect Josh, be the strong man for him. On the other hand, he wanted to be honest and vulnerable with him, needed him to know he was fucked up, too. Maybe more than he had realized, even.

When Josh had confessed his sexual trauma, Connor had realized they'd never work together. How could they when his damn cock was bound to hurt people? There was no way Josh would ever let him fuck him, not after what he'd been through.

Josh had been so fucking hard, though, undeniably aroused. Why would anyone want that monstrosity? Connor couldn't wrap his mind around it.

"What do you need to trust me?" he asked Josh once they were back in the parlor.

"Complete honesty. If you want me to trust you, you'll need to be willing to do a full disclosure. I promise I won't betray your trust, not even if things between us don't work out, but I need your honesty."

Connor leaned back on the sofa. Could he do this? Was he willing to give this man he barely knew the one thing he had never granted anyone? He'd never opened himself up, not to his family, not to his brothers in arms, not even to Lucas. Lucas had known more than anyone else, but even with him, Connor hadn't shared all. And instead of easing in, this guy was asking him to jump into the deep end from the start. Did he have any idea what he was asking?

"I suck at letting people in," he said.

Josh's face softened. "Tell me one thing you've told no one, and we'll take it from there."

Connor took a deep breath. He had to try. If he ever wanted to find someone to share his life with, he had to take this step. "I was taken prisoner by the Taliban. My best friend Lucas and I were held for five weeks until a SEAL team rescued me."

Josh's eyes hardened. "They tortured you."

"Yes."

"Lucas, he didn't make it? You said you were rescued, not the both of you."

Had he done it on purpose, to test if Josh was listening? Connor wasn't sure. But Josh had listened all right and had read between the lines. "No, he didn't."

Even if he could've talked about it, he wouldn't have, to spare Josh. His story was no bedtime story, especially not for a guy who had violence as a trigger.

Connor didn't know if it was something he'd said or how he had looked, but Josh got up from his chair and sat down at his feet, rubbing his head against Connor's hand like a kitten. Connor automatically put his hand on Josh's hair and stroked it. His hair was silken, the dark locks soft and comforting. It was a calming sensation to let the strands slide through his fingers.

"I am so sorry, Connor." Josh's voice was soft, his eyes closed as he leaned even farther into Connor's hand. Funny how a phrase that could have so easily been a cliché meant so much coming from Josh.

"Your hair feels nice," Connor said without thinking.

"Did you know it helps to touch something soft when you talk about a painful memory? It helps take some of the sharpness away."

He'd done it on purpose. Josh had known how hard this was for Connor and had offered him support in the best way he knew. That couldn't have been easy for him, what with his trust issues and sexual trauma. If Connor needed any more evidence of how sweet Josh was, it was right there.

"I didn't know. Thank you." On impulse, Connor bowed toward Josh, pressed a soft kiss on his head.

"What did you have in mind for our date?" Josh asked.

"I hadn't quite gotten that far. Wasn't sure you'd say yes in the first place."

"Connor, I ..." Josh pulled his knees up, hugging them tightly with his toned arms. He looked at the ground as he spoke. "I don't go out much, aside from shopping and therapy and running. People scare me easily, and I'm always afraid of having an episode. So I stay home, most of the time."

"It must've been hard for you to come to the station," Connor realized.

"Yes," Josh whispered. "But I didn't have your number, so I had to."

If Josh thought this would make him boring, Connor needed to set the record straight. "Josh, it's okay. I have a job where I'm out a lot of the times, and I have more excitement than I care for. When I get home, I'm more than happy to stay inside."

Josh raised his head, met Connor's eyes with a sweet smile playing on his lips. "You could come here, and I could cook for you, if you want."

"You cook?"

Josh nodded, almost eagerly. "It's a hobby."

"Good heavens, you're perfect," Connor said, then watched with amazement as another sweet blush crept up

Josh's cheeks. God, he was adorable. "That sounds like a perfect plan."

"What do you like to eat?"

"Anything and everything, as long as I don't have to cook. Household chores are not my forte, to be honest."

Josh flashed another sweet smile. "I don't mind doing them at all. Noah hates them, too, so I do everything."

Now that, Connor could believe. Noah didn't seem like the type who enjoyed doing the dishes. Not that Connor judged, because he hated them too. But it was interesting that Indy didn't have a knack for household stuff either. Or a willingness.

Josh jumped up. "Fuck, you need to leave."

Connor raised his eyebrows. Where was this coming from all of a sudden?

"Noah and Indy will be home any second, and you can't be here."

Connor got up as well, his mood darkening. "What's the problem? Did you lie about you and Noah? Why can't he see me?"

Josh stilled, then turned around to face him. "It's not that. I'll explain it to you next time, I promise. I'll cook for you, and we'll talk, okay?"

Everything in Connor screamed he shouldn't let this go, that something fishy was going on. Josh was hiding something from him, despite his talk about brutal honesty. Still, what choice did he have? Connor didn't want to risk running Josh off, not after they had connected so well.

He put his hand on Josh's cheek, raising his chin with slight pressure so their eyes would meet. "I'll text you later when I get home, okay? Don't wait too long texting me back, or I'll conclude you've changed your mind."

Josh's reply was quick and certain. "Yes, Connor."

And damn if that answer didn't make Connor's insides go all dominant as fuck. Nothing could've satisfied him deeper.

Maybe it would be enough, he mused on the car ride home, being with Josh, even if he could never fuck him. An image flashed through his head. Josh, taking his cock in his mouth, in that firm, toned ass. Connor groaned, repositioning his swollen shaft. He was a fucking idiot, setting himself up for disaster. Fuck, he was gonna get hurt. And so was Josh—and not in a good way.

3

Connor wiped his somewhat sweaty hands off on his dark blue slacks before he rang the bell. A quick check showed his crisp white shirt was all straightened and neat. You'd think a Marine who had been to hell and back would be cool about a simple date, but his nerves were killing him.

It had been a long week, waiting for the date to happen, meanwhile texting back and forth with Josh. He'd alternatively cursed himself and been excited, even though he knew it would never work. Not with his monster cock. Not with Josh's traumatized past. Not with him being all bossy and controlling and Josh so sweet and lovable. Fuck knew why he wanted to try anyway. Glutton for punishment, apparently.

Josh opened the door, and Connor let out an involuntary sigh at the sight of him. Dressed in a baby blue button-down and dark blue dungies that hugged his long legs, he made Connor's stomach do a little somersault.

"Hi," Josh said, not opening the door wide enough for Connor to step in.

"Hi." Had Josh changed his mind? Connor's stomach sank. "Can I come in?" he asked when Josh didn't say anything else.

"Shit, yes, of course," Josh stammered and threw the door wide open. Connor smiled. It looked like the guy was as nervous as he was, which was sweet.

"I brought you something," he said when they were inside, Josh watching him as he hung up his jacket and took off his beanie and boots.

He handed Josh the wrapped package. Would he like it? Connor held his breath.

Josh unwrapped it, then let out a little squeal. "The new Forza game! I wanted this. How did you know?"

A warmth Connor couldn't explain burned through him. He'd gotten it right. Damn, that felt wicked good. "It was a guess. I saw the Xbox last time and figured you were the one playing the most, so I went to the store and asked for a game without violence. The sales guy said Forza was a lot of fun, had beautiful graphics, and no gore."

Before he realized what was happening, Josh stepped in and kissed Connor on his mouth. "Thank you. Perfect gift."

An electric shock fired up Connor's system at the all-too-short sensation of Josh's lips on his. More. He wanted so much more. He swallowed. "You're welcome. Glad you like it."

He followed Josh into the living room, catching a satisfying look at his tight ass in those dungies. Damn, he could watch that butt for hours and not get bored.

"I made us some tapas as appetizers," Josh said, a hint of insecurity in his voice. He led Connor into the dining room where a sturdy wooden table had been set for two, complete with candles and napkins. White, small serving dishes in various shapes and forms held tiny little bites of beautifully arranged food. It all looked like it had been ripped from the kitchen of a three-star restaurant. Josh had gone through a lot of trouble for this date and didn't that warm Connor's heart? Whatever doubts he'd entertained after Josh had kicked him out last time vaporized.

"That looks amazing," Connor said. "You weren't kidding when you said cooking was a hobby."

A sweet smile flashed across Josh's face before he gestured toward one of the chairs. "What can I get you to drink? I forgot to buy wine, because Noah and I don't drink."

There was that insecurity again, as if he was scared Connor would get upset with him for not having wine. "I rarely drink, and I never do when I'm driving, so that's fine. It's probably gonna clash with these delicious dishes, but I'd love some more of your lemonade."

Josh's whole face lit up, his smile shooting lightning bolts through Connor. What was it about this man that made Connor want to protect him, pleasure him, and cherish him? All these warm and fuzzy feelings swirled around inside of him, and he didn't know what to do with them.

Josh sat down across from him after he'd gotten them both a glass of lemonade. "You said you liked everything, so I went a little experimental with the tapas. We have salad wraps with spicy chicken inside, homemade mini croquettes, Spanish ham rolls with melon, and gazpacho, which is a cold tomato soup."

"Wow. Tell me which one to start with."

Josh handed him the cold soup, served in a tiny glass. "It's a little spicy, but it's perfect to start with."

Perfect was the right word. A rich, full tomato flavor exploded in Connor's mouth at the first sip. It was fresh, spicy, and it tasted like summer despite the freezing cold outside. "Oh, man, that is so good. Love it."

"I'm glad you like it. It's Noah's favorite, too."

Noah. Connor couldn't help but like the guy, but what was the deal with him and Josh? No matter what Noah had said about him and Josh not being together, something was going on. Josh and Noah were living together, and Josh had been clear about him and Noah having sex as well. How did Indy fit into this picture? And was there even room for Connor? Still, he didn't want to start this date by asking the hard questions.

"Look, I know we're both new at this, so I did some research," he said.

"You did?"

"I figured we could start with 'Would you rather' questions to get to know each other."

A smile played on Josh's lips. "You're a bit of a control freak, aren't you?"

Connor opted for honesty, which seemed like a good strategy with Josh. "I am, and not even a little bit. I worried that between your shyness and my inexperience at this, we'd get stuck in uncomfortable silences, so I wanted to make sure we had a good time."

"I can appreciate that. You start."

Connor took another sip of his delicious soup, then fired off the first question. "Would you rather spend a year on a deserted island or in a cabin in the woods?"

"The cabin. I'm not a big fan of beaches, and I love hiking, so I'd take the woods. My turn, right?"

Connor nodded, curious what Josh would come up with. "Would you rather eat cereal every meal for a year or go without coffee for a year?"

"I don't drink coffee, not anymore."

Josh raised his eyebrows. "Why not?"

Connor hesitated, then surprised himself by going all in. "Our captors, they'd drink this rich, strong coffee all day. The smell permeated everything. I haven't had a drop since, and even the smell of coffee makes me nauseous."

Josh's eyes went soft. "Smell is a powerful trigger for memories, both good and bad ones."

Connor studied the kind blue eyes across the table. He'd never talked about his experiences. Even the trauma psychologist his CO had sicced on him had barely managed to get a word out of him. The thought of witnessing pity on people's faces, that they would see him differently, would treat him as damaged—it had prevented him from ever saying anything. But Josh, he understood. He'd been through his own version of hell, and he had survived. And Connor didn't see Josh as weak, damaged, or a victim. Even with the PTSD, Connor couldn't view him as anything else but a survivor, a strong fighter determined to get better.

"Next question. Would you rather go without books or without sex for a year?" Josh asked.

"Hey, it was my turn!" Connor protested.

"You waited too long, so you forfeited. Answer the question."

The guy was such an intriguing mix of shy and sexy, of awkward and flirty. And even after having had time to think it over, the size of Connor's cock wasn't deterring him. "Define sex," Connor said. "Are we talking all sexual acts or penetration?"

Josh smiled. "I like how you think. Erm, let's say all sexual acts."

"Yeah, I'll go without books in that case. Pretty sure my balls would explode if I couldn't jerk off for a year. How about you? You seem fond of your books ... "

"Not that fond, trust me. I'd have to agree with you on that one. Next. Would you rather fuck every day for the rest of your life, or get a blow job every day?"

"How come you get to ask another question? Isn't it my turn by now?"

"Nope, you used my own question about sex or books on your turn."

Connor shook his head, laughing. "You're a smart ass."

"Answer the question."

Connor had no hesitation this time, even though his stomach clenched. It would never happen, at least not with Josh. "Fuck. Hands down."

Josh nodded, a happy smile on his face. "I figured."

"I guess I'd have to alter the question for you a little," Connor said. "These salad rolls are amazing, by the way. Perfect combination of the crispy lettuce and the spicy chicken."

"What do you mean?"

"Would you rather be fucked every day for the rest of your life or give a blow job every day? That's what I should ask you, right?"

Josh frowned. "Am I so obvious?"

Connor reached out his hand, put it on top of Josh's. "You already told me you were a bottom, and that you loved sucking cock. I remembered because what you say is important."

Josh studied him, his blue eyes assessing. Connor stayed perfectly still. "Yeah," Josh finally said. "That's what you should ask. So are you asking?"

"No. Because I'd want to do both."

Josh's eyes glazed over. His Adam's apple bobbed as he swallowed. "I'd want that, too."

"Yeah?" Connor asked, his insides doing a happy dance.

"I want to do everything you ask me." Josh cast his eyes downward, fidgeted with his hands.

Connor stilled. *Is he saying what I hope he is? There's no way. No fucking way.* Could he at least hint at what was inside of him, this deep yearning? "All I want is to take care of you. You trigger a deep, dominant urge in me. I'm sorry if that offends you or scares you."

His eyes were trained on Josh, studying his every reaction. Josh's eyes lifted to meet his. "It doesn't."

What he saw in Josh's eyes made Connor breathless. "How does it make you feel?"

"Wanted. Safe." Connor's grip on Josh's hand intensified. "Indy says I have submissive tendencies. Do you know what that is?"

Connor swallowed. Holy crap. "Yeah, I do. Why do you think that?" His voice was hoarse.

Josh yanked his hand from under Connor's, directed his face to the floor again. It took a long time for him to speak. "Please, don't judge me, Connor."

Connor's alarm bells went off. There was more, but Josh felt scared to say it, feared Connor would judge and reject him. What could he offer to make him feel safe and secure?

He pushed his chair back from the table. "Come here," he told Josh in a warm, but firm voice.

Almost instantly, Josh got up. Holy fuck, Connor's instincts had been spot on. Josh hadn't hesitated even a second before obeying him. When Josh stood before him, eyes still glued to the ground, Connor reached forward with a slow motion and grabbed Josh gently by his hips. He pulled the man forward until Josh got the hint and straddled his ass on Connor's lap, facing him. Connor pulled him close, holding Josh loosely until he felt him relax. Josh put his cheek on Connor's shoulder, sending a sweet triumph through Connor's system.

It was almost surreal, this intimacy they were sharing when they hardly knew each other. Yet it felt so familiar, so right.

"What did you want to tell me, Josh?" he asked, rubbing Josh's back with his right hand.

For more than a minute, Josh was quiet but relaxed in Connor's arms. Finally, he spoke. "I like rough sex." Josh's voice was so soft it was barely audible.

"Okay."

"You don't think that's weird or perverse?"

"No, why would it be?" Connor had a good idea why Josh would think so, but he wanted him to come out and say it.

"Doesn't it mean I...liked what happened to me? That I somehow want to relive it?"

"Did you like rough sex before you were raped?" Connor wanted Josh to know he'd looked it up. It hadn't been too hard to find in the army records, not with the contacts he had. He figured it would help Josh if he was factual about it.

Josh let out a breath as if he'd been holding it in. "I think so. Never had much opportunity to experiment."

"Josh, what happened to you, it doesn't change who you are or how you're wired. You were gay before, and you still are now, right? In the same way, you had your preferences before, and those haven't changed. Doesn't mean you're some sicko deliberately reliving a trauma."

"Do you like it rough?"

"I think so. My cock isn't very sensitive, so it needs thorough stimulation for me to get off. But I've never really fucked another man, so I don't know for certain. But Josh,

I'm not sure if I could fuck rough and hard, with how I'm built."

It was easy to talk like this, with this sweet guy wrapped around him, Josh's face tucked away against his shoulder. It felt safe, like he was offering the man a cocoon where he could transform.

"Indy thinks I'm submissive, because I like being told what to do in bed. It fulfills me when I'm being bossed around and used. To me, it brings freedom, because I don't feel worry or stress. All I need to do is obey. And I think I like pain..."

Josh's voice trailed off, the last words barely audible. God, he was laying it all on the line, and it warmed Connor's heart. He made sure his voice was tender before he spoke. "It sounds like something you may want to explore further."

Josh sighed. "Yeah, I guess. It's not that simple for me, considering my...issues. Trust does not come easy to me."

Connor hmm'd, understood. He hadn't trusted anyone in his life. Not even Lucas, and he had been his best friend.

"Do you think this is maybe something you'd be interested in...with me?" Josh asked.

He still wasn't looking at him, and Connor was grateful. It made it easier, to be honest. Josh's hands were wrapped around Connor now, tracing unknown patterns on his back.

God, he wanted nothing more than to experiment together. Connor's dick had grown harder during the conversation, but the mere thought of being Josh's first in this aspect made his cock rock hard in an instant. But how could he risk it? Josh was vulnerable, and Connor didn't know shit about any of this. What if he ended up breaking him even more?

"Josh, I'd love nothing more, but I have zero experience with this. All I know is what I've seen in porn, and while I'll admit it exhilarates me, I'm not sure I'd be the right person for you to explore this with." He sighed. "I'm doing a wicked shitty job of promoting myself here, but I've been told I'm arrogant and dominant to the point where people have compared me to a steamroller."

Josh untangled himself, leaned back to look Connor in the eye. "And you see this as a problem why exactly? Isn't the whole point that one partner dominates and the other submits?"

"What if I'm too dominant for you? What if you don't say no, and I end up hurting you, physically or mentally?"

Understanding dawned in Josh's eyes. "You think I'm too fragile for you." His shoulders sagged. "You're right."

"No! God, no. You're not the problem, Josh, I am. Shit, I'm fucking this up, aren't I? It's all on me, I swear. Hell, you're not fragile at all, not after what you went through and came out of."

Josh's eyes fixed on him, those endless pools of blue. "Then what the fuck are you saying because I don't understand."

Connor sighed. "I'm scared of hurting you. I'm clueless about relationship shit. Plus, we're talking about exploring this submissive side of you, which I also know jack shit about. Look at my size, my whole body, my strength. And then there's the size of my dick... I could hurt you for real."

How could Josh not see this? Connor couldn't even bear to think about his attempts at fucking someone. It had been so damn humiliating it still made him sick to his stomach every time he thought about it. There was no way Josh would be able to take him without pain, and it could trigger so many bad memories for him.

"Connor, I'm no pushover. Trust me, I will communicate my limits loud and clear, don't you worry. But the last thing

I'm worried about is your size, and that includes your cock. I can take it. Take you."

Josh's eyes projected confidence, and Connor's heart sped up. Josh spoke like he meant it. But maybe Josh hadn't realized from that quick peek how big Connor's dick was. He'd seen only a glimpse. That had to be why he was still so confident. Connor's face fell again. God, this was hopeless. Absolutely fucking impossible.

"Since you haven't been weirded out so far, let me be even more honest. I love being fucked. I love it so much that I can come just by being fucked hard, without ever touching myself. Connor, I appreciate your concern for hurting me, more than you'll ever know, but I can take you."

THE DOUBT on Connor's face was easy to spot, but Josh picked up something else as well. Hurt. Shame. Connor's sexual experiences so far had been bad and humiliating, which was un-fucking-believable considering how sexy the guy was. Fuck, Josh found himself all but drooling at even the thought of taking that huge cock in. He couldn't be the only one who got off on that? How could he show Connor he was serious?

He raised his hand and put it on Connor's right cheek. Connor tilted his head sideways to lean into his hand. Josh let his fingers trail down Connor's strong jaw, swiping his thumb across his full bottom lip. As usual, Josh had stubble because he couldn't be bothered to shave every day, but Connor's face was clean-shaven, and it fit him. Mr. Control Freak who had prepared this date by doing research and by going through quite a bit of trouble to find the perfect gift for Josh.

It was a miracle the guy even wanted to date Josh. Josh knew he wasn't bad looking, but fuck, he was anything but a catch with his PTSD and everything else. Connor had done research there as well, had accessed Josh's military records to find out what had happened to him. And he had still shown up and had made every effort to make the date a success.

"Why did you wait so long to contact me, even after Noah told you he and I weren't together?" Josh asked. He kept exploring Connor's face with his hand, now sliding his hand through his high and tight brown hair.

"I wasn't sure if I wouldn't be too much for you and if I had enough to offer you."

Josh thought for a second Connor had to be kidding, but his face was dead serious. "I don't understand."

Connor sighed. "At the risk of ruining my whole sales pitch even more: you could do so much better than a closeted, sexually inexperienced cop who doesn't know the first thing about relationships. Plus, you know, there's the size of my dick and all the complications that brings."

Connor's face was calm and so was his voice, but Josh sensed the depth of his emotions. Connor was as traumatized as he was, if for completely other reasons. This beautiful, proud man had been rejected so many times it had done a serious number on his self-confidence. The dominance and arrogance he'd mentioned before, Josh almost laughed at that since it was not even close to being a problem for him—on the contrary. But Connor could not see past the problem of his size, no matter what Josh would say. It would always be an obstacle—unless Josh showed him it wasn't.

There was one thing he could do that would fix this problem once and for all and maybe take away some of the other doubts as well. And why wouldn't he when all that held him back was his own fear of being too easy?

Fuck that. Who cared anyway? He trusted Connor, he had from the moment they had met. Nothing he had learned about the man had changed that first opinion. Everything he had said and done had shown how careful he'd been with Josh to make sure he wasn't triggering anything. Who cared if they had just met? It wasn't like Josh needed to have a declaration of love before he was ready to have sex. He liked Connor, and he wanted him, plain and simple. Right now, that was enough.

"Ask me if I trust you," he said, increasing the pressure on Connor's cock with his ass. Would the cop get the hint?

Connor inhaled sharply, his body growing rigid, his eyes searching and finding Josh's. "Do you trust me, Josh?"

Oh yeah, Connor was following all right. His voice was soft, but his hands came around Josh's waist, pushing him down, creating even more friction between their bodies. "I do, Connor, and what's more, I like you. Time for rule number two: you have to ask for it. In this house, we don't assume. We ask. If you don't ask, you don't get."

Connor's mouth dropped open, and his Adam's apple bobbed as he swallowed. He shook his head almost imperceptibly as if he couldn't believe what Josh was saying.

"Ask me, Connor," Josh repeated.

Connor's voice trembled as he spoke. "Will you please try to let me fuck you, Josh?"

Josh thought he'd never been asked quite so nicely. "With pleasure," he said, fusing his mouth to Connor's.

After a minute or two of frantic kissing, Connor stood up from his chair, lifting Josh up with two strong hands on Josh's ass. Josh wrapped his legs around the cop, squeezing their crotches together. Oh, that cock, that beautiful, fat cock. He so desperately wanted to see it again, feel it, taste it. Josh's body hummed, gentle waves of energy pulsating through his veins.

Connor turned, backing Josh up against a wall, dove in deep with his mouth. Finally, a guy who loved kissing as well, Josh thought and attacked right back. Connor tasted so different from Indy. Indy was sweet, soft. His kisses made the butterflies in Josh's stomach do a happy dance. Connor was all male, powerful, spicy. He attacked, invaded, demanded Josh open up for him. It made Josh want to bend over and spread his legs. God, he wanted him. Craved him. Connor kissed him till Josh was a whimpering mess, his head spinning, his cock straining, and his body buzzing.

Connor unbuttoned Josh's shirt with nimble fingers. When it was loose, Josh obliged, leaning back against the wall so the guy could ungracefully yank off his sleeves. Their mouths met again while Connor's big hands grabbed Josh's butt again, kneading and groping. Too many clothes, they still had on too many clothes.

"Upstairs." He tore his mouth away from Connor, panting. "Let's go upstairs."

Connor held him tight, walking through the living room, then up the stairs. "You can't carry me," Josh protested. "I'm too heavy."

"Watch me," Connor grumbled, then took his mouth again. His tongue pushed in, dueled with Josh's until he surrendered, unable to think anymore. Josh's insides melted into a puddle as Connor carried him upstairs, step by step, their mouths never leaving each other. He kept his legs wrapped around Connor's waist, holding on, putting pressure on the treasure he couldn't wait to get his hands on. And in his mouth. Oh, sweet fuck, he was about to give that guy the blow job of his life.

"Which room?"

"Mine. Ours. Whatever."

Connor kicked open the door to Josh and Noah's room. He dropped them both on the bed, crashing his body into Josh's with a force that made Josh all weak inside. God, when this guy would let loose, it would get epic. He was about to get fucked harder and deeper than ever before, and he trembled in anticipation.

Josh kicked off his shoes, struggled to pull off his socks without losing Connor's mouth. He swore when he couldn't pull them off with Connor on top of him.

"Flip over," he panted, pushing against Connor's biceps. Connor held him tight, rolled over, pulling Josh on top of him.

With reluctance, Josh dragged his mouth away, sat up straddling the cop. It meshed their crotches tighter together, eliciting a moan from Connor's lips. Josh hummed with pleasure and gyrated his hips down.

Connor lifted his arms and let his fingers trail Josh's bare chest, stomach, back. "You're so sexy," he whispered. "I've wanted you from the second I laid eyes on you in that stupid store. I can't stop looking at you."

"Right back atcha, but I'm hoping you'll do a whole lot more than looking."

Josh unbuttoned his jeans and slid his zipper down, then discovered he couldn't take off his fucking pants while straddling Connor. He rolled off, muttering, dragging jeans and boxers down in one fluid motion. He might as well take care of Connor at the same time.

"You have way too many clothes on for this," he said, yanking Connor's shirt from his slacks and working the buttons free. Of course, he wore a T-shirt as well. Damn. Josh worked him out of both, dropping kisses on his taut muscles. His wide chest was hairless, with small scars scattered on his pecs and stomach. Josh licked them, kissed them softly with wet kisses.

He worked his way down, slipped a finger into the guy's waistband and popped the button.

It was like Christmas, and even though he'd seen a glimpse already, he couldn't wait to unwrap this package. He pulled down the zipper, teasing the massive erection underneath with his finger. Connor moaned low and deep.

Josh debated taking the slacks off first and teasing Connor even more, then decided he was done with waiting. He grabbed his slacks and boxers and signaled Connor to lift his hips, then slid them down Connor's legs. There it was, that beautiful, big cock, and it was even harder than he'd thought possible.

He licked his lips.

"First things first. Are you clean?"

"Yeah. I've always used condoms."

"So, you've never had a blow job?"

"No. It's okay if you don't want to." Connor's voice was once again dripping with insecurity. Josh longed to make that stop.

"Here's the thing," he said, letting his finger travel up Connor's leg till he reached his balls. "I love sucking cock, and I am exceptional at it." Connor shivered, and Josh removed his finger, let it wander up the other leg, evoking the same reaction. "But you're already rock hard, and you've never had a blow job, so you won't last long. I wanna let you know that's okay."

He cupped Connor's balls, squeezing them. Connor gasped. "Those things look like they hold a massive amount of cum. Don't hold back when you come. I want to take it.

Just don't hold my head because you may push in deeper instinctively."

Connor's eyes about crossed, and Josh hadn't even gotten started yet. The power of dirty talk—it never failed.

"Now lay back...and enjoy the ride."

Josh dropped on his stomach on the bed, putting his head above Connor's crotch. The cop's cock was so hard it was almost shivering, with droplets of precum at the top. Josh licked the head, savoring the salty taste in his mouth.

"You taste delicious," he said.

He treated the crown to little licks with his tongue, Connor's body trembling below him. He wasn't going to last long. Oh, well, there was always a next time. Josh opened his mouth and relaxed his tongue and throat. The guy wasn't going to know what hit him. He started with the crown, suckling it, teasing the slit with his tongue. Opening wider, he took him into his mouth, sucking him gently.

Connor bucked at the sensation, a hard moan echoing through the room. Josh increased the pressure, sucking harder, relaxing his mouth to take the guy in farther. He'd never be able to take this monster in entirely, but he would at least try.

He cupped Connor's balls in one hand—they spilled over—and the base of his cock in the other. That way, he could feel when the guy was coming. The balls were tightening already as Josh sucked and licked and worked the stiff cock in as far as he could.

God, he loved how that fat cock filled his mouth completely. There was something inherently dirty about stuffing your mouth with dick until your eyes watered and you ran out of breath. He fucking loved it, the pleasure and satisfaction radiating through his entire body.

Connor let out a deep groan. He bucked his hips again as Josh fisted the base of his cock. "I'm... Ohhh!"

Josh got the hint. He pulled back, and a splash of cum filled his throat, then another, and another.

"Ugh!" Connor grunted.

Connor shook as the ripples of a powerful orgasm tore through him. Josh swallowed and sucked and milked till there was nothing left. Much to his satisfaction, the continuous sucking left Connor hard—exactly what he'd hoped for.

He let go of Connor's cock and felt strong arms pull him on top of the man. Connor kissed him passionately, letting his hands roam over Josh's body.

"Shit, Josh, that was mind-blowing. Your mouth... Damn, that was so good."

He kept kissing Josh in between, clearly trying to convey his feelings. Josh smiled, his heart happy he'd been able to give Connor this pleasure.

"You feel perfect." Connor grabbed Josh's butt, put one cheek in each hand and squeezed. "Absolutely perfect."

Josh moaned as the strong hands grabbed him, stroked him. Connor's cock brushed up against his, and he ground his hips, twisting and gyrating to create a delicious friction.

"You ready for round two?" he whispered in Connor's ear, licking his neck and dropping butterfly kisses behind his ear.

"Don't you want me to ..."

Josh pushed himself up, found Connor's eyes. "I want you to fuck me. I want that big, fat cock of yours in my ass. Think you can accommodate me?"

"I'm so afraid I'll hurt you."

Josh kissed him. "You won't. We'll start slow, use plenty of lube. Did you bring a condom? I don't have your size."

Connor nodded.

Josh rolled off him to grab the lube while Connor got a condom from his wallet, then turned on his back, pulled his knees up. "Your job," Josh said with a sultry look, handing Connor the lube.

Connor climbed on the bed and sat on his knees. He rolled on the condom with fumbling fingers, which made Josh smile. Fuck, he was so perfect with all his inexperience. Connor applied a liberal amount of lube to his cock once he'd suited up. "Put some in my ass as well and finger fuck me, loosen me up," Josh told him.

Connor blinked twice, then hesitantly reached for Josh. This was not the time for endless foreplay. The longer they would draw it out, the more nervous Connor would get. His apprehension was already visible. No wonder when his previous experiences had been so disappointing.

Josh smiled a little when Connor did as he had told him, ignoring Josh's cock to focus on the task he'd gotten. Connor's finger slipped inside him, then another. He widened them, twisting and spreading them to stretch Josh. Connor was methodical about it, focused, his pupils dilated and sweat glistening on his forehead. It felt good, but nowhere near as good as that massive shaft would feel.

Classic Marine, great at following orders. Was he also good at giving them? Fuck, Josh hoped so. When Connor could get three fingers in with ease, Josh was ready.

"Connor." He waited till the guy looked at him, a mix of want and fear in his eyes. "You'll go slow, inch for inch. When I tell you to stop, you stop. When you're completely in, and you feel me relax, you take over. I told you I like it hard and deep. I want you to pound me, hammer me, drill me until you come so hard your eyes will cross."

Connor moaned, his cock releasing a bit of juice. "Dirty talk turns you on, huh?" Josh smiled.

The cop nodded, swallowed. "What about you?"

"Oh, don't you worry. Once you let loose, I promise I will come all over you."

Connor lowered himself on top of Josh, putting his weight on his arms. With a frown of concentration, he positioned the top of his cock against Josh's entrance, both slick with lube. He pushed inside, and Josh shivered. Even the guy's head was thicker than anything he'd ever experienced before. Josh put his hands on Connor's hips, signaled him to push farther in. He slid in another inch, his muscles trembling.

"Pull back and slide in back and forth a few times, but stay shallow," Josh said, his voice thick. He couldn't get that cock in his hole fast enough, but he had to take it slow, both for himself and for Connor. The guy was practically a virgin. Connor slid back his cock till the thick head was in the outer ring, then thrust forward again.

"Oh, fuck," Josh moaned, shivering with delight.

Connor repeated the move, slid in a little deeper. "You're so tight," he grunted. "It feels unbelievable."

Josh pressed Connor's hips again, pulled up his legs even higher. "Deeper," he said.

Connor's cock stretched him wider than ever before, and the sensation mixed intense pleasure with a burning sensation as his inner canal ached to adjust. He gyrated his hips, wanting to open wide enough to take in the rest. He only had maybe half of it.

When the burning eased, he signaled again. Connor slid out almost entirely, then pushed back in with a grunt. He had complete control over his muscles, not going deeper than Josh indicated.

"I can't believe you can take me," Connor whispered in awe. "And holy fuck, it feels perfect."

"Deeper." Josh focused on his breathing to relax, his inner sleeve achingly stretching even wider to accommodate Connor's girth and length. He rotated his hips again, moaning as the swollen member inside of him hit his sweet spot. Paradise was around the corner, so close he could almost taste it.

"Thrust a little."

The friction this caused triggered a deep ache in his balls, which were getting ready to unload. Not yet, dammit, not yet. He wanted more.

"Bring it home," he grunted, his forehead slick with perspiration. Connor pushed farther in until he filled Josh to the max, bottoming out.

"I'm in." The joy in Connor's voice hit Josh deep inside. "Are you okay?"

How Josh loved hearing these familiar words out of someone else's mouth. "I'm good, and I'm about to be great. Now, rotate your hips a little, like you're literally screwing me. Ohhh!" He lost his breath on a deep moan when Connor did what he asked.

Connor slid in and out with steady, graceful moves. Leaning on his arms, he was only moving his hips in a masculine, sexy way. Josh grabbed Connor's ass as the painful stretching morphed into a delicious burn and the most intense full feeling ever. Pain and pleasure were entwined, thundering through his ass. Every time Connor slid in deep, Josh's breath caught. Little specks danced in front of his eyes, his vision hazy with want. He let go of Connor's ass cheeks, reaching up to drag his mouth down for a hard kiss.

"Hard and deep?" Connor asked, his jaw tight with tension.

"Gimme all you got."

Connor started slow with rhythmic, deep thrusts, but he soon picked up the pace. Josh pulled up his legs as far as he could, opening his ass wide and fisting the sheets with both hands. "Fuck!" he cried out when Connor pulled back almost entirely, then slammed in balls deep. "Oh, God, yes!"

"You feel so good," Connor grunted, impaling him again.

This time, his cock hit Josh's pleasure spot, and he jerked. "Oh, my fucking—Ohh!"

Waves of ecstatic pleasure crashed into Josh as Connor cut loose and drove into his ass again and again. Their bodies collided with force, and Josh pushed back. Fuck, he wanted more. Harder. Rougher.

Connor threw his head back, grunting and growling, lips peeled. His arms quivered with the effort of holding up his weight. Every time Connor's cock drilled into Josh, it hit his sweet spot, and he was almost crying with pleasure. His balls pulled up tight, on the verge of detonating. He fought it, not wanting to lose this incredible feeling.

Connor grabbed his hips, pounding him with an urgency that alerted Josh he was about to blow his load. Josh couldn't keep it anymore. When Connor hit him once more so hard his balls thwacked against Josh's ass, his body spasmed, and he screamed as he unloaded all over Connor's chest. He wasn't even done spurting when Connor let out a strangled cry and rammed his cock in one last time.

"Ugh! Oh.... Fuck!"

Connor's cock pulsed, filling the condom with liquid. Connor stayed deep inside, grinding against Josh's ass, gyrating until he had squeezed every drop of cum out of his balls and dick. His entire body trembled with the exertion, and Josh was convinced he'd dead-drop his weight on top of him. Instead, he rolled over, taking Josh with him to place him on top.

Josh let his head rest on the man's massive shoulder, his arms around Connor's neck and biceps. Both their bodies were moist with sweat. He was too done to even lift a finger. God, this was everything he'd dreamed of and then some.

"Fuck, baby, that was unbelievable," Connor mumbled.

Even in his haze of ecstasy, Josh registered the unfamiliar term of endearment. Nobody had ever called him that and meant it.

"Hold on a sec," Connor said. He rolled Josh off him to take off the condom. He tried to tie it, but his trembling fingers failed.

"Throw it in the wastebasket," Josh said. "I'll empty it later."

Connor crawled back in bed as soon as he'd dumped the condom.

"Come here," he said, pulling Josh back on top of him. Connor's heartbeat slowed down under Josh's cheek as he kissed Josh's head, wrapping his arms around him and stroking his back. Josh turned his chin so their mouths could find each other again, lazy and wet. Their slick, soft cocks brushed up against each other, almost hugging and kissing too. For minutes they lay content, kissing and caressing.

"I love your cock," Josh said dreamily, tearing his mouth away and dropping his head on the man's shoulder again. It felt like such a safe spot with these strong, tight arms around him.

Connor chuckled. "I love your ass, baby. I cannot believe

you could take me. And your mouth too. You have to teach me how to give a blow job like that so I can do it to you."

"You'd want that?"

"Hell, yes. I wanna do anything you like."

Josh let that sink in for a moment. This was what it felt like to be with someone who was attracted to him. It was nothing short of a fucking miracle.

"A threesome with Noah?" he suggested.

Connor about choked on his breath.

4

If people had told Indy four months ago he'd be happy, he would have laughed them straight out of the room. Happy wasn't in the cards for him. Not now, not ever. Yet every time he so much as looked at Noah, his heart was doing a fucking Irish reel.

It was the longest he'd been in one place since he started running from the Fitzpatricks. He'd relaxed, but he was still on high alert every time he stepped outside. Duncan was looking for him, and one mistake could cost him everything. Now more than ever.

He should've left, of course. He told himself that every single day, wearing himself out with this constant internal debate and battle. He should leave them so they'd be safe, but how could he when the mere thought took his breath away?

He'd told them everything, Noah and Josh. Little by little, he'd shared what he'd seen and done, what had been done to him. It helped. He'd never imagined how healing it was to be able to talk. Josh had turned out to be an even better listener than Noah, maybe because unlike Noah,

Josh's own anger and temper didn't get in the way. Some-times Noah's emotions were so volatile that Indy stopped talking, because he felt guilty for making him angry or sad. When Noah had a night shift, he and Josh would talk for hours.

Not about Josh, though—at least, not about the specifics of what had happened to him. Indy guessed, but Josh had told him he wasn't ready to talk yet. Indy understood. How could he not? It had taken him a long time, too. Plus, Josh was an introvert by nature, unlike Indy, so that didn't make it easy for him to verbalize his emotions in the first place.

He'd worried about Josh the last week. Something was going on, and Josh wasn't talking. That crazy cleaning binge he'd been on today, that was not normal. Something had triggered it, but Indy had no idea what. Josh was more on his phone, exchanging messages with fuck knew who. Had Josh somehow met someone? It seemed almost impossible considering he hardly ever left the house, except for therapy and grocery shopping.

"I still think you rigged that coin toss," Noah complained from the driver's seat, dragging Indy out of his thoughts. They were on their way to the movie theater after a relaxed dinner in a pizzeria. Noah was driving since Indy was too scared of causing an accident or being pulled over. He still dressed like a woman most of the times he went outside, except for jiujitsu practice and running, the fear of being recognized too big.

Indy shot him a look. "Get over it. You lost fair and square, so I get to choose the movie."

Noah let out a dramatic sigh. "Why would you want to see some sappy romantic movie when there's an X-men movie playing? I mean, who does that?"

Indy laughed, reached out to put his hand on Noah's

thigh. "Tell me, which movie will bring me in the right mood for some fun afterward...the X-men movie that will scare the shit out of me, or a romantic movie that according to the reviews has some steamy love scenes? There's a reason the thing is rated R, you know?"

Noah's face lit up. "I hadn't thought of it that way. You're saying I will be rewarded for going to that movie with you?"

Indy snorted. "Now he's interested. Damn, you're so predictable. Besides, who says the reward will be for you? Maybe I'll let you satisfy me for a change."

Noah didn't respond with the expected quip, so Indy cocked his head to watch him. Noah's face was serious. *Uh oh.* Had he said something wrong? He thought back to his words, the joke of Noah pleasuring him. Was that how Noah felt already, like Indy was taking more than he was giving?

It was true to a certain extent. Indy still couldn't provide what Noah needed, which was where Josh came in. But when he could, he did try to please Noah. He'd never deprived him of a release when he was able to offer one. Every time he saw Noah was in pain, he'd been there for him. Was Noah not satisfied? Indy bit his lip.

Noah's hand covered his, still on Noah's thigh. "Stop worrying, baby. I'm not mad at you." His voice was soft, kind.

Indy released his lower lip. "You look a little put out," he observed.

"This may not be the best time to talk about it," Noah said. The fact that there was something to talk about caused Indy's stomach to swirl uncomfortably. He'd fucked up, somehow. He'd rather know now, otherwise it wouldn't let him go.

"Just spit it out," he said. His voice was filled with the same angst wrecking his body.

Noah shot him a quick look sideways before refocusing

his attention on the road. "Yesterday evening, when you gave me a blow job, did you want to?"

Indy frowned. What kind of question was that? "What do you mean? You came back exhausted from your shift, clearly in pain."

Noah sighed. "Remember when we had sex for the first time? You told me you wanted me to take pleasure, to not always make it about you. You wanted me to let go of the guilt, remember?"

Indy nodded, his teeth once again in his lower lip. Where was Noah going with this?

"You were right, and I've tried to change my attitude. But the other way around is true as well. Indy, you can't always make it about me. The fact that I'm tired or in pain doesn't mean you should have sex with me or even help me find release."

"I don't understand," Indy said, panic storming through his veins. What was Noah he saying? Didn't he like the sex with Indy? Was he doing something wrong? Oh, God, did he prefer Josh? For the first time, a red-hot jealousy raged in his system.

He yanked his hand from under Noah's, crossed his arms. "So it's okay when Josh does it, but not for me? Do you like the sex with him more?" The words flew out of his mouth, his filter obliterated in the pain and jealousy.

Noah gasped. "No! Baby, no. You're misunderstanding me."

Tears burned hot behind his eyes, but Indy refused to let them out. He stubbornly looked out the window, his fists clenched and his body tight with stress. If Noah was ending this, he'd damn well restrain himself from crying. He hadn't cried when Eric had raped him, so he'd not cry over this. He'd survive, somehow.

Noah suddenly took an exit, whipping the car onto the empty parking lot of the middle school. He yanked the shift in P.

Indy's body went on high alert. He stared at the door handle. Should he get out of the car? Noah was pissed off, so anything could happen. If he so much as touched him, he would—Noah's hand found his shoulder, and Indy reacted on instinct. His hands came up, dragged Noah's hand off his shoulder and bent it backwards until Noah yelped in pain. Whatever, he deserved it if he thought he could hurt Indy like this. He'd go down fighting.

"Indy, I love you. I love you, baby. I'm not angry with you. I won't hurt you. You're in fight mode, babe, but there's no need. I love you, so much."

Noah's words washed over him, creeping into his defensive armor. Noah kept repeating them, his voice soft and warm, battering against Indy's defenses until it registered.

Noah loves you. He isn't angry. He isn't hurting you.

He let go of Noah's hand, raising his hands in surrender. A sigh filled with pain echoed through the car as Noah rubbed his hand. Oh, God, what had he done?

The adrenaline seeped out of Indy, leaving him tired, so tired. He closed his eyes, hung his head as his hands fell limp to his legs. He'd fucked up big time, hadn't he?

"Baby," Noah said.

The tears he'd been able to hold back earlier now pushed their way through Indy's closed eyelids. He couldn't look at him, couldn't bear to witness what he'd caused.

"It's okay. I'm okay. I understand."

How could he when Indy himself didn't know what had come over him? Hot shame burned inside.

"Please, don't cry. I can't stand it when I make you cry. I love you. Please, Indy."

Noah's pleadings made little sense to Indy, but they rattled him enough to make him open his eyes and look at his boyfriend. Noah's face displayed none of the anger and reproach Indy had expected to see. Instead, he sported a pained expression, but his eyes radiated with love.

"I'm sorry," Indy whispered. "I didn't mean to hurt you."

"It was my fault. I shouldn't have started this in the car, and I damn well should've worded it differently. You thought I was telling you I didn't like the sex with you, correct?"

Indy nodded, bit his lip. "Do you?"

"Yes. Fuck, yes. So much. That's not at all what I was trying to say, and I'm so sorry."

"I don't understand. Why is it okay if Josh helps you find release, but not me?"

"It's not okay with Josh either, and I realize that more and more. I've established this pattern where I make others do something to make me feel better—and it's not right. What I was trying to say, was that I felt yesterday evening you weren't in the mood for a blow job. You were tired, and I was late from work again, and you wanted to sleep. But you felt obligated to help me, and it wasn't right. You shouldn't feel like you have to have sex when you don't want to, especially not you. It makes me feel like such a selfish bastard, and I don't want to anymore. With Josh, the guilt was always there, but with you it's unbearable. I can't do this to you, to us."

Every word Noah said hit home. "I hadn't even realized I didn't feel like it yesterday until you pointed it out," Indy said.

"I know, baby. And I'm even more sorry if that makes you feel crappy. You've been programmed to attend to the needs of others before your own, out of survival instinct, and it's a hard habit to break. I don't want that for us. I don't want you to ignore how you feel to please me."

Indy smiled, a sad smile. "You would've been an awesome shrink," he said.

"I'd rather be an awesome boyfriend. Promise me, baby. Promise me you'll say no when you don't want to do something."

"I can promise I'll try. But like you said, it's so ingrained that it's gonna be hard to break that habit." He hesitated.

"What is it?" Noah asked. The guy really could read him like a book.

"H-how will you cope?" He wasn't articulate, but he hoped Noah would understand him anyways.

"I don't know, but I'll have to find a way. I can't be using Josh like this anymore either. He deserves more."

Indy nodded. "He does. I would love for him to find someone, you know?"

His heart clenched painfully. God, he wanted to see Josh happy, but, he couldn't bear the idea of losing him. If Josh would move out, it would... No, he refused to think about it.

Noah sighed, rubbed his hand again. Red spots were still visible where Indy's fingers had dug in. "I'd hoped Connor would make a move, but I guess he chickened out."

He'd told Indy about their conversation in the hospital, about telling Connor Josh was available. Maybe the cop had decided coming out of the closet was too big a price to pay. Indy felt bad for Josh, but he couldn't deny he'd felt relieved. Josh cozying up with a cop from Boston was about the last thing Indy needed.

"You okay now?" Noah asked.

Indy grimaced. He'd completely overreacted. "Yeah."

"Can I touch you?"

He nodded. Noah pushed his car seat back all the way,

then held out his hands to Indy. Fuck, yes. He needed this, needed him. He climbed over the middle console and lowered himself on Noah's lap, his back toward the driver's window. Noah's arms circled him, and he put his cheek on Noah's shoulder, letting out a breath that released tension from his chest and shoulders.

"I love you," he said.

Noah kissed his forehead. "I love you, too, baby. I'm so sorry for triggering your fight mode. But I'm proud of you for fighting me, for being assertive. It eases my mind to know that you'll fend me off if necessary."

The thing that had gotten him into so much trouble was what Noah praised in him. His stubbornness, his feistiness, Noah wanted him that way. Indy relaxed even more, crawling deeper into Noah's arms. The sensation of those two strong arms holding him never failed to calm him, center him.

A sudden knock on the window made them both jump. Noah cursed. "Stay calm," he whispered in Indy's ear.

Noah lowered the driver's window. Indy stayed where he was, sensing Noah didn't want him to move. "Officer," Noah said.

Indy tensed. *Fuck. A cop.*

"This is not an appropriate place to make out," a stern voice said.

"We weren't making out, Officer. We were on our way to the movies when my girlfriend had a panic attack. I pulled into the parking lot here to help her calm down. Physical contact helps, but as you can see we are both completely dressed. I promise you, nothing untoward happening here."

Noah's voice was calm, steady. Indy never moved an inch, but his mind was racing. If the cop asked him to get out, what should he do? He'd be okay unless he somehow suspected him to be lying about his identity. But there was no reason, was there? Noah had identified him as a woman, so why would the cop think otherwise?

"Can you turn around, slowly, so I can see your face?"

Noah's hand squeezed Indy's side, communicating the cop was talking to him. Indy had to obey, his heart racing. He ungracefully turned around on Noah's lap, resisting the urge to straighten his clothes. His mascara had to be streaked from crying, but maybe that would only help. A flashlight shone in his face, and he blinked. It lowered, but Indy still couldn't make out the cop's face. He sounded young, but other than that Indy didn't have a clue. No Boston accent, though. Not that the odds of running into another Boston cop were high, but the odds had never treated him well.

"Is she of age?"

"Yes, sir. She's twenty. Do you want to see her driver's license?"

"That's okay. I believe you. I'll wait in my car until you're ready to move along, all right? I need to make sure you're leaving."

"I understand. We'll be out of here in a few minutes, Officer. Thank you for your understanding."

"Have a nice evening," the cop said, before walking out of their sight.

Noah closed the window. Indy let out a shuddering breath. Too close. That had been too close. One of these days, his luck was gonna run out, and someone would recognize him.

His stomach rolled in fear, but he pushed it back down. "Can we please go home?"

∾

CONNOR HAD NEVER DONE DRUGS, not even once in his life, having seen the destruction it brought to his family, but this was what being high had to feel like. On his back in bed, Josh resting on top of him, their slick bodies calming down, their hearts beating as one—no drug could beat this feeling.

A threesome with Noah. He'd known Josh was joking, well, after his initial shock, but it made him wonder again. What was the deal with Josh and Noah? They were lovers, Josh had said, yet Noah was involved with Indy—and had no qualms about Connor going after Josh. It didn't make sense at all.

"Can I ask you about Noah?" He tried to make his voice light, not wanting to go full interrogation on Josh.

"You can ask me anything after you just fucked me into oblivion."

The words coming out of Josh's mouth. Who would've ever thought an innocent-looking, cute guy like Josh would have such a mouth on him? The dirty sex talk had been a fucking turn-on. Not as much as his ass, though, greedily swallowing Connor's cock.

Ever since Connor had accepted he was gay, he'd come to see his cock as more of a curse than a good thing. Guys always bragged about their lengths and how awesome it was to be hung, but it wasn't helpful for backdoor entry. He'd never thought he'd be able to fuck someone, had more or less resigned himself to hand jobs forever—until Josh. That his lean body had taken him in, it blew his mind. And his balls.

He let his hands roam Josh's back, the soft skin still clammy under his rough fingers. "You and Noah, you are lovers, right?"

"We're fuck buddies. Have been for the last year, ever since he lost his leg."

"What's the difference between lovers and fuck buddies?" His hands found Josh's ass, stroked the taut muscles that shivered at his touch.

"Noah doesn't love me like that."

"But you love him." It was a dangerous statement to make to a guy you were holding in your arms after the best sex ever, but Connor had to know. Did he even stand a chance at Josh's heart or was it only about sex? "It's okay if you do. I'd understand. From what I've seen, he's a good guy."

Josh was quiet for a long time, but he didn't pull away from Connor's touch. Josh's hands were still around his neck and biceps, the fingers relaxed against his skin. He was thinking, apparently, and Connor understood. It wasn't an easy question he'd asked.

"I've loved Noah since the day I met him, and I wanted him, but I've always known we weren't meant to be lovers. So I've held back, giving him the part of me that I could without risking to lose too much. We're best friends with benefits, and he takes care of me, as much as I take care of him. But we're too codependent and fucked up together to be a couple. I'm happy he's found Indy, because they're perfect for each other."

There was something so sad yet sweet in Josh's words. If he loved Noah for that long, that much, maybe he could one day love Connor?

"So why did you start fucking?"

"He needed the physical release to distract him from his pain and to help him cope with his anger. Noah has been messed up in his head since…since our last tour."

Josh didn't say since the accident, or since losing his leg, which was what Connor had expected. Did this have to do with what happened to Josh?

"And you? Why did you agree?"

"Why wouldn't I? I'm gay after all, and I got the chance to fuck the man I had wanted all this time, right?"

The bitterness in Josh's voice made Connor's stomach turn. "Bullshit. You don't owe me an explanation, but don't try to feed me this crap."

"I just want to feel good, to stop thinking, to stop being scared. When Noah fucks me, I can forget about everything else," Josh said, his voice barely audible.

A thousand questions burned on Connor's tongue, but he held them in. It was hard sometimes to turn off the inter-rogation mode, the suspicious cop-mode, but it wouldn't do him any good to push Josh. He would tell Connor when he was ready. Instead, Connor let his hands explore Josh's body further. God, his skin was so velvety soft, and yet his muscles were so tight. Not as tight as his ass. Oh, god, Josh's ass. It was sheer perfection. His hands found the two cheeks again, caressing them, sliding a finger up and down his crack where Josh's hole was still wide open from being fucked.

"Did that work with me as well?" It was the closest Connor could say without saying too much, demanding too much.

"Baby, when your cock is in my ass I can't even think at all," Josh whispered, hitting Connor's heart.

And didn't that make Connor feel more wanted than he had ever been in his entire life? Even his cock stirred, and Connor hadn't thought it would rear its head again for hours at least, considering the fuck fest they'd had.

Josh chuckled. "You like that, huh?" Josh's hand squeezed between them, grabbed his shaft. "How the fuck can you get hard again? You came twice already. You got some serious stamina."

Connor groaned, as much in embarrassment as in pleasure. Josh had better not think it hadn't been good for him, that Connor wanted more. "Sorry, can't help it. You're so fucking gorgeous. Even touching you makes me hard again. But it's okay. I'm not expecting anything."

Josh slid his thumb over the head of Connor's shaft, teasing the slit on top. "Oh, I'm expecting much more. But I need to regain my strength first, so how about we clean up, grab a bite to eat, and we'll go for round two after that?"

Connor had no words. None. At least not words that came even close to expressing how he felt. Instead, he said, "Sounds like a plan."

They cleaned themselves with a washcloth and got dressed without the awkwardness Connor had expected. He followed Josh downstairs to the luxurious kitchen.

"I'd planned something elaborate, but I can't find the energy for that right now. So what are you in the mood for?" Josh stuck his head in the fridge. "Pasta? Steaks on the grill? Salad?"

"Whatever you want," Connor said, lowering himself on a bar stool so he could watch his lover cook.

Josh looked over his shoulder. "That's not how we roll here. Tell me what you want." He closed the fridge, walked up to Connor, parked himself between Connor's legs. "Stop being so damn careful with what you say. I'm not that fragile, you know. You're not being yourself, and I like you bossy and arrogant." He kissed Connor, then turned around.

He wanted bossy and arrogant? That could be arranged. Connor yanked Josh back by his arm, pushing him backwards on his lap so his cock was plastered to Josh's ass. He slipped his arm around Josh's chest, held him tight. "In that case, make whatever is the fastest so I can pound your sweet, tight hole again," he breathed into Josh's ear.

Josh went liquid in his arms, melting against him. "Fuck, you turn me on," Josh moaned, grinding his ass against Connor's dick.

"That's good, because I want to suck your cock...hard. I want you to come in my mouth, screaming my name."

"Damn, you're good at this," Josh said half-laughing, turning his head to kiss Connor. "Pasta it is."

Josh pushed against Connor's arms, and he let him go immediately. Connor followed Josh with his eyes as he walked back to the fridge, took out ingredients. The bulge of Josh's erection was visible in his tight jeans, and Connor smiled. Josh hadn't been lying. He did get off on Connor being the alpha.

Could it be that Connor had finally found someone where he could be himself? Where he could be gay and dominant at the same time, not being forced to bow to someone else's wishes? Oh, he didn't mind compromising, not one bit. But every cell in him had protested against submitting. He wanted to be the guy on top, wanted to be the protector, the strong one. Would Josh be the one who let him?

Josh cut small tomatoes in parts and threw them into a bowl, added some salad greens, bacon bits, and moist cheese he cut into small pieces. He pulled a plastic container from the fridge that contained cooked pasta. Salt, pepper, some herbs were carelessly thrown in, together with a hefty pour of what Connor assumed was olive oil. Grated cheese on top and the pasta salad was not only done but looked like something a restaurant would serve.

"Pasta salad with arugula, bacon, mozzarella, tomatoes, and Parmesan cheese," Josh said. "I hope you like cheese."

"I love cheese. Love all food, really. After eating MRE's for years, anything tastes better than that crap."

Meals ready to eat. If ever there was a rip-off, that was it. There was a reason Marines called them the three lies: they weren't meals, they weren't ready, and they sure as hell weren't edible. Lukewarm cardboard was how Lucas had described it. Or heated pillow stuffing. Warm wallpaper glue. He'd had dozens of creative terms to describe the absolutely shitty taste of the MRE's. God, he missed him. Would it ever go away?

"Amen to that," Josh grinned, bringing Connor back to the present. He didn't want to think about Lucas, not when he was with Josh.

Josh grabbed two bowls from a cabinet, dumped a little over half the salad in one bowl and handed it to Connor. "Eat up. You're gonna need it."

"Now how the hell am I supposed to want food when you say something like that?" Connor complained, laughing.

Josh deposited the rest of the salad in the other bowl, yanked open a drawer and grabbed two spoons. "Imagine how much harder you'll be able to fuck me if you've replenished your strength."

Connor's hand got stuck halfway to his mouth with a spoonful of the pasta salad. "Keep talking like that, and you'll find out how hard I can fuck you without eating a damn bit," he growled.

Josh's eyes sparkled as he laughed. Connor took a bite, almost moaning when the taste hit his tongue. The combination of the crunchy, salty bacon with the juicy tomatoes, the soft mozzarella, the slightly bitter salad, and the rich pasta—it was perfect. He'd never even known food could be that good, being a rather simple guy himself when it came to chow.

"Damn, this is good," he said, taking another big bite. "Sorry baby, your food wins over your ass. At least for now."

They kept teasing and flirting with each other throughout the meal. Josh stayed across from Connor, the breakfast counter between them. Wise decision because Connor could barely keep his hands off the guy as it was.

They discovered they had the same taste in movies and TV series, but Connor wasn't as much into books as Josh was. They were both runners, Josh preferring long distances while Connor liked short, intensive runs and hikes. The shy Josh he'd encountered at the Stewart's disappeared, but he was still as cute and sweet as he'd been then.

Connor finished his bowl of pasta with ease, licking his lips when he was done. "Delicious," he said, pushing the bowl away from him.

Josh picked it up, rinsed it off and set it in the dishwasher. Hmm, he was a little neat freak, wasn't he? Connor could so get used to that, liking structure and order himself.

He admired Josh's ass as the guy bent to put the plates and silverware on the lower rack of the dishwasher. How could he want him again so much? What was it that made Josh have such power over him? His dick had been hard the entire meal, never letting up. Every time Josh had licked his plump lips, closing his mouth around that spoon, Connor had imagined that mouth around his cock again.

"You like the view?" Josh said, catching his stare. He closed the dishwasher, his eyes burning into Connor's.

Connor didn't even try to hide it. "Come here," he said.

Josh's eyes never left his as he walked over to Connor.

"Drop your pants."

A powerful surge tore through him when Josh did as

Connor told him. Josh's face didn't show a trace of fear or hesitation, but pure expectation. Connor shoved the bar stool back, then yanked Josh toward him and with one move, lifted him bare-assed onto the counter. Oh, yeah, he had him exactly where he wanted him.

"Spread your legs."

Josh shivered but did as Connor asked. He pulled his bar stool forward until he was in the perfect position, his face in Josh's crotch. Josh's long, slim cock was solid hard, and he couldn't wait to get his mouth around him.

"Tell me how to suck you. I will do exactly what you tell me, but you have to give me detailed instructions."

Josh moaned, leaning back on his hands for support. "Kiss my thighs and work up to my balls."

Connor dropped butterfly kisses on Josh's inner legs, licking and scraping his sensitive skin with his teeth. Josh was already trembling under his hands.

"Can you give my balls some loving attention?" Josh's voice was hoarse.

Connor dragged his tongue over Josh's left testicle, then used his nail to tease the other. Should he suck them? Would it feel good? Josh hadn't done it to him, but the thought of Josh's hot mouth around one of his balls made his cock jump. He opened his mouth, licking and sucking around Josh' nut. Josh jerked, moaned. Encouraged, Connor took his entire left testicle in his mouth, sucking gently.

"Holy fuck!" Josh bucked, grabbed Connor's head with one hand.

Connor repeated the approach for the other testicle, Josh's groans cheering him on.

"God, you're good at this... Drag your tongue upwards from my balls all the way to the head."

Connor licked the entire length, going back and forth a

few times, sucking and dropping kisses and savoring this gorgeous shaft. His own cock was a beast, but Josh wasn't small either. He wasn't as thick, which was good because it would help Connor suck him better.

Connor lapped as if Josh's cock was a dripping ice cream cone he couldn't lick fast enough to prevent it from melting. Except the taste was different, salty and creamy. He took his time licking around the head, mixing his saliva with the precum that Josh leaked.

"Take the crown in your mouth and suck it. I'm—Oh!"

Connor dropped his mouth on Josh, took him in and sucked. He tongued the slit, then paid special attention to the sensitive area between the head and the shaft. He himself had about exploded when Josh's tongue had teased him there, so he was dying to return the favor. Josh's hips came off the counter, and he thrust into Connor's mouth.

Connor pushed him back down, let Josh's cock slide out of his mouth. "You getting impatient on me? Do you want me to stop?"

"Fuck, no, sorry... Please don't stop." There was actual remorse in Josh's voice.

"Baby, I wouldn't stop for the world," Connor said, then took Josh back into his mouth. He grabbed the base of Josh's cock with his other hand, squeezing and releasing. He never knew sucking cock could feel so good, in a way even better than having your dick in someone's mouth. Seeing the pleasure he was bringing Josh, it was an incredible rush.

"Slowly work your way down, see how far you can take me in."

Josh's hand caressed Connor's head, his hair. Josh had his head thrown back, his muscles tight with tension. Connor opened his mouth wider, taking Josh in deeper and sucking harder.

"Oh, fuck! Connor...ah!"

Josh's hips flexed again, but Connor felt him coming and relaxed his tongue, taking him in. Josh's balls tightened in Connor's hand. He was close. Connor pulled back, not wanting to choke on Josh's cum as he wasn't sure if he'd be able to swallow.

Josh grunted, swore, bucked, but Connor had an iron grip on the guy's hips. He kept sucking, kept moving his head up and down Josh's shaft.

"Connor!" Josh warned. He jerked his hips, spasmed, let out a deep, low growl as he shot his fluids in Connor's mouth. Connor swallowed, pushing back Josh's cock, then sucked and swallowed again. He didn't stop sucking and licking until Josh lay limp on the counter.

Connor dropped Josh's cock, then lifted him off the counter and sat him on his lap, hugging him. Josh was weak, still trembling from his release. Connor sought his mouth, kissed him deeply, stroking Josh's back, arms, and ass.

"Fuck, Connor, that was..." Josh leaned his forehead against Connor's, still panting. "You're a natural. Seriously. Perfect technique and A for effort."

"Only an A? Hmm, will have to try harder to get an A-plus next time."

"I won't survive an A-plus, not kidding. I'm pretty sure I drew cum from my toes."

Connor was ridiculously pleased with the praise. He'd been wicked scared to disappoint Josh, considering what a master the guy was at giving head, but also since he had so much more experience. The comparison with Noah wasn't fair, but it was there all right.

"Connor?" Josh leaned back to meet his eyes. "Why don't I catch my breath while you run upstairs."

Connor frowned. "To do what?"

Josh ground his ass on Connor's cock. "Take a guess."

"I don't expect you to... Are you sure? Isn't it still..." Connor stammered.

"The offer expires in 30 seconds, so make it snappy," Josh said and slid off Connor's lap. Connor wasted five seconds by staring at Josh in disbelief. He couldn't seriously be ready to...? Was he? Damn, he was. Josh wanted to be fucked again; the sheer lust on his face was obvious.

Connor shot to his feet and took a sprint through the kitchen, up the stairs, Josh's laughter following him. The lube was still on the bed and he grabbed it, then yanked a condom from his wallet and raced back down. Josh was waiting for him, his arms leaning on the counter, his underwear and pants on the floor, his legs spread wide. The invitation could not be clearer.

Connor dropped his pants and boxers in a second. He rolled the condom on with a little less fumbling than last time, though still not as quick and practiced as he'd liked. He flipped the top of the lube off with his thumb and took a healthy dose, rubbing it over his sheathed cock. With a quick motion, he threw the lube on the counter, a last bit of glob left on his right fingers.

He inserted a lubed finger into Josh's hole. It was still so stretched, that he easily added a second, then a third. He spread the lube around, circling and probing.

"Fuck me already," Josh snapped, pushing Connor's hands away. "I want your cock to fill me again."

Connor guided himself in with his right hand, circled his left hand around Josh's chest, pulling him close. "I want to feel you, hold you tight. That okay with you?"

Josh grunted.

"It's not too tight with my arm like this?" Connor checked again.

"Shut the fuck up and work that cock," Josh said, his voice low.

Sweeter words had never reached Connor's ears, and he eased in. Josh tensed up at first but quickly relaxed, and Connor's cock slid in without resistance. He did an experimental thrust, circled his cock to make sure Josh was ready. Josh's ass was completely relaxed, engulfing him in that tight way that transformed Connor into an animal with the desperation to breed.

"Brace yourself," he groaned.

"Finally." Josh pushed his ass back.

Connor forgot all about wanting to take it easy and slammed deep into him, holding Josh's body tight to protect him from the impact. Damn, standing behind him like that, he had the perfect angle to hit that sweet spot, too. His next thrust proved it as Josh moaned and jerked. He bowed over Josh, holding him down with some of his weight, scraping Josh's neck with his teeth as he rammed his cock into him, again and again and again.

"Fuck, your ass is heaven." Connor wasn't even sure if he thought it or had said it out loud. The roar in his ears prevented him from hearing anything else but his heartbeat in his head and the hum of ecstasy in his veins. He plunged in again, hard, pleasure surging from his toes to the core of his balls.

"Damn you, motherfucker, I will fucking kill you!" Connor was yanked back by two strong arms, spun around. He tripped over the pants at his ankles, still struggling to find balance when a fist hit him square in the mouth, and he went down hard. A large weight dropped on top of him, and he took another hit to the jaw that knocked him out cold.

5

One second Josh was writhing in pleasure, Connor's fat cock filling him to the max, the next Connor's dick was brutally yanked out of him, and he almost fell with the force of it.

Noah was yelling, furious.

What the fuck?

"Noah, no!" Indy screamed.

Disoriented, Josh stumbled. His entire body froze. Connor was on the ground, bare-assed, Noah beating the shit out of him.

Why? Oh, God, what is happening?

His eyes saw, but his mind would not follow. He pressed his palms against his temples, panic rolling through his belly, his lungs.

"Dammit, Noah, he's out! Stop!"

Why is Indy shouting?

Josh's mind seemed to detach from his body, and he watched as Indy dropped himself on Noah, wrapping his legs around Noah's head and putting him in a tight headlock to pull him off of Connor.

Stop!

Stop!

Bitter bile rose in his throat.

Nauseous.

Hot.

Where was he?

Rancid sweat filled his nose, mixed with dust. So much dust and sand.

He couldn't breathe, not with the strong hand clamped over his mouth. Mean fingers dug into his arms and legs, nails drawing blood, holding him so tight his circulation was cut off. A breeze of hot air touched his bare ass as his legs were forced apart.

"You sick little cock lover." The voice was spitting with hate.

He whimpered. Stop! Please stop. A massive hand forced down his neck, bending him over.

"Hold him tight, boys. I'll show this little faggot what happens when he eyes me in the shower. Fucking queer."

Three pairs of combat boots on the dusty floor. Three pairs. He stopped struggling. He didn't stand a chance.

"See? He wants it. The sick faggot wants to be fucked. We'll show him, boys, won't we? By the time we're done you won't ever look at another cock again."

He'd been beaten up so many times in high school before Noah had come to save him. It was how he had learned to retreat in his mind, to block out anything happening to him.

Noah, he would focus on Noah. Noah would save him. He always did.

He wouldn't cry.

He wouldn't scream.

He wouldn't beg.

He thought of Noah as the pain tore him in two, ripped him apart.

It hurts, oh, God it hurts, it hurts too much...

And then he stopped thinking at all and let himself fall into the darkness, finally letting out the screams of pain.

"Josh...Josh, come back to us. You're safe, Josh, no one is hurting you."

The voice pierced through the darkness, the fog in his head. His mind burned, stabbed. His throat hurt from screaming.

"Josh, you're home. You're okay. I've got you."

Home? Then why couldn't he breathe? His heart was drumming in his ears, his whole body so tense it hurt. Cold floor under his naked body.

"Breathe in deeply, Josh, recognize the smell? You're on the kitchen floor. You're home."

A wheezing breath entered his lungs. Finally, oxygen. The smell of citrus, vanilla. Not sand, desert.

"Noah?" His voice was broken, scratched.

"I'm right here, Josh."

Noah. He would recognize that voice anywhere.

"Noah!" A sob escaped, and he extended his arms with effort, not yet able to open his eyes.

Strong arms lifted him, Noah's familiar scent enveloping him. He was home. Noah was here. He leaned against Noah's chest, inhaling as Noah's safe arms held him, tucked him close on Noah's lap. He didn't care he was naked anymore—though he did seem to be wearing a shirt—because he was safe.

What had happened? Did he have a flashback while they were fucking? Noah held him tight, rocking him, caressing his head and cheek and hair.

"I'm so sorry, Josh," Noah whispered. "So fucking sorry. This was my fault."

Josh swallowed, his throat burning like a motherfucker. "What happened?" he managed.

"Can you get him some water?" Noah asked.

Footsteps. A cabinet opening. The sound of a glass being filled with water. Josh didn't open his eyes till he felt a glass being pressed into his hands. He took it, drank deeply, pressing away from Noah's chest. He slowly became aware of his surroundings.

He was on Noah's lap. They were on the kitchen floor, Noah leaning back against the dishwasher. Indy was standing close to them, his face taut with worry. And in the corner of the kitchen, dripping blood from his mouth and holding an ice pack against his jaw, sat Connor, half-slumped against the wall, wearing only boxers. A condom was on the floor next to him.

Josh was shocked back into reality.

He scrambled up from Noah's lap, stumbled to his feet, still dizzy from the experience. "You attacked him!"

Josh found his underwear and pants and put them back on with angry, uncoordinated moves. Indy sprang up, then extended a hand to Noah to pull him to his feet.

"Damn you, Noah! You can't do that!" Josh yelled. He shoved Noah back with two hands, didn't give a fuck Noah was off-balance without his crutches. "You didn't want me, okay? You chose Indy, and I was happy for you. But you can't turn into a fucking jealous asshole when I find someone as well. I like him!" He shoved Noah again, pushing him with his back against the counter.

"It wasn't like that!"

"Then why the fuck did you hit him? He's fucking bleeding! You knocked him out cold, asshole!"

"I didn't recognize him from behind, thought he was some guy raping you!"

Josh stilled. "What?"

Noah dragged his hands through his hair. "We walked in, and he had you bent over on the counter, holding you down with his weight, his dick in your ass. He had his pants around his ankles. I didn't see it was Connor. I thought... I thought it was happening all over again, dammit!"

Josh stared at Noah, at a loss for words. Noah buried his face in his hands. "I wasn't there to save you, and I'll never forgive myself for that, but I thought it was happening again. I only wanted to protect you."

Was he crying? Josh's suspicions were confirmed when Noah's body shook. "I'm sorry, Josh... I'm so fucking sorry."

They weren't talking about Connor anymore, he understood. How had he missed Noah's guilt all this time? "It wasn't your fault," Josh mumbled.

Noah dropped his hands with fury, his face tear-stricken. "Yes, it was. You were there because of me in the first place. The army was no place for you, and we both knew it. I was supposed to keep you safe, and I failed. I should've known, should've been there."

Noah's anger. His guilt. His fierce protectiveness of Josh. Things clicked in Josh's head. *Oh, God.*

"Is that why you fucked me? Because you felt sorry, wanted to make up for what you thought you'd done wrong?"

If Noah said yes, his heart would break into a million pieces. He could take Noah not loving him. He understood why they wouldn't work. But Noah using him to assuage his own guilt, that was a blow he would not recover from.

"No! Fuck, no, why would you think that?"

"Why wouldn't I? You never told me this, and we were

supposed to be honest with each other. You never said how guilty you felt for what happened to me. And for the record: it wasn't your fault, and I never blamed you. For fuck's sake, you went to your dad to make sure those three were court-martialed and thrown in jail. You made sure justice was served, and that they got what they deserved."

Noah clenched his fists, the veins in his neck bulging. His eyes showed a cold fury Josh had never seen there before. "They didn't get what they deserved. Every single day I regret going the official route. I should've done what I wanted in the first place, which was to lure them out one by one and beat the shit out of them. I should've fucking killed them for what they did to you."

Josh couldn't wrap his head around it. How could Noah feel so protective of him he'd be willing to kill for him? Where was this guilt coming from?

"Then why did you ask me to help you find release, that night at the hospital?"

"Because I wanted to. Because I had missed you the weeks before, had been worried sick about you, wanted to make sure you were okay. Dammit, because I wanted you... I had these weird dreams about you sucking me, about you riding my cock that felt so real and god, they were good."

Josh looked down, couldn't meet Noah's eyes.

Noah gasped. "They weren't dreams, were they? They were memories..."

"Yes," Josh admitted, his chest clenching tight. "It was one night, on my birthday, after you'd lost your mom. We were both drunk. I thought you didn't remember since you never brought it up. I was scared you'd be repulsed if I told you."

He still didn't look up, certain he'd lost Noah's friendship forever. Instead, he felt two strong arms embrace him. Noah hugged him for what seemed like a minute without saying anything, then pulled back and kissed Josh on his mouth. "Josh, I don't know anymore how to make you understand this... That repulsion you're always so scared of, it exists in your head alone. Ever since the day we became friends, I have never, ever been ashamed of you, repulsed by you, or embarrassed by you. I love you for who you are, and I would die to keep you safe."

He kissed him again with a gentle tenderness and Josh's throat got tight all over again.

"I asked you to help me because I wanted you and because I knew you wanted me too," Noah said. "Yes, I wanted to replace your memories with something good. I wanted you to experience sex with someone who loved you so that one day you'd be able to find the love of your life. You are so hung up on labels, so desperate to define what you are, what I am, who and what we are to each other that you missed the bigger picture. I wouldn't have survived this last year without you and your love. You helped me feel secure in my masculinity, even with my missing leg. You helped me discover parts of myself I never even knew existed. And dammit, Joshua, every single time we fucked, I have made love to you the best I knew how. I'm fucking jealous of you for remembering our first time, since I don't. I have never, ever used you without loving you right back, even if it wasn't the love you had pictured. I love, love, love having sex with you—and I'd be tempted right now to ask Indy for permission to fuck you senseless to prove it to you if I wasn't damn sure Connor would have an issue with that. You should see how he looks at you, as if you are the most beautiful, gorgeous, precious thing he's ever encountered. What you've been looking for, it's right there, Josh, but not with me. And I would apologize for that if I wasn't so sure that we wouldn't be good together in the long run. Not as partners, not like that. But I love you so fucking much."

It was the longest speech Josh had ever heard Noah make, and every word hit him like a jackhammer. Noah's eyes never left Josh's as he spoke directly to his heart.

Josh breathed in, out. In. Out.

It's time.

He stepped back from Noah's arms, but stayed close, his eyes never leaving those green, loving eyes.

"They attacked me when I came back from patrol. The other guys, they knew who you were, and they were too scared of your dad to mess with me much. Plus, I'd gained their respect as a sniper, since I was damn good. But this unit was new, and they didn't know you."

In. Out.

"I'd encountered them in the shower, days before. I was surprised because I didn't know them. I swear, I wasn't ogling them. Shit, I knew better than to draw that kind of attention to myself. Still, they took offense, called me a faggot, a fucking queer. I thought I'd apologize, make a joke of it. I thought that was the end of it."

He rubbed his neck, sighed. "They caught me with Dean two days later. Stupid bad luck. You knew Dean and I would mess around every now and then. I was sucking him off, and they walked in on us. Dean didn't know what to say, accused me of coming on to him. He didn't mean to throw me under the bus, didn't know what they would do. When I came back from patrol a couple of days later, they grabbed me, pulled me into an empty container. I stopped fighting when I realized there were three of them, knew it was useless."

He choked up, fought for control. Did he have the strength to finish it? Could he share for the first time what he'd been through? Not like this, not standing in the kitchen. He needed to feel safe, safer. He wanted strong arms around him when he broke.

Connor's.

His legs were too sluggish to carry him, and Connor was still on the floor, though he had put on his pants in the meantime. Josh dropped to his knees and crawled over to Connor, tears streaming down his face. Connor opened his arms wide, pulling Josh between his legs, folding those big arms around him. Josh leaned back against the broad chest behind him, letting his head rest against Connor's shoulder.

He breathed in. Out. It needed to be said.

"They called me names. Faggot, queer, cock lover...and they raped me. The pain was...it was so bad, and I passed out."

A sob tore through him.

"They left me there...like a used condom on the floor."

Connor kissed his head, tightened his grip on Josh. He pulled strength from that.

"They were probably scared after I'd passed out. I don't think they meant for that to happen; they just wanted to punish me. I woke up later, still bleeding. I didn't want to go to the CSH, knowing you'd be there, Noah... I knew you'd go after them, get yourself in trouble. So I went back to the barracks and took a shower. But the pain was so bad, and it wouldn't stop bleeding. I was scared of internal bleeding, terrified they'd torn me up inside, and that I'd bleed to death."

Noah limped over to where Josh and Connor were sitting, lowered himself to the floor as well, Indy following suit. Josh realized the boy hadn't said a word, but he'd watched them. Indy's sweet, brown eyes shone with tears. Seeing his own anguish reflected on Indy's face comforted

Josh. Indy understood. Their eyes met, and Indy smiled through his tears.

Indy nestled against Noah, giving him the support Josh knew he needed. Noah took a deep breath. "You passed out again before you made it inside the CSH. Some guy carried you in," he said, his voice raw. "Your pants were soaked in blood, and I thought I'd lost you. Fuck, Josh, you were so pale and so weak, and I thought you'd die right there. I didn't understand what had happened, thought you'd somehow been shot. When we saw... It took three guys to hold me back, did you know? Three guys pinned me to the floor because I was ready to find whoever did that to you and fucking kill him. They didn't let me go until I had a grip on myself. Until I had promised I would only hold your hand and nothing else. I claimed you, Josh, right then and there. There wasn't a single man in that hospital who doubted you were mine."

It was like Josh felt the wounds inside of him healing. He hadn't known, hadn't realized Noah had made him so much more than a friend even then.

"I held your hand when Graves operated on you, repaired what they'd done to you. It was superficial, though bloody, but the sight of you on that table... I was ready to go AWOL to take you home. It was Graves who convinced me to go up the ranks instead of going rogue. I told your CO what had happened, and when he didn't seem impressed, I went over his head all the way to my dad. He was furious, anti-gay as he is. He couldn't believe these guys had dese-crated the uniform like that and had done that to a fellow soldier. It took us only twenty-four hours to find them. Somebody had spotted them coming out of that container and ID'ed them. And you fucking refused to go home, to take the honorary discharge I'd gotten you. I was so fucking angry with you."

"I wasn't leaving you," Josh said. "I saw your pain for me, Noah, watched you push it deep inside. It killed you that I didn't want to talk about it, couldn't talk about it, not even with you. You were a big load of C4 waiting to explode. I wanted to tell you everything, but it hurt too fucking much. Maybe I was scared you'd see me differently, treat me differently, like I was even weaker and more of a victim than I'd been before. Just when I felt like I could maybe talk about it, you went on that fucking patrol, and I watched you get blown up through my telescope."

This was the last part and the hardest bit, even more difficult than talking about the rape. He'd known he would survive being brutalized, even as it happened, but seeing Noah explode… That had broken him.

"I should have seen it, Noah," he managed to say what he'd been feeling ever since, what had caused his break down in the first place. "I should've seen the irregularities on the surface, should've noticed there might be an IED hidden."

"Bullshit," Noah said forcefully. "Fucking bullshit and you know it. I was stupid, not paying attention."

"Because of me!" Josh cried out. "Because you were worried about me!"

"No! Because I was angry with myself for enlisting in the first place. Dammit, Josh, I should've never signed up, never. It wasn't my dream, and it certainly wasn't yours. I got blown up because I was trying to work out in my head when we could get a discharge, how I could make that happen sooner than later. I wanted both of us out, and I was thinking about that instead of paying attention to the terrain. I was careless, and I paid the price for that."

"And maybe it's time to let go of your guilt and forgive yourself for all of that, Noah." It was the first time Indy spoke up. "You're carrying a wicked amount of guilt, and it's fucking eating you alive. Josh decided to enlist; you didn't force him to. Instead of feeling so damn guilty, embrace the love behind that decision. You guys have had each other's backs for so long, but you're both feeling guilty for the consequences of that. Your brotherhood is beautiful, but there's no place for guilt in love, only remorse over mistakes —and that's what you forgive each other for...and yourself."

Josh and Noah stared at each other, Josh safe in Connor's arms and Noah holding Indy.

"I'm sorry for enlisting," Noah said, his voice thick and raw.

"I'm sorry, too," Josh brought out.

"I'm so sorry for what happened to you," Noah said. "More than anything, I wish I could've prevented that."

"I know. I don't blame you, not one bit. Thank you for standing up for me. I'm sorry for doubting your motives for sleeping with me. I should've known better."

"I understand. It's hard to feel loved when you've received so little of it before."

"And I'm sorry for not telling you we had that night together."

"I'm sorry for forgetting. The dreams were pretty sweet, though."

Josh's mouth curved upward. Peace. Finally. He leaned back, relaxed in Connor's arms. "How are you, baby?" he asked, turning his head and nuzzling his neck. "Noah hit you pretty damn hard."

"Much better now that I'm holding you. Besides, the guy hits like a girl."

Josh chuckled. Classic male pride at work.

"May I remind you that if I hadn't held Noah down, your face would have looked different?" Indy said, taking offense. "I had to take him in a tight headlock to get him to stop hitting you."

"Yeah, when I imagined my face between your legs, it was a little different," Noah said. Indy jabbed him in the ribs with his elbow.

Connor said, "Now that we've all kissed and made up, can somebody please explain why all of a sudden Indy is a guy and from Boston instead of from the Deep South?"

6

There was something eerily familiar about Indy, and it tickled Connor's brain. The first time he'd seen her in Stewart's she'd looked familiar, but he hadn't been able to place her. All of his alarm bells were going off now he realized Indy was, in fact, a guy. Where had he seen the boy before?

He trained his eyes on Indy. The boy's hands flew to his stomach, clutching it. He looked to Noah, then to Josh, who had frozen in Connor's arms. Something was wrong.

"Look, Connor," Noah started. He tightened his grip on Indy as if to prevent him from running off.

"No offense, but I'd rather have Indy himself explain. And I let you get away with hitting me, so don't give me any crap."

Indy's grip on Noah's arm was so hard, the boy's knuckles were white. That had to leave some serious bruises. What had the kid so scared?

"You're right, I am from Boston, South Boston. Grew up there." Indy shifted, wrung his hands. It was obvious he didn't want to tell this. "A couple of years ago I screwed up, got involved with the wrong guy. I was young, stupid, didn't know any better. I didn't see who he was until it was too late. He was a drug dealer, a nasty one. I got away but stole money from him, and he swore to take revenge, so I've been living under a false identity."

Lightning struck in Connor's brain. A nasty drug dealer from South Boston who was hell-bent on revenge. *Duncan Fitzpatrick. Holy fuck.* It was like he could finally connect the pieces, had found the right search term for his brain to recognize Indy.

"Stephan Moreau. Holy mother of all, you're alive."

Indy scrambled up, pushing himself off Noah, who let him go immediately.

"I'm on your side," Connor said loud and clear, realizing Indy was about to bolt out the door and would not come back. No wonder. He couldn't believe Stephan Moreau was still alive. He'd thought the Fitzpatricks had gotten to him, had silenced him forever and dumped his body never to be found again.

"Stephan, I mean, Indy, hear me out for five minutes, okay? Five minutes, that's all I'm asking. And if after that you decide you want to run, Noah can take my phone and keep me here under lock and key until you're safe."

Indy stood, one hand on the door to the garage. "Start talking."

Connor got up from the floor, untangling himself from Josh. He kept his distance from Indy, not wanting to spook him even more. "My mother is Brenda O'Connor, born Brenda Mary Fitzpatrick. She's the second daughter of Jeremy Fitzpatrick, Duncan's grandfather. Duncan's father Brian is my mom's younger brother. My mom, she wanted out, was tired of the violence, the risks. So she married a guy she'd met in high school, Anthony O'Connor, and got pregnant with me. She was still part of the family but wasn't involved in their dealings and neither was my dad."

Indy's face was so white, Connor feared he would faint. "You're a Fitzpatrick. I'm so fucked." His voice was barely audible, but the fear was palpable.

"I'm on your side, Indy, I promise. I never was a Fitz-patrick." How could he make Indy believe him? "I'm five years older than Duncan, and I was already in the Marines when he rose to power. I wanted nothing to do with it, and I'm no longer in touch with my family. Believe me, I abhor everything they stand for. It's why I joined the Marines, and it's also why I became a cop."

"If that's the case, then why didn't you ever come forward to testify against them? I didn't see your name on the list for the prosecution when the DA was preparing the case with me as the main witness."

Connor winced. He cut right to the core, didn't he? Fuck, once more he'd have to share more than he wanted to. It seemed to be the theme of his life at the moment. One look at Josh, still on the floor, staring at him with big eyes, made his priorities crystal clear. There was no way he was walking away from this man. He'd share whatever the fuck he had to to stay with Josh.

"I'd been in the Marines for years by then, overseas most of the time, and I had no firsthand knowledge of anything recent. But the main reason is that I was scared. They'd warned my parents, my mother especially, what would happen if one of us ever dared to turn against them. I knew what they were capable of..." His voice trailed off as he realized Indy knew better than anyone else. How weak his excuses sounded, compared to what Indy had been through and had still the courage to do.

He cleared his throat. "My mother contacted me in

Afghanistan, told me about the case. She begged me to stay away from it. She was scared I'd find out from someone else and would decide to testify against Duncan. After what happened to you, I was terrified of what they would do to my parents, maybe even my friends. When you disappeared, we all thought they'd gotten to you. I wrestled with my guilt for a long time. Fuck, Stephan, I am more sorry than you can imagine."

"My name is Indy. I buried Stephan Moreau a long time ago." Indy's voice was cold as ice. Connor nodded that he understood. He wouldn't make that mistake again.

"When I left the Marines, I left Boston as well. Never been back since. I wanted to stay far away from all of them, all of it. I broke off all contact with my parents, couldn't stomach it anymore. My dad passed away last year, but I didn't even go to his funeral. I'm not telling you this because you need to feel sorry for me, but I want you to know the facts."

You're not giving him all the facts. No, he wasn't. Because if he told Indy what he'd known, with Noah and Josh listening in, they'd kick him out the door. He'd been such a fucking coward. He swallowed back the bile of shame.

Indy said, "I need proof. I need to know one hundred percent certain you're not lying, because if you sell me out to Duncan, I'm dead. And don't even bother telling me you're a cop, because we both know how many boys in blue were on the Fitzpatrick's payroll. I don't trust cops, ever."

"I understand. Merrick, the DA who was on your case, is still there. You know he was not on their side. Ask him to check out my story. He's determined to bring the Fitz-patricks down."

Indy shook his head. "I can't call him. His phone may be

tapped, or they're monitoring his communications. Duncan has people everywhere, and I can't lead them here."

With anyone else, this would've been ridiculous and paranoid, but Indy was rightly worried. After the devastating blow he'd delivered the Fitzpatricks by killing Connor's cousin Eric, handing over sensitive information to the DA, and then escaping before he could be killed, he was their number one priority. If his family knew Stephan was still alive—and they had to know since they were the only ones interested in killing him and hadn't succeeded—they'd do anything to get their hands on him. Anything.

There had to be a big, fat contract out on the kid. No wonder he'd been dressed as a woman. Pretty damn effective, too, because even Connor had never seen through his disguise. It would've taken him a long time to connect the dots, if ever. It'd been hearing that all-too-familiar, thick Boston accent that had triggered his brain to make the right connections, and even then he'd only made it after Indy had supplied extra information.

"Do they have a contract out on you?" he asked.

"I don't know for sure, but I expect so. I took fifty grand, but it's not about that. It's about what I know and the fact that I killed Eric Fitzpatrick."

Connor scowled. "That sick motherfucker deserved everything you did to him, and then some. No jury would've ever convicted you of murder."

Indy shook his head. "For a cop who's related to the Fitzpatricks you're still damn naive. The prosecution would've painted me a whore, Duncan's whore. And who the fuck would've defended me, other than some washed-up pro bono attorney? I didn't stand a chance, which is why I sold Duncan out. Trust me, if I'd been able to walk away from that murder charge, I woulda kept my mouth shut."

Connor couldn't say anything, not when he himself had been too much of a coward to step up and do the right thing. No matter what Indy's motives had been, even if they had been self-serving, he'd been the only one willing to testify against the Fitzpatricks.

"I can reach out to the Boston PD, find out about a contract if you want. However you wanna do this, I'm on board."

"I need time to think," Indy said. He shot Noah a look filled with desperation. The kid had much to lose, and Connor's heart hurt for him.

"Look, I'll hand you my cell phone. If you'll allow me to call my boss, I can take off for the next few days to sort this out. My chief was getting on my case for too much overtime and accrued leave anyway. I'll stay right here where you can monitor me until you figure out what you want to do."

"Why would you do this?" Noah asked. "No offense, O'Connor, but what's in it for you?"

"I want them brought to justice. I grew up seeing and hearing what they did to people. They're monsters. It's why I enlisted, to escape them, to create a different future for myself. I was too scared to do this sooner, but I'm willing now. But to bring them down, the DA needs Indy. He's the only one who has the knowledge to do it."

"You mean the only one who's still alive," Indy said, the bitterness dripping from his voice.

"That, too," Connor admitted. "Witnesses do have a tendency to disappear. Though the DA has brought down a whole slew of bought cops in cooperation with the Boston PD. The Fitzpatricks don't have the clout and the reach they once had."

Indy bit his lip, studying Connor. He stayed calm under the boy's scrutiny. You couldn't blame Indy for being cautious. It's what had kept him alive the last two years. There were so many questions Connor wanted to ask him about that, like how he had managed to get a driver's license under a false name and with a different gender. But questions would make Indy distrust him even more.

"Josh ..." It was all Indy said, but Josh nodded.

"My first loyalty is to you, Indy," Josh said. He didn't even look at Connor, instead shot Indy a soft smile filled with love. Josh's words hurt Connor deep in his heart, even though rationally he understood. Of course Josh would side with Indy, but after what they had shared, it hurt. Would there ever be a time when he'd be number one on Josh's list, before Noah and Indy?

"For what it's worth, I trust Connor, and I think he's telling the truth, but I'll do whatever you want me to," Josh added.

"I agree, but it's your call, baby," Noah said.

Indy bit his lip again. "I'm too tired to think," he said.

"You can lock me in the guest bedroom for tonight without access to a phone. That way, you can sleep on it and decide in the morning," Connor offered. He had to be crazy to volunteer to be imprisoned, but he understood Indy's dilemma. Indy needed time to work it out.

Indy scoffed. "Dude, you'd burst through that window in a second if you wanted to, second floor or not."

Josh shot Connor a quick look. "I'll stay with him," he said to Indy. "You know Connor would never hurt me."

Indy's face softened for the first time since he'd found out who Connor was. "I know. But are you okay with that? Does he know about you?"

Josh stepped up to Indy, pulled him close and hugged him. "You're so sweet for worrying about me right now. It's okay, Indy, I'll tell him. Thank you." He kissed Indy on his mouth, and a stab of jealousy shot through Connor. What was it with all the kissing and the hugging here? First, he'd had to watch Noah kiss Josh and now this?

"Do you need me, Noah?"

What the ever-loving fuck? Was he jumping to conclusions or had Josh just asked Noah if he wanted to fuck him, in front of not just Indy, but Connor as well? From the low-key, almost automatic way Josh had asked the question, Connor deduced this was not the shocking question he perceived it to be. How the hell could he offer after what he'd shared with Connor today? Hadn't that meant anything to him?

"I'm good, but thank you," Noah said, pulling Indy close and kissing him on his head. The love Noah had for Indy was obvious, so how could everyone be so casual about Noah and Josh's sexual relationship?

"Problem?" Noah asked coolly, clearly witnessing the turmoil on Connor's face.

Connor jammed his hands in his pockets. "Nope, everything's peachy."

Josh looked at Connor, and his eyes widened as if he only now realized what he'd said. To Connor's satisfaction, the guy had at least the decency to blush.

"I'll go upstairs, seeing as it's close to ten." Connor desperately wanted to ask Josh to join him, order him to follow, but he held his tongue. He wasn't sure anymore where he stood with Josh, not after what had transpired. Maybe he'd attached more meaning to their fucking than he should have.

"I'll come with you," Josh said, avoiding Connor's eyes. His cheeks and ears were still flushed.

"Your phone." Indy held out his hand.

Connor dug his phone from his pocket, handed it over

without delay. "It's password protected, but the pin is 102704 if you want to check my email or anything else."

"October 27, 2004," Indy said. For the first time that evening, he smiled at Connor. "The day the Red Sox won the World Series and ended the Curse of the Bambino."

Connor nodded, not surprised Indy had gotten the reference. "Check anything you want on my phone. You'll see I'm telling you the truth."

He turned around and walked upstairs. His heart that had been so heavy did a happy little dance when Josh followed him.

Ten minutes later, they were in bed, their bodies not touching, both dressed in shirts and boxers. Connor had heard the door being locked—which was rather futile, seeing as one well-placed kick would get him out if he wanted to. He was okay with it, understood it was as much an extra measure as something to help Indy feel safer.

"You okay?" Josh asked.

"Yeah. You? What was it that Indy wanted you to tell me?"

Connor hated the physical distance between them but was hesitant to cross boundaries Josh needed him to respect.

"I have nightmares," Josh said after a spell.

That was to be expected, though Connor wondered if the nightmares were about Josh's war experiences or his assault. Probably best not to ask at this point. "What do you do to prevent them?"

"Sleep in the same bed as Noah and Indy."

"Oh, okay. Do you just need to be in the same bed, or...?"

"Connor, are we okay?"

"Why wouldn't we be?"

"Because I chose Indy over you and then offered myself to Noah."

Connor let out a breath. "That hurt," he admitted.

"The first or the second?"

"Both."

He felt Josh's hand seek his body, touch his shoulder. "Can I touch you?"

"Please," Connor said, probably way too eagerly.

In the dim light that spilled through the curtains, Connor watched as Josh sat up, whipped off his shirt. He lifted his butt, shoved down those sexy, tight, black boxers. What was he doing?

"I need to feel your skin," Josh whispered, pulling on Connor's shirt next.

Connor obliged and undressed. With a deep, satisfied sigh, Josh planted his head on Connor's shoulder, draping himself half over him. Connor circled his arm around the man, pulled him close and rested his cheek against the top of Josh's head. Naked skin on naked skin, that was something he could get used to.

"This is what I do to prevent the nightmares."

A loud moan erupted from the room next door. Josh giggled. "Noah is giving Indy a blow job."

Connor swallowed. "How do you know?"

"I recognize the sounds. I sleep with them, you know."

"They have sex with you in the room?"

"Sometimes. They try not to, to keep me from being embarrassed or plain horny, but it happens."

"And Indy is okay with Noah fucking you as well?"

"It's hard for you, isn't it? I'm sorry. I'm not used to explaining it, defending us. Yes, Noah still fucks me, mostly when he's too tired or fucked up to control himself. Sex is how he releases a lot of his pain and anger, and Indy can't take it. I can."

Connor let Josh's words sink in. The pieces of the puzzle started to make sense in his head. "I'm jealous," he admitted.

Josh's hand trailed to Connor's stomach, exploring the skin and muscles there. Connor shivered. "I don't mean to hurt you," Josh said.

Connor kissed the top of Josh's head. "Josh, do we have a chance? You and me, I mean. Will there ever be a day when you will choose me?"

He felt as if he was dangling from a rope, about to be dropped into an abyss. He'd fallen for Josh, way too fast and way too deep. It made him more vulnerable than he'd ever been in his life, and it wasn't a feeling he appreciated.

Josh lifted his head from Connor's shoulder and dragged his head down for a kiss that left Connor's head spinning. He wanted more, deeper, but couldn't with the angle of their mouths. He grabbed Josh by his arms, pulled the man on top of him and fused their mouth together again.

Josh's tongue met his, tangling, teasing, seducing. Short, quick breaths mixed with sucking sounds filled the room. Josh teased Connor's lower lip before biting it gently. A tremor tore through Connor's body. Holy smoke, the man could kiss.

Connor growled against Josh's mouth, dropping his hands to his ass to tug him closer. Josh squeezed his ass cheeks when Connor held him there, then let his legs drop on either side of Connor's as if to invite him in. Connor kept kissing him, dueling for control over Josh's mouth. He let his right hand slide through Josh's crack, felt his body shiver in response. He found the hole with his thumb, teased it, circled it. Josh pushed down, a clear invitation.

"Tell me what you want," Connor breathed into his mouth.

Josh whimpered when Connor pushed his thumb against his hole without entering.

The sounds from next door intensified, loud moans and grunts mixed in with an occasional thud against the wall. Connor smiled at the erotic sounds. It should've embarrassed him to hear Noah and Indy, but it didn't, somehow.

"I'm here, with you. Make me stop thinking, Connor."

Connor understood. Josh needed Connor to decide, to take over and make him submit. A powerful surge fired through Connor. Josh was his. He didn't know it yet, and Connor would have to be patient, but there was no doubt anymore. This gorgeous, sweet, submissive man was his. He wanted to be dominated? That could be arranged.

"Is there lube in this room?"

FUCK, yeah.

Josh trembled when Connor asked for lube. Finally, they would continue what they'd started in the kitchen. He climbed off Connor and yanked open the drawer of the nightstand. Nothing, except earplugs. He was sure there'd been a bottle of lube there, once upon a time, but somebody must've taken it. And damn, the door was locked, so what now?

He looked at Connor, spread out on the bed, his hands folded behind his head. Fuck, he looked perfect like that, all powerful, bossy male. Connor's beast of a cock stood at attention, all but demanding release.

Next door, Indy let out a hard moan. Josh hesitated. The

only way to get lube was to ask Noah to open the door, but that would be major awkward.

"If you want to be fucked, you'll have to get the lube. I have a condom in my wallet, but no lube," Connor said.

Josh leaned over to search for his boxers under the covers. The least he could do was put some clothes on.

"Uh, uh," Connor said. "I like you better naked."

The bed moved as Connor flicked on the lamp on the night table.

"Show me how much you want to be fucked," Connor said, his voice low and husky.

Dammit, the command pushed all those submissive buttons inside Josh. This, this was what he craved. He wanted to be told what to do, he needed to be used, and fuck it, he was desperate to take that huge cock in his ass again.

He shot Connor a sultry look and got up from the bed. "Noah!" He banged on the wall. "Stop fucking Indy for a second and open the door. I need something."

Next door, the noise quieted.

"Tell him what you need," Connor ordered.

Shame. That's what he should feel, right? Instead, Josh was filled with a strange, quiet peace. He felt no shame, only satisfaction, a deep need being met.

"I need the lube," he shouted, his voice more joyful than it should be.

Indy burst out in a giggle, followed by a deep grunt from Noah. Footsteps sounded, a door opened. Seconds later, the lock on their door was disengaged, and it opened. Indy—buck naked—threw Josh a big bottle of lube. "Have fun," he said with a wink.

"I will, trust me," Josh replied, catching the bottle with one hand. For a second they looked at each other and smiled. There was not a trace of jealousy on Indy's face, nor anger that Josh was quite literally sleeping with the enemy. The last bit of doubt inside Josh vaporized.

"Get your ass back in here," Noah yelled, though clearly not mad. "I wasn't done with you yet."

"Oh, pipe down, you," Indy shouted back, still smiling at Josh. "You can damn well wait till I'm good and ready."

"Get your ass back in bed," Connor said.

Josh knew what he was doing. Connor was deliberately repeating Noah's words. He was claiming Josh, showing Indy and Noah that he was the one fucking Josh, that he could boss Josh around. He was pulling Josh in with soft ropes, instead of just with words. Josh felt himself respond, didn't even want to resist.

"I have to go," he told Indy.

"Yeah, you do." Indy's smile was sweet and understanding as he closed the door and turned the lock again.

Josh turned around, faced Connor. Connor lazily fisted his rock-hard dick, his eyes fixed on Josh's. "Suck me," he commanded.

Fuck, yes. No decisions, no thinking, no doubting himself, or fear of showing too much, being too much. Josh walked straight up to the bed, dropped the bottle next to Connor on the mattress, climbed on.

"Sixty-nine," Connor said.

A deep thrill sent goose bumps all over Josh's skin. He didn't hesitate but lowered himself on Connor with his mouth on the man's dick and his ass almost in his face. Leaning on his forearms, he curled his fingers around Connor's base and raised his cock upright.

A first, tentative lick made Connor moan. Josh teased him with a hot breath, another quick lick. He ran his tongue over the crown, tasting Connor without taking him in. With a lazy stroke of his tongue, he lapped downwards, toward those huge balls. Connor's chest rumbled with something that sounded like a growl.

Josh's legs were spread wider, and he obeyed even though it left his hole wide open in Connor's face. He wouldn't...would he? Josh froze when he felt a hot, slick tongue on his ass. Teeth scraped his right cheek, his left. A finger dipped in his crack.

Fuck, yeah, Connor would. He did.

Seconds later, that moist heat traveled to his hole. Connor hoisted two arms under Josh's thighs, lifted him up like a buffet and dug in.

Rimming.

Connor was rimming him.

Josh melted, all his nerves shutting off except for the ones around his ass. God, that tongue. That mouth. Connor's smooth chin on his skin.

Connor's tongue pushed, and he let him in, welcoming him inside. It was unlike anything he'd ever felt before. When Connor sunk in deep, Josh let out a long groan.

"You like that, huh?" Connor's voice teased against his cheeks.

Like. That was the understatement of the year. He didn't like it; he fucking loved it, craved it.

Suck. He was supposed to suck Connor off. Fuck the subtle foreplay and the teasing. He couldn't concentrate with Connor's face in his ass. He opened his mouth, took Connor in as deep as he could and sucked.

Connor's hips bucked, but Josh had expected this, had put his weight on them so Connor couldn't push in too deep in a reflex. Fuck, he loved the sensation of that cock in his mouth even if it was too big to take in all the way. Maybe he'd do some research, see how he could train and practice to take him in deeper. God, his man would love that.

"Damn, baby, you're too good at that. Don't make me come yet."

With one last lap, Josh let go of Connor's dick, at the same time Connor pulled away from Josh's ass. Josh looked over his shoulder. "Don't you want to come?" he teased.

In answer, Connor reached for the lube, held it out to Josh. "Prep yourself. I'm in the mood to pound hard."

One sentence, that was all it took. The sheer mental image of Connor ramming into him was enough to not only make Josh even harder but to get him to scramble off Connor and yank the lube out of his hands.

He squeezed a generous amount of lube on his fingers, ruthlessly shoved them inside, knowing he was still stretched from their earlier fuck. Connor sat up against the headboard, watched him with burning eyes as Josh loosened himself and stretched, breathing away the burning sensation.

Connor rolled a condom on his monster cock, angled for the lube and coated it with a generous amount. "Ride me," he ordered.

Josh frowned. As much as he liked riding a cock since it allowed him to control the depth and pace, it was too passive a mode for Connor. He didn't want that man on his back doing nothing. Josh wanted him on top, fucking the shit out of him.

Still, he straddled Connor, reaching backwards with his right hand to position his cock. He lowered himself until the thick head breached him. Would he ever get used to this sensation, this deep anticipation of being filled?

Connor put his hands on Josh's thighs, holding him while Josh took him in, inch by inch. Yeah, he'd done a rush job with the prepping, and he was paying for it now, his body struggling to accommodate the thickness pushing inside him. But it wasn't merely pain. It was pain bordering on pleasure, burning with threads of pure ecstasy weaved in. He exhaled, relaxed, sunk lower, breathed out again.

Connor never moved a muscle, waiting for Josh to adjust, deeper and deeper. Finally, Connor was in all the way. Josh relaxed with a slow exhale, sat up, closing his eyes to revel in the fullness. This sensation of being full, of being complete, it was unlike anything he'd ever felt. It filled his body and heart at the same time.

"Ride me till you're completely loose," Connor told him.

He positioned two strong hands on Josh's hips, pushed him to raise and lower himself. The first few times, it still burned, but after a bit, all the pain was replaced by the familiar tingling. Josh sighed, opening himself completely. The thrill rolled over him, radiating from his ass outwards to the crown of his head. So fucking perfect.

Connor must've felt him relax because on Josh's next raise he lifted him off with strong hands. "Stand next to the bed, legs spread wide, with your arms resting on the bed," he told Josh.

A deep tremble tore through Josh's body at the words. He climbed off, did as he was told. He lowered his arms on the bed, resting his head on his forearms. It put his ass high up in the air, his hole wide and ripe for the taking.

Connor lined up behind him, put his hands on Josh's waist. "You might wanna hold on to something."

Damn, he knew how to push Josh's buttons. Shivering in anticipation, Josh grabbed the mattress with both hands and braced himself.

Connor slammed in deep, and Josh let out a hard groan. Fuck, yeah. That was what he wanted, what he needed. He lowered his body more, spread his legs wider, pushed his ass farther back shamelessly and canted it at the right angle. Anything, everything to invite Connor in.

The next thrust was so hard Connor's balls slapped against Josh's ass, the sound echoing through the room. Josh met Connor's surge with a ragged curse as he hit his prostate full on. Ecstasy rippled through him, all the way to his toes. He rubbed his cock against the sheets, delighting in the friction it brought. He was already leaking like crazy, and his cock throbbed painfully.

Connor set a steady pace of hard, deep thrusts and Josh groaned at every one, his voice drowned out by the obscene sounds of Connor ramming into him. He was so turned on, all his nerves were firing off pleasure, from his toes to the crown of his cock. He tensed, his balls pulling tight against his body.

"Don't come," Connor warned him.

"I'm so close," Josh all but wailed.

"Then hold it back."

Hot damn, Connor knew how to be dominant, didn't he? Josh clenched his teeth, fighting back his release with all he had. Sweat broke out on his forehead. He wanted to obey Connor. Dammit, he needed to, but he was so fucking close. He rocked his hips backwards, denying his cock the friction it sought. It helped, for maybe half a minute, but then he was right back on the edge.

Connor grunted as he thrust in and out of Josh. Josh closed his eyes, intoxicated by all the sweaty fucking, the erotic sounds filling the room. He shuddered, clamped down hard on himself.

"If you come, I'll have to punish you," Connor growled.

Punish. What would the guy do, put him over his knee and spank him?

The sheer image sent Josh over the edge, screaming as his release hit him with so much force his knees buckled. If Connor hadn't held him with such a death grip on his waist, he would've collapsed on the bed, but the man's strong hands held him up, even as a full-body shudder wrecked him.

"It's almost as if…"

Connor slammed home again hard and deep.

"…the thought of being punished…"

Another deep thrust.

"…turns you on."

Josh purred. He fucking purred. There was no other way to describe the sound escaping from his lips as his almost-limp body was being fucked into the mattress by this powerful man.

Connor's hips jerked, his fingers dug in deep, and with a loud roar he sunk in deeper than he'd been before and unloaded, every muscle tense.

Josh's body gave out, and he collapsed on the bed, Connor on top of him, catching his weight on his hands at the last second.

"That was …" Connor panted.

"Yeah …" Josh couldn't think in words, let alone say anything even remotely intelligent.

"Incredible."

"Yeah."

"Your ass is …"

"Yeah. Your cock, too."

Connor pulled out. He disposed of the condom with little finesse. With a grunt, Connor hoisted Josh on the bed, spooned him tight. He kissed Josh in his neck.

Josh's brain was rebooting, and the ability to form complete sentences returned. He snuggled closer to Connor, reached for the man's hand to lace his fingers through it. "Connor?"

"Yeah, baby."

"Thank you."

Connor chuckled. "You're welcome. Anytime."

"Are you gonna punish me for coming?" Josh asked.

"I'm sure we can find something that's satisfactory."

Josh's face cracked open in a big smile. "How do you feel about spanking?"

7

Connor woke up at o'dark thirty the next morning as usual. He'd always been a morning person, but ever since basic training, his internal alarm clock would wake him at zero five hundred. Even now, in a strange bed, he was instantly awake at that time.

Josh was still asleep, his warm body snuggled up against Connor's. His head rested on Connor's right arm, and he'd draped his knee over Connor's right leg. His warm breath tickled Connor's skin, making him all weak inside. A body could get used to this, he thought.

He'd never woken up with someone else in his bed, in his arms. Not that he minded. Hell, no. Josh was the best thing that had ever happened to him. Being needed, wanted, craved even, it was unlike anything he'd ever felt before. Connor had no intention of letting Josh go, not even with the whole Indy situation.

Indy's safety was the key in all this. He needed to find a way to keep Indy safe while bringing his family to justice. Both Noah and Josh had made clear the boy's wishes came first. Connor could respect that, but there had to be a way to accomplish both. Staying hidden was an understandable short-term strategy, but as a Marine, Connor had been taught to always take the long view. Indy would never be safe until Duncan and those loyal to him were in prison or dead. But the only way Duncan would ever be sentenced to jail was if Indy testified against him, which would put him in incredible danger. The question was: how could Connor help bring his family down while at the same time keep Indy safe?

Now that he had formulated the problem, he let it go. His mind worked best in the background, mulling things over while doing something else. So he focused on Josh and the mind-blowing sex they'd had the day before.

God, it had been amazing how Josh had not only taken him in all the way but had loved it. He'd come so hard from being fucked without even touching himself. What had Josh been thinking about that last time he'd come? Connor had mentioned punishing him, and Josh had erupted seconds later. It had been a heat of the moment, impulse remark. Connor had read about edging and how denying yourself release for a prolonged time would make your orgasm so much more intense. Since he had no chance in hell of doing it himself at this stage—fuck, the overwhelming sensation of being buried inside Josh was far too much of a turn-on to not come—he'd figured he'd let Josh give it a go. Obviously, he needed to work on his Dom skills. Or had Josh come because the idea of being punished turned him on rather than off? Hmm. That opened up all kinds of kinky shit they could explore.

Fuck, there was so much he wanted to try with Josh, so much he longed to experience for the first time with this man. Would he get the chance? Would they ever get the opportunity as a couple? He understood so much more about the relationship between Josh and Noah now, had seen how deep their love ran. It brought back all the reasons why he'd been hesitant to pursue Josh in the first place, this deep conviction that he had so little to offer the guy.

You can't compete with Noah, with the history they have, not even with the sweetness Indy has. They're better off as a three-some. It makes way more sense than Josh choosing you. And if they ever find out what you knew, they'll never want anything to do with you ever again.

A sliver of desperation danced down his spine. He'd tell them, but later. When they'd had a chance to get to know him, to trust him. If he told them now, he'd throw away any chance of a future with Josh. And fuck, he couldn't lose him. Not when he'd only gotten him.

Connor turned his head to watch Josh sleep. It was still dark outside, but the room was light enough he could make out Josh's face. His full lips were almost pouting, begging to be kissed until they were all swollen and wet. His dark stubble contrasted with his skin. It had rasped deliciously against Connor's thighs and stomach when Josh had sucked him off, had kissed him everywhere. Connor sighed. Josh was so cute, so hot. What could he possibly offer him?

Well, there was the Dom/sub dynamic. Josh craved to be dominated, that much had become clear. Peace had shown on his face, in his eyes, when he'd submitted to Connor. And fuck, it had turned Connor on. He needed to get more experience so he could bring more pleasure to Josh. And to himself, but in all honesty that came second. Maybe that would be enough to keep Josh interested? Because other than that...

Connor frowned. He was boring. His life was boring. Being a cop was fulfilling to a degree, but outside his job he had little that excited him. Meeting Josh had changed that.

He'd not been able to put him out of his mind after their first meet. His sweet, shy glances in that store, his awkward conversation and the light banter with Indy. Maybe love at first sight did exist, because if he'd been attracted to Josh initially, what he felt after spending one night with him was infinitely more.

Josh let out the softest sigh, and the pink tip of his tongue peeked out of his mouth to moisten his lips. The sight shot straight to Connor's balls. He wanted to kiss him until they ran out of breath, had to come up for air, and then do it all over again.

He reached out for Josh, pulled him closer and brought his mouth to Josh's lips for the softest kiss. It was a butterfly, feather light, a tickling tease of his tongue and lips. Josh moaned in his mouth, still half-asleep, and Connor kissed him again, with more pressure. Josh melted against his mouth, opened up. Connor slipped his tongue in, probed and coaxed until Josh responded.

He never opened his eyes, but Connor felt him wake up, become aware, then deepen the kiss. He rolled on his back, pulling Josh on top of him. There was something about the sensation of Josh on top of him that fired up every nerve in Connor's body. It felt so right, so perfect. Every hard angle of their bodies fit, naked skin teasing naked skin. Connor let his hands travel south, put them on that perfect ass he had pounded the night before.

Finally, Josh opened those crystal clear blue eyes. "Damn, Connor, that's how I prefer my wake-up call," he whispered against Connor's mouth after minutes of soft, moist kissing.

"I know it's still early, but I couldn't wait anymore," Connor confessed.

His words brought the sweetest smile to Josh's mouth,

his lips curving and his cheeks dimpling. He cupped Connor's cheek in a tender gesture, and Connor kissed his hand.

"You're ready for another round?" Josh teased.

"No!" Connor was way too loud, and Josh put a hand over his mouth. Connor nodded he understood, and Josh took his hand away. "No, Josh, that's not why...I wanted to spend time with you, that's all."

Five minutes. Josh was awake for five minutes, and already Connor was messing it up again. He sucked so badly at this.

"I know. I was teasing you," Josh said softly.

"I don't ever want you to think that it's about sex. Ever."

"But you liked the sex, right?" Josh asked, furrowing his brows.

"Fuck, yes. Shit, I'm fucking this up. I love the sex with you. You know it was mind-blowing. But I don't want you to think I'm here only because of that. I like you for you, not because you..."

He swallowed as images from the previous night flooded him. Josh's mouth on his cock, milking him till the last drop. Josh on top of him, lowering himself on Connor's cock. Josh leaning over the bed, Connor fucking the living daylights out of him. The two of them spent in each other's arms. As if his body wanted to fuck up the situation even more, he grew rock hard, his cock dangerously close to Josh's ass.

Josh chuckled. "You were saying?" he said, rubbing his crotch against Connor's.

"Yeah, sorry about that," Connor said, somewhat deflated.

"I think the Beast disagrees with you on how much you want another round."

"The Beast?"

Josh kissed him, smiled. "Your cock. I dubbed it the Beast."

"You named my cock the Beast?" Connor didn't know whether to laugh or be insulted.

"Aptly named, right?"

"Yeah, but shouldn't the honor of naming it fall to its actual owner, you know, me?"

"Did it have a name?" Josh wanted to know.

"Erm, no, not really."

"Then I think the honor falls to the guy taking it up his ass. The Beast it is."

Connor couldn't help but laugh. "Okay, you win. But you do understand considering the fairy tale, this makes your ass the Beauty, right?"

The expression on Josh's face was priceless, and Connor laughed again. Josh's look changed, softened. "You should laugh more often," he said. "You're damn sexy when you do."

For breathless seconds, they looked at each other. Then Josh lowered his mouth to Connor's and kissed him senseless.

JOSH WAS STILL CATCHING his breath after coming all over Connor's hand when the door of their room opened. The click of crutches gave away Noah's presence. What the hell did Noah think he was doing, barging in like that?

"Noah, get the fuck out of that room," Indy shouted.

Josh shot up in bed, covering Connor with the stained and crumpled sheets in a reflex.

"I just want to..."

It was clear Noah wasn't talking to them but to Indy who was in the hallway.

Indy yelled, "I don't give a flying fuck what you want. You don't barge into someone else's room when you damn well know they're busy. If you need Josh that urgently, you can knock and wait for him to answer."

"But I need him to..."

"Don't fucking lie to me. There's no reason you need Josh right now, except for this ridiculous urge of you to storm in and catch them in the act. Seriously, Noah, get the fuck out, or I won't let you touch me for a week."

"You wouldn't..."

Josh grinned despite his stress levels being sky high. "He totally would," he mouthed to Connor, who was equally tense.

"Try me." Indy's voice was cold as steel.

Two seconds was all it took before the door closed. "I'm sorry, baby." Noah's voice was muffled, making Josh suspect he was hugging Indy. Indy's reply was too soft to hear, as was Noah's low voice back.

"Sorry, guys!" Noah then called out, his tone not quite convincing.

Josh lowered himself again on his side, forcing himself to exhale and let out the tension in his body. "Noah doesn't stand a chance against Indy when he puts his foot down."

Connor relaxed. "I didn't think Noah ever backed down from a fight."

"He doesn't, but Indy knows his weak spots by now. Plus, he's steel covered in a small, pretty package. He calls Noah out on his shit."

"It seems they're well matched then."

Josh smiled. "They are. I'm happy for them."

Connor searched his face, then nodded. "I'm afraid we made a bit of a mess of this bed."

Josh shrugged. "That's why we have a washing machine. We have tons of sheets and covers for that reason." He blushed when his own words registered with him. Damn, he had to be more careful around Connor and not remind him of the sex with Noah.

"It's okay, Josh," Connor said.

Josh swallowed, composed himself. "Noah left the door unlocked. You wanna grab a shower?"

"Together?"

It wasn't what Josh had intended, but now that it was on the table, the idea appealed to him. Immensely. After all, Connor had jerked him off, but Josh hadn't been able to repay the favor because of Noah's interruption.

"Yeah. We'll use the master bathroom. It's got a huge shower that's big enough for the Beauty and the Beast," he added, laughing.

There was that smile again, that big grin on Connor's face that made Josh's belly all weak and fuzzy.

"Lead the way," Connor said, still smiling.

Josh got out of bed, groaning when his body protested. He flicked on the lamp on the night table, then stretched to work the kinks out of his stiff and achy body. Connor gasped.

"Josh, I'm so sorry."

Josh turned around, found Connor sitting on the edge of the bed, looking at him with eyes wide open. He looked down to see what had the man so flustered. His waist was covered in bruises, ranging from light to a few darker ones on his lower back. They perfectly matched Connor's fingers.

"I bruise easily," he shrugged. The slight throb of the

bruises bothered him way less than the sting in his ass. Yup, he was now paying for the sloppy prep before their last fuck. It was a painful reminder he needed to do a better job loosening himself considering the size of the Beast.

Connor was studying him in silent horror, his shoulders sagging and his hand rubbing his chin. "Connor, it's okay," Josh said.

"How can it be okay? I hurt you. Damn it, Josh, you should've said something."

Josh stepped in between Connor's legs, put his hands under Connor's jaw to make him look up. "I loved every second yesterday. I didn't feel these when you made them, I swear. And if I did, it only contributed to my arousal. I wanted you to be rough, and when you fucked me that hard, I saw stars, okay? A few bruises seem like a small price to pay."

Connor's eyes narrowed. "You're walking carefully, which means you're hurting inside as well."

Josh should've known nothing escaped the observant cop. "Yeah, my ass stings. But I did that myself, okay? You told me to loosen myself and prep, and I rushed it, was impatient to get fucked. That turns out to be a bad idea considering your size. Lesson learned."

"I don't want to hurt you."

Josh leaned in and kissed Connor. "What if I want you to?"

"Do you?"

"The idea of you spanking me made me get off yesterday... Baby, I like a bit of pain with the pleasure." Josh bit his lip. Would Connor think he was perverted?

You are. Shit, he has no idea of what you want him to do to you.

"You want me to spank you?" Connor's voice was hoarse,

but it wasn't disgust on his face. It was pure, unadulterated lust.

Josh nodded.

Connor dropped his hands to Josh's ass cheeks and rubbed them. "Here?"

Josh could barely breathe, nodded again.

"Okay."

Josh stilled, searching for Connor's eyes, insecure he'd misunderstood. "Yeah?"

"Yes. What else would you like, baby?"

Josh cast his eyes down, shivers dancing on his spine. Connor had reacted well to the spanking. Maybe he was into this shit as well? Could he risk it?

"Maybe tie me up?"

"Okay."

Emboldened, Josh raised his eyes. God, Connor's eyes were on fire, devouring him. Josh asked, "You'd like that?"

"Fuck, yes. You have no idea what I want to do to you, with you. But I wanna do this right, so we'll research, okay? We'll figure it out together."

"Together," Josh repeated, pretty sure he had the goofiest smile ever on his face.

"Now get your beautiful ass in that shower so I can stare at it more. Haven't had my fill yet."

It took them half an hour to shower, get dressed, and show up downstairs. It would've been way less if they hadn't gotten distracted by hand jobs and kissing and more rubbing and jerking and kissing. They were like teenagers who couldn't keep their hands off each other, Josh mused as they made their way downstairs.

Noah was in his usual spot, reading the paper, while Indy was cutting up ingredients for an omelet, the tip of his tongue sticking out between his lips. In the months Josh had been teaching him to cook, he'd gotten handy in the kitchen.

Josh walked over and hugged him from behind. "Hey, gorgeous," he said. Indy leaned back, turned his head sideways and kissed him on his mouth, as they so often did. They both stilled as they became aware of Connor.

"Sorry," Indy said, stepping away and shooting an apologetic look Connor's way. "Force of habit."

Josh cringed when he realized he hadn't filled in Connor on the details of his relationship with Indy.

"It's okay," Connor said, much to Josh's surprise. "I understand that Josh is kind of a package deal with you and Noah."

"And you're okay with that?" Noah asked.

Josh held his breath, waiting for Connor's answer. "Yes. But Josh has to ask me for permission if he wants to do anything more than kiss either of you."

Damn, Josh felt Connor's authority reach deep inside him, pushing all those needy submissive buttons.

Noah raised his eyebrows, looked at Josh. He wouldn't accept Connor's words at face value, would want to make sure this was what Josh wanted. "Does he now?"

Josh didn't hesitate for even a second. He nodded happily. "I do." He turned to Connor, shot him a look of pure gratitude. "Thank you."

Connor held out his hand, and Josh stepped in, took it, allowing himself to be pulled close to his man. Because that's what Connor was, his man. He was communicating in crystal clear terms that the pecking order had changed and that Josh was his now. And damn, if that didn't make Josh all gooey and giddy inside. But would Noah accept it?

Josh found Noah's green eyes studying him and Connor, assessing. Josh tensed. Please, Noah had to be okay with this. He couldn't do it without Noah's blessing, even if it was implicit. If Noah and Connor would be bickering all the time, it would be impossible for Josh. He couldn't live with that kind of constant friction.

"Okay, then," Noah said. He focused on Connor, narrowing his eyes.

Connor sighed dramatically, rolling his eyes. "I know. If I hurt him, you'll feed my balls to wild dogs or something equally appealing. I get it."

The corner of Noah's mouth pulled up. Josh smiled. Noah liked Connor, even if he hated him a little bit at the same time. They were two alphas determining a pecking order when it came to Josh, and that wasn't easy.

"I'm glad we understand each other," Noah said, not quite pulling off the menacing look he was aiming for.

Connor pulled Josh's head in for a slow kiss that was obviously meant to yank Noah's chain. The first three seconds, Josh was painfully aware of Noah and Indy watching them, but then he forgot about them and sunk deep into the kiss. When Connor broke off the kiss, Josh let out a contented sigh and stayed safe in those strong arms for a few seconds more.

"If you guys are gonna be like that all day, we'll lock you right back up," Noah said.

"Oh, shut up, you. We were just as bad in the beginning," Indy came to their defense.

Josh turned in Connor's arms to face his two friends, leaning back against the powerful body behind him. "Worse," he confirmed, not embarrassed in the least.

Indy giggled. "True. You watched us fuck on more than one occasion. Does that mean you'll return the favor?"

Before Josh could say anything, Connor's hand clamped down hard on his shoulder. The warning was clear: this was not something he should joke about. The openness about sex he had with Noah and Indy was a foreign concept to Connor. Josh understood Connor's insecurities, respected them enough to obey. Not that obeying hadn't been his first instinct anyway. Damn, it was scary how deeply ingrained his need to submit was.

Josh smiled at Indy but didn't respond. Instead, he reached for Connor's hand and squeezed it to signal he understood. Connor mumbled a low "Thank you" in his ear.

"What do you want for breakfast, baby?" Josh asked, changing the subject. "Indy is preparing an omelet if that's what you want, but I can fix you anything else. Pancakes, waffles, a fruit smoothie, or a yogurt with granola and fruit."

"Waffles and a fruit smoothie sound good, thank you." Connor kissed Josh one more time and let him go.

With a bounce in his steps, Josh got the ingredients. Connor lowered himself on a bar stool next to Noah, who held out a section of the newspaper. It was as good as a peace treaty, and Josh sighed with relief. Thank fuck Noah had decided to cooperate. Now, all they needed to do was find a solution to Indy's dilemma so they could all live happily ever after.

His hand was halfway to the blender with a hand full of frozen strawberries when it hit him. He wanted a happily ever after with Connor. How the fuck had he fallen for the guy that quickly? It was ridiculous. Nobody could fall in love that fast. It had to be the mind-blowing sex, the fact that he'd finally been fulfilled in that craving to be fucked hard and rough, to be dominated. That had to be the reason for this weird, deep connection with Connor.

"Josh?"

Noah's voice pulled him back.

"I'm good," he said, smiling despite his inner turmoil.

Connor shot Noah a look, raising his eyebrows. Noah hesitated for a second, then gave in. "If Josh freezes like that, it could mean something has triggered an episode in him. If that's the case, and you recognize it early, you can usually bring him back with your voice. You'll learn to read his body language over time."

Connor nodded, focusing his attention back on Josh. Fuck, Josh felt like a total nutcase now, with two men discussing his weaknesses. Well, he was a total nutcase.

Josh turned back to the counter, threw the strawberries in with more force than needed. The noise of the blender drowned out any other noise, but not the angry voice inside him.

Why can't you be normal, like everyone else? Noah got blown up by a fucking IED, and he doesn't have PTSD. Indy has been raped and abused, and he's able to function like a normal person. And Connor has been held hostage, tortured, and watched his best friend die, and he's a cop for fuck's sake. Why is everyone but you able to deal with the shit in their lives?

He was such a loser, reluctant to go outside most of the days. How could he ever expect to keep a man like Connor happy? Sure, Connor had said he was okay with staying home, but at some point, he'd want more than a boring homebody. Now that he had discovered how good sex could be, wouldn't he want to look for someone healthy to share his life with?

Dammit, he needed to show Connor he could be fun, spontaneous. What was it his therapist had advised him last week? Right. He had to engage in playful battle situations. Well, here was his opportunity. He pushed his anger down and took a deep breath. "I want to go paintballing today," he announced. "With the four of us."

He looked at Noah, who opened his mouth as if to say

something. "You fucking owe me after hitting Connor and storming in this morning," Josh said and watched with satisfaction as Noah clamped his mouth shut again.

He turned to Indy, pleading with his eyes to be on board with this, despite everything. "I'm keeping Connor's phone," Indy said, his face tight. "I'm not taking any chances."

Josh nodded that he understood.

He swiveled again and faced Connor, who smiled. "Whatever you want, baby."

NOAH WINCED as he rolled the liner and prosthetic sock on his stump. It was so damn irritated and hurt like hell, even after putting lotion on it. Not that he would ever admit that to anyone but himself. Indy especially couldn't know, not after everything that had happened the day before. He'd been a fucking idiot for bringing up the sex thing in the car. The conversation had derailed horribly, and then that cop knocking on the window had only made things worse.

Coming home and finding Josh being fucked... He now understood what people meant when they said their vision went all red-hot and hazy. He'd been on him in a second, had never even recognized Connor. To be true, he hadn't been expecting him either. Why the hell had Josh felt he'd had to keep his relationship with the cop a secret? How often had they met before without him or Indy knowing? It left a sour taste in Noah's mouth, that his best friend hadn't trusted him.

And the fact that Connor had not only known Indy's true identity but was in fact connected to the family that had made his life hell. At first, Noah had been ready to beat the shit out of Connor all over again. But when the cop had explained, every word had sounded sincere. He wasn't lying —at least, as far as Noah could tell. He couldn't blame Indy for wanting to make sure.

He'd tried to talk about it with Indy last night, but he'd waved Noah off. He wanted a distraction, not a conversation. So Noah had given him a blow job and had made love to him after. The sex had been great, but it had been hell on his stump, especially the constant friction with the sheets. He'd woken up from the throbbing pain a few times that night.

He'd checked it when he was alone. An old friction wound at the bottom of the stump had opened up again last week and had gotten a bit infected. This morning, it had looked worse, fiery red and hot to the touch, but he'd have to ride it out. There was no way he was having it checked out, not when Indy and Josh were depending on him to keep them safe. Noah wasn't going anywhere until he knew for a fact Connor wasn't about to screw Indy over.

He'd taken a triple dose of Ibuprofen minutes earlier, as well as a couple of acetaminophen. The first should help with the infection and the latter with the slight fever he suspected he was sporting. God, he hoped they'd tide him over when they were playing paintball. What the hell had Josh been thinking when he came up with that asinine idea? He slid his limb into the socket and rolled up the sleeve to create a seal with the liner. He had to fight back the tears of pain that sprung to his eyes. Hot damn, this was gonna be a long day.

"You okay?" Indy asked. Noah hadn't even heard him step into the bedroom. "You look like you're in pain."

"Yeah, a little. The painkillers should kick in in a few minutes."

Indy frowned. "You took painkillers?"

"Uhm, yeah? That's what they're for, you know. You're supposed to take them when you have pain."

"Don't get smart with me. I've never seen you take them before."

Noah shrugged, cursing the fact that Indy was so fucking perceptive. There was little that escaped him, and this was one of those times Noah wasn't too happy about that. "I'm careful because I don't want to get addicted. It's all too easy when you're in actual pain."

Indy lowered himself on the bed next to him, his brows furrowed. "Are you sure paintballing is a good idea for you right now?"

Noah rolled his pants over his prosthesis, shot Indy an apologetic look. "Probably not. But I can't refuse Josh this, not after what I did to Connor. And there's no way I'm letting Connor out of my sight, not until we know for sure he's not a threat to you."

Indy snuggled close, lowered his head on Noah's shoulder. "You're a good man, Noah Flint. I don't always appreciate that ego of yours, especially not in combination with that massive amount of guilt you carry around, but your heart is pure gold, baby. I love how you take care of us."

Noah's heart filled with joy. This. This was what he did it for. The knowledge that Indy was safe, with him. "How are you feeling?" he asked.

Indy sighed. "Scared shitless."

Noah looked at his watch. They had an hour before they had to leave. "Let's lie down for a few minutes, talk."

He bit back the pain that stabbed through his leg as he maneuvered himself down on the bed, pulling Indy close. Indy's head rested on his left shoulder, and the boy's left hand found his favorite spot under Noah's shirt, on his belly. Indy loved to play with his belly button, for some reason. It could drive Noah wild with want, but he endured it like he tolerated so many other things Indy did that affected him deeply. Indy had no idea, and Noah kept it that way. At least for now while he was still vulnerable.

"What are you scared of, babe?" he asked.

Indy was quiet for a long time. "That they'll find me. Torture me before they kill me." He shivered, and Noah kissed the top of his head, pushing back the anger inside. The idea of anyone hurting his Indy, it was almost too much to bear. "But I'm most of all scared they'll find me with you and Josh. They'll kill you, too, and if they ever find out what you mean to me, they'll use you against me."

His voice broke. Noah held him tight, at a loss for words. There was nothing he could say, for they both knew how real that threat was.

"Do you believe Connor?" he asked finally.

"Yeah, I do. His surprise at finding out who I am was genuine. If he'd been close to the Fitzpatricks, he would've made me after the robbery. There's no way he wouldn't have known what I looked like, because finding me has got to be a priority for them."

Connor had mentioned a contract on Indy's life. Somehow, that was even scarier than the threat of the Fitzpatricks finding him. With them, you knew what you were looking for. With a contract, it could be anyone they met.

"Plus, his whole career in the Marines. He's highly decorated, you know. You don't serve that long, that well if your character isn't morally sound," Noah added.

"I agree, but I need to be one hundred percent certain. I'll have to work on a way to contact the DA and get him to verify Connor's story. Fuck, I wish Josh would've chosen a different boyfriend."

A fresh wave of guilt hit Noah. "I'm sorry for my role in

that. I sort of pushed him in Josh's direction, without ever thinking about the threat he'd be to you. It was thoughtless of me."

Indy's index finger found his belly button and played with it. Noah's cock stirred in response, but he ignored it. "It's okay. I like him, and I calculate he'd be good for Josh."

"He'd better be," Noah said darkly.

"Oh, fuck off. Josh can fight his own battles when it comes to his love life. He doesn't need you to complicate it even more. Besides, you said it yourself: Connor looks at Josh like he hung the frigging moon."

Noah sighed. The thought of Josh and Connor together made him feel weird. Not jealous, thank fuck for that. More like sad, melancholy. It was the end of an era, and it also meant he was in serious shit, because there was no way Connor would allow Josh to be fucked by Noah. Not that Noah could blame him. The fact that Indy was okay with it was a fucking miracle.

"Did you see Connor's cock?" Indy whispered.

"No. I was preoccupied at the time as you may recall. You had me in a pretty effective hold, by the way. Impressive."

Indy giggled. "His cock is huge. Seriously, I'm talking absolutely ginormous."

Noah's eyes widened. "How big are we talking? Give it to me in inches."

"Fuck, I dunno. Maybe, what, nine, ten inches?"

Noah whistled softly between his teeth. "Damn, that's impressive."

Indy let out the cutest snicker. "He's thick, too. Huge balls. The whole package is fucking intimidating. Must make Josh happy, though."

Noah frowned. "Why would that make Josh happy?"

Indy pushed himself up on Noah's chest to look at him. "You're kidding, right?"

"No. What am I missing?"

"Josh likes it rough. He craves a little pain with his pleasure, you know that. That's why he gets off on you fucking him so hard when you're stressed out. A cock that size, man, that has got to fulfill him. Plus, Connor looks like he may be the kind of dominant Josh needs."

Indy put his head back in his previous spot. Noah subtly rearranged himself, his cock having grown even harder after their conversation. Of course, he'd known Josh liked it hard. He'd simply never connected the dots that way, had never realized Josh would want more than being fucked hard. It made sense. And if Connor was into that kind of shit, power to him.

Indy's hand trailed lower on his stomach and slipped under his boxers. Noah groaned involuntarily. "You're such a horny fucker," Indy teased. "You'd think you never got off, but I'm pretty sure you came hard last night."

"All that sex talk got me excited, so sue me. I'm a guy, you know," Noah made light of it.

Indy's hand found his cock and scratched it with his nail from the base to the tip. Noah shivered. Fuck, he hoped Indy was willing to do more than tease. If not, he'd have to jack off before they left.

"Well, I'm a guy, too. So what do we do about this?"

The tone of Indy's voice told Noah he was down for a round. Thank fuck. He wriggled his left hand between their bodies, reaching for Indy's dick to find it equally hard. "I say we make it fast and dirty. We don't have much time."

Indy laughed. "I like the way you think."

He sat up to yank down his pants, didn't even bother with his shirt. Noah dragged his zipper down, shoved his pants over his hips and left them there. Too much trouble to take them off. Plus, it would be way too painful to doff the prosthesis again.

Indy angled for the lube on the nightstand and managed to reach it with his fingertips. He squeezed out some gel on Noah's fingers and took another dollop himself. They worked fast, Noah coating his cock, jacking off till he was hard as iron, and Indy loosening himself up. He'd gotten good at relaxing and only needed a little prep before Noah could take him.

Indy slung one leg over him and straddled him. "I'll ride you."

It was what Noah had wanted to suggest because there was no way he could put weight on his leg right now. Had Indy sensed it? Noah didn't know, but he was damn grateful.

Indy positioned himself, spreading his ass wide open. Noah watched as he lowered himself on Noah's cock, taking him in inch by inch. It never failed to take his breath away, this slender man filling himself with sheer lust on his face. Noah had no doubt Indy wanted him. This wasn't out of obligation or guilt. This was pure desire, want.

He let out a contented sigh as his cock was engulfed in that moist, hot cave. So tight. So deep. So fucking good.

Indy gyrated his hips, sighing deeply. He took his own cock in his right hand, raised his hips and lowered himself with precision. His eyes closed, his jaw set tight with concentration. He was lost to everything and anything, it seemed, except for the sensations riding Noah delivered.

Noah put his hands on Indy's hips to help lift him up and push him down. He arched his back and closed his eyes, too. His cock throbbed, his balls were already tightening. Tingles of pleasure raced over his hot skin. He needed this release. Badly. *Please, let it help with the pain.* Even now, his limb was throbbing.

He opened his eyes again, not wanting to miss out on watching Indy ride him. "You feel amazing," he said, his voice raw. "You're perfect on my cock. So damn tight."

Indy smiled a hot, sexy smile. "You're perfect in my ass. So damn full."

Indy's body jerked as he sank down, probably from Noah hitting his sweet spot. Little drops of sweat pearled on his forehead. His hand jerked his cock with rough gestures, keeping rhythm with his hips.

"You're so beautiful," Noah said in awe. "I could watch you ride me for hours."

Indy laughed with abandonment, never faltering in his pace. Up and down those hips went, sucking Noah in again and again in that perfect warm spot. "Not gonna last that long."

Noah's balls pulled up, the tension in his body building. Maybe the release would bring him some relief from the pain. *Oh, God, please.*

Indy shifted, moving his legs a few inches farther down. One second Noah was gasping with pleasure, his cock taken in even deeper, the next, white-hot pain assaulted his body. Indy's foot had grazed his stump, causing a torture so blinding it took his breath away. He yelled out, his body cramping up.

"Fuck! I'm sorry, Noah..."

Indy climbed off, careful not to touch his leg again, but it didn't matter anymore. Noah closed his eyes, waiting with clenched fists for the pain to subside.

Oh, fuck, fuck, motherfucking hell. This was bad. What the fuck was wrong with the stump? It should not be hurting this much.

His stomach rolled in protest. He would not throw up, dammit. His cock had gone instantly soft, agony overriding all pleasure. Finally, he managed a shaky intake of breath, forcing his muscles to relax.

"Dammit, Indy, you have to be more careful."

The second the snarky words left his mouth, he regretted them. It wasn't fair to take this out on Indy.

"I'm so sorry, Noah..." The anguish in Indy's voice broke his heart. Fuck, he was such a bastard.

The bed moved, and seconds later, Indy was out of the room. Noah covered his eyes with his hands, his soul hurting as much as his body. Would he ever get it right with Indy? The man deserved more than a crippled boyfriend with anger issues. Fuck, he was failing everybody.

First, he'd fucked it up with Indy with that stupid move of bringing up the sex when they were on a date. Dates with him were rare since he was not keen on going out in public. But Noah had convinced him, had assured him he was fine with Indy dressing like a woman. What the fuck did he care as long as they were together? Well, that had gone well, with them going home before they even got to see the movie.

Then he'd beat Connor up, and in the process, managed to piss Josh off. It had led to them saying shit they should've said ages ago, but still. He'd fucked things up again this morning by wanting to walk in on them. Shit, he didn't even know what had come over him. He'd heard them having sex and had wanted to catch them in the act. What the hell was wrong with him that he would do something like that? It hadn't even been jealousy. Not in the sense that he was jealous Josh was with someone else. It was more that he wanted to let Connor know who was boss. Pathetic, now that he thought about it.

And now, he'd hurt Indy. Again. He'd been in horrible pain, but that was no excuse.

"Fuck!" he shouted, then again, "Fuck!"

He dragged himself off the bed, biting back the gasps of pain. He was not canceling on Josh, not after what he'd done to him, but he needed more painkillers if he was going to make it through the day.

With effort, he made his way into the bathroom and opened the medicine cabinet. His hand hovering, he hesitated. He'd been legally prescribed them, but he knew how addictive they were. Was this a smart choice? Fuck it, he needed them. There was no way he would survive today without something stronger than over-the-counter painkillers.

He grabbed the Oxy, popped one before he could change his mind, swallowing it dry. He palmed two more and put them in his pocket. That would last him through the day. After that, he'd see about his leg. It would have to wait until everything had calmed down.

8

Connor had never been on a paintball range before. He wasn't sure what he'd expected, but it wasn't the huge terrain in the middle of nowhere where they parked. The field on his three o'clock had knee-high grass, with bales of hay spread out to hide behind. It didn't look like much of a challenge.

Near the entrance was another field, much bigger. It was a mix of frozen mud and sand, with sparse bushes thrown in as well as ramshackle walls, sheds, and half-collapsed structures, and a few rusty cars. Some buildings had second stories, with wooden stairs giving access. Everything was covered in bright splatters of paint, resulting in a colorful, yet eerie appearance.

Noah and Indy were walking in front of Connor, Noah kissing Indy's head. It seemed like they'd made up after what had obviously been a fight earlier that morning. Connor didn't need to guess what that had been about—undoubtedly his name had fallen a few times. He was so damn sorry for the shitty circumstances in which he'd met Indy. He seemed like a great guy, but Connor's connection to his fucked-up family overshadowed anything else. Connor couldn't blame him, not with all he knew about his family. They were monsters, every single one of them, but Duncan especially. And from what he'd heard, it had only gotten worse since Stephan had disappeared.

"Welcome to PB Extreme. You guys ever been here before?"

A young guy, maybe twenty, welcomed them with a big smile. They were the only customers even though it was much warmer than the previous days, and last week's snow had already melted. Guess few people wanted to be outside anyway. Connor didn't mind. The cold was better than the desert heat.

Noah shook his head on behalf of all four of them.

"Okay, my name is Cory, and I'll be explaining the rules today. Any military experience amongst the four of you?"

Josh casually pointed them out. "US Marine. Army medic. He's got no military experience, but he's a badass shooter."

Connor hadn't realized Indy could shoot well. It made sense, being around a Boston crime family. And he'd been able to identify that robber's gun in an instant.

"And yourself?" Cory asked Josh.

"He's one of the best snipers the Army has ever seen," Noah said with audible pride.

Connor expected Josh to blush as he so often did when he was embarrassed, but he didn't. Interesting. Apparently, he wasn't flustered by Noah's high praise. Connor couldn't wait to see Josh in action.

"Well, that will make my explanation a hell of a lot shorter," Cory grinned. "Since there's only four of you, we'll let you use the pinball guns with clips. It holds twenty paint bullets, so aim well."

Ten minutes later, they were all suited up in camouflage gear, complete with jackets, helmets, and gloves. It felt different from his Marine cammies, but still more familiar than he'd expected. Josh inspected the paintball rifle they had all received. They carried clips with extra ammo in the side pockets of their pants. Connor watched in fascination as Josh brought the paint rifle to his shoulder, felt the trigger, seemed to get used to the weight and feel of it.

"You guys made teams yet?" Cory asked, checking their gear.

"Yes." Josh's voice was strong and clear. "It's me and Indy against Noah and Connor."

"You want me on the opposing team?" Connor couldn't hide his surprise. He'd expected him and Josh to team up, had counted on it.

"Yes. I'm the best shooter, so it makes sense to team me up with the weakest. No offense, Indy. Plus, I need you and Noah to learn to work together, so you can get over this exasperating alpha male rivalry you got going."

Indy's eyes went big at those words, Connor noticed, but the guy wisely held his tongue.

"Okay," Connor said. He turned to Noah, studied him with assessing eyes. Technically, he outranked him, but he didn't want to appear to treat Noah differently because of his leg. It seemed to bother him even more than usual today. He was clearly keeping his weight off it as much as he could, and every now and then he winced. "Lead the way, Corporal."

They broke into two pairs, Josh and Indy jogging in one direction and Noah leading him the other way.

"Is Josh that good a shot?" Connor asked.

"Better. It's uncanny, the way he becomes one with his

rifle. They wanted him to apply to the Rangers as a sniper. He would've gotten in, but he refused."

"He wanted to stay with you."

"I would've followed him," Noah said. "Or at least, I would've tried."

"What's our strategy here?"

"Josh will try to make a sniper's nest somewhere. High ground, preferably. He can climb anything, has no fear of heights. And he's got more patience than Job. I've watched him spend over eight hours high up in a tower once, never moving a muscle until he got his shot."

Connor let it sink in, this unfamiliar side of Josh. "Won't he expect you to predict his strategy and do something else?" he asked, his eyes tracking the various structures on the terrain. If Josh was going for higher ground, he'd have the choice of a few trees, but they were bare, or a few structures on an elevation that couldn't even be called a hill.

Noah halted and shot Connor a begrudging look of respect. "Look, my guess is you defaulted to me because you didn't want to make me feel crappy about my leg. You not only outrank me, O'Connor, you're way more of a soldier than I'll ever be. I was a medic first and foremost, and while I'm a decent shot and I've seen my fair share of combat, I'm no Marine Sergeant. So, lead."

Connor nodded. Thank fuck Noah was being reasonable about this, or they would get their asses handed to them. "Okay. My guess is Josh will try to use Indy as a distraction. No matter how good of a shot Indy may be on a gun range, he has no combat experience. Josh will use him to draw us out, betray our positions. This terrain isn't suitable for a fixed sniper's nest. He'll stay mobile, wait for us to give away our position and expose ourselves and then take us out. Like you said, he's got patience, so all he has to do is wait for one opportunity to nail us."

"What do you suggest?"

"We're gonna do the same. Josh is counting on you to make noise since your leg makes it hard to move quietly. You'll need to find a spot where you're hidden but have an excellent overview. There."

Connor pointed toward a half-collapsed metal structure.

"Lay on your belly, let your gun rest on the lowest piece of metal. You're in the shade, so reflection isn't an issue. You should be able to stay invisible until they're close. I'll try to draw them out and make them come to you. When you see Indy, don't shoot. We gotta take out Josh first."

Noah nodded. "Damn, you're good at this."

"Get comfortable. It's gonna be a while."

Seconds later, Noah had disappeared in the structure. Connor waited till he saw the barrel appear in the spot he had indicated to Noah. Good, the guy knew how to follow orders. That would make things a hell of a lot easier.

He made his way toward the far end of the terrain, taking notice of the different structures. He walked till he found a collapsed shed that would offer him enough cover. Connor ducked between the shed and a low wall made of loose stones. He'd better not touch it, or it could come down on him and betray his position. A whistle pierced the sky, the sign the battle had started.

Josh might be a world-class shot, but Connor had a little trick up his sleeve as well. He closed his eyes, forced his breathing to slow down and focused on nothing else but what he heard. At first, his ears buzzed like they always did when he tuned in, but then he distinguished sounds. A car passing by on a road a couple of hundred yards to his six o'clock. Something rustling in frozen leaves on the ground to his eleven o'clock—probably a squirrel.

He listened harder, deeper, forcing his ears to reach out all the way. A hearing test when he'd entered the Marines had confirmed what he knew already, that his hearing was exceptional. It was a handy thing in situations like this. He didn't have to see anything; all he needed was to eliminate his other senses as much as possible and focus on his hearing.

It took close to five minutes before he heard the first sound. A soft crunch, like boots on stones, coming from his two o'clock. If Josh was as good as Noah claimed, he wouldn't make that much noise. It had to be Indy, trying to draw him and Noah out. Noah had better follow orders and stay put, or this battle would be over in no time.

A shot rang out, the wet plop echoing loud in the relative silence. A fraction later, paint splattered on a structure at least a hundred feet away from Connor. Connor tensed. Who was shooting? Indy? The shot seemed to come from a different direction than the footsteps he'd heard. It didn't make sense.

His ears had to readjust, and it took him a spell to refocus. Another crunch—this time more to his three o'clock and far closer. Indy again? Connor crawled forward on his belly without making a sound. If he stuck his head around the corner, he might be able to see something.

Another shot. He dropped down, not moving a muscle, trying to pinpoint where the shot was coming from. It was hard to gauge the direction since the sound was distorted between the buildings. The splat of the paint was on his right side, and it sounded close to where he'd heard the steps. Had Noah moved? Was that why the noise was so obvious, because of his leg? It would make sense, except for the fact Connor had told him to stay where he was.

If it was Noah moving around, it had to be Indy shooting at him. Josh wouldn't miss, if the reports were true. That meant he had to locate Josh before he could take out Noah, which wouldn't be hard if he kept making so much damn noise. Fucking asshole. Was it that hard to obey an order? No Marine would've ever disobeyed a direct order.

He heard the sound again. Fucking hell. He would kill Noah for making them lose this battle. It might be a game, but fuck it, he hated losing, especially for a stupid reason like not listening. He raised himself up on his arms and crawled soundlessly forward until he had reached the corner of the wall. He listened for a full minute but didn't hear anything.

Connor stuck his head around the corner, helmet first, then the rest. Nothing happened. He scanned the terrain, didn't see anything move. From his vantage point, he had a clear view of Noah's hideout. Was he still in there or had he moved against Connor's order? It was hard to see from this distance without binoculars.

The crunching sound again, way too close to his three o'clock. He dropped down on the ground, just as a shot rang out.

"Fucking hell, asshole!"

Noah. From the direction of where he'd been hiding. Connor crawled forward. What the hell was going on? Had Noah been hit? How the fuck was that possible if he'd stayed inside that shed?

Shit. Misdirection. Josh was playing him. The shot rang out, and he knew. The paint bullet hit him on his left shoulder blade, would have shredded his heart had it been real. Instead, it merely stung.

"Dead!" he shouted, adhering to the rules.

"Fuck it!" A loud noise came from where Noah was hiding. "Surrender." Noah's voice sounded pissed as hell. If Noah hadn't been fatally hit, why was he surrendering?

"Accept." Indy's voice was giddy. He came walking toward Connor from the direction where he'd heard the crunching sound.

Connor got up and dusted himself off. Damn, it stung where that bullet had hit him. That was going to leave a nasty bruise for certain. He bent to brush off his knees.

"Accept," Josh said from behind him.

Connor spun around. Josh smiled a big grin, his rifle casually slung over his shoulder. "Nice ass," he said.

Connor shook his head. How had Josh spotted him? He'd been between a shed and a wall. Josh shouldn't have been able to see him, so how the fuck did he pull it off?

Noah came stomping toward them, fired a murderous look in Josh's direction. "You fucking cheat, you disabled my gun!" Noah all but shoved the rifle in Connor's face. "Look what he did, he shot straight into my barrel, rendered it useless. And I have the bruise to prove it, 'cause the force of the impact slammed it into my cheek."

Connor turned around. "You fired a paint bullet exactly into his barrel?"

Josh shrugged. "He shouldn't have stuck it out if he wanted to use it."

"It was you shooting all that time," Connor realized. "You pretended to shoot at Indy, making me think it was Noah."

"I needed to get a sense for the rifle, judge its accuracy, or rather, lack thereof. Plus, I knew you'd hear the noise and would assume it was Noah."

"Why? At first, I thought it was Indy."

Josh smiled. "Not after I started shooting. You reasoned it was Noah, ignoring what you had told him to do, and Indy trying to shoot him as a result."

"How did you... When we split up, Noah was in charge. How did you know that would change?"

Josh raised one eyebrow. "You really need me to answer that, Marine? Noah is a fucking medic, not a rifleman. This is what you do, what you're trained for. Noah may be bossy, but he's not stupid, and I knew he'd default to you. He wants to win too much to not sacrifice whatever pride he has about this. I also knew you wouldn't trust him to obey your orders, not really. I figured once you heard the walking noises and the shots, you'd jump to the conclusion Noah was being a stubborn ass and would try to nail his shooter."

Connor was speechless. He got his ass handed to him by an army sniper, and it stung more than he wanted to admit. He swallowed down his wounded pride, allowed himself to be filled with admiration for Josh. "How did you spot us?"

"The both of you, you're specialized in warm-weather conditions. For my sniper training, I did a six-week stint with NATO somewhere in Norway in the dead of winter. They taught us to recognize breath patterns and lead them back to a location. I got lucky today, because there's practically no wind, so your breaths gave you away. I'll admit, I had trouble determining the exact position of your body because you were between two structures. Smart choice. But once you started moving, I had you."

Connor raised his hands in defeat. "That's impressive," he admitted. As much as his own pride hurt, the deep satisfaction on Josh's face got to him.

"I'm gonna get a replacement rifle, and then we're gonna do this again. We'll get this right, Marine," Noah said, his face tight.

Connor nodded. "Oorah."

JOSH NAILED them four more times before Noah and Connor finally got the best of him. Josh didn't say it, but they lucked out because Indy messed up. Otherwise Noah and Connor would've never caught him. But Josh was okay with it. It wasn't about winning in the first place, though he was competitive enough to care, but about getting Noah and Connor to trust each other. If they kept up the constant alpha posturing, Josh would go crazy with the tension. Plus, he also wanted to show Connor he could have fun, too, that he wasn't as boring as he appeared.

"Nicely done, O'Connor," Noah said, extending his hand to Connor.

Connor took it. "We got lucky," he said with a nod to Josh.

Josh smiled. He knew.

"I don't care," Noah said. "You got him."

It was Connor who'd managed to get a kill shot in with Josh, nailed him in the chest. Connor's eyes found Josh's. "I sure did."

The double entendre was hard to miss, and Josh grinned. "Yup, he nailed me, all right."

"Oh, fuck off, you two. Seriously. Not everything is about sex, you know?" Noah muttered.

Indy launched himself into Noah's arms, who caught him effortlessly. Indy wrapped his legs around Noah's waist and kissed him hard. "It's not? That's not what you said last night when you were..."

He never got to finish his sentence, because Noah kissed him to shut him up. Josh laughed. It was good to see his plan had worked, that some of the tension at least had dissipated. Noah and Indy clearly had a row that morning, and he was happy to see they'd made up. He couldn't stand it when they fought.

His guess was Noah had lashed out at Indy in anger for some reason. He'd seen the tension on his face, in his body. He was in pain. Fuck, what if Noah needed him? He'd do it, but what would it mean to Connor? He'd said Josh needed permission to do more than kiss. Connor would give it, no doubt. He'd know he couldn't refuse, not this early in their relationship, not when Noah was in so much pain. But how would it affect him, affect them? It was all so fucking complicated. Josh wanted Connor, more than he'd thought possible, but he still felt tied to Noah and Indy as well.

He grabbed his gear and walked back toward the entrance. Connor caught up with him and fell in step. "You're a phenomenal shot," he said.

"Thank you."

It shouldn't matter to Josh, but it did. No matter how morally wrong it felt to be outstanding in killing people, the fact was that he had exceptional skills with a rifle, and it made him feel accomplished. He'd never been good at anything in particular, had so often felt like a failure, especially to his parents. But the one thing the army had given him was a sense of skill.

"How was this for you?" Connor asked.

"My therapist suggested it. Said it might be helpful for me to engage in playful combat or some shit like that. And it was good, fun even."

"You're not merely a master sniper. You kept winning on strategy, kept anticipating what Noah and I would do."

Josh raised his eyebrows, shot a sideways glance at Connor. "You say it as if it surprised you."

"It did. Somehow I'd gotten the impression that you didn't do well in the army, but from what I've seen you must've been one hell of an asset."

Josh pondered the thought. "If I hadn't been gay and so damn sensitive, I think I would've loved every minute of it. The routine, the rules, they fit me well."

Connor grabbed his shoulder, stopped him. "What do you mean, sensitive?"

Josh lowered his eyes, stared at the ground. Did he really have to say it?

"Josh, you're not talking about your PTSD, are you?"

He bit his lip, nodded, still gazing downward.

"That's bullshit." Connor lifted his chin up with a finger, forced him to meet his eyes. "You know that's not true. Having PTSD says nothing about how strong you are."

Josh swallowed. "You don't have it. Noah doesn't have it. Indy went through hell and back, and he's okay."

"Again, bullshit. None of us are okay; it manifests in different ways. You said it yourself: Noah has anger issues and hasn't found a healthy way to cope with his emotions. I don't know Indy well enough, but I'm sure he's got emotional scars judging from the way he flinches from touch. And as for me..." Connor stopped and sighed. "I'm a hot mess, Josh. You have no idea."

Josh frowned. What was Connor talking about? "I don't understand. You're a cop. You have a solid life, are functioning without problems."

Connor closed his eyes for a second, and when he opened them again, a deep, unexpected sadness radiated from him. "I'm a robot, Josh. That's how I'm coping. I'm a fucking robot. I show up, do my job, go home. I have no friends, no life, nothing. I don't talk about what happened to me. I don't talk, period. Shit, I've told you more in the last week than I've told anyone, ever. That whole honesty thing and all the talking you guys do? It scares the shit out of me, okay? Trust me, Josh, I may not have PTSD, but I'm seriously fucked up."

Josh saw it in Connor's eyes: every word he said was true. And it cost him to say it, this proud, strong man who humbled himself for Josh.

"You're lonely," Josh said, reaching out for Connor's cheek with his hand.

"You have no idea. I have zero experience with relationships, even with friendships. Sure, I had my brothers in arms, but I never allowed them to get too close, except for Lucas. And when he...when I lost him, that was it. I've been alone for so long I think I've forgotten how to be human."

Suddenly, it all made sense to Josh. Why Connor had waited so long before pursuing Josh. Why he had been so scared, so insecure. It also explained part of the jealousy he had of Noah, which was about more than just the sex between Josh and Noah. It was about their friendship, the level of comfort they had with each other, and with Indy. The banter, the teasing—Connor didn't have that. Didn't even know how to do it, maybe.

His hand still on Connor's cheek, Josh leaned in to kiss him. He wrapped his arms around Connor and hugged him tightly.

"Josh, promise me one thing," Connor whispered in his ear.

Josh leaned back so he could see his face but held his arms around Connor's neck.

"If I fuck up with you, if I hurt you with what I do or say, tell me. Please tell me so I can try and make it right. I'm winging this, Josh. I don't know what I'm doing with you or how to be in a relationship, but I want to learn to take care of you, okay?"

Josh nodded. "Does that mean we're in a relationship?" he asked. He didn't want to pressure Connor, but he didn't want to hide either. If Connor wanted them to be together, he'd have to come out and say it, own it.

"Yes. You're mine, Josh, and I'll say it to anyone you need me to."

"Your work?"

Connor swallowed. "I'll tell them."

Joy sparked in Josh's heart. Connor was willing to come out of the closet for him. He was serious about them. "Did you mean what you said about Noah and Indy this morning?"

"Yes. I get that you need them, even if it's hard for me to not be jealous. But Josh, anything more than kissing and you talk to me first, ask me for permission."

Yup, there it was again. That authoritative tone that made Josh want to bend over and take it. "Yes, Connor," he said. The satisfied look on Connor's face was beautiful. "Will you spank me if I disobey?" Josh teased.

Connor laughed. "I'm not sure that would be effective as a punishment, seeing how much you're looking forward to it. I'll have to find something else more deterring, like not fuck you for a week."

Josh's eyes went big. "Damn, that's cruel. You know how much I like the Beast."

Connor brought his mouth so close to Josh's their breaths mingled. "The Beast likes you too, Beauty. But if you disobey me, I will deny you the pleasure, even if it costs me, too."

Josh was sure it was really, really fucked up that this turned him on. For fuck's sake, he was throbbing hard. The slight sting in his ass had bothered him all day, a reminder of their session last night. Josh had told himself to wait at least twenty-four hours before letting Connor fuck him again, but right now, he'd drop his pants and spread his legs in an instant to take him in again, pain be damned.

"That dominant thing comes pretty naturally to you," he said, his voice hoarse.

"You have no idea how much you submitting turns me on. Every time you say 'yes, Connor', I want to rip your pants off and fuck you senseless."

Yup, Connor could fuck him right here, and Josh wouldn't mind one bit.

"Are you two lovebirds about done?" Noah shouted.

"Not even close," Josh whispered.

9

Connor woke up the next morning at oh-five-hundred sharp with a naked Josh draped all over him. Josh's head was on his shoulder, his breath breezing over Connor's nipple. Connor didn't move, too scared he'd wake him up. He sighed with contentment. God, he could get used to this.

By unspoken agreement, nobody had mentioned the Fitzpatrick situation yesterday evening. Instead, Josh and Indy had cooked dinner—a pasta dish with some delicious spicy sausage, fresh tomatoes, and basil—and they watched a movie. Noah and Indy were lounging on the couch, their bodies intertwined—though Indy had been careful to not touch Noah's leg. It was bothering him more than usual, Connor had noted. Noah kept wincing whenever he moved, and Connor had seen him pop a pill—presumably a painkiller.

He and Josh had been in one of the reading chairs. Josh had started on the floor, leaning against him, but had moved to his lap where they had kissed and snuggled. During a fiery love scene in the movie, Connor had looked up from having kissed Josh senseless to find Noah's hand buried deep in Indy's unbuttoned pants. Seconds later, they'd gone upstairs where the subsequent loud moans left no doubt as to their activities. Connor and Josh had followed suit and had managed to keep the fresh sheets clean with a satisfying mutual blow job.

Josh had begged Connor to take him again, but Connor had refused. He'd seen the slight cringe on Josh's face throughout the day whenever he exerted himself too much. There was no way Connor would exacerbate that pain, so the answer was no. When Josh had whined a little, Connor had gotten firm and had threatened to withhold for a day extra for every time Josh whined. That had shut him up.

How he had loved spending this time with Josh. Every minute with him, he felt more alive, more human. It had made him painfully aware of his loneliness, the unbearable emptiness of his life until now. He was proud of his time in the Marines, and he was grateful to serve as a cop, but he'd been sleepwalking. Josh had awakened him to a different life, one where he could feel, experience, love.

He jolted when the door was unlocked, and someone stepped inside. Indy.

"Everything okay?" he whispered.

"No. It's Noah. He's in incredible pain, and I don't know what to do. I need Josh."

Connor's breath stilled. He knew what Indy was implicitly asking. God, he'd known this would come up at some point, but he'd hoped to have more time to reconcile himself with the idea. How could he let Josh be used by Noah when he wanted him so desperately for himself? Still, he had no choice. Josh would never forgive him if Connor didn't allow him to be there for Noah.

He kissed Josh, stroking his head. "Josh, baby, wake up."

Josh's eyes opened. "Hey, baby," he whispered. "Impatient for me to wake up again?"

"Indy needs you. It's Noah."

Josh shot up. "Is he okay?"

"His leg is killing him. I don't know if he overdid it on the paintball range or what, but it's bad. I figure he has a fever, too." Indy sounded close to tears.

Josh scrambled up and climbed out of bed without so much as a glance at Connor. He followed Indy into the hallway, and Connor heard them walk in the other bedroom. Connor sat up with clenched fists, forcing a breath through a constricted throat.

You're losing him. He'll always choose Noah above you.

He dragged himself out of bed and got dressed. What else could he do? If they want him to stay much longer, they should at least let him pick up fresh clothes. He was wearing Noah's boxers, and though they fit, it was awkward as hell. Not as awkward as the sounds he was about to hear, though. Maybe he should go downstairs so he wouldn't have to listen in. How could Indy be okay with this, let alone watch? If they'd force him to watch, he'd fucking kill Noah. There was no way in hell he would be able to look and do nothing while another man was touching Josh. His Josh. But he wasn't truly Connor's, now was he? He would always be Noah's first.

Fully dressed, he sat down on the bed, his head in his hands, waiting for the proverbial ax to fall. Josh's voice was audible. Connor raised his head, tried to make out the words.

"I don't give a fuck what you want, Noah. This is not your decision anymore. We're taking you in, right now."

Take him in? What the hell was going on?

Josh stormed into the room, buttoning up his jeans, and

his socks in his hands. "Good, you're dressed. You need to carry Noah down. We're taking him to the ER."

Connor's mind shifted into operational mode. "What's wrong?"

"He has an infection on his stump that's spreading. The stubborn asshole has kept it from me, tried to self-medicate it. He's a fucking PA, and he should know better!"

The last words were clearly aimed at Noah, who responded from the other room with an equally loud "Fuck you!".

"Get the car ready and grab essentials for him. I'll bring him down," Connor said.

"He won't like it," Indy said, stepping into the room. His face was pale, and he was fidgeting with his hands.

Connor shot him a reassuring smile. "I can handle it. Go downstairs."

After putting his shoes on, he walked into the other bedroom without hesitation. "Let's go," he said.

Noah was still on the bed, naked, with a big scowl on his face. "I'm not going anywhere. Josh is overreacting. It's nothing."

Connor crossed his arms. "What you mean is that you'd rather he pity-fuck you so you can go back to feeling sorry for yourself."

Noah narrowed his eyes. "Wouldn't you prefer Josh's sweet, tight ass over a hospital?"

Noah was baiting him. And dammit, it was working. Connor bit down on his temper. "I would. But no matter how sweet Josh's ass is, it will not heal an infection," he said coolly.

"It's just irritated, not infected."

"Really? So you're requesting a pity-fuck at oh-five-thirty over a mere irritation of your skin?"

"Fuck you!"

"No, but thanks for offering. You've got two choices, Flint. You can go to the hospital as naked as you are right now, or you can go wearing clothes. The choice is yours. But I will take you to the hospital, and I'll knock you out cold if I have to. You still owe me a couple of punches anyway."

Noah was fuming, his face tight with anger and pain. "Close the door," he bit out at Connor between clenched teeth.

Connor thought he could've asked nicer but decided to let it go. The man was in pain, so he could cut him some slack.

"I know it's infected. But I didn't want to go to the hospital."

Connor saw more on the man's face than mere pain and frustration. Fear. A deep sense of duty. "You didn't wanna leave Indy and Josh alone."

"They need me. I know that sounds like a massive ego thing, but it's not."

"I get it," Connor said.

Noah let out a muffled curse, and his face distorted with pain. "I need to know I can trust you."

"I love him." Connor wasn't even sure why he told Noah, but he meant what he said. "I don't know why or how it happened so quickly, but I love him. I would die before I'd hurt him, at least intentionally."

Noah nodded, accepted. "And Indy?"

"I don't know how to prove I mean him no harm, other than to keep saying it. I hate my family, Noah. I hate who they are and what they did to him."

"Okay, then." Noah let out a shaky breath. "I'm trusting you to take care of them, O'Connor. Don't let me down." Connor nodded. Was Noah's voice weaker, or was that his imagination? He looked flushed, sweaty, his eyes glazed. "Grab me a shirt and some boxers, would you?"

Connor opened a random drawer, found boxers that matched the ones he was wearing and assumed they were Noah's. In the next drawer there was a stack of white shirts. He threw them at Noah, expecting him to catch them, but they fell down on the bed.

Noah smiled weakly. "I fucked up," he said.

Hesitantly, Connor walked over to him, grabbed his shoulder to pull him up. Noah's skin was burning hot under his hand. "Oh, shit," Connor said, his eyes growing big. "Fucking hell."

"Sepsis," Noah brought out, blinking slowly. "Tell them sepsis."

Noah went weak as jelly under his hands, then passed out. Connor grabbed the cell phone on the nightstand, dialed the all-too-familiar number. "Dispatch, this is Officer O'Connor, badge number seven-eight-five. I need an ambulance over at two-four Dearborn for a civilian with life-threatening fever due to infection."

"Ten-four, O'Connor, ambulance en route to two-four Dearborn. Which hospital do you prefer?"

"Albany General. Please alert the staff they have a colleague coming in, physician assistant Noah Flint. Infected amputation stump resulting in high fever, possible sepsis."

"Ten-four. Ambulance is four minutes out."

"Thanks, dispatch. I'll have someone stand outside to guide them in. I'll call you back when I'm outside."

He wrapped the sheet around Noah, not bothering with more clothes. It didn't make sense when they were about to treat him anyway. Noah was passed out, his whole body burning up with fever. Oh, God. Please let him be okay. Josh will not survive if Noah doesn't make it.

Connor folded his arms under Noah's body and lifted him off the bed. Josh was waiting in the hallway, his face white as the sheet around Noah. "He passed out. Ambulance is on the way. Tell Indy to stand outside and guide them in. And I need my phone and wallet, please."

Connor carried Noah down the stairs, out the front door. Josh was outside in the driveway with a flashlight, and he'd turned on all the lights around the house. In the distance, sirens wailed.

"Where's Indy?" Connor asked.

His muscles trembled with the effort of holding Noah up. Normally, he would've slung him over his shoulder which would have distributed his weight better, but he was scared it would rub the stump and hurt the guy even more. With the fever he was sporting, his system couldn't take much more.

"I don't know," Josh said. "Your phone and wallet were downstairs on the kitchen counter. I have them on me."

"Are you okay?" Connor checked. The last thing they needed now was for Josh to get hit with an episode.

"Yeah, but keep talking to me, please."

Connor made senseless small talk until the ambulance pulled up, lights blazing and sirens on until they pulled up in the driveway. Noah was transferred to a stretcher and wheeled in in no time. Connor's muscles were screaming in relief, and he rubbed his arms hard to get them to relax.

"Is one of you riding with him?" the paramedic asked.

"I can't," Josh said, panic visible in his eyes.

"You guys go. We'll drive to the hospital," Connor decided. Josh handed him his phone and wallet. He punched in the number again "Dispatch, this is O'Connor again, seven-eight-five. Ambulance has arrived. Thank you."

"Ten-four, O'Connor. Out."

"Okay, let's find Indy, and we'll head for the hospital."

They hurried inside, expecting to find Indy there. Two minutes later they had searched the entire house, and he was nowhere to be found.

"He's gone," Josh said, dragging a shaky hand through his hair. "How could he do that? Noah needs him."

Connor sighed. "He had a lot to deal with the last two days with me discovering who he was. Maybe it was all too much. He'll come back, baby. He loves Noah, and you, too."

Josh closed his eyes and drew in a ragged breath. "I can't lose him, Connor."

Connor didn't hesitate but pulled him close and hugged him tightly. "Don't allow your mind to go there. You'll break if you do. Stay grounded in the now, okay? I'm right here with you."

Josh leaned in, nodded with his cheek against Connor's.

"Let's go to the hospital. We'll leave the back door open so Indy can get in if he comes back."

He kept making small talk in the car, constantly drawing Josh back to reality. Fuck, if he slipped into an episode, things would get fucked up. He parked the car—luckily the parking lot was all but empty at this time—and held on tight to Josh's hand as they walked inside. It hadn't even occurred to him he was in a way coming out as gay until he ran into a colleague.

"O'Connor," Mack said. His eyes widened as they trailed to Josh's hand, entwined in Connor's. "What brings you here?"

"Mack," Connor nodded. Josh's hand stilled in his. Connor had expected to be nervous when the time came, but he wasn't. All he felt was a deep inner peace, a sense of doing the right thing. "This is Josh, my boyfriend. A friend of ours was brought in, so we're checking up on him."

To Mack's credit, he didn't react in any way other than that slight widening of his eyes. "Nice to meet you, Josh, though I'm sorry it's under these circumstances. I'm Oliver Mack." He didn't extend his hand, but maybe that was because Josh's right hand was in Connor's.

Josh merely nodded, his body tense.

"Captain said you took a few days off," Mack said, his voice trailing off at the end. His curiosity wasn't unexpected as Connor had never taken a day off so far.

"I needed to be there for our friend. Listen, Mack, we need to go. I'll talk to you soon." Connor was firm, gave Mack a courtesy nod and walked on. Josh followed him wordlessly.

"Josh!" A petite, fifty-something woman in nurses' scrubs spotted them and hurried to them. She halted awkwardly when she noticed them holding hands. Of course, people would stare. This was Noah's workplace, and they all thought Josh was Noah's boyfriend. Noah would not have brought Indy here, what with everyone having met him as a female patient. Shit, what should Connor do? He didn't want to let go of Josh's hand. First of all because he wanted to claim him, but also because he needed him grounded. Still, he loosened his grip, signaling to Josh it was his choice. As a reaction, Josh held on even tighter.

"How is he?" Josh said, the first words he'd spoken since the car ride.

"You know I'm not allowed to say anything as a nurse," the woman said.

"Come on, Judy, you know as much as any doctor here,

at least that's what Noah always says, and you know he doesn't give a shit about you breaking rank," Josh said.

She smiled. "No, he wouldn't," she relented. "He's not doing well, honey. I'm sorry. His fever is spiking, and they suspect the infection is spreading. They're doing rush blood work. Owens has called in the surgical attending."

Josh clamped Connor's hand so hard, he was bound to have bruises tomorrow. "What's the worst-case scenario?"

Judy put her hand on Josh's shoulder. "Worst case it develops into sepsis, and his organs start shutting down. Or it spreads too far in his leg, and they have to amputate the entire leg."

"That fucking idiot," Josh let out. "Sorry, Judy."

"No worries, honey, it's nothing I haven't heard from Noah before. Why don't you wait in the family room, and I'll let Owens know you're here."

With a last curious glance at their hands, Judy left, and they walked into the family room. It was blissfully empty. Connor found a spot on a comfy reading chair. Without hesitation, Josh crawled onto his lap, resting his head against Connor's shoulder.

"Josh, I know you need my physical presence, and I love holding you like this, but do we need to be worried about what people here will think and say? It's Noah's place of work, and I don't want things to get awkward for him."

Josh closed his eyes, leaned in even farther and snuggled up against Connor. "I don't give a shit, and neither would Noah. We don't explain ourselves to others, you know."

It was an approach that was foreign to Connor. In the Marines, he'd done everything he could to keep his sexual orientation a secret. He'd never said anything, not even to Lucas, had not even approached those who were known or rumored to be gay. Fuck, he'd hooked up with a few fellow

Marines, but even with them, he'd never talked. Lucas must've known, but they had never discussed it. Connor had kept his head low, hadn't wanted to make waves.

When he became a cop, he'd done the same. Until he'd run into Mack ten minutes ago and had claimed Josh as his boyfriend. Even then, he'd done it more to show Josh he was making good on his promise to be open about it than because he wanted to come out as gay. To him it had always felt like an either/or situation: either you pretended to be straight, or you came out as gay. Maybe there was a third way: doing what you wanted, not explaining anything and not giving a damn about what people might think or say. It seemed to work for Noah and Josh.

They sat there for maybe fifteen minutes in complete silence, Connor rubbing Josh's back, when an older guy in scrubs stepped in. "Josh, how are you holding up?" He extended his hand to Connor, completely ignoring the awkwardness of finding his employee's boyfriend in the arms of another man. "Owens, the ER attending, and Noah's boss. You look familiar."

"O'Connor. I'm with the Albany PD, so I've been in a few times. How is he?"

Owens pulled up a chair. "Not well. He was in and out of consciousness but not alert. We've put him in a medically induced coma, for now, to give his body rest. His fever is high, and we're worried about the infection spreading further and resulting in multi-organ failure. He's on high-dose antibiotics right now. If we don't see an improvement in the next couple of hours, we need a plan B. Josh, Noah's health care proxy lists you as his agent for medical decisions, so you need to let us know what you want us to do."

Josh turned his head toward Owens, but he never left his spot on Connor's lap. It gave Connor a strange satisfaction he mattered enough for Josh to do that, to not care what people would say or think. "What are the options?"

"I fear we may need to amputate more of his leg. The stump is badly infected, and it's spreading. The previous amputation was at his knee, but the orthopedic surgeon thinks we'll need to go mid-thigh, and I agree with him. That may be our best shot."

"Does waiting longer increase the risk?" Josh wanted to know.

"Unfortunately, yes. If amputation is a feasible option for you, sooner would be better. But I can have the orthopedic attending explain this to you since he would be the one doing the surgery."

"No need. Do the amputation."

Owens' eyes widened at Josh's fast answer. "Are you sure that's what Noah would want?"

"Listen, doc, the choice is simple. He can live without his entire leg. He cannot live without his organs. The stump has bothered him ever since the amputation in the CSH. He's been in constant pain, and even with the prosthesis, it was always a struggle. He said more than once it never fully healed. Maybe a higher amputation will give him more mobility instead of less."

"I agree with you when it comes to the risks. However, an amputation now is far from ideal. Cutting when there's already an infection is high risk, as the surgery itself could spread it. I would be remiss if I didn't make you aware of that risk."

"I appreciate that, but my decision stands. And, doc, you know Noah has a living will. He's an organ donor and doesn't want extraordinary measures if it would mean a permanent vegetative state."

Owens' eyes filled with compassion. "Let's hope it

doesn't come to that. I'll send Judy in with some papers for you to sign, but for now, I've got my marching orders. Hang in there, Josh. It's gonna be a long day."

Connor didn't know what to say to Josh. What was there to say at this point? Even if they weren't together in the conventional sense, Josh and Noah were closer than many lovers, spouses even. If Noah didn't survive this... Connor didn't even want to think about what that would do to Josh.

And Indy. He should be here, should be involved in these decisions. It was understandable his name wasn't on any official papers, what with their relationship being new and Indy living under a fake name, but he should have a say in this.

Josh was still on his lap, his face hidden against Connor's chest, his body tense. How could Connor provide him with what he needed to get through this? There was so little he could say or do to make it even remotely better.

Josh mumbled something Connor didn't hear. He kissed the top of his head. "Sorry, baby, what was that?"

"I need you to fuck me."

NOAH IS DYING.

It was all Josh could think of, again and again and again. Noah was dying. His best friend was dying. The thought was so big, that it threatened to take over, hold him captive. Josh clenched his fists, struggling to stay grounded and not let himself sink into the maelstrom of emotions.

"I don't understand," Connor said.

"Make me stop thinking. I'm going mad, Connor. Help me."

So he was a sick bastard for wanting to get fucked while

his best friend was dying. Whatever, he didn't give a shit. It was either that or surrendering to the madness threatening to take him. Pain and pleasure, both would help him stay grounded. Yet he didn't dare to look at Connor, fearing the rejection and judgment in his eyes.

"Not here," Connor growled.

Josh leaned back, found Connor's eyes. He saw understanding, love. Relief flooded him, made him tingle. "You'll do it?"

"We wait till you've signed the papers, and we go somewhere else, leave our cell numbers."

"Our house?"

Connor shook his head. "Mine. I live close by."

Connor's house. Or apartment. Josh didn't even know where the man lived. How disturbed was that? He called Connor his boyfriend, yet he didn't even know the basics, like his address. Or his date of birth.

"How old are you anyway?"

"Noah didn't tell you when he did his little research into me?"

"He did what?"

"You didn't know? Typical. Noah checked me out after I'd been to your house. I guess he wanted to know who he was dealing with. Come to think of it, he never made the link to the Fitzpatricks. He must have seen my mother's maiden name."

Josh leaned back against Connor's chest, reveling in the safety it brought him. It was like hiding behind a strong wall. "Indy hadn't told us back then, so it wouldn't have meant anything to him."

"That makes sense. I'm thirty-two by the way."

Four years older than Josh. He felt older, somehow, even though he didn't look it.

"What's your favorite color?"

Connor chuckled. "What's this, twenty questions?"

"I don't know the first thing about you."

"You know the most important things," Connor interjected.

"True. But I'd like to fill in some of the details. Humor me."

"Marine blue."

"Movie?"

"Gladiator."

"Music?"

"I barely listen to music. I dunno, eighties rock?"

"First kiss?"

"Dana Rogers, eleventh grade, after my high school football team won the state championships. She was the head cheerleader, and I scored the winning touchdown. Obviously, I didn't want to admit I was gay yet."

"First time sex?"

Connor laughed. "Dana Rogers, eleventh grade, after my high school football team won the state championships. Yeah, she was what was known as easy, and I was a nervous virgin who wanted to experiment. Awkward doesn't even begin to describe it."

Josh smiled as he felt some of the tension leaving his body. "You've learned a thing or two since then."

Judy came with the papers, and Josh signed each one without hesitation. This was the right thing to do. Noah had never been a proponent of the wait-and-see approach. He was a man of action, wanted to do something rather than leave things to chance. He gave Judy both their cell numbers, had her promise to call them if anything changed.

"I need to make a quick call," Josh said. "Noah's dad.

They haven't talked to each other in almost a year, but he needs to know."

Connor nodded. "Make the call."

Josh called the general, didn't use more words than necessary to update the man on Noah's condition. He hung up in a little over a minute, relieved that was done. "Let's go," he said.

Wordlessly, they drove to Connor's house. More precisely, Connor drove, and Josh watched him. No, he didn't know many of the basic details yet, but Connor had been right. Josh did know the most important things. The fact that Connor was calm in a crisis, decisive. That he was protective as hell when it came to Josh and would do anything to shield him. Connor was a rock he could lean on, take shelter behind.

Connor parked in the lot of a widespread apartment complex. Josh followed him as he opened a door, walked up one flight of stairs to a dark blue door. No name shield, nothing to make it personal. If Josh had to take a guess, he'd bet the apartment was sterile inside, empty of anything personal.

Connor closed the door behind them, turned the bolt into place.

"Strip," he told Josh.

A shiver tore through him. "Here?"

"That's one strike. Three strikes and you'll pay."

Fuck, yes. This.

This was what Josh wanted, what he craved. For Connor to take over so he could shut his brain down. He kicked off his shoes, not bothering with the laces. He unbuckled his belt and shoved his jeans down his hips, taking his boxers with him. His socks and shirt came off next, and he stood naked before Connor, his cock already growing hard.

"Undress me."

He reached for Connor's belt, but Connor's hand grabbed his wrist. "Yes, Connor," he commanded.

Tears of relief burned in Josh's eyes. How did this man know what he needed? Did it feel as good for Connor as it did for Josh when he submitted? If it did, he wanted nothing else but to obey. It felt so right.

"Yes, Connor."

He reached again for Connor's belt, and this time, he was allowed. Josh unbuttoned the jeans and pulled them down. Shoes. He should have taken Connor's shoes off first.

He kneeled, not in the least embarrassed by his nakedness, untied Connor's shoelaces and took off his shoes. After that, the jeans and socks followed suit. Connor's jacket came off. He lifted his arms so Josh could pull his sweater and shirt off. All that was left were his boxers. Well, Noah's boxers.

Josh put both his hands on the waistband and pulled them down. Connor's massive cock sprung free, halfway hard already. He dropped to his knees again to let Connor step out of his underwear. It brought the man's cock in his face, and he couldn't resist a quick lick.

Connor stepped back. "Two strikes. Did I say you could touch my cock?"

Josh stayed kneeling, waiting for further instructions. "No, Connor."

Connor opened a door that led to his bedroom. A dark mahogany four-poster queen-size was perfectly made with a dark blue comforter. It looked like it had never even been slept in.

"On your back on the bed, your head hanging over the edge. I wanna fuck your mouth."

Josh made his way to the bed. If Connor wanted Josh to

suck him off, why didn't he let him kneel? He climbed on, lowered himself on his back and scooted over until his head hung over the edge. Immediately, he realized what the idea was. He'd seen it in enough porn videos. This position allowed Connor to fuck Josh's mouth deep, deeper than in another position. It gave Connor almost complete control. Fuck, he was vulnerable like this. If Connor pushed his monster cock too far in, he could hurt Josh. He wouldn't be able to breathe, not with the Beast stuffed in his mouth.

Connor would never hurt you. This knowledge filled him, gave him peace of mind. Allowing Connor to be dominant meant trusting him to know what was best. He would never hurt Josh in a way that didn't bring pleasure. The peace returned, and Josh surrendered.

"Yes, Connor."

Only then did he realize Connor had waited for his submission, his permission. He hadn't done anything until Josh had signaled his agreement with those two simple words.

"Open up," Connor said, a deep sound of satisfaction in his voice. He positioned himself above Josh, his legs spread wide to get the right height.

Josh opened his mouth, relaxed. The crown of the Beast teased his cheek, then his chin.

"You want it?"

"Oh, please, Connor."

To Josh's deep delight, Connor brought his cock in line with Josh's mouth, entered it. Josh licked, shivering when the saltiness hit his tongue. Fuck, yes. He started sucking, licking, drawing Connor in deeper until his whole mouth was filled with cock.

Connor kept a close watch, pulling back when Josh ran

out of breath. Still, his eyes watered with the pressure and saliva was pooling out of the corners of his mouth.

"Damn, you look good with my cock in your mouth, baby," Connor grunted.

Even if Josh had wanted to say anything, he couldn't. All he did was moan when Connor pulled out his cock, allowed him to catch his breath and stuffed it right back in. He never pushed in too far, never got so deep it hurt, though Josh's jaws tensed up with the constant pressure. At the same time, he was getting mighty hard by sucking off Connor. His right hand sneaked lower to grab his own dick.

"Did I say you could touch yourself?"

Fuck. Was that the third strike? No, no, no!

He whimpered when Connor pulled out of his mouth. "I'm sorry, Connor. Please, please let me suck you till you come."

Connor's face was blank. Damn, the cop was good at hiding his emotions.

When Connor walked away to the corner of the room, Josh thought he'd lose it. If Connor would punish him by not fucking him, he'd go mad. He didn't dare to move and watched upside down as Connor lowered himself into a sofa chair. He gestured Josh to come with a single index finger.

Josh scrambled up, almost tripping over himself in his haste to obey. Connor spread his legs. Did he want Josh to resume sucking him there? He would, but he wasn't sure that was the plan. Until he knew for certain, he wasn't moving, not wanting to incur Connor's disapproval.

Connor gestured to his right knee. "Bend over," he said. This time he wasn't quite capable of preventing the gleam in his eyes.

Holy fuck, he was going to spank him. Josh held back a

smile, biting his lip in anticipation instead as he lowered himself over Connor's knee.

"Twenty strikes, count them out and say 'thank you, Connor' after each one."

Hot damn, how did he come up with this stuff? Was Connor a natural, or had he done research? Josh closed his eyes, tensed as he awaited the first slap. Connor made him wait, Josh's body shivering with need and nerves.

Slap!

He jerked off Connor's knee as the strong hand hit his right butt cheek full on. Fuck, that stung.

"One," he said. "Thank you, Connor."

The second one came fast, hit his other cheek.

"Two. Thank you, Connor."

A pause before three, four, and five came in rapid succession. By now, his ass was smarting something fierce.

"Five. Thank you, Connor," he managed between clenched teeth.

Number six forced tears from his eyes, but after number ten something strange happened. It was as if his body went into a different mode. His cock, which had softened during the first strikes, became rock-hard again, and all his nerves were on fire. His ass stung like a motherfucker, but it felt somehow good at the same time.

"Eleven. Thank you, Connor."

He heard himself say it, detected the sincere gratitude in his voice. More tears came, started falling for real.

Fourteen, fifteen. His body was shaking, and to his surprise, his balls were pulling tight as if about to release. What the fuck was happening?

Twenty.

"Thank you, Connor," he all but whimpered. Ecstasy.

His body was ecstatic, his cock throbbing hard. How the hell was this possible?

He felt Connor's left hand on his ass, way colder than the right one he'd used to spank Josh. "You are so beautiful," Connor said, his voice full of admiration. "Fuck, Josh, your ass right now... It's on fire, and it must be hurting, but it's never beckoned me more."

Josh's muscles gave in, and he would have slid off Connor's knee if the man hadn't grabbed him. He lifted Josh with ease, carried him to the bed and lowered him on his belly. "Stay there. I'll be right back."

Josh couldn't have moved if he wanted to. His limbs were like elastic bands, his muscles weak and useless. He jolted when he felt something cold and wet on his butt. Had he fallen asleep? He'd never heard Connor walk away, or return. A wet, cold washcloth was draped over each ass cheek, soothing the pain.

"Thank you, Connor." The words fell out of his mouth automatically, much to his surprise.

Connor chuckled. "That's a good boy."

Josh felt the words in the very core of his being, like they were what he had been waiting for all this time. Rain on a barren desert, the dried-out trees rejoicing in the first few drops of water.

He must've dozed off again, though it felt more like dreaming awake than sleeping, but he woke up when the wet cloths were replaced by a towel that patted him dry. It still stung, but way less than before. Cool moisture hit his bottom, and he jerked in shock.

"Don't move." Connor's voice was back to authoritative, and Josh settled back down.

Connor's hand rubbed a cold lotion into his skin, circling his cheeks with gentle moves. Josh relaxed, pushed his butt into Connor's hand. His eyes closed, he reveled in the sensation of the warm caress, the cool lotion, the tingle in his ass that kept spreading. This felt so good.

Connor's finger found his crack, traveled all the way up... and down. Josh shivered. Cold liquid dripped in his crack, found a slow-dripping way down, down, down, into his hole. The lotion smelled of coconut, triggering images of white beaches and a blue ocean, happy cocktails with those cute paper umbrellas.

Connor's finger followed, teasing his entrance until Josh whimpered. In a reflex, he spread his legs farther, pushed back his butt.

More teasing, probing, circling. Fuck, didn't the guy realize what he was doing, that he was driving Josh crazy?

Finally, finally, Connor's finger slipped in, only to disappear just as quickly. Josh let out a frustrated groan. He opened his eyes, turned his head sideways and aimed a get-the-fuck-on-with-it look to Connor, who didn't seem inclined to speed things up.

"You're a needy little bottom, aren't you?"

Josh whimpered again, couldn't seem to stop the desperate sounds coming out of him. "Yes, Connor. Please, Connor, please," he added, not too proud to beg.

"Please, what?"

"Please fuck me. Please, I need you."

"Jerk me off. I want to see you covered in my cum."

Later, Josh realized that was the moment his mind found complete peace. He stopped thinking as there was nothing to think about. All he needed to do was obey. His only thought was what Connor wanted.

He came up on hands and knees and turned around. Connor's cock was thick and quivering. Josh grabbed some lotion, used it as a lubricant and fisted Connor.

"Harder. I like it rough, remember?"

"Yes, Connor."

He jerked him off with one hand. It barely fit around the thick member, and he used his other hand to cup Connor's balls. He squeezed, jerked, fisted. Hard. Connor came with a roar, shooting his fluids all over Josh's face, chest, and hands.

"Clean me up."

"Yes, Connor."

He opened his mouth, let his tongue out and licked him clean.

"On your knees, ass toward me and high in the air. Spread those legs wide."

Josh turned, assumed the position, letting his head rest on his hands, still sticky with cum.

"Whatever I do, you cannot come, you hear me? I don't care what you have to do, but you are not allowed to come."

"Yes, Connor."

A heartbeat later, Connor's face was in his crack, his tongue deep inside his hole. Josh howled in pleasure, reaching for his cock and jerking it once, twice. Then he remembered Connor's command. He would obey. No matter what it cost him, he would not disappoint Connor.

He pulled the skin forward over the crown of his cock, pinched so hard tears sprung to his eyes while his body shivered at the same time with delight at the sensation of Connor's tongue. Every time he felt himself come close, he pinched again. Pain and pleasure, they tormented him while Connor was eating him out like a death row inmate devoured his last meal.

Connor let go of his hole with a loud smack. "You're doing good, baby."

Balm for Josh's tormented body. He melted into the mattress, let go of his dick for now.

A cap opened, a squirting sound. Connor's fingers returned, pushed inside without hesitation. Finally. Josh relaxed, opened up, invited Connor in. Two fingers, three, then four were asking for entry. He tensed for a second.

"Let me in, baby."

He bore down, accepted them all the way in. Connor spread him wide and didn't stop until all the pain was gone.

"Attaboy."

Connor pulled out his fingers. A condom package ripped open. More squirting, then the glorious feeling of that monstrous cock against his hole. He pushed down, opened wide. Connor surged in deep, was halfway in on the first thrust. Josh let out a contented sigh.

Four thrusts and Connor was in all the way, a testament to the care he'd taken in prepping Josh. His body was liquid fire, every nerve burning with desire. His ass felt like it was ready to explode, so deliciously full. Connor's dick pulsated inside him, demanding he surrender. God, Josh was seeping precum, his cock weeping for attention.

"Brace yourself and remember: you cannot come."

Josh dug into the mattress with one hand, grabbed his cock again with the other, pinched hard. Connor pulled almost completely out, thrust back in hard and deep, hitting Josh's prostate full on. Josh was teetering on the brink, his balls strained and his cock ready to blow.

Oh fuck, oh fuck, oh fuck. He would never make this. It was impossible. His breaths came in ragged gasps as his ass was ravaged, owned.

He needed to distract himself. Anything but the thought of coming.

Connor pumped so deep, his balls bounced against Josh.

Heat raced up and down Josh's spine. Fuck, he was stretched to his limits, and it felt so damn good. But he couldn't come. Connor had told him he couldn't, and he wanted to obey.

He'd do a field strip, the procedure to disassemble and clean his rifle.

Connor slammed in, made him almost lose his balance.

"Dammit, hold on," Connor snapped.

Josh let go of his cock, leaned farther forward and rested his face on his arms, braced himself with both hands. "Yes, Connor."

Connor surged, plunged, sunk in deeper than should have been possible. Josh made a sound of torment. Oh, God, dammit, fucking hell.

He disassembled his rifle, cleaned it, reassembled it.

Connor slammed, rammed, fucked. Josh's body soared. So. Fucking. Close.

He checked his rifle, tested it.

Connor grunted, switched gears. His thrusts became more vigorous and shallow. Josh had to hold on with both hands to stay in place. The pleasure was almost too much to bear, bringing tears to his eyes.

He loaded the ammo, checked to make certain it was in place.

Connor's hips jerked, his fingers dug deep into Josh's hips, and with a last desperate shove, he came inside Josh. The long growl of pleasure Connor let out send a wave of emotion through Josh. Oh, fuck, he'd done it. He hadn't come. He'd obeyed.

Connor dropped his weight on him, and Josh buckled, his legs sinking into the mattress. Connor kept fucking him lazily, his cock still hard until he slipped out with an erotic plopping sound. Josh stayed where he was, fucked into complete surrender.

The weight disappeared. Rustling sounds, Connor disposing of the condom. "On your back."

He didn't have the strength to answer anymore but dragged himself halfway up, only to sink down again on his back. Eyes closed, he pulled up his legs, canted his ass to invite Connor back in.

His eyes shot open when he felt Connor's slick hand on his cock. That single touch brought him back though his eyes were still unfocused, and he had a hard time concentrating. Connor jerked his cock hard. "Come for me, Josh."

That was all it took. Josh cried out, wrenching a moan from his toes and came so hard his whole body jerked and spasmed. He shot his cum all over himself, including on his cheeks where it mingled with the tears that still fell from his eyes.

Connor sat himself upright against the headboard, jammed a pillow in his back. He pulled Josh towards him, then raised him up on his knees. This time, he rolled a fresh condom on with ease.

"Open your ass."

Josh relaxed, positioned himself above Connor's cock and sank down, taking him in again. He wrapped his leg around Connor, hid his face against the strong chest. Connor held him while he cried, emptied himself out, meanwhile softly thrusting. The comforting rhythm calmed Josh, brought him back to reality. He shifted, angled his body so that Connor hit his sweet spot. God, his ass hurt.

"Can I come again?" he asked, his voice hoarse and broken.

"Yes. Take what you need, baby."

Josh rode the Beast until he came again, another violent orgasm that had him collapsing into Connor's arms. He fell asleep instantly, only waking up when Connor carried him into the bathroom. He lowered them together in a deep bathtub, the water warm and smelling of the ocean.

Josh could barely keep his eyes open as Connor washed him, ever so tenderly. He shampooed his hair, kneading the last bit of tension out of Josh's scalp, rinsing it out with the hand showerhead. He carried him out of the tub, patted him dry, then wrapped a big towel around him and lowered him back on the bed. Somewhere in between, Connor must have changed the sheets because the linens smelled fresh and clean. Josh sighed, too worn out to move a muscle.

"I love you," he said, searching for Connor. When he found his strong body, he cuddled up against him, pushing the towel aside to feel his naked skin. "I love you, Connor," he repeated.

"I love you, too, Josh."

10

Indy's stomach rolled and lurched. It wasn't the kind of sick where your stomach wanted to get rid of something bad you ate, but the kind of unease that informed you about a spectacularly bad decision.

He'd taken off.

Noah was in the hospital, in wicked bad shape, and Indy had split. What did that say about him, about his character? What kind of boyfriend was he if he wasn't there when Noah needed him the most?

This is why he'll choose Josh over you. Well, he would if it wasn't for Connor. You don't deserve him, either of them.

He bit his lip as he drove the I-87 eastward toward New York City, more by chance than by plan. He'd taken off on instinct, and now he had no idea where to go. God, he sucked, both as a boyfriend and as a human being. Who took off like that, without saying anything?

He'd been so damn scared. When he'd woken up from Noah thrashing in the bed, he'd known something was horribly wrong. Noah had been out of it, so hot. He hadn't known what to do, except to get Josh. Josh had told him they would take Noah to the ER, that he was way sicker than he'd let on.

In hindsight, he should've known something was off. The stump had been bothering Noah the last few days, more than usual. Noah never took painkillers, and Indy had noticed him take one twice on the paintball range. Afterward, he'd been out of it. Indy recognized it from how he'd felt after the acid attack. They'd sedated him at first to cope with the pain, but after that, he'd been on heavy painkillers. Industrial strength, the treating physician had called them. They worked well to block the physical pain, but they also made you numb emotionally. That's what he'd seen in Noah, that flat emotional state. Like nothing got through to him.

They'd had sex, even, the night before. The movie had been nice, with them cuddling on the couch. He'd been careful not to touch Noah's leg again, but Noah had assured him it was fine. He'd apologized up and down for that morning, had said it was all on him and not on Indy. Indy had believed him, had figured it was a weird fluke with his leg. After all, they'd had sex. But even during the sex, something had felt off. Noah had been performing on autopilot. He'd been emotionally switched off. Damn, he should've known then. Should've said something.

When he'd heard Connor call that ambulance, he'd bolted straight out the door. He couldn't do this. He couldn't watch him die. He'd observed from across the street as Connor carried Noah outside. Noah's body had hung limp and unresponsive in the cop's arms, and Indy's heart had stopped. The way he'd looked, so deadly still, Indy knew it was bad. Really bad.

Suddenly the thought of something happening to Noah had been too real. Many times he'd feared what would happen if Duncan ever found him, what he'd do to Noah and Josh. And now Noah was dying, or what looked like it, and it was all too real. All he'd been able to think was that he needed to get the hell out of there.

He'd watched Connor and Josh search for him, call out. He'd stayed hidden until they'd left, presumably to the hospital. As soon as they were gone, he'd gone back to the house, had cleared out his stuff. It was pathetically little, but it had hit him how much more it was than before. Noah and Josh had bought clothes for him, shoes, a new phone, a warm winter jacket. He'd thrown it all in his ratty weekend bag, had added food and drinks. Then he'd changed into his female outfit, and minutes later, he'd taken off.

He'd left him.

His stomach rolled again, and he swallowed back bile, his hands shaking on the wheel. He took in a raspy breath, forced it down to his belly. It would be okay. He would be okay.

Another breath.

What about Noah, will he be okay, too? You left him. How could you do that? He'll never, ever forgive you.

His stomach wouldn't settle. He yanked the car over to the shoulder, got out just in time to empty his stomach onto the grass. He shivered, both from the cold and from the bitter taste of bile residue in his mouth. His stomach had been empty. He hadn't even had breakfast yet, for fuck's sake.

He placed his hands on the roof of the car, made himself breathe in. Steady, now. He had to keep it together. Otherwise he'd fuck up.

A plan. He needed a plan.

New York City was good. Anonymous. He'd take an airport motel. Newark, easiest to get to from where he was.

Once he was there, he'd contact Houdini. He needed a new identity, in case this one was compromised and would lead back to Noah and Josh. Noah was helpless in the hospital, so Indy would need to stay away and leave no trace behind. That also meant selling his car and buying a new one as soon as he had his new identity.

Someplace neutral, this time. Far away from Boston. Unremarkable. The Midwest, maybe? Ohio. Ohio sounded good.

Okay, that was better. Having a plan eased his stress. Next up was getting something in his stomach. He got in his car, grabbed a health bar, and took a bite while he merged back on the New York Thruway.

A little over two hours later, he checked into some crappy motel in Jersey. It smelled musty with a faint trace of tobacco smoke lingering. He bolted the door, closed the burgundy curtains that were faded from the sun. His car was parked at the main entrance, not near his door. He never parked in front of his room. It would be too easy to find him if they'd ever made his car.

The room was outfitted with a tiny microwave and fridge. Perfect for his needs. He heated a cup of water to make tea. That would help him calm down. As soon as it was ready, he settled on the creaky queen-size bed. The burgundy-and-pink flowery bedspread had stains he did not want to know the origins of, and it, too, smelled dusty. Whatever. He'd only be here a day or two, tops.

He opened his laptop, hoping the motel's promise of free Wi-Fi would check out. He could make his phone into a hot spot, but it would cost him valuable data. Luckily, the Wi-Fi worked. Not only that, it was faster than he'd expected. Probably not a lot of people here at ten-thirty in the morning. He'd been lucky the motel even allowed early check-in.

He'd given the front desk receptionist some story about his flight being canceled, but the man had barely listened.

He shot off an email to Houdini.

NEED NEW ID. Female. White, common name. Same pic. Ohio. Different DOB. 21. Including SSN, HS diploma. Pick up NYC.

NOW, all he had to do was wait. Houdini would reply in exactly one hour. That man was a godsend. He wouldn't have survived without him.

What felt like ages ago, but in reality was maybe three years before, he'd met an associate of Duncan's. Associate being a loose term here, as the man was being blackmailed into doing work for the Fitzpatricks. He was a con artist specialized in fake documents that could pass any test. Drivers' licenses, passports, birth or death certificates, this man could produce anything you wanted for a price. Houdini was his moniker, as he could make people disappear with what he did.

He'd possessed more morals than the Fitzpatricks had counted on though, and when Duncan had asked him for fake IDs for a bunch of underage girls he aimed to pimp out, Houdini had refused. Being a Fitzpatrick, Duncan didn't take kindly to the word 'no', and he'd kidnapped Houdini's ten-year-old daughter to get what he wanted and to show him who was boss.

Stephan had overheard what Duncan had done and had been repulsed. Who the fuck would kidnap a ten-year-old to get to her dad? Pretty sick if you asked him. But when Duncan and one of his lieutenants joked about raping her, he knew he couldn't idly sit by. It might've been brash talk, but who the fuck knew what they would do. Everyone knew Duncan liked them young. Stephan had done some discreet digging, discovered where they kept her and had sent an anonymous text to Houdini with the location. Within an hour, a group of armed men had freed the girl from the house where she was being held.

A few weeks later, a simple piece of paper had been dropped in Stephan's pocket with an email address. He'd emailed it, curious as he was and had found out it was Houdini, promising him to deliver anything he wanted if he ever needed it. Somehow, Houdini had found out it had been Stephan who'd helped him even though Duncan had never discovered it. Thank fuck for that. Houdini had given him specific instructions on how to contact him. When Stephan had gone on the run and had become Indy, he'd contacted Houdini, and the man had delivered an ID in his new name within forty-eight hours. With his help, Stephan Moreau had become Indiana Baldwin. Without him, Indy wouldn't have stood a chance.

He played games on his phone to pass the time. At the expected time, an email came in.

NO PROB. 34. tracks. rose & jack.

INDY EXHALED IN RELIEF. Houdini would come through. The delivery instructions were coded, but Indy understood without a problem. The handover was always in a Starbucks where he'd order a tall latte macchiato if everything was okay, and a grande espresso macchiato if he knew he was being tailed. Houdini delivered exactly forty-eight hours from sending his reply unless he indicated otherwise in his email. The 34 meant the Starbucks was somewhere on 34th Street, but the tracks narrowed it down to Penn Station, which was on 34th Street. Rose would be his codename, and he'd be meeting 'Jack'. Houdini had a fondness for movies, always picked duos from movies, he'd told Indy.

Indy closed his laptop. Two days from now, he'd have a new name, a new identity. A new future.

Would Noah and Josh be in it? He honestly didn't know.

WHEN CONNOR and Josh got back to the hospital, Noah had been wheeled out of his surgery. A nurse told them they could see him as soon as he woke up, which should be in about an hour. They settled in the waiting room again, which was now fuller. They encountered some raised eyebrows when people spotted their entwined hands, but nobody said anything.

Josh had been quiet since he'd woken up after a two-hour nap. At first, Connor had thought he'd needed time to wake up, or maybe process, but when Josh still had said nothing an hour later, Connor worried. Had it been too much, too soon? Had he gone too far? He'd been winging it, after all, going by sheer instinct and a deep desire to give Josh what he needed. What if he'd fucked up? Josh had said he loved him, but maybe that had been the endorphins talking?

"How did you know?" Josh said.

"How did I know what?"

"That I needed for you to..." Josh looked around, lowered his voice. "...to take over, fuck me senseless. Literally."

The old adage of a weight being taken off your chest got a whole new meaning for Connor. It was like he'd been carrying a ton of bricks that disappeared, filling him with sweet relief.

"Instinct," he said, not capable of keeping the joy and satisfaction out of his voice.

"I've never felt like that," Josh said, a sense of awe in his voice.

"How did it feel?"

"Tranquil. Serene. My mind came to a complete sense of peace, of fulfillment, somehow. It felt so right, perfect even."

Connor smiled, squeezed Josh's hand a little tighter. Thank fuck he'd gotten it right.

"How did it feel for you?" Josh asked.

Connor grinned. "You really are a girl, the way you talk about your feelings."

"Baby, I think I proved to you today I am anything but a girl," Josh whispered and oh, so innocently, brushed his other hand against Connor's cock. It hardened instantly. How the hell was that possible? He'd never had this kind of sexual appetite, but with Josh he was aroused all the time.

He grabbed Josh's hand, shot him a dark look. "You're playing with fire."

Josh smiled. "Yes, Connor."

The words alone were enough to bring back the sweet memories of earlier that day. The incredible surge of power and control Connor had felt every time Josh had submitted. His hand on Josh's ass as he spanked him, which had turned him on as much as it had Josh. Pounding Josh so hard he'd almost fallen off the bed. Josh weak and trembling in his arms after being fucked senseless, as he put it. He'd never even imagined it could be like that, that he would love so wholly and completely.

"I love you." The words rolled out of his mouth.

Josh's eyes searched his. "I wasn't sure if you meant it, or if you said it because I did."

"I meant it. You're mine, Josh, and I love you more than I'd thought possible. I know it's ridiculously fast and messy and complicated, but it's real."

"I love you, too. I want to be with you, Connor, more than anything."

Connor couldn't resist and leaned over to kiss Josh quickly. It was Josh who held his head when he wanted to pull back and deepened the kiss.

"Stop that, right now!"

Connor didn't realize the cold, hard voice was aimed at them until he felt Josh freeze.

"It's disgusting! Making a display like that and going behind my son's back. You should be ashamed of yourself!"

Connor broke off the kiss and looked past Josh to find a general in full uniform shooting him a look that was meant to kill. General Flint. Wasn't that nice of him to drop by? He squeezed Josh's hand, then let go as he rose.

"Keep your voice low, General. There are children present," he said through clenched teeth, rising to his full height.

"Who the fuck are you?"

The general took a step closer, undoubtedly an effective intimidation technique with others. Connor wasn't impressed. He didn't give a shit who the man was, other than he was being an ass. Besides, he had a trump card that would make Flint do what he wanted, and he wasn't above playing dirty. The guy fucking owed him.

"O'Connor. I'm a police officer with the Albany PD. Again, I will ask you kindly to mind your language."

"I will do whatever the fuck I want, especially when it

comes to my son. I will not allow him to be treated with such disrespect by this...this morally subversive excuse-for-a-man who corrupted him."

An ice-cold temper crept through Connor's veins. Nobody insulted Josh and got away with it. This time, he took a step forward, bringing him nose to nose with the general. The man's eyes narrowed in anger and surprise at Connor's brazenness.

"That's my boyfriend you are insulting, Sir, and I will not stand for it, nor for your combative behavior in a hospital. You will back off now, or I will have you arrested."

Flint smirked, a look that left no doubt whom Noah had inherited it from. "You and what army?"

Connor's voice was so low, no one else but him and the general would hear it. "That would be the United States Marine Corps, Sir, where I was a sergeant until you fucked up an operation that left me and a fellow Marine in enemy hands, which led to his death. Do the names O'Connor and Martins ring a bell? Operation Clear Blue Sky? I know you buried it deep, but I haven't forgotten. Sir."

Connor had the distinct satisfaction of watching the general pale. "Now, get the fuck out of my face before I start singing like a fucking mockingbird and blow your pristine reputation to smithereens."

One. Two. Three seconds. That was how long Flint tried to keep his composure before he stepped back and walked out without another word.

"Sorry about that, folks," Connor said, looking around the waiting room and sending everyone his standard "don't worry I'm a cop, so everything is under control" look. Satisfied that no one would cause any more issues, he sat back down.

"Holy crap, now I want to let you fuck me all over again," Josh whispered, looking at Connor with unbridled lust.

And, Connor was hard again. He sighed, fighting back a smile. "Your ass is way too tender, baby, but if you're good, I'll let you suck me later."

"Yes, Connor."

JOSH COULD NOT TAKE his eyes off Connor. Something had happened between them that he had no words for. He loved him and felt Connor's love for him, but it was more than that. It was like they had clicked as puzzle pieces. They had found the roles, the positions they were supposed to have. Dom and sub, commanding and obeying, deciding and following. It felt so right, more right than Josh could've ever imagined. It brought peace. Freedom.

The way Connor had defended him toward Noah's father, it had been unbelievable. Josh didn't know what he'd said to the man, but it had been damn effective in getting him to scram. Aside from Noah, Josh had never met anyone who dared to disobey or even displease General Flint. It made Connor even hotter in Josh's eyes.

Violet, a nurse Josh knew, walked into the waiting room and sought them out. "Noah is asking for you," she said. "For the both of you."

Noah was awake? Oh, thank God.

Violet's tone alerted Josh the gossip machine in the ER was in full swing, with people speculating who Connor was and what they both were to Noah. Josh didn't give a shit. As long as Noah was okay, he couldn't care less about anything else.

They followed Violet into the post-op area where she

brought them to Noah. He was hooked up to all kinds of monitors, but he was breathing on his own, so that had to be a good sign. God, Noah was deadly pale, but he was sending them a weak smile, blinking his eyes as if he was groggy. Well, he probably was, having just woken up from a serious surgery.

Josh walked over, put his hand on Noah's head. He kissed him on his mouth. "How are you feeling?"

"Like crap, but I'm alive. I'll take it."

Josh's stomach cramped. Did Noah realize yet what had been done to him? Would he blame Josh? "I'm sorry, Noah."

"You made the right call." Noah gestured at his leg, or what was left of it. "I fucked up, Josh."

Josh bit his lip. "Was it the right decision to amputate?"

Noah let out a shaky breath. "Yes. I'm not saying it doesn't suck because it does, but you did right by me. I was contemplating getting another surgery already because the stump kept bothering me. I wouldn't have quite gone this far, but I fucked up by ignoring that infection."

"Yeah, you did. You should've told me, told us. God, I was worried about you. I wasn't sure you'd make it..." Josh's voice broke, and Connor put a hand on his shoulder. He reached for it, held on to his rock.

Noah's eyes flashed with guilt. "I know. I'm so sorry. It was...inexcusably stupid." His eyes found Connor. "Thank you," he said.

Josh looked over his shoulder to Connor, who simply nodded at Noah.

Noah swallowed. "Where's Indy? Was he afraid to come here?"

Josh closed his eyes for a second. He couldn't lie to Noah, but how did he tell him? Connor said, "Indy took off, probably scared of what was going on with you, but he'll come back." The quiet reassurance in his voice encouraged Josh, but would it be enough for Noah?

Noah closed his eyes, sank back against the pillow. "Yeah, I fucked that up, too."

Josh didn't say anything. What could he say? Meaningless clichés wouldn't help.

When Noah's eyes opened again, they focused on Josh. "How are you holding up?"

"I'm good."

Noah's eyes narrowed. "You look remarkably relaxed."

Color crept up in Josh's cheeks. He shot a help-me look sideways to Connor, who still had his strong arm around his shoulder.

"I provided Josh with what he needed. He's mine now."

Connor's calm words were a balm to Josh's torn soul. He exhaled. The truth was simple. For a second, he feared another pissing match between the two men, but Noah smiled. "You worked him over good."

"I did." Connor's face lit up with a slow, sensual, and fucking proud smile. "Didn't I, Josh?"

He never even hesitated. "Yes, Connor."

"That's good. That's really good." Noah's eyes saddened. "Look, you don't owe me anything, but—"

"We'll do whatever we can to find Indy while protecting his identity," Connor said. "He loves you, Flint. He'll come back."

Noah did a weak-ass attempt at looking assured. "His self-preservation instinct may trump whatever feelings he has for me."

Josh so wanted to reassure him, but he didn't know how. Lying wasn't the answer, and no matter how badly he wanted to tell Noah Indy would be back, Josh wasn't certain. Indy loved Noah, there was no denying that, but would it be enough to overcome his fears? And could you blame him considering the circumstances?

"I have more bad news," he finally said.

"Spit it out," Noah said.

"I called your dad to let him know. He stopped by but was upset when he caught me and Connor kissing."

A flash of disgust clouded Noah's face. "I'm assuming upset is too mild a word here?"

"He wasn't happy. Connor had to step in."

Noah's eyebrows rose. "How did you get him to back off?"

Huh. What had Connor said to the general to make him leave? It had been effective, but what had been the trick? He turned to watch Connor, whose face closed off completely. What the hell?

"Let's say I can be persuasive when I want to be," Connor said, his voice as dismissive as could be. Wow, this was not a topic he was willing to discuss further. That, of course, made Josh even more curious what had happened—and he didn't need to see Noah's face to know his friend shared that feeling.

"You shouldn't have called him," Noah said to Josh, his voice friendly, though decisive.

"He's still your dad, Noah. He had a right to know."

"On that, we disagree. He lost all rights after the way he treated you."

Josh knew arguing was senseless. This was something he and Noah had never seen eye to eye on. As much as he feared the general, Josh felt he was still Noah's father and deserved to be treated with respect, but Noah disagreed. As far as he was concerned, his father could go to hell and stay there, roasting for all eternity.

"So how are you going to find Indy?" Noah changed the topic.

"I can't use any traditional methods, like putting out a bolo for his car or driver's license since that would leave a trace in the system others could track." Connor's face was pensive. "My first step, I guess, is to find a safe way to contact the Boston DA and ask him to affirm my story. That way, if we find Indy, at least he'll be certain I'm not out to screw him."

11

They'd fallen asleep almost as soon as they had undressed and cuddled up in bed. No wonder, it had been an exhausting day, though a satisfying one.

Holy crap, the images of Josh draped over Connor's knee, that strong hand coming down on his ass. Connor fucking the living daylights out of him. Josh kept playing them in his head as he took off the bedsheets in the master bedroom and walked them over to the washing machine. He'd never experienced anything like it. It was like he was born to be with Connor, like his body was made to accommodate his. Though in all honesty, his ass did still sting. No wonder with that pounding he took.

He added detergent and fabric softener and turned the machine on. At least Noah would have a clean bed when he came home. Whenever that was. With the infection still in his system, he wouldn't be leaving the hospital anytime soon. It could be a week, they'd said, maybe even longer.

Josh had worried about being by himself and what that would do to him, but Connor hadn't even hesitated. He'd asked Noah if he could move in to take care of Josh, and Noah had gladly accepted. It should make Josh feel weak that he needed this, that two men were so focused on taking care of him, but it didn't. Instead, it made him feel loved. Safe. And wanted.

He and Connor had shared a quick breakfast this morning before Connor had booted up his laptop. He'd taken some clean clothes and personal stuff from his apartment before they'd gone back to the hospital, including his laptop. Josh could've monitored him, but what was the point now? Indy was gone, and besides, Josh had no doubt about Connor's intentions.

Josh was on his way to clean the master bathroom when the doorbell rang. His heart jumped up with joy. Indy!

He all but ran down the stairs, only to come to a full stop. A tall, lanky man stood outside, his face hidden by a faded Orioles cap, but Josh would recognize him anywhere. What the fuck was Aaron doing here?

Connor stepped up behind him and took a quick look outside. "You know him?"

Josh sighed. "Yeah."

He opened the door. Aaron looked up, and Josh's breath stopped. Aaron sported a blackened eye, a thick, bloodied lip, and a bruised and swollen face. Holy crap, he'd been worked over good.

"What the fuck happened to you?"

"Hi, Josh. Can I please come in?" Aaron's voice was hesitant.

Josh threw the door open wide and gestured. With careful steps that indicated more injuries, Aaron came inside—stopping abruptly when he saw Connor.

"Aaron, this is my boyfriend Connor. Connor, my brother Aaron."

To his credit, Connor didn't even blink, merely shook Aaron's hand with care. Had he even told Connor he had a brother? Josh wasn't sure. He might've, but then again, his family wasn't a priority to him, so who the fuck knew.

Minutes later, they were seated in the living room—Aaron lowering himself ever so gently onto one of the chairs, with Josh and Connor hip to hip on the couch.

"What the fuck is going on? What happened?" Josh asked.

Aaron didn't meet his eyes, but kept staring at the floor. "I got beaten up."

"That much I surmised myself, genius. But by whom and why? And what the hell are you doing here in the first place?"

Josh knew he didn't sound friendly, but then again he wasn't feeling magnanimous. It wasn't like Aaron and him had been close. Sure, as kids they had been tight—the two years separating them ensured they'd played a lot together. But after Josh had come out as gay? Aaron had sided with his parents and had barely even talked to his older brother. And when he had, it had been to spew anti-gay sentiments and recriminations.

"Mom and Dad kicked me out," Aaron said, meeting Josh's eyes for the first time.

"What?" Josh shook his head in disbelief. Aaron, the golden boy, had been kicked out? What the fuck? "Why? I can't see you doing anything so horrific that would warrant their hate. Surely they keep all of their loathing stored up for me, their heathen, perverse son."

Aaron hesitated. "I've been living on my own for a while, but I lost my job, and it's been hard."

Josh's eyes narrowed. Something was off. He might not have been close to his brother for a long time, but he knew him, and something was different. Aaron had always been a brash, arrogant little shit after Josh had come out, and their parents had blatantly favored him. But now he was much more subdued, vulnerable. Broken, even. What had happened?

"I'm sorry to hear that, but it doesn't answer my question. Why did they kick you out? And what made you get over your disgust of your gay brother to show up here?"

Nope, still not friendly, and he wasn't a bit sorry. Karma was a bitch, wasn't it?

Aaron took a long time to answer, his eyes looking everywhere but at Josh and Connor. "I'm gay," he finally whispered.

Josh froze. He misheard. There was no way... "You're what? What did you say?"

Aaron's eyes traveled up, met Josh's dead on. "I'm gay," he repeated, firmer this time.

Gay.

His conceited, judgmental little brother who bullied him mercilessly for being gay, who sided with his parents against me every single time, was gay.

Holy fuck.

He closed his eyes. Was he sorry for Aaron? His brother had to be confused as shit. Hurt, too, after being rejected. But God, he fucking deserved it, didn't he? After all he'd done to Josh, there was a strange sense of justice that he'd had to experience the very thing he'd preached against. Dammit, he'd never said sorry, never asked for forgiveness. He'd never even shown up after Noah had gotten hurt, after Josh had been...

No, don't go there. Fuck, the fog is coming. It's coming. It's so hard to think. Too much to think about. What the fuck does

Aaron want? I'm not helping him. He can go fuck himself. My head hurts, it hurts.

Josh pressed his clenched fists against his head in an attempt to make it stop.

"Josh, stay with me, baby."

Connor's voice pierced through the fog in his head. He fought back the cloud enveloping him, wanting to stay in the present, stay with Connor.

Strong arms lifted him, and he was parked squarely on Connor's lap. "I'm right here, baby. Stay with me."

In a reflex, Josh leaned back, felt the safety of the muscular body surrounding him. "That's it," Connor said, his mouth close to Josh's ear. "Lean on me. I'm right here with you. I'm gonna kiss you now, okay?"

The words wouldn't come yet, and his eyes wouldn't open, but Josh knew he'd made it through. Connor's breath danced over his lips, and then his warm, firm mouth settled on his. Hell, yeah. Within seconds, he was back, relaxing into the kiss. Connor was such a terrific kisser. His mouth was like the rest of him, big and firm and hot as hell. And his tongue...the man could work magic with it wherever he put it.

Connor pulled back his mouth but kept Josh close. "You good?"

Josh nodded. Swallowed. "Yeah. I'm back. Thank you."

As soon as he opened his eyes, Josh had to face Aaron. How embarrassing he'd seen him this weak, this vulnerable. Josh pushed back that thought as utter bullshit. Aaron had no right to judge at all. Plus, Josh didn't give a shit what his brother thought or felt about him.

He opened his eyes, ready to combat whatever judgment he'd see in Aaron's eyes. Instead, he found his brother studying him with worry.

"Are you okay?" Aaron asked.

"I have PTSD. I don't deal well with shock."

Aaron looked uncomfortable. "I'm sorry. I didn't know."

"You would've if you'd bothered to come see me after my discharge. How long have you known you were gay?"

"A couple of years. I knew for sure after you'd enlisted, but I didn't want to believe it. I didn't want to accept God would be so cruel as to make us both gay."

Josh grimaced. "At least you've dropped the whole rhetoric on men choosing to be gay, choosing this lifestyle. That's what you and Mom and Dad kept telling me, that I chose this for myself."

Connor's arms tightened around him as if to signal he was safe. He leaned back more, let himself be supported by Connor.

"I know that I can never make up for what I did to you. All I can say is I'm so sorry, so very sorry."

The sincerity in Aaron's words was easy to spot, but Josh wasn't sure if it was enough. Would there ever be a way he could forgive Aaron? Move past this? His life had been hell at home, and his brother had been a part of that.

"What happened to you to get you looking like this?" Connor asked.

Aaron shuffled his feet, shifting in his chair. "I got beat up two days ago."

"I can see that. Why?" Connor said patiently.

"I went to a bar. Someone took offense to me being gay."

"A bar close by?"

Aaron sighed. "O'Flannigan. I wanted to relax a little, find the courage to come here. Look, I didn't know, okay? I met this guy. I thought he was flirting with me, and I flirted back. When I asked him to meet me out back, he showed up with his friend, and they beat the crap out of me."

Connor shook his head. "O'Flannigan is about as redneck as you can get it up here. They don't like gays on principle. We get called in regularly for fights and assaults there. Not that much ever sticks as they all defend each other till kingdom come. Still, you should press charges."

"Connor is a cop," Josh explained when he noticed Aaron's confused expression.

"No, thanks. I know a lost cause when I see one. So, no offense, Josh, but what happened to Noah? Did you guys break up?"

Understandable as the question was—Aaron knew from Josh's teenage years how close he and Noah had been—Josh had no intention of explaining anything. "I get that you're sorry, Aaron, and I believe you mean it. Doesn't mean it wipes out everything you did to me. And it certainly doesn't mean that now you're gay, too, we're best buddies. You haven't earned the right to ask me anything about Noah."

Aaron's shoulders slumped. "I know. It's... I didn't know where else to go. I've run out of options, and you were my last resort. But I understand you don't want anything to do with me. I deserve that."

Josh studied Aaron to see if he was playing the woe-is-me card, but his words rang true. "I didn't say that. You can stay here, at least for a day or two till you figure out your next step. Just don't ask too many questions."

"Thank you, Josh. I mean it. I won't be a bother."

CONNOR WAS WAITING in bed till Josh was done taking a shower. His offer to take one together had been kindly rejected as Josh had indicated he needed some time to think. As an introvert, Josh needed alone time to recharge.

Connor understood all too well, being introverted himself, but he couldn't help being disappointed since it had been such a tense day. He would've loved to relax together in the shower.

Josh had made up a fresh bed for Aaron in the guest bedroom and had moved Connor's stuff into the master bedroom. Connor seemed to be taking Noah's place in several aspects. He tried to let go of the weird vibe surrounding that. It wasn't like Josh could do anything about his brother showing up out of the blue.

Connor had insisted on checking Aaron out physically. He wasn't a doctor, but he knew enough to spot the signs of possible trouble after a beating like that, like broken ribs or internal bleeding. It looked like Aaron had gotten away with mere bruises—though an impressive number.

Aaron had slept part of the day, no doubt exhausted by both his injuries and a lack of sleep in the last few days. He had said little, but Connor got the impression he'd been living in his car. Things had to have been desperate for Aaron to throw himself on the mercy of the brother he'd treated like crap.

It had been scary, watching Josh slip away like that. Connor had remembered what Noah had told him, how your voice could be enough if you caught it early. He'd figured kissing Josh couldn't hurt either. It had certainly worked for Indy.

Josh's earlier confession of having slept with Indy made more sense now that Indy turned out to be a guy. But it still left Connor with questions. Why had Indy slept with him when he was in love with Noah? Josh and Noah, Connor could understand. He didn't like it—and that was an under-statement—but he understood why they'd needed each other. But Indy and Josh? Why would Indy do that?

Unless Indy had a reason to choose Josh over Noah. Josh was softer, easier. A bottom.

Connor remembered what had happened to Indy, or Stephan as he'd been back then. The story of how Duncan had set him up with their vile serpent of a cousin Eric and how Stephan had taken the guy out—it had broken Connor's heart and filled him with a deep respect at the same time. He was nothing if not a survivor. But there was no doubt an experience like that had resulted in sexual trauma. And who better to help him overcome that than another survivor? Josh must've offered to let Indy fuck him, to show him how different it could be. Connor sighed with relief as the puzzle bits fell into place.

It was a little disconcerting, this complete focus of his mind and body on Josh. Connor had felt nothing like this, not even close. He'd been attracted to men before, but he'd never, ever felt this deep need like he did with Josh. What had started out as simple attraction in that Stewart's store, had morphed into something much more complicated and intense. A constant desire to be with Josh, to be near him. A powerful need to take care of him and protect him. A pressing want that burned through his veins and made him almost crazy at times.

Love. This had to be what love felt like.

Josh stepped into the room timidly, a towel wrapped around his waist. "Sorry, it took me a while to relax."

Connor smiled. "It's okay, baby. What's not okay is that towel. Why are you depriving me of the most fantastic view ever?"

A shy smile spread across Josh's lips. "You're saying my body is better than, say, the skyline of Boston? Or some breathtaking mountain lake view?"

Connor chuckled. "Baby, your ass tops anything I've ever seen. Hands down. Now ditch the towel."

His two favorite words echoed through the room as Josh unhooked the towel and let it slide to the floor. "Yes, Connor."

"Much better," Connor let out, his voice hoarse. "Turn around."

Josh obeyed, flashing Connor a full view of those gorgeous long legs and that amazing tight butt. Connor hadn't been joking: Josh's ass was a sight to behold. Those two curves were so perfectly tight and soft at the same time.

"How's your hole?" he enquired. Josh hesitated, and Connor's eyes narrowed. "Do not lie to me, Joshua."

He watched a powerful shiver tear through his lover's body. "It's still tender. But I want you, Connor. It's okay, baby, I can take it."

Damn, Josh all but pouted, and it made Connor's insides go liquid. "No," he said firmly. "I'm not taking you when you're still sore."

Josh pushed his bottom lip out into a full pout. "Before Indy came, Noah would fuck me every day. I don't need to wait."

"Really? You thought that a comparison to Noah would make me give in? Dumb strategy, Joshua. Last time I checked, Noah's dick wasn't on equal terms with the Beast."

Shit, had he referred to his own cock with that term? Josh would never let it go now.

A slow, seductive smile played around Josh's lips. "True. The Beast has no equal. Nothing feels as good as your cock inside me, baby."

Oh, fuck. If Josh kept that strategy up, Connor was toast. He had to do something, because he was serious about not fucking Josh until he was completely recovered. He wasn't taking any chances.

"I'll tell you what, baby, how about we do a little wager? I haven't come all day, and to be honest, I'm horny. If you manage to make me come five times tonight, I'll prepare a session for you later this week that will make yesterday pale in comparison."

Josh's eyes grew big, and a delicious blush crept over his cheeks. "And if I lose? Which I won't, but out of curiosity."

Connor put on his stern face. "If you lose, I won't fuck you for another week. Fair's fair, right?"

"And I can do whatever I want to make you come, correct?"

Connor had to swallow. What was Josh planning? The gleam in his eyes promised little good. It didn't matter. Even he with his stamina couldn't come five times in a row. "Anything, except making me fuck you."

"Oh, you're so on. Trust me, you'll see actual fucking stars by the time I'm done with you. Now, lay back on the bed and enjoy the ride."

IT TOOK a little over a minute for Connor to blow his first load. Josh licked his lips as he sucked the last bit of cum off the Beast. Making Connor come with a blow job was almost too easy as the guy still wasn't used to the sensation of his cock in Josh's mouth. Josh had no doubt the second and third orgasm would be doable as well, knowing Connor's insatiable stamina. The fourth and fifth, however, now that would be a challenge. He'd have to come up with something special...and he knew just the thing.

He jacked Connor off for a second load, which took

slightly longer, then went to town on another blow job for the third one. It took more effort, but seeing Connor's deep satisfaction when he came had been worth it. It was time to take it to the next level.

He brought a warm washcloth from the bathroom and cleaned Connor up. If the man had any inkling what was coming, he never said a word.

"Relax," Josh said, still buck naked. "The next round will take a while."

Connor's eyebrow rose. "Anything you'd like to share?"

Josh smiled. "Not really. Turn on your stomach, spread your legs and let me do my thing."

Obeying orders did not come easy for his man, not even after years in the service. He shot Josh a look stuffed with warnings, which Josh happily ignored, but turned around.

Josh grabbed a bottle of massage oil and heated the lavender-infused oil in his hands. He straddled Connor's broad back, let his bare cock brush against Connor's skin, causing him to get goose bumps. Josh smiled. He hadn't even gotten started.

He began at the top, kneading Connor's neck and shoulders, then made his way down. God, his man was built, every muscle solid and perfectly defined. Connor had expressed his admiration for Josh's ass, but holy fuck, his own ass was damn fine, too. And those thighs... They should video having sex sometime. Watching that massive body of Connor's pound the shit out of him had to be the best view ever.

He showered every inch of skin with loving attention from his hands, stroking, massaging, rubbing, and petting. Connor let out a stream of happy moans and groans, and his muscles relaxed under Josh's ministrations.

When he reached Connor's lower back, he felt the

muscles quiver in anticipation. He dropped even lower, massaging the muscles connecting those strong butt cheeks with the lower back. Connor tensed despite the relaxing massage. Josh smiled, withdrawing his hands. He scooted down, grabbed Connor's right foot and started kneading it. Connor let out an unhappy mewl.

Again, Josh worked his way up, hitting every inch of Connor's legs. When he reached his thighs, Connor spread them even wider without being asked. Josh ran his hands up the inside of Connor's right thigh. Connor's ass contracted, his body expecting the much-anticipated touch—but it never came. Connor had to be cursing him.

Another growl escaped Connor's lips as Josh switched to his other leg, repeated his move. Again, Connor's body went on high alert, almost inviting Josh to dig in higher, deeper, further. Josh bit back a smile at the blatant invitation Connor was extending. Nope, it wasn't happening. He had other plans. With a lightning-fast move, he climbed off Connor.

"How did that feel?" he asked.

Connor raised his head, shot him a look so dark it would have made milk turn sour. "Pretty fucking unfulfilling."

"You're welcome," Josh said, smiling broadly. "Turn on your back again, sit up against the headboard. I've got something for you to watch. Watch, mind you, not touch."

Grumbling, Connor did as Josh asked. Josh grabbed something from the drawer in the nightstand, hiding it from Connor's curious eyes. He threw a bottle of lube on the bed as well before climbing on and maneuvering himself on his knees, facing Connor. He wasn't gonna stay that way, though. If his man thought Josh's ass was heaven, he would love this next part. Or not.

Josh squirted lube on his hands and rubbed them

together to heat the liquid up. He grabbed his cock—which had become rock hard from pleasuring Connor—and with slow, almost lazy moves began to jack himself off. He caressed his balls with his other hand, rolling and fingering each one before giving extra attention to the sensitive spot behind his balls. He stroked, fisted, pumped, his eyes never leaving Connor's. Much to Josh's satisfaction, the Beast was fully awake. Apparently, it appreciated Josh's little peep show. And man, he was only getting started.

He rubbed his thumb over his crown, making circles, then pushed on the slit. That never failed to make him shiver in anticipation. Euphoric bliss blazed through him, ending in his weeping cock and strained nuts. Fuck, he wanted to come so badly. But it wasn't time yet. He needed Connor with him, and he wasn't there. Time to level up.

He turned around, spread his legs wider and brought his ass back far and low. Connor was getting a prime view. The low groan he let out suggested he was enjoying it. Josh's right hand trailed to his ass and stroked, teasing his own hole. He scratched it with a nail, made himself shiver. It contracted, ready for more.

He dipped his index finger in, swirled it around. With his fingers slick with lube, he added a second finger. He pulled out, explored his crack, squeezed his own butt cheeks, kept grazing his back door. Fuck yeah, it was a little weird to do this with an audience, but a quick peek over his shoulder confirmed Connor was mesmerized.

With a satisfied grin, Josh grabbed what he'd hidden before: a slim, black vibrator that despite its size, packed a serious punch. He lubed it up before bringing it back. He trailed it down his crack...and back up again. He repeated the move, swiping his hole, surprised by a violent shiver when his body was denied what it wanted. His cock was dripping with precum and his ass quivering for more. Enough with the teasing.

He dipped the vibrator lower again, this time not stopping when he reached his back entrance. With a slight push, it slipped in, and he couldn't hold back a sigh of relief. He pushed in and pulled back, each time a little farther and deeper than before. His own moan of pleasure mingled with a grunt from Connor, who shifted on the bed. Josh dipped his head low, looked between his legs and caught Connor repositioning his cock. The Beast was, as Josh had counted on, once again ready for action.

Josh spread his legs wider, let his head rest on his left arm and brought his ass up high, while his right arm kept up the push and pull with the massager. It had nowhere near the effect of the Beast, but it still felt fucking good. If he kept this up, he'd come in minutes, probably less. But the little toy had one advantage over Connor's cock, a nifty little feature that had brought Josh to screams of pleasure many times before.

The bed moved again, and Josh brought his head up to see what Connor was doing. He'd gotten the lube and was squirting a healthy amount in his right hand. Josh's smile became a low groan as the vibrator hit his pleasure spot. His hips jerked and his ass tightened around the slim shape. Fuck, how he wished it was Connor's dick in his ass. And as much as he enjoyed pleasuring Connor and teasing the hell out of him, he'd ten times rather have his man be in control, ordering him around.

Slick sounds alerted Josh that Connor had started to jack himself off—exactly as Josh had hoped. And perfect timing, too, as he was oh, so ready to blow his wad. He positioned the massager against his prostate, then turned it on. It pulsated and Josh moaned. When you had that thing in the right spot...another deep groan...it was unbelievable.

His channel was electrified, shards of pleasure stabbing him. Sweat pearled on his forehead, and all his muscles contracted, fighting the intense pleasure and at the same time, embracing it and wanting more.

Connor's breathing became labored, and he let out a stream of mumbled curses, a perfect symphony with Josh's grunts and moans. Josh's balls pulled up even farther, painfully full. He hadn't come all day, so it would be a nice amount. He licked his lips, fought back the release with all he had. Connor wasn't there yet. One more minute. The vibrator teased and prodded, electrifying his body. A full-body quake wrecked him. He couldn't take it anymore. He had to come. Now.

He pulled it out fast and scrambled around to face Connor, who was fisting himself furiously, his heated face tight with concentration. Josh threw the massager on the bed, grabbed his cock with his right hand and matched Connor's rhythm. A few seconds later, Josh exploded. He threw his head back, stretching his body as far as it would as he jerked ruthlessly, spraying his cum all over Connor.

"Fuuuuuuuuuck!"

His body shivered, spasmed, and shot off the last squirt of fluids. Josh brought his head back and watched with intense delight as Connor came hard, his face twisting in a mix of agony and pleasure. His cock shot out a meager amount of cum—no wonder after coming three times already. And they still had one more round to go. Poor Connor, he might come to regret his impulsive bet.

"Dammit, Josh, that was...intense," Connor said when he'd caught his breath.

Damn, but the man looked sexy, all flushed and covered

in both their cum. Josh's thick fluids—easily distinguishable from Connor's cum as it was way less translucent—were dripping off Connor's abs and massive chest, even on his thighs, and a few drops seemed to have landed on his biceps.

"You look damn good covered in my cum," Josh said in a throaty voice.

"That was quite the show. Good thing my heart is in master shape, because weaker men might've had a heart attack."

Josh was ridiculously pleased. "You liked it?" he asked, stupidly smiling.

"Baby, come on, you had me jacking myself off, despite the bet. Smart move."

"You know me, always the strategist."

Connor pushed himself up straighter, apparently not bothered by the smeared semen on his body. "You only got me to four. I'm so spent, you'll never get me to come a fifth time."

Josh smirked. "You should know better by now than to doubt my abilities."

Connor's eyes narrowed. "What do you have in mind?"

"You'll find out. Turn on your stomach."

Connor shot a pointed look at the mess on his upper body. "You wanna clean that up first?"

Josh grinned. "Not really. I like you like this. Tonight, you're my cum slut, aren't you?"

Connor's eyes spewed fire. "You will so pay for this," he said between clenched teeth.

"You know, that would scare me if I wasn't so damn sure I will enjoy your punishment. Besides, if you dare me to make you come five times, you deserve to look like this."

A hint of a smile teased Connor's lips, but he didn't say

another word and turned himself on his stomach. Josh noted he spread his legs, which was as clear an invitation as he was going to get.

"Put this under your hips," he said and shoved two pillows Connor's way.

Connor was too much of a Marine to show fear, but the slight tremor that shimmered through his body told Josh he knew what was coming. Still, he didn't say a word, and that trust warmed Josh's insides. He scooted over, kneeled next to Connor on the bed.

"If you tell me to stop, I will," he said, putting a hand on Connor's ass. The muscles contracted under his hand. He let a finger trail over the taut, muscular cheeks. Fuck, Connor was so beautiful. So strong.

"I know," Connor said, not lifting his head from his arms.

Josh let his index finger travel to the top of Connor's crack. "Spread your legs wide, baby. Open up for me."

Without a second of delay, Connor did as Josh asked.

"You're so beautiful," Josh said, his voice dreamy. He splayed both his hands on Connor's ass, one on each cheek and squeezed. "Your ass looks like a Greek statue, all toned and muscular. I love how big and strong you are, you know? Makes me feel safe and protected."

He bent over, kissed the right cheek, then the left. Because he loved feeling the thick muscles react to his touch, he kissed some more. Then licked and bit ever so gently, taking his time to cover every square inch of that perfect ass. Connor responded to every little touch. His dick might be worn out, but the rest of his body was still wide awake.

He took position between Connor's legs, lowered himself on his stomach and landed his face where he wanted it to be. "Pull your knees up." Connor moved, and his crack opened for Josh. "Perfect."

He took a tentative lick at the top of Connor's ass, then worked his way down to that deliciously quivering hole. With every swipe of his wet tongue, Connor tensed up more. Josh reveled in the musky taste of Connor, the salty sweat that was so distinctively male. He didn't have much experience rimming, but damn if he didn't love every second.

He blew a hot breath on Connor's entrance, smiled as it contracted in response. "You ready for me baby?" he whispered.

Connor grunted in what Josh assumed was agreement. He teased the puckered hole with the tip of his tongue. After dripping some saliva on it, he pushed. Connor tensed up and Josh retreated. "Relax, baby. This is gonna feel good, trust me. Push back against my tongue."

On his next try, he felt Connor push back, opening him up. Josh slipped his tongue in, circled the hole with enthusiasm. Connor shivered, moaned. Josh pushed and probed with his tongue, persuading Connor to relax and open wider. God, he could do this for hours. His face buried in Connor's ass was beyond good. It was fucking dirty and damn perfect.

He pulled back. "How's that feel, baby?"

"Good. Don't stop."

"Wasn't going to." He did, however, grab the lube and squirted some on the fingers of his right hand, before digging in again into the buffet that was Connor's ass. He fucked him with his tongue, pushing in and out until Connor was pushing back by himself, opening up for more. When he did, Josh replaced his tongue with his index finger, slipping inside with ease.

Connor uttered a muffled curse, which made Josh smile.

Connor had a bit of a trauma when it came to bottoming, but seriously, the man needed to learn how good it could feel. Not that he had any intention of permanently switching positions, but in situations like this when Connor flat out refused to fuck Josh 'cause he was still too tender, it'd be great to have an alternative.

He added a second finger and felt Connor close up and tighten. "Uh, uh. Push back. Bear down on me, baby. It's only going to get better."

It took a few seconds, but Connor relented and let him in. He finger-fucked him for two minutes or so before grabbing the vibrator. He cleaned it with a sanitary wipe. Would Connor be okay with him doing this?

He hadn't realized he'd stopped moving until Connor raised his head from his arms. "Stick it in already."

Josh swallowed. "You knew?"

Connor raised his eyebrows. "After the show you put on? Yeah, I had a good idea of what was next on the menu."

"And you're okay with it?"

"Does it look to you like I'm protesting?" He dropped his head back on his arms as if to say, "Hurry the fuck up and get it over with."

Josh lined up the little toy against Connor's entrance, pushed it in an inch or so. Connor tightened around it, but after a few seconds, Josh felt him relax. He slid the slim massager in and out, going deeper and deeper until he had it in almost entirely.

"This is where I need your help, baby. Tell me when I hit the right spot."

Josh slid it in and out, hitting different spots inside Connor. He twisted the toy to aim at a different spot, shoving it back in. Connor's butt came off the mattress, and he forced out a long moan.

"Jackpot, baby."

Josh tried again, wanting to make sure he hit it exactly. Another loud growl from Connor confirmed the position. He flicked on the button, held the vibrator tight. "You may want to hold on to something," he teased.

Connor's head shot up as the vibration started. "Holy fuck!"

Josh clamped down on the toy, trying to hold it in position as Connor shook and trembled with the impact.

"Oooohhh...fuck...Josh...argh!"

The stream of guttural sounds coming from Connor's lips was almost inhuman as if Josh brought him to the brink of sanity. Well, that's what it had felt like the first time for Josh. It was a pleasure so intense, it bordered on pain. More than once, he'd jerked so violently, he couldn't hold on to the toy and had to start again.

Connor rubbed his dick against the mattress in desperate need for friction, Josh guessed. Anything to make the pleasure peak. There was no stopping now, he would come a fifth time, and they both knew it. Except in this position, Josh wouldn't be able to see it—and wouldn't that be a shame? He pulled out the massager, turned it off.

"What the fuck?" Connor's voice was almost aggressive. "No more games, Josh."

Oh, now wasn't that interesting? Strong, proud Connor was ready to beg...and that after having already come four times. Still, Josh didn't have it in him to prolong the man's suffering. Not for long anyway.

"On your back. I want to see you come."

Lightning fast, Connor switched on his back, propping the pillows under his ass and pulling his legs up wide, giving Josh even better access.

"Such a needy little bottom," Josh teased him, positioning the tip of the vibrator against Connor's hole but not sliding it in.

"Joshua, you are so gonna regret this. I swear, I will fuck the shit out of you."

"Is that a threat or a promise?"

He didn't wait for Connor's answer but shoved in the vibrator, enjoying the breath of relief Connor let out. His bossy top was enjoying the experience, wasn't he? He poked around until Connor bucked, then turned the thing back on. In this position, he could see the myriad emotions playing over Connor's face. His eyes were closed, his face tight with concentration. Whenever a strong vibration hit him, he grimaced in a tantalizing mix of pain and pleasure.

Connor's right hand traveled to his cock, but Josh swatted him away. "My job," he said.

He looked at the position he was in, on his knees between Connor's legs. Could he...? He shifted, changed the angle of his hand holding the massager without losing position. Yeah, that would work. He spread his own legs wider, stabilizing himself on the mattress before bringing his head down. With one move, he took the Beast into his mouth again.

Connor yelped, probably as much in surprise as pleasure, and Josh went to work. Holding the vibrator in the right position with Connor's hips thrashing and bucking was a challenge, but even more so with his mouth around the man's cock. Josh tightened his hold on the toy, used his weight to hold Connor down, all the while sucking hard. Well, it wasn't so much sucking as positioning his mouth right to let Connor fuck it. He still had his left hand around the base, in case Connor forgot about his size and tried to ram it in too hard in the throes of passion. Because man, he was far gone, his whole body quivering, begging for that final release. If he'd come four times while fucking Josh, this would have been impossible, because his dick would've been way too tender. Even now, Josh could see slivers of pain mixed in with the intense pleasure on Connor's face, no doubt caused by a sensitive head.

His jaw ached from opening wide, but he fucking refused to stop. Connor was so close, he could feel it. He would win this damn bet if it killed him. Or both of them. But for fuck's sake, could the guy come already? Even his hand was cramping from the repeated movement.

Connor grabbed Josh's head with both hands and fired off a round of hyper-fast thrusts into Josh's mouth. Josh let go of the vibrator, couldn't get his worn-out muscles to hold it anymore. With a roar that had to be audible all the way in the basement, Connor came, spasming hard. A few droplets of cum landed in Josh's mouth, and he swallowed.

Connor dropped on his back, his hands sliding off Josh and his legs falling down. With effort, Josh climbed over Connor's legs and nestled against him, his arm around Connor's sticky chest. Tired as he must be, Connor still reached out and pulled Josh even closer, making him rest his head on Connor's shoulder.

"Remind me to never make a bet with you again," Connor said, at least three minutes later.

Josh smiled sleepily. "You didn't enjoy it?"

A soft laugh rumbled through Connor's chest. "Baby, you almost killed me. I don't think I would survive another bet."

"I won," Josh said, not even trying to keep the triumph out of his voice. "You'd better come up with something good. I fucking earned it."

"Oh, don't you worry. I did research online today, and you're gonna love it."

Josh's eyes, which had drifted asleep, flew wide open. Should he be worried? Nah. Connor wouldn't hurt him, not more than would bring pleasure. "I love you, baby," he whispered.

Connor's arm tightened around him, and Josh felt himself falling asleep.

"I love you, too, Josh."

12

As if it wasn't weird enough to be living in the same house as his brother again, now Josh had to deal with the fact Aaron had undoubtedly heard them yesterday evening. Yeah, Connor and he had both forgotten about the little detail of Aaron staying in the guest bedroom when they started their sexual extravaganza. Fuck, Aaron must have gotten quite the audio show.

Josh hesitated a little before going downstairs even though Connor had long since gone down to face the confrontation. He'd been up early as usual and had jumped in the shower without even waiting for Josh to wake up. No wonder, the man had to be sticky and itchy from yesterday evening as they'd both been too worn out to bother cleaning up. He'd better change the bed sheets today, Josh thought. Again. Luckily, he and Noah had bought quite the collection as there were weeks where they went through a fresh set daily.

Taking a deep breath, Josh made his way downstairs. Connor was dropping a few slices of bacon in the skillet while Aaron was at the counter, looking ten kinds of nervous. Huh, maybe he was dreading this conversation as much as Josh?

"Hey, baby," Connor said.

Almost automatically, Josh walked over to him, leaning in for a kiss. He would never understand how and why, but Connor grounded him. Just feeling his body, hearing his voice made Josh connect with the present.

"I hope I didn't wake you, but I desperately wanted a shower," Connor said softly, holding on to Josh's neck with his hand. There was a twinkle in his eyes.

"I can imagine," Josh said, exhaling. It would be okay. He and Noah had never given a fuck what others thought, so why would he start now because it was his brother?

Connor gave him a quick kiss, then turned his attention back to the stove.

"Go sit," Josh said. "I got this."

"I can do it. It's okay."

Josh gently pushed him. "No, it's not. This is my kitchen, and you're my man, so I prepare your breakfast. What else did you want aside from bacon?"

Connor beamed Josh a smile that was so full of pride and love it made him all gooey inside. "Eggs. Protein. Lots of protein. Gotta replenish my strength."

The accompanying wink made Josh blush. He shook his head, buried it in the fridge while gathering ingredients for a hearty omelet. A couple of eggs, ham, he'd throw in some avocado and kale and finish it with cheese. That had to be enough, right?

He set everything on the counter, then remembered Aaron. "What can I get you for breakfast?" he asked. Yeah, so it wasn't cordial, but he was trying, okay?

"Anything is fine. I'm not a picky eater," Aaron said.

"You never were. Tell me what you want: cereal, yogurt with granola, oatmeal, something warm?"

"Whatever is easiest for you."

"Fuck, Aaron, tell me what the fuck you want, okay? You probably mean it well, but it's annoying the shit out of me." He met Aaron's eyes, saw a flash of temper. He crossed his arms, narrowed his eyes. "And if you have a problem with my fucking language, you can pack your fucking bags and find some other fucking place to stay."

Aaron clenched his fists. "I don't have a problem with your f-fucking language as you put it so eloquently. I do, however, have a problem with the fact that everything I do frustrates you. I get that you're still angry with me, Josh, and you have every right to be, but I'm trying, okay?"

Josh sighed. "That's the first time I've ever heard the f-bomb coming out of your mouth."

Aaron shrugged. "Lots of first times these last few months."

"Like hearing your brother have gay sex," Josh threw in there. Aaron swallowed. Josh straightened, stood ramrod tall. "If you have an issue with that..."

"I don't. I swear," Aaron interjected him. "I didn't want to make it awkward by saying anything."

"Yeah, 'cause the fact you heard us wasn't awkward enough in the first place," Josh muttered.

"I found ear plugs in the drawer and put those in so I could give you guys your privacy."

"Oh." Josh wasn't sure how that made him feel, but at least he appreciated Aaron's effort. He didn't know what to say, so he started cutting up the ingredients for the omelet.

"If it's not too much trouble, I'd love some of whatever you're fixing for Connor," Aaron said softly.

Josh didn't look at him. "No problem."

Breakfast was peaceful, with Aaron reading the newspaper while he and Connor chatted over nothing.

"I thought maybe we could go over to Indy's jiujitsu studio, find out if his professor has seen him. Indy was supposed to train yesterday, and he never misses, so maybe he went, and the guy knows something," Josh said after breakfast. Aaron had gone upstairs to shower, so it was just him and Connor.

"Sounds good. What about Aaron?"

"He'll have to come with us because I don't want to leave him here by himself."

Connor looked at Josh inquisitively. "You don't trust him? He's your brother."

Josh grimaced. "Yeah, my brother who has made my life hell ever since I came out. No, I don't trust him."

"Okay. We'll take him with us, but we won't explain anything. He can't know about Indy, agreed?"

"He can't stay long. If Indy scouts the place because he wants to come back and sees a strange face, he's gone," Josh stressed.

"We'll figure something out."

As a Bostonian, Indy was genetically programmed to hate New York City. The truth was that he appreciated certain aspects of the city. The Yankees sucked, obviously, and New Yorkers had to be the rudest people on the planet. But Central Park was lovely in the summer, the shopping was unparalleled, and he loved the weirdness of this city. Right now, more than anything, he appreciated the busyness, the hustle and bustle, which assured no one was paying attention to a slim, young woman.

Fuck, he hardly recognized himself. He'd gone for a complete makeover. Colored contacts had transformed his brown eyes into pale blue ones that were forgettable, and a wig with straight, blond hair covered his curls. He'd put on some makeup, but not so much it would stand out, and wore the most nondescriptive jeans, top, and shoes ever. He wasn't attractive enough to pay attention to, but also not so odd or flashy people would notice him for different reasons. He completely blended in.

He'd driven to Newark Station, had parked his car there and caught the Jersey Transit to Manhattan. Easy peasy since it brought him straight to Penn Station. He looked around casually as he disembarked the train. No one seemed to pay attention to him, and no one stood out to him.

It was decent weather, considering it was mid-December. It was chilly, but not freezing cold. That could change quickly. Being from Boston, he knew what winter could look like here in the northeast. One nor'easter and you'd be paying good money to move south.

He'd already searched online to find the Starbucks and walked straight to it. He glanced around when he entered. There were about half a dozen people in line, professionals judging by the suits and office outfits, and he took his spot. Most of the tables inside were occupied, which was not uncommon this time of day. Everyone seemed to be hunched over a laptop or was texting.

"Good morning, welcome to Starbucks. Can I take your order?"

He gave the forty-something barista a quick once-over. He was a gorgeous lumberjack type if that was your thing, with a carefully trimmed beard. Indy's eyes went to his name tag. Jack. Well, that made it easy. "A tall latte macchiato please."

"Absolutely. What's the name?"

"Rose."

"All right. Four-sixty, please."

He gave him a five-dollar bill, and Jack handed back his change with a large, yellow envelope. The barista barely looked at him as if it was the most normal thing in the world he was doing. Indy took the envelope, stuffed it straight into his backpack.

"Thank you," he said.

"Sure thing, Rose. Your coffee will be a minute."

It was tempting to walk out since he had no intention of drinking the damn coffee, but he didn't. That would arouse suspicion, and everything had to look normal. He never looked back at Jack while he waited for his order to be called out. Two minutes later, he was back outside. He held on to his coffee until he was four blocks away and certain no one was watching him. Only then did he dump it in a trashcan.

He circled back to Penn Station, then took the train again to Jersey. As soon as he had returned to his motel, he opened the package. An Ohio driver's license in the name of Laura Downey tumbled out. It was the same picture as he'd used for his Indiana Baldwin one, with his curls and the blue contacts, wearing tasteful makeup. He'd debated using a complete disguise—much like he was wearing now—but it was too cumbersome to keep up. Wigs could sag, be too obvious. Plus, it was hard to keep that disguise up all the time. This way he had more flexibility, could disguise when he wanted to but still use the license. In the unlikely event a cop pulled him over, he could say he liked wearing wigs.

There was also a high school diploma from Neil Alden

Armstrong High School in Columbus, Ohio. A quick Google search taught him Neil Armstrong was from Ohio. That made sense, then.

Laura Downey.

He rolled the name on his tongue. It was boring, nondescriptive. Exactly what he needed. He'd be sad to leave Indy behind, though. He picked that name himself. Indiana after Indiana Jones, obviously. Indy had been secretly fascinated with the man who was smart, inventive, and sexy all in one.

At first, he'd chosen MacGyver as his last name, after another hero of his. The show had been from way before his time, but he'd watched every episode. It was cheesy, but he loved it. Had learned tons, too. But he'd decided the combination of two well-known names would stand out too much, so he'd picked a last name by pointing a finger at a list of names in an ad for a legal firm. Baldwin, it was.

He studied the driver's license from every side. He didn't know what Ohio licenses looked like, but like his previous Georgia one, it appeared legit. Now all he had to do was sell his car, buy a new one, and register it to Laura Downey. He'd have to decide where to go first as he'd need to register it in the state he would be staying in.

Indy laid down on the bed, flat on his back. Was he really gonna walk away from Noah, from Josh, from all of it? Could he?

Sooner or later, you'll have to. You know this can't last. Sure, Noah will miss you at first, but it will be better for him in the long run. Kinder. You have nothing to offer him. A relationship with a guy who's on the run, who you can never publicly claim, what kind of future is that for him? Plus, your very presence endangers Noah and Josh, even Connor.

A man like Noah deserved more. Better. If he broke it off

now, Noah would be okay after a spell. The longer he waited, the harder it would get. But the thought of leaving Noah, of never seeing him and Josh again... Indy's throat tightened, and swallowing was painful. These three days without him had been hell. Indy hadn't realized how much he'd come to depend on Noah's strength, his care. Between him and Josh, Indy had felt loved and taken care of. That first night at the motel, he hadn't even been able to fall asleep in the empty bed, used as he'd gotten to sleeping between the two men.

He hadn't thought it was possible in such a short time to get that attached to someone, but his aching heart was proof. God, he loved him so fucking much. He missed him with a physical pain he'd never experienced before. And Josh. He missed being part of their unit, a family.

Hell, he even missed Connor. The man had such a stabilizing effect on Josh, much like Noah, only deeper somehow. Those two were a perfect match if he'd ever seen one. If only he knew for certain he could trust the cop. That would at least eliminate one obstacle.

There was no way he was contacting the DA. If they were monitoring Merrick, he'd be dead. You could change a lot of things, but changing a voice was hard. He could fake an accent, but the chances of someone recognizing his voice were too high. No, he'd have to find another way. Maybe Connor could contact Merrick. As long as he didn't mention Stephan, that would not raise suspicion, right? He could ask the DA to vouch for him, maybe spin a story about a job or something.

How would he get a message to Connor? He couldn't call him, not directly. If the cop was crooked—though Indy doubted it after what he'd seen from him—he'd sign his death warrant. And if he wasn't, Indy wasn't ready for the

questions, the accusations even. They had to be pissed he'd
taken off.

No, they won't be.

The thought popped into his head, crystal clear. Josh
wouldn't be mad at him. He'd understand. He'd know it had
gotten to be too much. Hell, no one knew better about over-
loads of stress than Josh. Josh wouldn't get angry. He would
plead with Indy to come home. As a matter of fact, he was
probably already looking for him, though low-key. Where
would he look?

The answer was clear, easy. Professor Kent. There was no
way Josh would not look for him there. All he had to do was
get a message to Connor through Kent. The only thing Indy
wasn't sure of was how long it would take Josh to get there.
Noah's surgery and everything that had happened could've
affected Josh's PTSD. For all Indy knew, Josh could be out of
order. Still, his gut said Connor wouldn't let that happen,
that he would find a way to keep Josh safe and healthy. No
matter the doubts surrounding Connor, the man's love for
Josh was hard to miss.

Like Noah's love for him.

Sometimes Noah looked at him with so much love, it
took his breath away. He still couldn't comprehend what
had happened, how it was possible that this wonderful man
had fallen in love with him. But he had. Noah loved him.

It wasn't always easy for Indy to remember that, especially when his fight or flight took over, like in the car. Or
when he was hurting, like after Noah had lashed out at him.
When he was that stressed or emotional, he wasn't capable
of reminding himself Noah loved him. It was like he'd short-
circuit, somehow.

But afterwards, he knew. Noah had apologized profusely,
and Indy had seen his sincerity. He'd forgiven him without

hesitation. That's what you did when you loved someone. Because he loved Noah, too. There wasn't a sliver of doubt anymore. What he felt for Noah was so big, so deep, that he couldn't deny it. Surely Noah had to know how much Indy loved him, too.

Did he? Would he, after the way he left him?

His heart cramped in sudden distress. What if Noah thought he'd left him for another reason? What if Noah thought he was at fault because of his temper, or their row over the sex and everything else?

No, no, no. Oh, God, would he blame himself?

He'd see every reason to. Noah didn't know why Indy had run. He couldn't do this to him. Not right now, not while he was recuperating from that infection. He had to go. He had to see with his own eyes that Noah was okay, and he damn well had to make sure Noah knew he loved him. Even if he had no other choice but to leave him, he couldn't do it like this. Not without saying goodbye. Noah deserved at least that much.

Indy left his old identity papers in the motel, hidden behind an air vent. If he got arrested, he didn't want to get caught with two sets of papers.

He shouldn't take his own car. If he'd been made, somehow, he'd be too easy to spot. No, he needed to rent a car, using his new ID. That wouldn't trigger any alarms.

He drove to Newark airport, parked his car in a long-term parking lot close to the airport and took the provided shuttle bus to the terminals. Half an hour later, he drove out with a silver Honda Civic—the most boring car ever.

He didn't even try to find out about visiting hours and shit. If there was one thing he had learned in the last year, it was that people didn't question who you were and what you were doing as long as you looked like you knew where you were going. If you looked legit, went about your way with confidence, nobody batted an eye. Indy had called ahead to the hospital to find out Noah's floor and room number and walked straight in.

Noah was in a private room, his face turned toward a big window where pastel yellow curtains had been opened. Indy swallowed back the nasty taste in his mouth hospital smells always brought.

"Noah," he said softly.

Noah's head whipped around. To his credit, he recognized Indy instantly under the disguise. "Indy..."

The joy in his voice brought tears to Indy's eyes. Tears that he pushed back hard as he closed the distance to the bed. His eyes fell on the covers, a flat area where Noah's stump used to be. God, what had happened? Had he lost his entire leg? "How are you?"

Noah smiled. "Much better now you're here." His face turned serious, anxious even. "What happened? Why did you take off? Is everything okay? Fuck, I was worried sick about you."

Indy pulled a folding chair close to Noah's bed, not wanting to perch down on the bed in case a staff member would walk in and find them. How the fuck would Noah explain that one? As soon as he sat, Noah reached for his hands. His fingertips trailed the soft pink nail polish on Indy's manicured hands.

Indy bit his lip. "I'm sorry, Noah. I didn't mean to worry you. I needed time to figure things out."

Noah's hand enclosed his in a firm grip. "What things? What had you spooked, was it Connor?"

"I'm almost positive his story will check out, but I've sent a message through Professor Kent to send me proof," Indy said.

"Smart. But if that's not what you were worried about, why did you run?"

Noah's face didn't show mere worry. Indy had been right. Noah was blaming himself, for whatever reason.

"I can't do this," Indy blurted out. "I can't love you more every day, knowing it can't last."

"What do you mean, it can't last? Indy, I love you. You know that. I'm not going anywhere."

And how amazing was that? Here he sat, two days after he'd run off on a whim, dressed like a woman, and the man still told him he loved him and wanted to be with him.

"I'll have to leave at some point. It's one thing to fear for my own life, but I can't risk you and Josh. If Duncan ever finds me, he will not hesitate to hurt the both of you to get to me. You don't know what he's capable of."

"Damn it, don't you think I know that? I've known ever since I found out who you were. And I still wanted you to stay, and so did Josh. We know the risks, but we choose you anyway. I choose you. I want you. I love you too much to let you go."

"I'm sick with worry half the time that Duncan will find me and will hurt you... What kind of life is that?"

Noah's hand clamped his in an iron grip. "Are you sure that's the only reason you want to leave?"

Indy frowned. What other reason could he have? Noah was everything he'd ever dared hope to find in a man. If not for that stupid fuck Duncan, he'd be permanently glued to Noah's side. Well, as long as the man wanted him.

"Of course it is."

"This has nothing to do with my surgery?"

At first, Indy didn't even understand what Noah was asking. What surgery? His confusion must have shown because Noah added, "They had to amputate higher, cut out the infection. I'll recover, but I'm missing an entire leg now. It'll be a huge adjustment, you know, and I have no idea if I'll be able to get back to my job."

When the realization hit, Indy blew up. "Who the fuck do you think I am if you think I would leave you over that? I love you, Noah. I don't give a shit about your leg other than I'm fucking sorry for you. And whether or not you go back to working as a PA, as long as you're doing something that brings you joy, I'm good with it. I'm not with you because of your paycheck, even if you do support the three of us. I don't want you for your money. I want you for you."

He hadn't realized how deeply he meant it until he saw the impact his words had on Noah. It was hard to comprehend, but the man had worried Indy would reject him over his leg as much as Indy had worried about Noah rejecting him because of his background, his scars, or his female disguise. Fuck, they were perfect together, weren't they?

Noah released the death grip on Indy's hand, brought it to his mouth instead and kissed it. "Please, Indy, don't give up on us yet. We'll take it one day at a time, okay? For now, let Connor get his proof from the DA so you can let that part go, and we'll figure it out from there. Together."

His eyes burned into Indy's, and how could he say no to that? How could he let go of the one man who loved him for who he was, with all his hang-ups and luggage and scars, emotional and physical?

He nodded, let out a breath he hadn't realized he'd been holding. "Okay."

"Don't go home yet, okay? Josh's brother showed up unexpectedly, and he's staying at the house. They're trying to find him a different place to stay, but it will take a few days. Do you have a place to stay? Are you good on cash?"

Indy hesitated. After his passionate speech of a minute

ago, how stupid would it be to ask Noah for money now? Still, after buying a new car and the new disguise, he was low on reserves. He'd have to get a job at some point, as Laura. He'd have to work hard and be careful to pull it off, but fuck, he needed the money. Houdini had provided him with a nice new social security number and credit history that would stand up to a standard background check, so he should be okay.

"There's a couple of prepaid Visa cards in the top drawer of the night table. I asked Josh to drop off a few in case you came and needed money. Please, Indy, take them. Let me take care of you as much as I can. I feel so fucking helpless already."

Again, Indy nodded, too emotional to say anything. Fuck, he was so tired of it all. Tired of running, of hiding, of pretending. How he wanted to rip off that stupid wig, take out those contacts and wipe off the makeup—and crawl into bed with Noah. He longed to feel that big body close to his, to feel those strong arms come around him. Instead, he leaned in for a quick kiss that burned its way straight into his gut.

Noah held his head when he pulled back. "I'll be home in a few days, and I want you there, Indy. I need you there. Promise me you'll come back."

Indy gave up. How could he stay away now? "I promise."

Just then, Noah's cell phone rang. He grabbed it from the night table, scowling when he saw the number.

He muttered a curse, then answered the call. "What do you want?".

His eyes narrowed at whatever the person on the other end was saying, and then he let out a colorful tirade of curses. What the fuck was going on? Was something wrong with Josh?

Noah's face was tight, his jaw clenched. "Thank you for letting me know, Dad. I'll take care of it."

Dad? That was the general on the phone? What did he want?

Noah threw his phone back on the nightstand where it sailed dangerously close to the edge before coming to a stop just shy of falling off.

"Noah, what's wrong?"

"The three guys who raped Josh, they've been granted their request for an appeal. That not only means they're released awaiting the appeal but also that there will be another trial. Josh will have to testify again, this time before the Military Court of Appeals."

"Noah, he can't," Indy brought out. The thought of sweet Josh having to relive his worst memories made him sick. "He won't survive mentally, not even with Connor's help!"

"I know. Fuck it!" Noah brought his fist down on his bed. "And I'm stuck in this damn bed and can't do a fucking thing!"

"But why is there an appeal? I thought it was an open-and-shut case? They had physical evidence and all."

"From the beginning, they claimed the sex was consensual. Said Josh approached them, asked them to fuck him rough. The defense painted a picture of Josh as a sick fuck who had fantasies of being raped. They claimed to have gotten scared when he passed out, regretted they'd gotten too rough but insisted he initiated it. The jury didn't buy it and convicted them, but now their lawyer states he has new evidence Josh asked them to rape him."

Indy's fists were clenched, his body rigid. A holy anger burned through his veins. How dared they blame this on Josh? What sick motherfuckers raped a man till he passed out and then claimed he wanted it?

"I'm sorry, baby. I wasn't thinking... I shouldn't have told you, not after what you went through yourself. I'm so angry, and I feel so fucking helpless."

Indy blew out a slow breath, steadied himself. "It's okay. I share your anger. How the fuck can they do this to him? Let me handle this, Noah. There's little you can do from here. Let me tell Josh, or do you think his lawyer told him already?"

"No. My dad called him and asked him to wait a day so I could tell Josh. He's a major bastard, but I gotta give him credit for this. Are you sure you want to do this?"

"Yes." A wild idea formed in Indy's head. An idea that was not even close to being legal, which is why he wanted Noah nowhere near it. Those fuckers would not get away with this. He'd killed once to protect himself, and he had no qualms about using violence again to protect someone he loved. He forced a neutral expression. "I'll take care of it, Noah. Trust me."

Noah's face was so full of pain that Indy couldn't help but offer. He wasn't even sure if he could take what Noah would dish out, but seeing Noah's pain was too much. "Noah, do you need me?" He deliberately used Josh's words, knowing Noah would understand the code.

Noah's jaw set. "No. Thank you for offering, baby. God, I love you."

"I want to help you. I can't stand to see you in pain."

Noah's face softened. "I know, baby. Damn, you and Josh are so much alike in that aspect. I know how much courage and love it took for you to offer, but I can't. One thing I've realized is that I need to take my responsibility. I can't keep using sex as some sort of painkiller, or even a distraction or outlet. If we want to make it work between us, and fuck knows I want nothing more, then I need to find a healthier way of dealing with my pain, both physically and mentally. I've signed up for a pain management course that's being offered by an anesthesiologist and a psychiatrist together, here in the hospital."

Indy didn't know what to say. He hadn't dared to suggest it to Noah earlier, not wanting to seem jealous of what he and Josh had—and above all, not wanting to come between them. "You're not going to use Josh anymore?"

Noah shook his head. "No. It's not healthy for us, and it's not good for him either, especially now that he's with Connor. I won't deny it's gonna be hard to let him go, but it's the right thing. He belongs with Connor, like I belong with you."

13

J osh told Aaron they were going somewhere, and Aaron didn't comment. He simply put on his jacket with a careful move, indicating he was still in pain and got into the back of the car.

"How's the pain?" Connor asked, backing the car out of the garage.

"It's okay. Coughing hurts. And I have a mild headache all the time."

"Probably a minor concussion and bruised ribs," Josh said. When Aaron looked surprised, Josh said: "You pick up a thing or two from living with Noah."

If Aaron thought it strange Josh mentioned Noah so casually in front of Connor, he didn't say anything. "Can I ask you a question about your PTSD?" he asked Josh instead.

"Can't guarantee I'll answer it, but sure."

"What are things I shouldn't do around you, to, you know, prevent problems for you?"

Josh let that question sink in. It showed more kindness and consideration than he'd ever expected from Aaron. He cleared his throat. "I don't deal well with surprises or shock. And violence is a big issue. No violent movies, games, or even play."

"Ok. I'll remember that."

It was hard to reconcile his memories of Aaron with the man he was now, Josh thought. He remembered Aaron as arrogant and spoiled, but he spotted little of that now. Aaron seemed lost, broken. It made sense considering what he'd been through, but it didn't mesh with Josh's image of him. He sighed. Best to let it go. Aaron wasn't his problem, after all.

When they entered the parking lot near the jiujitsu studio, Josh scanned it, searching for Indy's car. It wasn't there. Of course not. That would've been too easy. Still, he harbored hope Indy's professor would know more. Kent wasn't the friendliest guy, so Josh could only hope he'd be cooperative.

Kent was in the hallway when they stepped inside, talking to an older guy. It appeared they were in the goodbye phase, and the man left with a friendly nod in their direction.

"Hi, Professor Kent," Josh said.

"You're Indy's friend," Kent said. "Josh, correct?" His eyes traveled to the two men behind Josh, then narrowed. "What happened to you?"

Josh could only assume the question was directed at Aaron, considering his visible injuries.

"I ran into some trouble, sir," Aaron answered.

"With these two?"

Josh almost took a step back when he realized what Kent meant. "What the fuck?"

Kent shot him a cool look. "In case you didn't know, this is a registered safe haven for victims of domestic abuse.

When a guy comes in looking like that, I ask questions until I am satisfied he's safe, no matter who he's with."

"Josh is my brother, sir, and Connor here is a cop. They took me in as a matter of fact after I got beaten up. It was my own fault, sir."

Wow, he was being awfully polite. It felt genuine, though.

Kent's face relaxed. "That's where you're wrong. Getting beat up is never your fault. No matter who you are or what you do, other people should keep their hands off you." He nodded as to underscore his words. "You a cop?" he turned toward Connor.

"O'Connor, I'm with the Albany PD. We okay here?"

"You have your badge on you?"

Connor reached for his wallet, showed his badge and ID. Kent studied them for a few seconds.

"We're good," he said. He looked at Aaron, gestured toward an open door at the end of the hallway. "Can you wait in my office for a minute? I need to talk to Josh and Officer O'Connor."

Josh tensed. What was going on? Before he could say anything, Connor grabbed his hand and squeezed it. As soon as Aaron was out of earshot, Kent looked at Josh.

"Everything is okay. I have a message for you from Indy, but I needed to verify Connor's identity first as I'd never seen him before."

"From Indy? Oh, thank fuck. How is he? Did you see him? Is he okay?" Josh fired off. Connor's hand squeezed his again. Slow the fuck down, it seemed to say.

"He asked me to tell you Connor needs to leave proof from the DA here. Indy will contact me, and I'll get it to him. He said you'd know what that meant."

Josh breathed a sigh of relief. "Tell him Noah is recovering well considering the circumstances, but that he misses him like crazy."

"And I've contacted the DA through safe channels, and I'm awaiting his response," Connor added. "I'll let you know as soon as I hear anything."

Kent nodded. "I'll give him the message. Josh, about your brother. I run a ten-week course in basic jiujitsu skills aimed at self-defense. It may be a good fit for him."

Josh studied the man. If you got past his rather stern attitude, he wasn't bad looking. He had dark hair, kept a tad too long so it curled at his neck, and piercing blue eyes that stood in sharp contrast with his olive skin. Must be some Mediterranean blood in him. He was as tall as Josh, but more muscular, though nowhere near Connor's size.

"He got beat up because he was gay," Josh said finally.

Kent raised his eyebrows. "And that matters because...?"

"Because the first time Indy came here with Noah, you didn't seem to take too kindly to them being a couple. I wanted to make sure it wasn't going to be an issue."

"I didn't have a problem with them being gay or a couple. What I saw was a young guy, maybe still in his teens, coming in with an older guy while clearly being hurt. A broken arm and bruised ribs are classic injuries in domestic violence, so I was on the lookout for any signal Indy was being abused."

"He's not. Noah would never hurt him," Josh said.

The corner of Kent's lip pulled up. "I know that now, but I didn't at the time, and as I said, this is a safe place for victims of domestic abuse. Some of them show up with their abusers, counting on me to pick up on their hidden signals and keep them safe."

Josh couldn't help but admire the guy for what he was doing. From his point of view, it made total sense. Considering how young and innocent Indy looked and how they'd shown up here, you couldn't fault Kent for being suspicious. "I'll tell Aaron about the self-defense. Not sure if he's planning to stay, though, as he's out of a job and can't stay with us."

He cringed as his own words registered. He didn't mean to sound so cold, but Kent didn't seem to take issue with it.

"If he needs a place to stay, have him talk to me. I live close by and have several rooms available for short-term emergencies. We can work something out."

"Thank you," Josh said, surprised. "I'll be sure to tell him."

"You want me to move in with a complete stranger?" Aaron asked in the car after Josh had filled him in. The indignity in his voice was obvious, and it got Josh's back up.

"Oh, I'm sorry, I didn't know you were in a position to be picky," he snapped. Connor put a calming hand on his thigh, and Josh took a breath, exhaled slowly. God, he was worked up today. The stress of everything was getting to him for sure.

It took Aaron a minute to reply, but Josh refused to watch him in the mirror. "You're not wrong," his brother said. Wow, Aaron was admitting Josh was right. Call the fucking press.

"What job did you get fired from?" Connor asked.

"I worked in DC as a staffer to Senator Fremont from Georgia. He's an old-fashioned, fire-and-brimstone Republican from the South who's in his fifth term. He fired me when I came out as gay, said I was an abomination. Of course, he found a different legal and official reason, but we both knew better. And since I was fired without a recommendation, I couldn't get a job with anyone else in DC. It's a small town in that sense."

Connor entered their driveway, and Josh couldn't help but hopefully check for Indy's car. Nope, still nothing. God, he missed him.

"I'm sure you should be able to get a job somewhere else," Josh said. "I mean, even if it's waiting tables, it'll pay the bills."

"I know, but I have a master's in political science, and aside from the fact that Fremont was a judgmental asshole, I loved that job. I'd hoped to find something similar."

"There's enough governing going on here in Albany," Connor said. "And it's a hell of a lot more liberal than the Deep South. You should be able to find something here."

"I hope so. It's hard to figure out where to start."

Holy crap, what the fuck was wrong with Aaron? Did he think employers would line up for him? The passiveness he radiated irritated the shit out of Josh. "I'd say you start with accepting the first job you can get so you make some money and go from there."

"Do you work?" Aaron asked.

Josh's head shot up. Was Aaron taking a dig at him being home because of his PTSD?

"Aaron, do not go down that road," Connor said, his voice cold as ice. He parked the car in the garage, turned off the engine and met Aaron's eyes dead on in the mirror. "Your brother has served his country with honor and paid a high price for it. Don't you dare belittle that, or you'll discover how fast I can kick you out. I will protect Josh from you, you understand me?"

"I wasn't... I didn't..." Aaron sighed. "Never mind."

He carefully got out of the car. As soon as Aaron had closed his door, Connor turned to Josh. "Don't let him get to you, baby. He's not your problem."

Josh reveled in the warm feeling in his belly Connor's

words inspired. Fuck, how he loved it when the man went all authoritative as shit.

"Yes, Connor," he whispered, just to let him know what he was doing to him. He was rewarded with a stare from Connor that made his cock hard instantly. It seemed his submissiveness turned Connor on as much as Connor's dominance affected him.

Fuck, he couldn't wait for that session Connor had promised him. They'd have to get rid of Aaron first. Josh was not planning on letting Aaron know about that part of his relationship with Connor. It was bad enough he'd heard them fuck. Not that he gave a shit what Aaron thought, but it felt too personal, too raw to share.

He wasn't even sure how much he wanted Noah to know. His best friend had to suspect something after their conversation in the hospital and Connor's admission he'd worked Josh over good. After all, Noah knew how much Josh loved the rough sex and how he got off on Noah ordering him around in bed. But they'd never even gotten close to what he and Connor had shared, and he wasn't sure Noah would understand, let alone approve.

"You okay, baby?"

Connor's soft question yanked him from his thoughts. "Yeah. Looking forward to my reward."

Connor's eyes clouded over, and he swallowed. "Me too, baby. Me too."

INDY HAD no intention whatsoever of informing Josh about the appeal. Instead, he had Noah call Josh's lawyer. Noah had assured the lawyer he'd inform Josh and had asked him because of Josh's PTSD to contact Noah first if there was any news. Because Noah was still listed as Josh's health care proxy and had power of attorney in case Josh wasn't able to make decisions, the lawyer had agreed after some persuading. That was the first step in Indy's plan.

Next, he needed to talk to Connor without Josh finding out. It was a risk he was taking, meeting the cop alone while still not one hundred percent sure of his intentions, but he had little choice. Josh's safety and well-being came first. So the next day, he'd called Connor, had asked him to meet later that day at the studio, without Josh. Connor had agreed, even if he'd been clearly reluctant to keep it from Josh.

Indy had checked out from the motel in Jersey and had found a similar one near Albany airport. He'd managed to sell his car the day before and was now using a rental. The money from his car, combined with the prepaid credit cards from Noah would tide him over for a little while.

Indy stood close to the entrance to the studio and watched Connor walk up. The cop gave him a cursory glance, then proceeded to go inside. Indy smiled. He couldn't have asked for better proof his disguise worked.

"Connor," he called out.

The cop whipped his head around. His eyes widened when he recognized Indy. "Fuck, you're good," he said with obvious admiration.

"Thank you. I'll make this quick, because you must hate leaving Josh alone right now."

"I sent a message to the DA. He should have something for you today, tomorrow at the latest," Connor assured him.

"Okay, but that's not what I need to talk to you about." He took a deep breath, hoped Connor would keep his cool. "The three guys who raped Josh have been released, pending an appeal. General Flint got a heads up and let Noah know. Josh doesn't know. Yet."

Other than a tightening of Connor's jaw, the man didn't react, something Indy could appreciate. Where Noah's temper ran hot and instantly, Connor's ran cold and long. Indy wasn't sure which he preferred, but in this case, his money was on Connor. There had to be little the cop wouldn't do to protect Josh.

"Noah spoke to his lawyer, got him to agree to not contact Josh directly because of his PTSD. It's not legal, but neither is what I'm about to propose to solve this issue. You gonna have a problem with that?"

"Does it involve killing these three motherfuckers?"

"Sadly, no. But it might break a few bones, and more importantly, it will result in a more satisfactory punishment and get them to drop the appeal."

Connor nodded. "Spill."

In quick sentences, Indy explained what he had come up with. When he was done, Connor shook his head and whistled softly. "You have three times the brain the Fitzpatricks ever gave you credit for."

Indy shrugged. "Duncan never gave a shit about what I thought. All he wanted was to fuck me and brag about fucking me. I was nothing more than a hole for him to use."

Connor's hand landed on Indy's shoulder and squeezed gently. "You're so much more than that, so don't ever believe otherwise. Noah loves you for who you are and rightly so. Look at what you're willing to do for Josh. He's damn lucky to have a friend like you."

"You know he let me fuck him, right?" Indy figured he might as well clear the air on that one. If Connor was going to become a fixture in Josh's life, Indy wanted to make sure they had things out in the open.

Connor swallowed. "Yeah, he told me. Can't say I like it, but then again I like the idea of Noah fucking him even less."

At least Indy could offer peace of mind there. "He won't. Not anymore."

Surprised flashed over Connor's face. "Did you...?"

"No, that was all him."

"How were you okay with that? The thought of having to watch Noah and Josh... I don't think I could. As a matter of fact, I'm sure I couldn't. I'd rip Noah's heart out. How could you stand it?"

"When I met Noah and Josh, they were a unit. I don't think they realized it, but they were a couple. A dysfunctional couple, but they were most definitely together. They needed each other, and they were nowhere near ready to let go. If I had forced it, I would've lost them both. And it didn't bother me, watching them together. It still doesn't. I calculate it woulda been way worse to not see it. This way, I could see it for what it was, and not let my imagination run off. And in all honesty, it was becoming less and less frequent. Plus, Josh needed something Noah couldn't give him...and I suspect you can."

Connor cleared his throat, and Indy bit back a smile. The cop was clearly not used to discussing his sex life. "Josh told me you had suggested he might have submissive tendencies."

Indy lifted his eyebrows. "Does he?"

"Yah."

"And I take it you like to be dominant, then?"

Connor looked everywhere except at Indy. "Yah."

"Well, that's good then, that you both can find fulfillment."

"Can I ask you a question about that?"

It had to be a hell of an important question for the cop to overcome his reluctance to discuss such private matters. "Sure."

"I'm looking for a way to become more...proficient. I want to fully satisfy Josh's needs, and I need to learn how to dominate him better. There's a ton of stuff online, but I'm not taking any risks as some of it seems dangerous. He's too important to me. Any suggestions?"

Indy sighed inwardly. How the fuck had he become the go-to person for kinky sex? The irony wasn't lost on him. "Find a local Dom who does couples' sessions. There are Doms that specifically teach partners the Dom/sub relationship. Find one you connect with, that you trust and go together."

Connor's eyes lit up. "That's a thing? I thought those Doms-for-hire were, like, a sex-club thing, or for subs who needed a Dom. Thank you, I'll look into it."

"You're welcome. Now, back to our plan. You'll need a solid alibi and not from Josh. You'll be the first one they suspect. Noah too, but they'll clear him because of his surgery."

Connor smiled, amused. "You realize you're talking to a cop?"

"Sure, but you wanna know how often cops get caught for doing stupid shit, like accepting bribes? You'd think they know better, and they don't. I'll let you know when I leave, but it will be in a day or two. I want to get this done before Noah comes home."

"Other than the alibi, do you need anything from me?"

"Money." Indy breathed out. He hated this part. "I'm low on cash, and I need to travel without arousing suspicion, using several rental cars and motels. Plus, I need to hire a PI to dig up shit on these motherfuckers."

"Cash or a prepaid credit card?"

"Both, preferably. Thank you. I hate asking, but I can't pull it off otherwise."

Connor shook his head. "No, don't thank me. I owe you for this. The money doesn't mean shit to me, and I'd pay anything to keep Josh safe."

"I don't like IOU's. Consider it an act of love between friends. We're good. But Connor, the money is not the only reason I informed you." He searched for words.

"Noah can't know, so you needed to inform me in case something goes wrong. I get it."

Indy breathed out in relief. "Noah would try to stop me, and I understand where he's coming from. But I have to do this for Josh. I can't stand the thought of him having to go through this again."

Much to his surprise, the cop closed the distance between them and bent over to hug him. "Thank you for that. But know that if I ever find a way to repay you, I will. And please, Indy, be careful."

14

Aaron had to go. Connor was sick and tired of Josh being on edge all the time, which was only exacerbated by Aaron's lazy-ass attitude toward everything. It wasn't that he was a bother, but he sure didn't do fuck. Plus, Noah was coming home tomorrow, which meant Indy probably wanted to come back as well. He'd texted Connor to say he'd left to carry out his revenge plan, but he promised he'd return as soon as he was done.

More importantly: Connor wanted his sex life back. He and Josh hadn't had sex since their bet, aside from a fast mutual blow job. Connor wanted to fuck Josh properly, and there was no doubt Josh needed to be worked over well. He was so tense Connor kept having to yank him back out of a starting episode. He'd already found a solution for today, but it was time to get their privacy back.

He'd waited three more days to see if Aaron got the hint himself, or for Josh to say anything, but when neither moved into action, Connor decided he was done. They were having breakfast, as always prepared by Josh. He'd fixed Connor oatmeal with nutty toppings as he called it, which meant a crunchy layer of various nuts and seeds he'd baked in the oven, with some maple syrup on top. Connor loved how Josh insisted on making a hearty meal for "his man", as he dubbed Connor. The deep satisfaction that expression gave Connor had no equal.

"Aaron, what's your plan for today?" Connor asked.

Aaron jerked up from the newspaper he'd been reading. "Erm, hadn't really thought about it."

Connor held back a sigh. What else was new? "I can't help but notice that seems to be a recurring event."

"What do you mean?"

"You've been here six days, and I've seen no indication of you getting a job, or even moving any closer to obtaining one. You haven't contacted Professor Kent about that room either."

Aaron had the decency to look embarrassed. "Yeah, I know. Noah is coming home tomorrow, right? Well, I figured I could maybe use your apartment, Connor, since you're staying here, or if you guys wanted to go to your place, I could stay here with Noah."

Out of the corner of his eye, Connor caught Josh freezing to his spot. Before he could say anything, Connor put his foot down. "No. You're not moving into my apartment, and you're not staying here any longer. We gave you time to get your act together, but you seem to think that's an ongoing invitation. It's not. Deadline is tomorrow. When Noah comes home, you're gone." Having said his piece, Connor took another bite of the delicious oatmeal concoction Josh had made for him. Damn, the man could cook.

Aaron's spoon clonked out of his hand, splashing milk over the breakfast bar. "But where am I supposed to go? You can't just put me out on the street. And it'll be two days before Christmas then."

"I don't give a fuck, and sure we can. You've had plenty of time to find something. It's not our fault you didn't use it. Call Kent and ask if you can stay with him. Book a motel. Or sleep in your car. I don't care as long as you're gone in two days."

Aaron paled and Connor almost felt sorry for him. He wasn't a bad kid, but holy fuck, he was spoiled as all get-out. He needed one hell of an attitude adjustment.

"I'll figure something out," Aaron mumbled. He quickly finished his cereal and went upstairs, leaving his bowl on the counter.

If there had been any doubt in Connor's mind about Josh's opinion on what he'd told Aaron, it was gone when he was rewarded with a fierce kiss.

"Thank you," Josh whispered in his ear, hugging him tightly. "God, I need you, Connor. I need you bad."

Connor kissed him hard. "I know, baby. I have a surprise for you today. I need you dressed in comfortable clothes and ready to go after lunch, okay? Don't eat too much. I promise, it's a good surprise, and you're gonna love it."

Josh's eyes lit up, then sobered. "What about Aaron?"

"I'll tell him to entertain himself outside of the house this afternoon. Maybe he can go job hunting. I don't care, but I'll make sure he's gone."

He felt good enough about what he had planned with Josh that he interpreted Aaron's muffled remark when he informed him of their plans as enthusiastic consent. It even helped to suppress his worry about what Indy was about to do. Indy was wicked smart, and his plan was solid, but it still had risks. If one of the men reacted differently, if they got violent... Indy knew how to defend himself, but what would happen if he accidentally gave away his identity?

Still, Connor didn't see another way. The sheer nerve of

these guys to request an appeal communicated loud and clear what caliber men they were. The lowest. Connor had no doubt they would sink to unfathomable depths to get off —and in the process not only blame Josh but destroy him. He couldn't let that happen. And as much as he believed in justice and the system, he also knew this was one of those cases where being innocent didn't mean you had the law on your side. No, what Indy was doing had Connor's whole-hearted blessing. He could only hope he would be okay.

At one o'clock, Aaron left with an expression that tempted Connor to slap it off, but he let it be. He wanted to save his energy. "Come on, baby, let's go."

Josh hadn't asked once where they were going. Despite his aversion to surprises, he trusted Connor enough to surrender completely. Not that Connor wasn't planning on springing this on him, but he'd thought it best to wait till they were in the car.

"You curious where we're going?" he asked once they were on their way. It was a twenty-minute drive, he'd seen on Google Maps.

Josh nodded. "But the fact it's just us is reward enough. Fuck, Aaron was getting on my nerves. Thank you so much for stepping in."

Connor smiled at Josh's trust. "I'll tell you anyway since I don't want to blindside you. I've booked us an appointment this afternoon with Master Mark, as he calls himself. He's a Dom who gives private lessons to couples to teach them the Dom/sub relationship."

Josh's head whipped around. His mouth slightly agape, he was clearly trying to digest what Connor had told him. "He's gonna dominate you, too?"

The mix of worry and indignation in Josh's voice made

Connor want to pull over and kiss the man senseless. How telling it was that Josh's first concern was for Connor.

"No, baby. He's going to teach me to be a Dom and you how to be a sub since we're both newbies at this. I filled out this entire list of preferences, and he emailed me a contract that states what he can and cannot do. He won't sexually engage us for instance, only help us pleasure each other. You didn't think I'd be content watching another man touch you, or let you touch him, did you? You're mine, Joshua."

Josh put his hand on Connor's thigh. "I don't want to have sex with Noah anymore," he said softly. "Will you please be there when I tell him?"

Connor's entire body glowed at these words. Josh chose him over Noah. He'd never expected it to happen so soon. Of course, Noah felt the same, but Josh didn't know that. Maybe it would be better for Josh's self-confidence if he was the one to break it off, not Noah? Connor would have to think on that, maybe discuss it with Indy and Noah. He wanted to do what was best for Josh.

"Thank you, baby. You have no idea how happy that makes me. I'm sure Noah will understand, and we can tell him together. How do you feel about my surprise? We can cancel if you want to."

"Fuck, no, I don't want to cancel. I can't wait. You surprise me, though. You're always so private about sex, and this is a huge step. You sure you'll be okay with it?"

"I'm a little nervous, but mostly because I want to do right by you. I figure being so private about sex was to protect myself since I wasn't out and my experiences were so disappointing. I have no qualms about fucking you in front of this Master Mark if it helps me to take better care of you."

They drove in silence for a few minutes when Josh spoke

up again. "Connor, would you be open to ditching condoms?"

Connor shot him a quick look sideways. "Is that what you want, baby?"

"Noah and I never used them because we were exclusive, and I would love that with you, too. I love the sensation of cum dripping out of me, and now that we're exclusive, too, I thought maybe you'd... I dunno, am I going too fast here?"

Connor reached for Josh's hand, which was still on his thigh. "I'd love that. We'd need to get tested first, right?"

"I had my check up the week before we started...dating, I guess we could call it? I could show you the results. Noah, too, since we always go at the same time."

Connor smiled. "I believe you, baby. I get tested monthly because of my job. I'm due next week, actually."

Josh sent him a careful smile. "Does that mean we could go without today? I'd love that."

Connor thought it over. He wasn't taking any chances of passing anything on to Josh, but the reality was that he hadn't had a hook-up in months. Barebacking Josh... He was hard just thinking about it. "I reckon we can go bareback today."

THEY PULLED up to a nondescript single family home that lay back from the road, surrounded by trees. Huh, not what Josh had expected. He'd figured it would be some seedy sex club or an industrial building of some sort. Since Connor seemed confident they were at the right place, they got out and rang the doorbell.

The door was opened by a forty-something guy with friendly blue eyes, a wide smile, and long, dark hair pulled into a ponytail. "Hi guys, come on in. You must be Connor and Josh. I'm Mark."

Josh shook his extended hand. "Nice to meet you," he said.

"You too. We're gonna go down into the basement, so follow me."

Josh reached for Connor's hand, finding himself unexpectedly nervous. Connor gave him a reassuring squeeze and led Josh down the stairs into a softly lit area. Two leather couches were positioned across from each other with a sturdy-looking wooden coffee table between them.

"Grab a seat. We're gonna start by going over your preferences and getting to know each other a little bit. Feel free to ask me anything. In order for this to work, you guys need to feel like you can trust me, so ask whatever you need."

Josh lowered himself so close to Connor their legs were pressed together.

"You're the sub, Josh, am I correct?"

Josh blushed, cursing himself as his cheeks reddened. "Yeah. I guess Connor told you?"

"He did, but it was clear from your dynamic as well. You were looking to him for reassurance and guidance. That's a good thing, by the way. It means you already have the natural urge to follow his lead. Neither of you has much experience with this, correct?"

Josh shook his head. "I was talking to a friend about... sex, and he mentioned I might have submissive tendencies. When I met Connor, I told him, and we wanted to explore it."

"Well, you've come to the right place." Mark shot them a friendly smile. "Let me start by explaining a little. There are many misconceptions about BDSM or the Dom/sub relationship. What many people call BSDM is merely being creative in bed, like spanking, or using restraints. Even when one partner is dominant, technically it's still not BDSM. True BDSM is a lifestyle that most of the times happens outside the bedroom as well."

Josh looked at Connor, suddenly uncertain. Had they misunderstood?

"No, don't worry, Josh, it's all good. From what I understand you guys are at the beginning of exploring your need for submission and Connor's wish to dominate. I'd love to help you with that. Maybe you'll both be happy with a little more Dom/sub dynamic in your sexual relationship, and maybe along the way you discover you want more. Either way is fine. I wanted to make sure you understood the terms we use."

Josh nodded, sighed in relief.

"To keep it simple, I'll refer to Connor as the Dom and Josh as the sub, though those may be terms you'll never fully grow into. Now, I don't know if you're aware, Josh, but there are several types of subs. Some get off on being humiliated, treated like crap—sometimes literally. We're talking licking boots, being chained up like a dog, or similar scenarios. Others are about physical domination, wanting to be physically subdued. They crave feeling weak and want the Dom to physically overpower them. This is where bondage comes in, being tied up or restricted in some way. Then there's a group who likes pain, ranging from mild to extreme torture. And lastly, there's a group that just wants to be dominated in a general sense, without going to extremes. They relish relinquishing control without taking it too far. If you had to put yourself in a group, Josh, which one would you pick?"

Josh's head automatically turned to Connor, but when he realized it, he stopped. This wasn't something Connor could and should decide for him. This was about him, about what he craved. "The humiliation thing is definitely not me. Anything with bodily waste, and I'm out. I like some pain, but I don't know how much. And I love it when Connor takes over, makes me stop thinking. So maybe the last group?"

Mark nodded as he wrote down notes on a clipboard. "Have you guys experimented with pain?"

This time, Josh did look to Connor for permission, but before he could say anything, Connor answered. "A little. I spanked Josh, and he almost came from just that. Plus, he digs it when I take him hard and rough."

Josh couldn't help but smile at the pride in his man's voice. He realized how healing this was for Connor, the man who had such negative experiences with sex. For him to bring such pleasure to Josh, that had to feel so good for him.

Mark noted something down again, smiling. "We'll definitely explore that more, then. Anything else you want to add, Josh?"

Josh swallowed. Fuck, this got so personal. "Two things. One is that I have PTSD, and violence is a trigger."

Mark nodded. "I'm aware. Connor gave me the necessary info. We'll make sure to stay away from anything that could trigger you. I work with multiple veterans with PTSD, and they've all seen improvement in their symptoms. The release and relaxation you find through your sub experience with Connor will help you find more balance elsewhere as well."

Josh's heart flooded with love all over again. He should've known Connor would think of it, would know his needs. He always did. "Thank you, baby," he said, leaning in for a quick kiss.

"What was the other thing?" Mark asked. "You said you had two things."

"Right. Well, it's three, actually. I've discovered I like it when Connor uses me to get off. Like, when he fucks my mouth or my ass and forbids me to come. It gives me a rush to make him come, I guess."

Mark nodded. "That makes sense, considering your profile. You're a sub with a deep need to please and pleasure, Josh. It's important Connor learns to utilize that without feeling selfish. And the last thing?"

Despite Mark's friendly and casual attitude, Josh wasn't sure about the last topic. Connor had shown more openness than he'd ever had before, but would he be okay with this? On the other hand, Mark would notice anyway as soon as they'd undress.

"Connor here is...erm, well endowed." He shot a quick look sideways, but Connor's face was stuck in neutral. "Oh, fuck it. Look, his cock is huge, and I love it. I can take him, and it feels incredible, but it means prep is crucial. Whatever we do, we need to factor that in."

Mark's eyes shifted to Connor. "You didn't mark that on your online application. Any reason?"

Connor's jaw ticked. "It's not something I like to talk about."

"You don't like to talk about it, or you don't like that your cock is big?"

Josh almost held his breath. Mark was getting awfully personal. "It's been nothing but a nuisance, so no, I don't like it." Connor's voice was gruff, but he was talking, which Josh considered a major victory.

"I love it," he piped up.

"You don't see it as a problem?" Mark asked. "You can be honest."

"Hell, no. As Connor said, I love it when he takes me hard and deep, and with his cock, well, it's always hard. The only downside is the time we need to take to loosen me up, but no, I don't see it as a problem at all."

"If I hear you correctly, you're seeing it as a good thing since you love the mix of pain and pleasure it brings you," Mark said.

Josh nodded. "Damn right."

"This isn't sex therapy, Connor, but I want you to think about what Josh said. Maybe your size has resulted in some negative experiences before, but Josh loves your anatomy. It brings him exactly what he needs, so maybe you can learn to see yourself in a new way."

Mark looked at his notes. "You're both physically healthy, correct? No physical injuries or limitations we should take into account? How's your sexual stamina?"

Josh let out a giggle, his mind wandering back to the night of their bet. "Connor has exceptional stamina," he reported.

Mark raised an eyebrow. "Wanna expand on that? This could be interesting to play with."

Josh didn't dare look at Connor. "I made him come five times a few days ago. The first three times were easy, but after that, I had to work for it."

Mark whistled between his teeth. "That's impressive. Definitely something to work with. Okay, we need to talk a little more about you, Connor. How do you see your role as a Dom with Josh?"

Connor cleared his throat. "My goal is to bring pleasure and release to Josh. I like bossing him around, and I get a kick out of using him sexually or disciplining him, because he loves that. But I won't do anything that could be harmful to him, physically or emotionally. So for me, the whole humiliating thing is a big no as well, and so are all the extremes."

"Sounds like you guys have figured out what you want from this. Connor, you filled out the extensive list of things you don't want to do here. Did you talk about these with Josh?"

"No. I didn't tell him we were going here until we were in the car."

"Okay. In that case, Josh, I need you to approve what Connor filled out for your limits, okay?"

Josh shrugged. "I don't need to. I trust him."

Mark smiled. "I'm glad you do, but consent is the foundation of BDSM in any shape or form, and consent can never be implicit. I'll give you guys a few minutes to read the list and sign it both, okay? When you're done, strip and go through that door. We'll start with a low-key session where we experiment with some discipline. Sounds good?"

They both nodded.

"One last thing. I'll also need you to come up with a safe word, Josh. This is something you can use in a scene when you want to stop, or when you're close to your limits. You can use green, yellow, and red to indicate being fine, getting close to your limits, and stop immediately. If you want to use different words, that's fine, but make sure they're not something you're likely to use in everyday life."

Mark disappeared after handing Josh a set of stapled papers. It was a long list of all kinds of elements and sexual tools, Josh guessed, you could choose or choose not to do with Master Mark. Spanking, paddling, handcuffs, being gagged, cock rings, what the fuck was a humbler? And more importantly, how the hell was he supposed to choose when he didn't know anything about this?

Safe words. Limits. He had no limits when it came to

Connor, only a blind trust Connor would take care of him. Maybe that was too naive when they started considering things like being gagged and cock rings.

"I figured we'd start conservatively, go from there," Connor said, his voice sounding as insecure as Josh felt inside. Somehow, that made Josh feel less of a wimp.

He read through the list, saw which ones Connor had ticked off as 'yes.' Being blindfolded, that sounded like it could be fun. Spanking and paddling were a definitive yes. Handcuffs were fine, as were silk ropes. Cock rings and other restrictive devices...Well, he figured Mark knew his shit and wouldn't do anything that caused permanent damage, so why the hell not?

He noticed Connor had crossed out penis-enlarging devices. Yeah, good choice. The Beast would suffice. Reading through it all, he didn't disagree with Connor on anything. He grabbed the pen, signed at the bottom and handed the paper to Connor, who studied him with a guarded expression.

"What?" Josh asked.

"I should've asked you if you wanted to do this, instead of deciding for you. It's hard sometimes to distinguish between dominating you in the bedroom and in everyday life. I'm sorry I crossed that line."

Josh didn't think, just did what came naturally and climbed on Connor's lap. "We're good, baby. Did you see I agreed with every single thing you checked on that list? I trust you because you know me well. I'll let you know if you ever go too far, okay? You know I'm no pushover."

He leaned in and brought their mouths together. Connor's mouth was hot and impatient, wanting more. When Josh pulled back, Connor's hand came around him, dragging him close again.

"Connor, we have to..." Josh managed before Connor plundered his mouth again.

Josh gave up and dove in deep. When Connor scooted forward, he wrapped his legs around his waist, locking his arms tight around his neck. Connor stood up, two strong hands holding Josh's ass, pressing him close.

"I need you," Connor growled.

"But Mark is..."

"I don't fucking care. All this sex talk has me horny as fuck. I'm about to explode, and I want to do that in your ass."

Connor put him down on the coffee table where Josh unwrapped his legs, somewhat dazed. Connor yanked off his shoes and within seconds, had dragged Josh's jeans and boxers down. Without a word, he produced a package of lube from his back pocket, almost threw it on Josh, who was still wearing his shirt. Connor's belt came off. Next, he popped his fly and reached for his cock, kneeling in front of Josh.

Josh didn't even think but scooted down toward Connor, pulling up his legs and opening wide. Fuck, yes, this was what he needed. Connor lubed up his cock, then his fingers. Josh pushed down at the first contact, allowing Connor entrance. This truly was the one downside to Connor's size, their inability to do a quick fuck.

He moaned loudly when Connor added a second finger and hit him deep, grazing his sweet spot. His hips moved, rocking back against Connor's fingers. "Don't you dare come, you hear me? You're not coming until my cock is all the way in," Connor ordered.

Three fingers. How the hell had he gotten so horny so quick? All he could think of was that cock inside of him. Mark had to be wondering where they were, would probably come to check on them at some point, and yet Josh didn't care. He needed Connor too much. All this because of his shitty excuse for a brother. Josh did a quick mental check. Fuck, he hadn't come in two days. No wonder he was so fucking on edge. And Connor, too.

Connor loosened him up with little finesse, but Josh couldn't care less. He was as impatient as Connor, wanted to get the fuck on with it. Finally Connor lined up his cock against Josh's hole, pressing gently as if asking permission to enter. As always, Josh cringed a little when the head pushed in.

Connor's hands circled his waist to drag him even lower. Josh didn't need to be told to hold on to the edges of the table. He pushed down, inviting Connor in. Inch by inch Connor slid home until his entire dick created that indescribable sense of fullness. It felt different, without a condom. Nothing between them anymore. God, he loved it. Josh let out a long sigh that mingled with a low grunt from Connor.

"I see you guys have gotten a head-start on things," an amused voice commented. They both froze. "No worries, you're not the first couple that gets their game on in here. I always consider it a good sign, means you're excited for things to come. But let's move it into the chamber, shall we?"

15

Connor was oh, so tempted to tell Mark to fuck off so he could finish. His cock still throbbing, buried to the hilt inside Josh, it was not only embarrassing to have to pull out but pretty damn impossible. They were both so close. One more minute and he could've made them both come. Damn.

He looked at Josh, whose face was still frozen in shock. Then his eyes twinkled, and before Connor knew it, they were both grinning like kids caught with their hands in the cookie jar.

Connor pulled Josh close and pushed his legs down so he'd clamp them around Connor's waist—which he did. He leaned back on his heels, found his balance and pushed himself up. It was a credit to the strength of his legs and his core that he managed to stand up while holding Josh, never pulling out. He'd listen to Mark but on his own fucking terms. He wanted to stay inside Josh just a little bit longer.

Josh held on tight, dropping kisses on Connor's neck and shoulder. "You know it makes me all weak inside when you carry me, right?"

Yup, he made the right choice. He followed Mark, who was sporting a toned, tattooed body in tight leather pants, into what the man had dubbed the Chamber—and almost dropped Josh when he saw the impressive range of tools the guy had amassed there. Holy fuck, it was like a sexual-dungeon dream come true.

Sturdy black metal rings in various sizes were screwed into the wall on one side while the other side was decorated —if you could call it that—with various benches that looked like mini-prisons. One cabinet held an assortment of paddles, crops, and whips, another every dildo, vibrator, and sex toy you could imagine, including at least two dozen Connor had no idea how to use. There was another glass-door cabinet with serious torture devices, from the looks of it intended to put on your cock and balls. He swallowed.

"Connor, why don't you put Josh down here."

Mark pointed toward a bench that would have Josh kneel on a soft, padded ledge, with his stomach on another padded part, at the perfect height to be fucked, legs spread wide and ass sticking backwards. Despite the alluring picture it put in Connor's mind, it was hard to obey, Connor discovered. Had to be the Dom inside him. Every instinct he had told him to ignore the man, to keep on fucking Josh until they both came.

Josh whimpered as Connor pulled out. Connor put him down gently, holding on to him till he knew for certain Josh had regrouped.

"Connor, I will only talk to you this session, okay? You'll have to tell Josh what to do. You are his Dom, not me."

Connor nodded as a strange sense of destiny settled over him. He wanted this to work, wanted to get good at this, for Josh.

"What does Josh have to call you when you're sexually

engaged?"

"He has to reply with 'Yes, Connor.'"

Damn, even the thought of Josh submitting had his cock twitching. It was hard to focus on Mark when his eyes kept trailing to Josh, wanting to be buried in him all over again. He should've jacked off before they came here. He hadn't been thinking, had figured he needed to be horny when in reality, it was impossible to think when his balls were itching to unload.

"Make sure to discipline him every single time he forgets. And, more importantly, he has to earn the right to come. He can't orgasm without your permission, so if he does, discipline him. That's also a great way of seducing him to break the rules. Tell him not to come and then keep doing what you know will make him come. He'll hate and love you at the same time."

Connor resigned himself to confessing the embarrassing truth to Mark. There was no way he could do this, not in the state he was in.

"I need to come first. I'm sorry, I should've jerked off before we came. I'm too on edge right now, can't think." If Connor had been anything like Josh, he would have been beet red at this confession. But Mark wasn't irritated or even surprised in the least.

"Don't tell me, tell Josh."

Josh stood still, eyes fixed on Connor as if he was waiting for orders. He was, Connor realized. He breathed in. Despite Mark's presence, which took some getting used to, they were still Connor and Josh. If he played it right, Josh would come too, and would thus earn punishment. He would have to do it fast so Josh could take a second round. He didn't want to have to prep Josh again, though. Maybe Mark had...?

"Do you have a butt plug, one that approximates my

cock size?"

Mark smiled. "I sure do. Good choice." He walked over to a cabinet, pulled something out. "This should do the trick."

Connor took the black silicone plug that was thick with a pronounced flared end to prevent it from being sucked in. He held it next to his cock, saw it was shorter but even thicker than the Beast and shot Josh a kinky smile. "Think it's about the right size?"

Josh's eyes grew big. "Holy crap, I can't take that in."

"Strike one," Connor said, not able to keep the satisfaction out of his voice.

"But Connor," Josh stuttered.

"Strike two."

Josh visibly swallowed. "Yes, Connor."

Damn, those words reached deep in him. He let out a satisfied sigh. "On your knees on the bench and spread wide."

It took two seconds before Josh complied. "Yes, Connor."

He kneeled clumsily but spread wide open. Mark handed Connor a big bottle of lube, and Connor lubed up the plug liberally, then put it aside for now. Connor noticed the bench had rings to tie someone down, but he didn't think that would be necessary now.

Connor didn't think about it but took a solid stance behind the bench and plunged his cock inside Josh's ass as soon as Josh had found a good hold on the bench. Fuck, yes, this felt good. Josh yelped, probably as much in surprise as in discomfort. Connor sunk in all the way, bent over to bring his mouth close to Josh's ear. "You heard the man: you cannot come until I say so. And I say no. Do not come, Joshua, you hear me?"

"Yes, Connor."

He pulled out, ignoring Josh's whimper as he did. "Fuck, you're beautiful like this, all spread out for me." He kneaded Josh's ass with his right hand, slapped it playfully. "Your ass, baby, it never fails to entice me."

Josh's hole twitched, winking at him, and Connor let out an appreciative groan. He lined up again, pushed back in, making sure to hit Josh's prostate. Josh's moan confirmed he'd aimed correctly. He gave five, six thrusts, only pulling out a bit before slamming back in, nailing the perfect spot every time. His body hummed in pleasure. No, he wouldn't last long, but that was okay.

Josh let out a muffled curse, and Connor smiled. "You okay, baby?" he teased.

There was a muttered expletive before Josh obeyed. "Yes, Connor."

He leaned back without pulling out, teasing Josh's sensitive crack with his index finger. "You know what I was thinking, baby?" He stroked both ass cheeks with a feather light touch, reveling in the goose bumps that appeared. "I'm gonna fill you with my cum and then plug you. That way, you stay nice and wide with all of my juices inside you. And then when I want to fuck you again, I can yank the plug out and fuck you senseless. What do you think?"

Josh shivered. "Yes, Connor."

By his calculations, Josh had to be as close as he was. There was no way he was not coming now, which was exactly the plan. Connor pulled out almost entirely, then slid in deep. Fuck, he was almost there. One, two, three more thrusts and with a low growl, he unloaded what felt like a mother load of cum in Josh's ass. As he did, Josh's ass contracted around Connor's dick, his muscles spasming with Josh's own release.

Connor shook his head to clear it. Man, that had felt

good—though he was nowhere near finished yet. He pulled out, slid in the butt plug without hesitation, closing Josh's hole completely. His cock was still half-hard, ready for more.

"Did you come by any chance, Josh?" he asked casually.

Two seconds hesitation. "Yes, Connor."

"Get up," Connor ordered.

Josh scrambled off the bench, his head hanging low and avoiding Connor's eyes. His cock was still dripping juices.

"Clean me up, baby."

Without a word, Josh sank to his knees and licked Connor clean. Connor sighed. Way better than the towel Mark had offered him.

"Thank you, baby," he said. "Nice job on the cleaning. But you disobeyed me, didn't you?"

Josh lifted his eyes. "Yes, Connor."

"That means you deserve discipline."

"Yes, Connor."

"I'm gonna ask Mark what he thinks I should do with you, okay?"

"Yes, Connor."

Connor had lost all awkwardness of being naked around Mark even though the guy was sporting one hell of a boner in his pants. Apparently, he had liked the show, and who could blame him?

"Any suggestions?" Connor asked.

Mark walked over to the cabinet with the paddles and crops and chose a sturdy looking wooden paddle with several holes in it. "This is a good one for beginners." He showed it to Connor, then handed it over. "It's light, but it packs a punch, so be careful. The key to good spanking and paddling is buildup. You want to rub the ass cheeks first, to get the blood flow going. You can even massage them with oil or lotion. Once they're supple and warm, alternate both cheeks when spanking and build up in intensity. You can also go the other way and start hard and get less intensive. Start with bursts of five or six, then pause to rub and massage more and do the next series. Keep a close eye on Josh to see when it gets too much. He shouldn't have to say anything. It's your job as Dom to know his limits."

"What's a good position?"

"If you ask me, nothing beats an over the knee spanking. I have a spanking chair right here, which is nothing more than a soft leather seat for you with a foot bench to raise one foot so you can lift Josh's ass a tad higher. It also has straps for Josh to hold on to if he wants, and we'll put a pillow on the floor for him."

Connor sat down on the chair and motioned Josh with his index finger to come. He came, his face red with most likely a mix of excitement and fear.

"When you spank him, aim for the softest parts of his cheeks. Also, don't hit the plug. It won't harm him, but it will distract him and prevent him from entering subspace, the pain-pleasure zone," Mark instructed. "Not that I expect him to get there as this takes time and training, but it's a good habit to build."

"Over my knee," Connor ordered.

Josh didn't hesitate, which told Connor he wanted this. He rubbed Josh's cheeks. "You looking forward to this, baby?"

"Yes, Connor." Josh's reply came out on a sigh of surrender. Connor saw him grab the straps and loop his wrists through them, holding on tight.

Connor kneaded both cheeks, rubbed and massaged them till they were warm and ready. "Ten counts, Joshua, count them out."

"Yes, Connor. Thank you, Connor."

Oh, damn, those words were so hauntingly beautiful. Did Josh realize how precious a gift his surrender was, every single time anew? He raised the paddle, aimed for the right butt cheek, waited long enough to make Josh squirm—then brought it down with a resounding slap.

Josh jerked in his straps, his butt lifting from Connor's knee before settling down again. "One. Thank you, Connor."

The second slap hit the other cheek, making a nice zing as it flew through the air. It left a distinct red spot.

"Two. Thank you, Connor."

He slapped again, and again. Josh's ass was pinking up beautifully, and Connor almost stopped to admire the view. Almost. He brought down the paddle again, a tad harder.

"Five. Thank you, Connor."

He put the paddle down and put his hand on Josh's ass. It was glowing like he had a fever, all red and cute as hell. Connor sighed as he rubbed both cheeks, stimulating the blood flow again. Josh moaned, his body all but limp over Connor's knee.

Connor straightened, took the paddle again and smacked out the next five in rapid succession, Josh barely keeping up with the count.

"Ten. Oh, fuck, thank you, Connor."

Josh's voice had that dreamy edge again, as if he wasn't completely there. Connor accepted the cool cucumber lotion Mark handed him and rubbed in a generous dollop on Josh's ass.

"How's that feel, baby?"

Josh didn't reply, and Connor was about to reprimand him when Mark put a hand on his shoulder. "You did great with the paddle, nice buildup and perfect placement. There are two things I would suggest. The first is that you don't decide up front how many times you're gonna spank him. Sometimes he'll be able to take ten, other times twenty or even more. Make it flexible. Related to that is this: right now, Josh is in the zone. It's a place where pain and pleasure become completely intertwined and where he can take almost anything you give him. Making him answer you would yank him out of it, so leave him be. This is the perfect state of mind for something that will bring more pain and pleasure to him. Wanna do a little experimenting?"

Connor nodded. Mark walked over to the cabinets, grabbed a few items.

"Let Josh stand up," he told Connor.

"Stand up," Connor ordered.

Josh came up, his eyes glassy.

Mark showed him what he had in his hands. "Let's start with these. They're nipple clamps, the softest ones. They'll bring a constant pain-pressure that Josh should appreciate. Want me to show you how to put them on?"

Connor couldn't say no, but even the thought of the other guy touching Josh send a wave of jealousy through him. Despite his zombie-like state, even Josh appeared to freeze a little.

"Explain it and I'll do it."

Mark nodded. "Make sure the nipple is hard and pull it forward. Put the clamp on the entire bud, not just a part of it and release it gently so it doesn't spring."

Connor did as he was told. Josh let out a hiss when the clamp set. Connor did the other side, then stepped back to admire his work. Josh looked up at him with big eyes, less glossed over than before, probably because of the unfamiliar feeling.

"Another suggestion would be to experiment with some

sort of cock or ball restraint for Josh so that he can't come when you fuck him. Since it appears you have a lot of stamina, you could come several times and then give him an intense orgasm that's been building up that whole time."

Connor smiled when Josh's eyes lit up. "You like the sound of that, huh, baby?"

Josh nodded.

"How do I prevent hurting him, though? I mean, I've always been afraid to fuck him too long or too intense out of fear of hurting him, either at that moment or the day after."

Mark looked down at Connor's cock. "Well, I don't want to make you uncomfortable, but your size is rather impressive. It's a beautiful cock, though, with a perfect upward curve and well proportioned with your balls."

Connor grimaced. It couldn't get much weirder than this, right? "Eh, thanks, I guess?"

"It's a shame you guys aren't into sharing, because I would love to get fucked by you."

Connor's eyes widened. "You're a bottom?"

Mark smiled. "I'm vers. I enjoy both. But like your Josh here, I like it hard and rough when I'm being fucked, so your cock would be heaven."

"It is," Josh suddenly said. "When he's inside me, it's this intense full feeling unlike anything else. And when he lets loose, holy fuck, you feel so perfectly powerless and wanton at the same time."

Not until Connor let out a stern "Joshua!" did Josh seem to realize he'd spoken out of turn. Josh blushed, but something told Connor he wasn't entirely sorry.

"You know what, a cock ring sounds great," Connor said, shooting Josh a fiery look. "Maybe we can gag him as well?"

Mark laughed. "Whatever you say."

Connor yanked Josh toward him by his neck, smashing

their mouths together in a fierce kiss. Josh all but melted against him, which proved once again how much he enjoyed Connor taking control. He broke off the kiss. "The next time you embarrass me, I will gag you, you hear me?"

Their bodies plastered together, Josh's hard cock poking in his stomach, Connor once again heard the words that made his skin tingle. "Yes, Connor."

"Why don't you get on your knees and suck me off, while I talk to Mark? I need to come a second time so I can fuck you hard and long after that."

The glint in Josh's eyes affirmed he was down with the plan. "Yes, Connor."

He dropped to his knees in an instant and took Connor in, who hummed in pleasure. "Damn, baby, you're so good at that."

Mark looked down at Josh's mouth working hard on the Beast. "I have to say, I enjoy watching you two. The love between you is palpable, but so is the natural Dom/sub dynamic you got going. You've got the classic sub here, Connor. Use him well."

Connor widened his stance, strangely proud to let another man watch Josh at work. Watch, mind you, not touch. His sigh transitioned into a deep moan when Josh tongued his slit.

"To answer your previous question, good lube is crucial, and there's no such thing as too much. Careful prep is another aspect, but you said that yourself already. I can teach Josh more techniques to completely relax and how to angle his body. Is it his hole that's hurting the day after, or his muscles? If the latter, a simple painkiller or muscle relaxant could help. If it's on the inside, you could experiment with giving him an anal douche after fucking and then applying healing oils with a small dildo. It's a lot of work, but it can be pleasurable, and some of my clients report great benefits."

Connor nodded, distracted from the pressure building in his balls.

"He doesn't gag?" Mark asked, curiosity lacing his voice.

"Nope. But I don't push in. He holds my base with one hand, always, so he can dictate how much he takes."

Mark hummed in admiration. "He's really good at this, considering your size. Lots of people would gag continuously."

Once again, Connor had this weirded-out sensation, like he had stepped out of his body. It had to be a different Connor that was standing there, naked, being sucked off by his boyfriend, with another guy watching. He'd never expected to like it so much to have somebody watching. It felt good. Not as good as Josh's hot, wet mouth, though. The familiar tingle built up in his balls, radiating to the tip of his cock.

"Babe," he warned, as he always did.

Josh pulled back and opened wide. Connor threw his head back and came with a contented moan. Without being asked, Josh licked him clean, then licked his own lips as if he didn't want to miss a drop.

It felt so much better to get the edge off. Now that he'd come twice, he could focus on Josh instead of constantly having to push back his own need to come.

Josh's body was on fire. Every nerve was tingling and aching. The two clamps on his nipples were burning, his jaw and mouth were achy from sucking Connor off, the humongous butt plug was stretching his ass, and his butt cheeks were glowing with the aftereffects of the spanking. He had never felt so alive. He wasn't sure what was next, but fuck, he hoped it would involve getting pounded by Connor.

Still on his knees, he waited for Connor to give instructions.

"Let's go with something that will prevent him from coming, or at least, make it a lot harder," his man said.

Mine. Connor is mine. And I'm his.

How had he ever gotten so lucky to find a man like Connor who not only loved him, but accepted his weaknesses and his kinks as well? He wanted nothing more than to please Connor. If the man would ask him to suck him off again, he'd do it in a heartbeat. The peace this surrender brought, there was nothing like it. When Connor was ordering him around, telling him what to do, using him—everything else faded away. He had no fear of having an episode, of dragging up bad memories, of fucking up in whatever way. He had no fear, period. All he had to do was what Connor told him.

Mark came back with a stainless steel device in his hands. Josh's eyes bulged when he figured out what it was. A cock cage. An actual, fucking cock cage. Oh shit, this would get mighty uncomfortable. His eyes traveled to Connor's face, which broke out into a fat smile.

"Get up, baby," he told Josh, who rose with care as not to stimulate the plug in his ass even more. He was already half-hard, and something told him that wasn't going to be pretty when they tried to stuff him into that thing.

"He'll be able to get a little hard, but nothing more. Which should have him nice and ready for an explosive orgasm when you take it off," Mark said, a gleam in his eyes.

Josh eyed the contraption again. Was he really going to do this? His eyes found Connor's. "Step closer," he told Josh.

Josh relaxed. He still had a choice. Connor wasn't deciding this for him, he was still giving him an out. Suddenly, he understood the need for those safe words. Green, he was still green.

He surrendered all over again and stepped in, trusting Connor to know his limits. "Yes, Connor."

Connor and Mark both kneeled, which brought Josh in the somewhat awkward position of having two guys at his feet. As long as Mark wasn't going to touch him, he was more than okay with the guy being there. Even more, it seemed Connor got a kick out of it. The irony of Connor being an exhibitionist wasn't lost on Josh.

"He's too hard to get it in," Connor said.

"Pinch him," Mark said. "For uncut men, the head is sensitive, so pinch him there. He'll become soft almost instantly."

Josh braced himself but still let out a sharp hiss when Connor pulled back his skin and pinched his cock. As Mark had said, his cock went soft immediately. Cold steel surrounded his dick on every side, and before he knew it, his whole length was wrapped in steel circles.

"This one has a lock so you can lock it and keep the key. That way, you can prevent Josh from jacking off by himself or from coming when you fuck him. I know quite the number of subs who wear one twenty-four seven."

The cage closed, and Josh was afraid to move, afraid to breathe even. Mark better have made sure this fucking contraption was the right size for his dick, because he was quite attached to it.

"How's that feel, baby?"

Josh discovered he'd closed his eyes and slowly opened them, letting out an experimental breath. Between the plug in his ass, the clamps on his nipples, his cheeks smarting, and now this iron cage pressing into his cock, his body was throbbing with low pain. He needed something, shivering restlessly. More, he needed more. He wanted Connor, needed him. He wanted to go back to that zone where he didn't think at all, where all he felt was Connor.

"It hurts," he whispered. "Please, Connor."

"Do you want me to take it off?" Mark asked Connor.

Connor extended a finger and raised Josh's chin so he could study him, search his eyes. A slow smile painted his lips. "No."

He looked around the room, searching for something. When he'd found what he'd been looking for, he grabbed Josh's hand. He let him to a broad bench with what looked like soft padding. Above the bench, attached to the wall was a horizontal beam with several leather straps.

"On your fours, hold on to the straps," he told Josh.

Josh climbed up, wincing as pain radiated everywhere. He planted his knees wide, grabbed the straps and hung his weight in them, canted his hips and spread his ass wide. The thought of Connor fucking him again made his cock jump up, but it was denied by the cage. A sweat broke out on Josh's body.

"Fuck, you're so beautiful, Josh. I love you so much, you know that, right?"

"Yes, Connor...Please, Connor, please." His voice broke.

Connor's warm hand cupped his ass. "I've got you, baby. Let go. Let me take care of you."

Josh relaxed. With all the pain humming through his body, he relaxed against Connor's hand.

Mark said something Josh couldn't make out. "I appreciate the suggestion, Mark, but this is where you can stand back and enjoy the show."

Josh closed his eyes, waiting for what he needed more than anything else right now.

Connor's cock brushed his thighs, then his ass. "Hard and deep, baby, hard and deep."

Josh's hole clenched when he felt Connor pull on the butt plug. It took him a few seconds to relax and let go. It popped out with an obscene sound, releasing Connor's previous juices that trickled down his crack.

"Damn, baby, you should see yourself now. Your ass on fire, my cum dripping out of your hole, your gorgeous cock all caged up for me... You're mine, Joshua. I love you, so much."

Josh had about a second to brace himself, feeling Connor line up his cock, and then he slid in. He gave a careful thrust, testing to see if Josh could take him. Josh canted his hips even more, pushed his ass up, bore down and took him in all the way.

Connor let out a grunt when he was fully inside. Two strong hands grabbed Josh's hips. Connor bent over and kissed his neck. "You know it's gonna take a while for me to come again, so you're in for a hard, long fuck, baby. I'm gonna hammer that perfect ass of yours till I'm done, and maybe I'll drill it some more after that. You're so tight and slick and hot, I may never wanna stop fucking you."

Every word out of Connor's mouth danced over Josh's skin, teasing his nerves, his brain. The images conjured up by Connor's dirty little speech... Right now, he didn't care if Connor wanted to fuck him for hours. He'd die a happy man. Not even the fact that he couldn't come himself made the pleasure any less. All he wanted was that thick cock in his ass, pounding him hard. Impatiently, he pushed back his ass, urging Connor to get a fucking move on.

"Such a needy little bottom." Josh could hear the smile

in Connor's voice at these all-too-familiar words. Fuck, yeah, he was needy. And he didn't give a shit. He moved his ass again.

Connor laughed, a full-out belly laugh that made Josh smile—a smile that disappeared when Connor pulled back and thrust in hard and deep. Fuck, yeah..

The rhythm Connor set was steady, but each thrust was deep and so powerful Josh had to hold on with all he had to prevent himself from being fucked off the bench. It hurt, but it hurt so good. Everything else faded away. Connor's fingers dug hard into his hips—probably leaving bruises.

That was the last coherent thought Josh had as his brain disengaged, and he stopped thinking. His whole being centered on his body where every nerve was being assaulted in the most delicious way. His ass completely full, his cock stinging something fierce, his balls furiously throbbing and tight, his nipples and butt cheeks smarting like a mother-fucker—he was in heaven.

He lost all concept of time, had no idea how long Connor had been nailing him when his lover upped the speed and fired off a furious round of thrusts before erupting inside him all over again. A growl of ecstasy filled the room, followed by almost desperate grunts as Connor fucked him relentlessly to squeeze the last drops of cum out.

Limp, Josh hung in the straps, barely able to support his own weight on his legs. He didn't react when Connor pulled out, just hung on till his man would take care of him. He didn't have to wait long till familiar hands unhooked his wrists and hands from the straps.

"You were amazing, baby," Connor praised him, as Josh collapsed in his arms.

His body was turned over. Josh heard a click, then the pressure on his cock disappeared as the cage was taken off.

It was replaced by Connor's hot mouth, taking him in as far as he could, sucking hard. Josh clenched his eyes as the pressure that had built up in his balls forced its way out to his cock. Within seconds, he spewed into Connor's mouth. His hips jerking, his back arching to fuck Connor's mouth as deep as he could. His vision went white, his heart rate furious as he shook violently from his release. Spent, he dropped back onto whatever he was laying on.

Eyes closed, he let himself be picked up, carried to wherever. A bathroom. Steam heated his skin, the smell of sandalwood tickled his nose. Seconds later, Connor lowered them into what had to be the mother of all bathtubs, filled with perfect warm water. Connor laid back and positioned Josh on top of him, looking up. The tub was so deep, they were both underwater to their neckline.

Suddenly, the clamp on his right nipple was removed, quickly followed by the left. Tears trickled down his face as the pain hit.

"Ssshhh, I know, baby."

Josh kept his eyes closed, melting against Connor who started to wash him with a sponge. "You did so good. I'm so proud of you, Josh."

The words washed over him, warming him as much as the water did, soothing his frayed nerves. Tender hands spread his ass cheeks, washed him clean. The pain in his nipples subsided to a dull throb.

He fell asleep as Connor kept whispering sweet nothings to him, holding him lovingly. He half-woke as he was lifted out of the tub, patted dry. Cool lotion was rubbed into his buttocks, another flowery-smelling oil into his hole where Connor's finger pushed it in deep. Josh let it wash over him, completely spent.

16

By all standards, Indy should be tired. He'd driven the entire day yesterday, bringing him from the Empire State all the way to the south of Virginia. Blacksburg, Virginia was new to him, and yet as familiar as many southern towns.

He turned his drawl back on, had switched cars in Roanoke and had insisted on Virginia plates. He was a redhead today—well, this morning. His eyes were green, his wig a deep red that suited his pale skin well. His make up was classy, befitting the Army JAG uniform he was wearing. It was amazing what you could buy online if you were willing to pay for it. He looked rather stunning, if he did say so himself, and damn fucking professional.

And he wasn't tired at all. On the contrary, a holy fire of revenge burned through his veins, and fuck, it felt good. He had dozens of problems he could do nothing about, but this one he could fix. He could do this for Josh and dammit, he would.

Ty Beaufort was where Indy had expected him to be: working at the Fast-Lube car shop. He was a big guy with a buzz cut, narrow blue eyes, and a permanent scowl. Indy recognized him from the pictures the PI had provided. He skipped the receptionist, walked straight into the shop.

"Mr. Beaufort?"

The guy looked up, his scowl lessening as he took in Indy's appearance.

"Yes, ma'am. How can I help you?"

"I'm with the Army JAG Corps, tasked with preparing your case. I need a few minutes of your time, please."

Beaufort's eyes lit up. "No problem. Yo, Casey, I'm taking my break," he shouted to another guy who was putting new tires on an F150 truck. The guy waved, which Indy assumed was consent.

"We can talk in the office," Beaufort said. He gestured toward a small office in the back of the shop.

"Thank you," Indy said, ever polite.

He took a seat across from Beaufort, who lowered his tall frame in a squeaky desk chair. "What can I do for you?"

Indy folded his hands, smiled. "Am I correct it is your intention to file an appeal in your case against specialist Gordon?"

"Yes, ma'am."

"On what grounds? Merely checking facts here."

"On the grounds that the rape charge was bogus since it was consensual sex. He asked us to do him, said he liked it rough."

Indy nodded, fought to keep a professional smile on his face. "And when you say 'us', I assume you refer to privates Winters and Moloney as well?"

"Yes, ma'am."

"All right. And you do understand that by confessing to consensual sex, your public army record will reveal you are a homosexual?"

"What? No! I'm no faggot."

Indy leaned forward, still smiling friendly. "Mr. Beaufort, your defense is that it was consensual sex, that you willingly had anal intercourse with Mr. Gordon. I'm not sure how else this can be interpreted but you being a homosexual."

"Fuck, no, I'm no faggot. Pardon my language, ma'am. It's an army thing, you know. Half the guys there fuck each other. There's hardly any women, so what else can we do to get off? It doesn't mean nothing. Gordon wanted to be fucked, and we obliged. Doesn't mean we're queer."

Indy nodded as if he understood, then opened the leather briefcase he'd been carrying. He pulled out a large, yellow envelope, opened it while Beaufort looked increasingly nervous. Did he have any idea what was coming? Fuck, Indy hoped not. He wanted to shock the shit out of him. He pulled out the first picture.

"Are you sure you're not a faggot, in your words?"

Beaufort's eyes dropped to the picture on the desk, and his color changed fast, the blood draining from his face. "How did you... Where the fuck did you get this?"

"And 'this' refers to the picture of you and a gay prostitute who goes by the name of Devious Devin? It's a screenshot taken from a very...entertaining video of you and Mr. Devin. For someone who claims he's not a faggot, you sure seem to be enjoying yourself, Mr. Beaufort."

Small bubbles of spit pooled in the corners of Beaufort's mouth. "What do you want?"

"I'd hoped to have to convince you with the dozens of other pictures I have in this envelope, but I see you already understand there's an ulterior motive. Too bad. I especially like the pictures where you're fucked by—what was his name again? Right, Juicy Justin, a friend of Mr. Devin—while you're sucking off Mr. Devin."

Beaufort was barely able to restrain himself. "I will fucking kill you," he spat at Indy.

Indy leaned back in his chair. "If you want these pictures to become public, by all means, go ahead. I'm sure you've realized by now I don't work for the Army JAG. I need you to listen to me carefully, Mr. Beaufort, because I will only explain this once. If you continue with your appeal, these pictures will become public. I will personally send them to every media outlet in Virginia after I've sent them to your wife, your parents, and every one of your brothers, sisters, and cousins. You have quite the extended family here, Mr. Beaufort, and they're all so active in the Southern Baptist church. I can only imagine how well you being a faggot would go over with them."

Beaufort's hand reached out to snatch his wrist, but Indy was faster. Within seconds, he'd dislocated the man's thumb, causing him to yelp out in pain. If looks could kill, Indy would have been reduced to ashes right about now.

"You're not listening, Mr. Beaufort. If you continue the appeal, I will expose you for the flagrant hypocrite you are. If something happens to me, these pictures will become public. But that's not the worst of your concerns. Ask me what is."

Beaufort shot him a murdering look but didn't say anything. With a lightning-fast move, Indy dislocated his index finger. Beaufort screamed in pain. Luckily, his coworker wouldn't be able to hear it over the noise of the radio and the tools he was using. "Let me try again. Ask me what you should be concerned about, Mr. Beaufort."

He was sweating now, probably from the pain. "What should I be concerned about?" he said between clenched teeth.

"If you continue this smear campaign on specialist

Gordon—and let's face it, we both know you're lying through your teeth—you will experience firsthand the meaning of the Biblical expression 'an eye for an eye'. We will find you, Mr. Beaufort, and we will do to you what you did to Joshua Gordon—times ten. By the time we're done, you'll be shitting in a bag for the rest of your life. Please tell me I'm making myself clear."

Beaufort, white as a fucking ghost, nodded.

"Words, Mr. Beaufort. I need to make sure you understand me. This is not a threat. This is a promise, a given. Withdraw the appeal, or you will pay tenfold for your crimes."

He swallowed visibly. "I understand." He hesitated. "What about Winters and Moloney?"

Indy smiled. "Don't you worry about a thing, Mr. Beaufort. We'll take care of them." He let go of the man's hand and rose. He straightened his uniform, then patted Beaufort on his shoulder. "I'm glad we could come to an understanding. I will check in with Army JAG Corps tomorrow, but I'm sure you'll cooperate, won't you, Mr. Beaufort?"

He didn't wait for an answer but walked out. He'd parked around the corner, giving him the time to drive off before Beaufort would even gather his wits to try and make his car.

One down, two to go.

Winters took even less convincing than Beaufort. The PI had said he was a follower, would do what Beaufort said. Still, Indy wanted to make sure Winters understood the consequences should he deviate from the plan.

"I didn't even touch him," Winters whimpered after Indy had detailed the Biblical threat to him.

Somehow, that pissed Indy off even more than Beaufort's actions. He reined in his temper. "And you think that makes you innocent? Two United States soldiers raped a man while you watched and did nothing. He was your brother in arms, your fellow soldier—and you let it happen. I don't care whether or not you touched him. You're equally guilty."

"I know. Believe me, I know. I've had nightmares about it. I deserved to be in jail, you know? But Beaufort managed to get us out, and he threatened to pin it all on me if I didn't cooperate."

Indy shook his head. What a pathetic excuse for a human being. "My advice to you: grow a pair. Men like you are what's wrong with this country. Now get out of my sight and do not forget what I told you."

"No, ma'am. I won't. I'll call the JAG corps right now. I'll do the right thing."

"The right thing would've been to prevent it from happening in the first place," Indy muttered as he left, but there was no point arguing this with Winters.

Beaufort and Winters had lived about a hundred miles apart, but Moloney was a little farther out. He had settled in Memphis and had found a temporary job as a dishwasher.

When he planned this, Indy had wondered if Beaufort would warn the other two. Winters probably wasn't worth it to him, but Moloney might be. These two were clearly the brains of the operation. If Beaufort had warned his friend, Indy could walk straight into a trap.

That's why he hadn't been a redhead with Winters. He'd been a blond girl in a skanky skirt and a tight top where his boobs were all but spilling out. It was a fucking miracle what a good push up bra and some fake boobs could get you. Winters had been drooling and had invited him in right away. With Moloney, he'd have to be even more careful.

～

HE'D BEEN DAMN lucky he hadn't paid for his stupidity with his life, Noah thought as he managed to get in the passenger seat of Connor's car. Sweat pearled on his forehead from the exertion. Fuck, the surgery had taken a lot out of him.

What the hell had he been thinking, keeping his infection a secret? He'd known it was a biggie but still hadn't said anything. If Indy hadn't woken up from Noah's feverish restlessness, if he hadn't gotten help, if Josh hadn't put his foot down and sent him to the hospital... Noah shuddered to think how close to death he'd been. Sepsis. He knew better. It shamed him, being this reckless with his health, his life.

"You comfortable?" Josh asked, buckling Noah's seat belt.

He nodded. "Let's go home."

Connor slid in behind the wheel, and Josh folded his long legs in the back of the car.

"How's Aaron doing?" Noah asked. He couldn't believe Josh's asshole brother had shown up out of the blue. The kid had some nerve after the way he'd treated Josh. Noah wasn't the forgiving type in general, but he held a deep grudge against the brother who'd gone out of his way to make Josh's life hell.

"He never came back, sent us a message he'd taken Kent up on his offer and was renting a room from him."

Noah huffed. "Renting, with what money? Does Kent know he's flat broke?"

Josh shrugged. "I don't know, and honestly, I don't care. Not my problem."

"I can't believe you let him even stay that long," Noah said.

"Connor kicked him out or gave him an ultimatum, more correctly. I guess he got the message as he packed up and left that same day."

"Good job, man," Noah said to Connor.

The cop nodded. "He's not a bad kid, but he needs a serious attitude adjustment."

"He needs to be taken down a few pegs, is what he needs," Noah muttered.

"The DA came through with the proof of Connor's story," Josh said. "We gave it all to Kent, so Indy should have it by now. I can't wait for him to come home."

Noah closed his eyes, drowsy from the painkillers he was still taking. Home. He'd missed it desperately. Indy first of all, but also Josh, their routines, the privacy. How would this work now that he was coming home? Would Josh move in with Connor? The cop had an apartment close to the hospital. The thought of losing Josh clenched his heart. They'd been together for so long, inseparable in many ways. Living without Josh was something he didn't know how to do, didn't want to, not even now that he had Indy. He'd have to, at some point, but god, it would be hard.

He cleared his throat, opened his eyes again. "Have you guys talked about what you want to do about living arrangements?"

"Living arrangements?" Josh said. "You sound like a commercial."

"I have some ideas," Connor said. "But we can talk about that later."

Noah guessed that to be code for "not in front of Josh", which was wise as Josh tended not to take change well. He shouldn't have even brought it up. His head was still so fuzzy from the meds that it was hard to think straight.

"I don't understand, what living arrangements?" Josh asked.

"We don't need to do this now," Noah said. Oh, crap. He was a fucking idiot with his big mouth.

"I'm asking what you're talking about, not to give a three-hour discourse," Josh said, clearly irritated.

"Baby, Noah will want to move back into the master bedroom. It's his house, after all," Connor said in a placating tone.

"Yeah, so? We can sleep in the guest bedroom. What's the problem?"

Noah almost smiled. Josh could be so naive. "The problem is that Connor has a home, an apartment, with his own stuff. He may not like being relegated to a small guest bedroom."

Noah looked over his shoulder, saw Josh freeze. Apparently, reality hadn't hit until now.

"You want to move back into your apartment?" Josh whispered to Connor, his tone dripping with hurt.

The cop's jaw set. "Technically, I never moved in. I brought some essentials, but most of my things are still at my place."

Noah cringed. That might not be the smartest thing to say right now. Josh was silent as they pulled up into the driveway. Noah knew what was coming, hoped Connor could handle it.

"If that's what you want, then you should go back to your apartment. I'm staying here with Noah and Indy," Josh said, then got out of the car and shut the door.

Connor threw his door open, all but jumped out, leaving the door wide open. "What do you mean, you're staying here?"

Josh turned around in a second, his eyes blazing. "You thought you could order me to come with you and I would say 'yes, Connor'?"

Josh probably didn't mean it the way it came out, but Noah felt for the cop. That one had to hurt.

"No, you stubborn fool. I wasn't planning on leaving in the first place. I know you need to stay with Noah and Indy for now, that you need that stability. I had an idea, but I wanted to discuss it with Noah first."

"Behind my back," Josh fired.

"Not behind your back, but considering the house is in Noah's name I thought it the right order to talk to him first. Damn it, Josh, I'm trying to look out for you, for all of us."

Stuck in the car since he couldn't get out without help, Noah had no reservations about listening in on their fight. He wondered what the cop's big plan was.

"I want to know," Josh said. "The fact I let you boss me around when we're having sex doesn't mean you can walk all over me."

Noah filed that one away as something he needed to grill Josh about later. Or Connor. Or both.

"For fuck's sake, Josh, how can you trust me with sex and not trust me with this? If you want to know, I was gonna propose to Noah we sell this house and buy a ranch that's for sale a couple of miles north of us. Noah will need something more accessible to him, and if we're gonna stay in a house with four adults, we need two master bedrooms and bathrooms. We're nut to butt in this house, and we need more room. This ranch is a completely renovated farm. It's big, in solid shape, quiet, with a new kitchen for you and a nice garden where you could plant a vegetable garden. The asking price is reasonable, and Noah and I should be able to afford it easily."

Noah's mouth went slack. That was a big proposal Connor had blurted out to Josh. Holy crap, the man had clearly given this some thought. Noah hadn't even thought about his limited mobility and what it would mean for his housing situation.

"You want to buy a house with Noah. For all of us to live in." Josh's voice was soft, incredulous.

"Yes."

"You're okay with sharing a house with Noah and Indy."

"I love you, Josh. I would do anything for you, but it's not a sacrifice. I know you love them both and you're not ready to leave them yet, if ever. You being looked after when I'm at work, that's important to me."

Josh stared at Connor as if he couldn't believe what he was hearing, his mouth open. Noah couldn't blame him. He was flabbergasted himself by Connor's proposal. The fact that the cop was willing to do this, to not only pay half a mortgage but allow Josh to stay with people he'd had sex with, wow. Noah could only hope Josh realized the depths of this man's love for him, because that was a big gesture.

"And it's got room for a vegetable garden?" Josh's voice quivered.

Connor sent him a soft smile. "I thought you might like that. I saw you had some books from the library on growing veggies in raised beds, figured it would be important to you in a new house. And it's got a huge kitchen, brand new, with all these shiny appliances you would love."

Josh stepped in, hid his face against Connor's shoulder. "I'm sorry."

Connor's arms came around him. Noah smiled as he watched the obvious love between the two men. His belly went weak. God, he missed Indy. He was damn happy for Josh he'd found Connor, but watching them made him painfully aware of Indy's absence. It was as if life was darker without him. Heavier.

Connor held Josh tight, then let go and cupped Josh's cheek. "I didn't intend to do anything behind your back. I wanted to talk to Noah first because I wasn't sure he'd be on board with this."

"He is!" Noah interjected from the car. If he waited any longer, they were going to kiss and make up, and he'd be stuck there even longer.

Josh disentangled from Connor's arms, shot Noah a guilty look while Connor laughed and pulled him right back to kiss him again. Laughing, they broke it off to help Noah get out.

Minutes later, they were seated in the living room. Noah had swallowed his pride and had let Connor carry him inside. He was still too weak to use his crutches, scared he would lose balance and hurt himself even worse.

Connor had grabbed his laptop. "I'll show you some pictures."

The dozens of photos depicted an old farming ranch, painted in the familiar dark red typical for the area, with white accents on doorposts and beams. It looked freshly painted, new and classic at the same time.

"The house is from the turn of the century, but it has been completely updated." Connor clicked, showed them a picture of a huge kitchen with an island. "The kitchen was redone two years ago. Because they had their parents live in, they added a second master suite to the original structure. They also built a wrap-around porch and a sunroom."

Noah hmm'd. "So, two bedrooms?" he asked.

"No, two master suites plus two extra bedrooms. There's also a study, a formal dining room, a family room, a living room, a finished cellar, a garage with room for three cars and a barn-shed structure. Plus, the lot is so big you could easily add to the house if you wanted to. The whole house is level, with the exception of the cellar, obviously."

Noah whistled. "Lots of room."

Josh bit his lip, sending off waves of guilt toward Connor. "I'm so sorry I doubted you, baby. It's beautiful."

"You like it?" Connor sounded like a kid who had bought presents for someone and couldn't wait to see if he got it right.

"Do you like it, Noah?" Josh asked, insecurity lacing his voice. It had to be hard for him, feeling like he had to please two men. Maybe even three if you counted Indy.

Noah said, "I love it. We should book an appointment to have a look."

Connor nodded. "We'll work out the financial part."

"I can put up half of the down payment, assuming we sell this house fast."

"No rush. I have enough to finance the down payment. You can pay me back later. We'll work out a contract."

Noah's eyebrows raised. "You live in some shitty apartment when you have enough money to buy that? Why?"

Connor's eyes saddened. Josh seemed to know what was coming or suspect it at least, because he took the laptop off Connor's legs and set it on the table. He parked himself on Connor's lap, and the cop's face softened as Josh snuggled up close to him.

"My best friend died in combat, and he left me his life insurance since he didn't have immediate family, except for a biological dad he hadn't seen in years."

About a dozen questions burned on Noah's tongue, but he held back, sensing this was not something to push. "Your friend, what was his name?"

A look passed between Connor and Josh, with the latter nudging Connor to share. "Lucas, he was a fellow Marine. We were held hostage by the Taliban, and he didn't survive."

A shock wave went through Noah as he put things together. "Operation Clear Blue Sky, that's you."

Connor's face darkened and closed off. "What did dear old Dad tell you, the official story that my unit fucked up? He's a fucking liar, and he should've been held accountable for this. It was his arrogance that cost Lucas his life."

Waves of anger were rolling off the man, his body tense as if gearing up for a fight. Josh cringed on his lap, making himself as small as possible. Before Noah could say or do anything, Connor noticed, too. His face relaxed, and he kissed Josh on his head.

"It's okay, baby. I'll calm down, okay?"

Connor reined in his temper quickly, Noah noted. His hand made soothing circles on Josh's back. Thank fuck he was putting Josh's needs before his own. The man had every right to be livid, but he couldn't show it in front of Josh. The fact that he got that scored him major points with Noah.

Noah waited until he saw Josh was relaxing again. "He didn't tell me anything. I was in his office two years ago, waiting for him, spotted a copy of a report that had top secret stamped all over it. Naturally, I started reading. I never was able to resist a red button. It said that an operation to capture two top Taliban leaders had gone horribly wrong since it was based on faulty intel. My dad gave the okay even though unit commanders had advised against it, believing it to be a trap. They were right, because the Marines unit that went in was all but slaughtered. Fourteen were killed, countless were wounded. Two men who were taken prisoner, including the sergeant who had led the mission. When intelligence had finally figured out where they were being held, a SEAL team was sent in to rescue them, but one of them had passed away already."

Connor held Noah's gaze, his face tight even though he was still cuddling Josh, stroking his back. "They used our own enhanced interrogation techniques, thought we could appreciate the irony. Lucas died from water boarding." He swallowed. "They threw his body back in with me until the smell of his decay got too bad for them to handle, even for a few minutes a day. Lucas was buried in a hole, somewhere. They're still trying to recover his body to give him the proper burial at Arlington."

"And the army buried the truth, denied responsibility." At Connor's surprised look, Noah said, "I read the report, remember? I know what happened. I also heard the official version, which couldn't be further from the truth."

"Your dad is a fucking asshole and a first class liar."

"I know."

"At least we agree on that."

Noah's face softened. "We agree on more, Connor. What you're doing with the ranch, it's a beautiful gesture, man. I deeply appreciate it, both for myself and Indy, as well as for Josh."

"I meant what I said. I would do anything for Josh. So you're on board?"

"Hell, yeah. Let's have a look at that ranch ASAP to see if it fits our needs, but it looks great. I like that the two masters are somewhat separate so we still have some privacy." He grinned, knowing it wouldn't be him and Indy needing privacy. Josh met his eyes and shot him a saucy smile that affirmed he knew what Noah was referring to. Noah wasn't sure what those two were doing together, but it wasn't plain vanilla sex, that much was clear.

Connor ignored Noah's remark, apparently feeling the sudden urge to study his hands. It was amazing how uncomfortable the cop was with talking about sex. Well, being around the three of them would cure him of that, for certain.

Josh was squirming on Connor's lap. "You okay, baby?" Connor asked him.

Josh bent over to whisper something in Connor's ear. The sad look the cop had been sporting transformed into a look Noah recognized with ease. Pure lust. Whatever it was Josh had whispered, Noah would bet all his money it had been about sex.

"Excuse us," Connor said with an admirable attempt to keep his voice level. He got up from the couch, yanking Josh up as well. "Josh and I have something to do upstairs."

Noah grinned, couldn't resist teasing Connor a bit. "Is that what you guys call it: 'something to do'? Admit it, O'Connor, you want to fuck your boyfriend. We're all adults. There's no need to be secretive."

For a few seconds, nobody said anything, and then Connor smiled a big, fat smile. "Oh, I'm gonna do more than fuck him. First, I'm gonna make him suck me off. Maybe twice. Then, I'll find an excuse to punish him and spank him until his ass is all red and hot. After that, maybe I'll let him rim me or fuck me with this vibrator he's got. Next, I will fuck him so hard and deep he will moan himself hoarse. And then, only then, I will take off his cock cage and let him come. That enough details for you, Flint?"

Noah's mouth dropped. What the hell? One look at a fiercely blushing Josh and Noah knew every word had been true. "Holy fuck, are you serious?" he managed. "You like that?"

Josh straightened, his hand searching for Connor's. "Every second of it."

The pride in his voice was unmistakable. Indy had been right then when he'd guessed Josh was a sub. Noah couldn't even imagine doing that. It had been one thing to order Josh to come, but doing what the cop had described? Way out of his league. But man, was he happy for Josh he'd found someone to share that with.

"You're wearing a cock cage?"

As if he needed more proof of the dynamic between Connor and Josh, Josh looked to Connor before answering that question, asking for permission. Wow. Just wow. Connor nodded, and Josh unbuttoned his fly and dropped his pants and boxers, revealing his cock all wrapped up in a sturdy contraption. A cock cage. He was wearing an honest-to-God cock cage.

"Doesn't that hurt?"

Josh smiled. "It's a constant pressure that gets a little worse when I get hard, but I love it. We bought it yesterday, and I've been wearing it since."

Noah shivered. "You'd better get to it, then. I'll put on headphones with some music so I won't hear anything."

"You can listen in," Josh said. "Connor doesn't mind, do you, baby?"

There was a teasing tone that made Noah smile, realizing Josh was intentionally revealing more than Connor would've wanted.

"Joshua!"

Yup, you could've seen that one coming.

"Strike one."

Noah bit back a laugh, realizing those two both wanted to get to strike three. Good for them.

"Yes, Connor."

"Get your ass upstairs, right now. When I come up, you had better be butt naked, on your knees, waiting for me, you hear me?"

"Yes, Connor."

With a last cheeky look at Noah, Josh dashed upstairs.

Connor cleared his throat. "You okay with this?"

"Yeah. I could say I'd kill you if you hurt him, but that would defeat the whole purpose, wouldn't it? I can tell it's what he needs, so yeah, we're good. Did you tell him I won't need him anymore? I know Indy told you of my decision."

"No. I wanted to ask you to not say anything. Josh has decided he doesn't want to have sex with you anymore."

Understanding dawned. "You want him to tell me instead of the other way around."

"It would save him feeling rejected and empower him in making his own decisions."

"No problem. Go upstairs, Connor. He needs you, and I'll be fine here. I'll catch a nap."

Connor nodded, put a water bottle within reach for Noah as well as his pain meds and his cell. "Text us if you need anything. We'll come."

Oh, too easy to resist. "I'm sure you will."

Connor rolled his eyes more perfectly than any teenager could have ever done and disappeared upstairs. Noah whipped off his shirt and with grunts of pain, managed to remove his sweatpants as well, leaving him in his boxers. He settled in on the couch, pulling a blanket over himself. He needed a nap. Fuck, he was still so weak and tired. And lonely. His heart was aching for Indy. He'd promised he'd come, so where was he?

INDY HAD SWITCHED CARS AGAIN, in Nashville this time. He always chose airports because the sheer volume of people there would make people less observant. As a result, they'd be less likely to remember him. Or her, as was the case. He'd rented the car as Laura Downey, same as in Virginia, but he'd changed his appearance again at the first rest stop along the Interstate. The blue contacts were the same, but he tied his hair up under a Nike cap so it looked short. He'd bought loose Nike pants, high tops, and a hoodie. It made him look like a teen boy—nothing like the sleek, sophisticated woman who had visited Beaufort, or the buxom blonde with Winters. Hopefully, Moloney would be expecting a woman, not a teen boy.

He drove straight to the restaurant where the PI had reported him working. That woman had been a godsend. Indy had emailed Houdini, asking for a referral to a PI who did fast and anonymous work and who was located in the south. Houdini had recommended a PI by the name of Jeanette Baker who was based in Atlanta. Within forty-eight hours, she'd given Indy what he needed to nail these assholes. It had cost him—or Connor, more accurately—but it had been worth every penny.

Bella's Burgers was a classic southern diner, nothing special. Indy studied it from a safe distance. It had the old-fashioned railcar appearance, with shiny silver plates nailed against the exterior, rounded corners, a lighted sign, and that whole sixties-vibe. According to the handprinted signs in the windows, they sold the best shakes south of the Mason-Dixon line and the best burgers in Memphis. Good to know.

Two men walked up the street toward the diner, passing Indy's car. They glanced inside his car at him but looked away again. Indy's eyes narrowed. Both had short buzz cuts, fit builds. They walked ramrod straight in the same cadence, screaming former military. Had Moloney asked army buddies of his for help?

Their quick dismissal of Indy told him that if they were Moloney's friends, they were looking for a woman. In that aspect, his disguise had worked. But how would he get close to Moloney to deliver his message?

He could forget about it, go home. Winters would do the right thing for certain, and it would surprise him if Beaufort still aimed to go through with the appeal after Indy's rather graphic warning. But if that was the case, why had he alerted Moloney? No, he wasn't fully convinced, yet.

Or he had changed his mind after the immediate threat had passed. People tended to do that once the shock and adrenaline wore off. They'd start to reason, argue with themselves. Giving up the appeal meant going back to prison, and Beaufort clearly wasn't attracted to that concept. Maybe he was hoping Moloney would be able to grab this woman, and either threaten her until she'd give up, or maybe even kill her. After all, men who were capable of brutally raping another soldier would have no qualms about using force against a woman. To be fair, she'd threatened them with quite the amount of violence as well.

The more he mulled it over, the more Indy was convinced Beaufort and Moloney were on some foolish mission to get their way, which was to stay out of prison. He had to make it clear he meant business without executing his threat, because then they'd have nothing more to fear and would have no reason to do his bidding anymore. It was like what he had experienced with Eric. His biggest fear had always been what Duncan would do to him, but once he'd lived through that, had survived it, it was no longer a threat. Now he feared what Duncan would do to those he loved— and he hoped he'd never have to live through that.

The two men had gone inside, but a few minutes later one of them came outside again. He stood on the front steps of the diner, scanning the street in both directions. Oh, yes, he was definitely on the lookout. Jeez, could he be any more obvious? Indy resisted the urge to duck. That would only make him look suspicious. He needed a plan B.

The man went back inside, and seconds later, Indy saw him sit down at a booth that gave him a good view of the street. Only in one direction, though, unless he craned his head to look behind him, and it wasn't in Indy's direction. He was watching the front entrance, but nothing else. But where was the other guy?

Two minutes later, he had his answer. Guy number two stepped outside and walked off in the opposite direction to where Indy was sitting. He, too, was obvious in the fact that he was watching his environment. Not a casual stroll, then, and definitely not taking off. No, he was on patrol. Indy would have to wait and see what he was up to.

As soon as he'd rounded the corner, Indy got out of his car. There was a cell phone shop right behind where he'd parked, and he ducked in there. It wouldn't be a strange place for a teen to be, he reasoned. While pretending to compare the two latest Samsung phones, he watched the patrol guy round the corner and come up the street again. To his credit, the man was observing everything around him, but he was looking for something that didn't exist anymore. He kept on walking, apparently prepared to keep circling the block on foot.

Next to the diner was a small alley, with an Indian restaurant on the other side. It was almost dinnertime, and things were getting busy. Indy pursed his lips. He would have no trouble getting into that alley unseen, but how would he get inside the diner?

Maybe he didn't have to. All he needed was for Moloney to come outside. But how? He needed to get into that alley first, get closer.

He waited till patrol guy had passed for the second time,

then exited the cell phone shop, crossed the street and walked into the alley. The guy inside the diner hadn't even turned his head. Indy hurried through the alley until he had reached the end where it broadened. Both restaurants had large dumpsters there with trash bags sticking half out. Indy ducked behind the dumpster of the Indian restaurant, wanting to make sure he couldn't be spotted from the street.

He looked at the back of the diner. It had no windows, but it did have a door, and the Indian restaurant was the same. That had to be an emergency exit, probably for the kitchen staff since the kitchen had to be located in the back. He checked the roofs, the walls, and anything else where a camera could be hidden but didn't see anything. It seemed they weren't monitoring the back.

An idea popped into his head and he smiled. Moloney would be in the kitchen, being a dishwasher. He was expecting trouble to walk in through the front door, not the emergency exit in the back. Big mistake.

He waited till patrol guy had passed again, then pushed the trash containers as quietly as he could farther into the alley. He put three side by side so they were blocking the alley. Someone had thrown a stack of paper placemats in the diner's dumpster—presumably because they were replaced with newer ones. Indy grabbed a lighter from his backpack—he was like a fucking boy scout, so prepared—and put it in his pocket. Now all he had to do was wait. If patrol guy was any good, he'd notice the dumpsters and would come investigate.

It took him three rounds before he noticed, but when he did, he walked straight into the alley. Indy was counting on him not warning the others before he knew there was something to be concerned about. Hopefully, the guy inside the diner hadn't seen his friend enter the alley. Indy hid behind another dumpster, one he hadn't needed. Footsteps crunched on the asphalt. When they were close, he stepped out.

The guy had his back turned toward him, studying the dumpsters.

"Surprise," Indy said.

The guy whipped around, but Indy was faster. He jumped up, hand and leg in perfect coordination. The guy was down on the ground before he could even utter a sound. A solid kick to your carotid artery would do that.

Indy dragged him away. Damn, that guy was heavier than he looked. He needed to be far away for the next phase of the plan. Behind the dumpsters was a shed on the Indian side, and he dumped the guy there, then tied his arms and legs with tie wraps. For good measure, he took off the guy's steel-toed shoes since some brainiac had made a YouTube video about escaping from tie wraps using your shoelaces that had gone viral. Indy wasn't taking any chances.

He duct-taped the guy's mouth, made sure his breathing was okay. He'd come around in a minute or so, but that was fine. He wouldn't be going anywhere. Time for phase two.

Indy crumpled the paper placemats and spread them out on top of each of the three dumpsters. He got out his lighter and lit them, one by one. Within seconds, each of the dumpsters had a nice fire going. Now all he had to do was make a phone call. He grabbed his phone and dialed the number.

"Bella's Burgers, how may I help you?"

"There's a fire in the alley next to the diner. I'm across the street, and I can see it. You need to pull the fire alarm, now!"

The flames were spreading inside the dumpsters, and heat was developing. The fire department better hurry the fuck up. Indy pulled back behind the diner and hid behind stacks and stacks of empty crates. Seconds later, an ear-splitting shrieking noise started. The back door burst open, and three men stumbled out. He recognized Moloney right away from the PI's pictures.

"Damn it, someone set the dumpsters on fire," one of the other two guys shouted. "We need to get a fire extinguisher."

He and his colleague ran back inside, but Moloney hesitated long enough for Indy to spring into action. He jumped Moloney from behind, put a chokehold on him and brought him to the ground. He had seconds at most. Moloney was too stunned to respond, and Indy dragged him behind the crates. He put another chokehold on his neck and brought his mouth to the guy's ear.

"If you try and fight me off, I will kill you right now." He wouldn't, but the guy didn't need to know that. Hell, he even had qualms about using this much violence, especially since he was using jiujitsu techniques that were meant to be defensive, not offensive. Still, he had to believe that in the bigger picture, both justice and karma would be on his side.

"What the fuck is wrong with you guys? Was the warning to Beaufort not clear?"

No southern drawl this time. Instead, he did his best imitation of a New York-Italian "Are-you-talking-to-me" accent. He held Moloney's eyes away from his face as much as he could, didn't want to give him more to possibly identify him on.

"Use words, asshole. I can't read your fucking mind."

"I'm sorry, okay? We thought…" Moloney stopped, probably reconsidering.

The two cooks were running outside again, both holding

a fire extinguisher. Indy had three minutes, at most, before the fire trucks would show up. It would be enough.

"You thought you could jump whoever was coming to warn you off, maybe prevent this whole shit from going down? No such luck, asshole. Did Beaufort tell you what we threatened him with?"

Once again, Moloney waited too long with answering, so Indy tightened his hold, making him gasp for breath.

"He said...you'd rape us."

Indy loosened his hold. As much as he wanted to punish the guy, he didn't want to kill him. "Tenfold, dipshit. Remember that. You two lowlifes raped Gordon until he bled, and we will do that tenfold to you. You will never, ever want to have sex for the rest of your life, you feel me?"

Moloney's answer was barely audible, but his frozen body told Indy the message had been received. "Yes."

"Did Beaufort tell you about the pictures?"

"What pictures?" Good, he was learning fast.

"Of Beaufort with his male whores. The guy is a bona fide faggot in case you missed it. Wanna know what we have on you?"

"No. Yes."

Indy smiled. "Pretty sure your wife doesn't know about your son, does she? The one with that blond tramp from Nashville? And the blond tramp doesn't know about the wife, now does she? Also, you told them both you went to prison for theft, not rape."

"Fuck, please. I'll do whatever you want."

"You will withdraw the appeal, or I swear to God, we will fuck up your life first, and then come after you. You've seen how easy it is for us to get to you. By the time we're done, you'll dream of being back in prison. Tell me you understand me."

"I promise. God, please, I'll do what you say."

A sour smell permeated the air, and Indy crinkled his nose. What the fuck is that? He looked down. Holy fuck, Moloney had pissed himself. Revenge wasn't sweet at all. It smelled like dirty urine.

"You have twenty-four hours. If I call the Army JAG Corps tomorrow and you haven't withdrawn the appeal, your life is over, do you feel me?"

"Yes."

"Good," Indy said, then tightened his hold until the guy passed out.

In the distance, sirens announced the impending arrival of the fire department. Time to get the fuck out of there. He peered around the crates. Both cooks were still busy putting out the flames, getting help from their Indian counterparts. Good.

Indy got up, eyeballed the wall next to him, then jumped up and hoisted himself over. It was the back side of a coffee shop of some sorts, and he strolled through the connecting alley to the front. The guy who had been watching the street from the diner stood at the entrance to the alley between the diner and the Indian restaurant, agitated because he couldn't get to the back. He had his phone to his ear, was probably trying to call one or both of his friends.

Good luck with that. Indy slipped out into the street. He circled the block till he got back to his car. By now the fire department was arriving, two big trucks parking in front of the diner. He waited till the trucks had passed him, then drove off without a care in the world.

Three down.

17

J osh's heart broke for Noah. The day after Noah had come home, Indy still hadn't shown up. Josh didn't even want to consider the unthinkable, that Indy had decided not to come back.

He'll come back. He has to. He loves Noah too much. And he knows how much we love him.

Josh's chest constricted, and he pressed a fist against his heart. It felt egocentric, but he missed Indy, too. Horribly, if he was honest. He missed his sweet presence, Indy shadowing him when he was cooking, or the two of them cuddling on the couch. Without him, Josh felt incomplete somehow, like a part of him was missing.

What if Indy never...Fuck, no, stop it. Don't let yourself go there. Indy will come back.

His phone dinged, mercifully yanking him out of his thoughts. Noah needed him upstairs. Connor had gone to his apartment to pick up more clothes and personal stuff, leaving Josh to take care of Noah. He'd been an easy patient so far, mostly sleeping and resting.

Connor had brought his TV over earlier so Noah would

have something to watch and installed it in the guest bedroom where Noah had taken up residence. Noah had indicated Josh would be better off in the master bedroom, which was true since Josh slept better there. Anything unfamiliar threw him off his routine.

Josh took the stairs a few steps at a time, burst into the guest bedroom. "You okay?"

Noah had dragged himself into a sitting position, leaning against the headboard. "Yeah. Bored, but more importantly, I'm in desperate need of a shower. I stink."

Josh smiled. "You do, a little."

"Think you could help me shower?"

His first instinct was to say "Sure, no problem", but then he reconsidered. Showering Noah would mean getting naked in the shower. With Noah. Would Connor be okay with that?

Also, he hadn't told Noah yet about his decision. Since Indy hadn't come back yet, Noah might ask him for help, and what would he do then? He had to tell Noah first, but could he do that without Connor being here? Was he strong enough for this, to face Noah's reaction?

Noah was watching him, his lips curved into a soft smile and his eyes understanding. Did he suspect what Josh was about to tell him?

"Noah, I have to tell you something," Josh started. He sat down on the bed, careful not to touch the stump.

"You can tell me anything, you know that."

The kindness in his eyes gave Josh the strength he needed. "I won't have sex with you anymore."

"Okay."

"Okay? That's it?" Josh dragged a hand through his hair. Not the reaction he'd expected.

"You want me to tear out my hair in grief, put ashes on my head, and dress in burlaps?"

Josh smiled. Classic Noah. "No, Mr. Drama Queen, but I thought you might be disappointed or mad, or at least ask why."

"You forget how well I know you. You love him, Josh. It's easy to see, and even easier to understand. You're his now, I get it."

Tears formed in Josh's eyes. On impulse, he crawled toward Noah on the bed, seeking his arm on his good side. Noah pulled him close like he had done so many times before, and Josh found his favorite spot on Noah's shoulder. "I still love you," he mumbled, overcome with emotions.

"I know. Your heart is big enough for the both of us, or I should say the three of us, Indy included. But Connor deserves first place, Josh. He's a good man."

Josh's heart expanded, relieved of the weight of telling Noah this. He should have known Noah would understand. "I love him so much."

Noah kissed the top of his head. "He's good for you."

Josh sighed. "He is. He grounds me, even more than you do. Sorry, I don't mean to compare."

"It's fine. Though you two are two kinky fuckers, dude," he joked.

Josh snickered. "You have no idea. We went to see a Dom together. He's teaching us how to grow in our Dom/sub relationship." He told Noah what he had experienced in his session with Master Mark.

"Wow," Noah said. "Just, wow. I had no idea. I can tell you're really into this."

"I love it," Josh said simply. "There's a peace in submitting to Connor that completely relaxes me. I always fall asleep after a session."

Noah snorted. "No wonder if the guy fucks you that intensely. Indy saw his dick when I decked him in the kitchen. Said it was huge."

"Trust me, it is. And I take every inch of it and fucking love it."

"You are a kinky little fuck, aren't you?"

How liberating it was to talk about this with Noah. Josh had feared losing this aspect of their friendship, the ability to talk about anything and everything without judgment from either of them. But here he was, sharing what was in his heart with his best friend. If only Indy would come home, life would be perfect.

"Have you heard from Indy?" he asked, almost fearing the answer.

Noah let out a long sigh. "No. What if he doesn't come back?"

How Josh wanted to reassure him, but he couldn't. "Do you have any reason to believe he won't?"

"He's so scared, Josh. Scared of being found, but even more of being found with us. He fears what those fuckers will do to me, to you, to anyone Indy loves. And how can I blame him for that? Connor checked, and there is a contract on his head. Two hundred grand. Alive. They don't want him killed. They want to torture him, then kill him. With an amount like that, there's got to be some bad people looking for him everywhere."

"He'll never be safe as long as Duncan Fitzpatrick is alive," Josh concluded, his heart heavy all over again, if for a different reason.

"Or in jail," Noah said.

"Would Indy be willing to testify after all?" Josh thought out loud.

"I don't know if I want him to. It's a catch-22, you know.

Testifying could get him killed, but not testifying means being on the run forever. There's no solution here, at least, not one that I can see."

If there was a way out of this, Josh didn't see it either. Until Indy came home, there was little they could do.

"I'll text Connor and ask him if I can help you shower," he said, raising his head and kissing Noah on his lips.

"Thank you."

Connor's answer came fast. "Fine. Keep your cage on."

Josh smiled. "Let's go get you cleaned up, because you really do stink."

Minutes later, they were both in the shower. Noah was leaning heavily on the handrails while Josh was attending to him. He'd put a plastic bag around Noah's leg and had taped it off so water couldn't come in. Noah groaned as Josh lathered his hair with shampoo, giving a little scalp massage while he was at it. "Damn, that feels good. It's been, like, a week since I washed my hair."

"You need a haircut."

"Yeah, amongst other things."

"Lean back so I can rinse it out."

Noah shook his head when it was clean. "So much better."

Josh grabbed a sponge and squeezed out a healthy amount of Axe shower gel. He inched past Noah to get behind him so he could wash his back. Noah was fully aroused already, which was no surprise. His body remembered. Josh's own cock wanted to stir as well but had no way to go with the cage around it.

"Connor makes you wear that?" Noah asked.

"I want to. It's part of the dynamic. And I like that I can't even get hard without Connor's permission."

"Damn right," Connor's voice said.

Josh found him leaning against the wall, studying the two of them with burning eyes. "Hi, baby," he said, happy.

"Sure, walk right in. It's not like I'm naked in the shower, or anything," Noah muttered.

"With my boyfriend. And you have zero right to talk, considering how you let your own boyfriend watch while you fucked another man."

Josh had stopped worrying about this dynamic between Noah and Connor. Apparently, they both got a rise out of teasing each other like this. Whatever, as long as they got along.

"True," Noah admitted. "Wanna return the favor? I could watch while you ravish our Josh here."

Josh grinned, squeezed past Noah again and washed his front.

"I wouldn't do that to you," Connor said.

"Oh, you think I would get jealous?"

"No. More like performance anxiety and feelings of inadequacy," Connor said with a straight face.

Josh's body shook with laughter, and Noah smirked, too. "I heard rumors," Noah said.

"Did you, now? Then you know why I want to protect your fragile ego, Flint."

"Fragile ego, my ass," Josh muttered. He'd reached Noah's cock and kneeled. He grabbed it, washed it without even thinking about it.

"You like watching your boyfriend on his knees, washing my dick?"

Josh froze. He shot a quick look over his shoulder. Had he fucked up? Connor's smile assured him he was fine. He continued, curious how Connor would respond.

"Not particularly. But let's see how you like this. Josh, come here."

Josh dropped the sponge immediately and walked out of the shower stall, dripping wet. What was Connor's intention?

"You did good, babe, asking me for permission. As a reward, I'm gonna let you suck me off now."

Josh's eyes grew big. Was Connor serious? Hell, yeah, he was. Oh, damn, payback was a bitch. His answer came swift and definitive. "Yes, Connor. Thank you, Connor."

He sunk to his knees on the plush bath mat, unbuckled Connor's belt and unzipped him. Seconds later, he held that beautiful cock in his hands. Noah gasped behind him, but Josh ignored him. He took a tentative lick from the base to the tip, licked his lips at the delicious salty taste.

He dragged Connor's pants farther down so he had full access. He dropped kisses on the massive shaft poking in his face, then licked Connor's balls, making sure to tongue the hypersensitive area between his balls and his hole. Connor loved that, and he proved it by moaning loudly when Josh put his wet tongue there, swirling it around. Damn, he tasted so good. Sweaty. Musky. All male.

He licked Connor's testicle again, lapped it like a dog, then switched to the other one. Josh dribbled saliva on Connor's cock to create lube, then jacked off at the base while he licked around the crown. He tongued the slit, extracting another obscene moan from Connor.

Connor spread his legs wider, pushing his cock in Josh's face. The message was clear. He wanted more. Josh lived to please. He sucked on the crown, scraped it ever so lightly with his teeth.

"Oh, fuck," Connor groaned. "Damn, you're so good at this, baby."

He'd just gotten started. Josh took him into his mouth and sucked. He teased him a little, but when Connor's hands dropped to his head and pulled him closer, he obliged and went to work. His mouth opened wide as he took him in and sucked hard. His head bobbed as he slid back and forth on Connor's cock, taking it as deep as he could. As always, he held the base to protect Connor from jerking in too deep.

His head found peace even as his own body surged with desire. God, he loved giving head. It was so perfectly dirty, with the kind of discomfort that would've made him rock hard if not for the cock cage. He hummed around Connor's dick, knowing that drove his man wild.

Connor moved with him, fucking his mouth with deep thrusts. Josh's eyes watered, but he had enough air, so he ignored it. Spit dribbled out of his mouth, onto his chin, but he didn't bother wiping it away. It wouldn't take long anyway since they hadn't fucked yet this morning. The first orgasm was always fast with Connor.

Behind him, the water shut off and the sounds of someone jacking off were unmistakable. It seemed Noah was enjoying the show.

"Babe," Connor growled.

Josh pulled back, and a big squirt of cum painted his throat. He swallowed happily, waited for more. Connor moaned again, then erupted in another prolific surge of fluids. Before he'd swallowed it all, Josh was yanked up under his arms and Connor kissed him deeply. Josh closed his eyes, moaning at the dirty kiss. Behind him, Noah groaned and sighed, presumably coming.

Finally, Connor broke off the kiss and pushed Josh back, turning him sideways with one strong hand on his shoulder. He slapped Josh on his butt, hard. "Towel Noah off and get him dressed so I can carry him downstairs. Make sure he has everything he needs because we're not done yet."

"Yes, Connor."

With a triumphant look at Noah, Connor strode out of the bathroom. Josh turned to face Noah, who hung against the handrail. The shower wall was painted with his cum, and his cock had gone soft.

"You weren't kidding about his size," Noah said.

Josh grinned. "Told you." He stepped back into the shower and turned it on to clean off the wall. With quick, efficient moves he cleaned Noah up again.

"I hadn't pegged him for the type who'd let others watch," Noah remarked.

"He's an exhibitionist, but he's only starting to discover and accept it. Secretly, he loves it when others get to watch us."

Josh toweled Noah off first, then grabbed another towel for himself. He shivered. Time to get dressed. Or get busy.

Noah leaned on him heavily as they made their way back to the guest room where he lowered his friend on the bed.

"Let me get some clothes for you."

He came back with boxers, a shirt, and jogging pants.

"Only the boxers right now. I'm gonna take a nap," Noah said.

Josh didn't even bother putting anything on himself, not with what Connor had planned.

"Connor," he yelled downstairs. "He's ready for you."

He could help Noah downstairs, but it was way easier for Connor, who carried him without breaking a sweat. It had to be embarrassing for Noah, but if it was, he didn't show it. Instead, he thanked Connor once he was settled on the couch in the living room. Josh brought him a glass of lemonade and a bottled water, set out some nuts and baby carrots with ranch dipping for him.

"You need anything else?"

Noah shook his head, smiled. "Go, obey your man. Have fun. I'm gonna take a nap."

On impulse, Josh bent over him, kissed him on his lips. "He'll come, Noah. He loves you. I don't know when, but Indy will come back."

INDY SIGHED as he stepped back into the house, coming in through the back door. He kicked off his sneakers, hung his jacket in the closet near the back door and walked inside. The house was quiet, at first. When he listened a little harder, he picked up rhythmic noises from upstairs. Connor and Josh, in all likelihood. Would Noah be upstairs as well? Indy didn't think the cop was the type to let someone watch, but you never knew with people.

Familiar smells tickled his nose. The lemon-scented cleaner Josh always used. The vanilla from the scented candles on the kitchen counter. Cinnamon, left over from something Josh had cooked. Fresh herbs, from the cute little pots in the kitchen window.

Home. This was what home smelled like.

He'd stopped by the jiujitsu studio. Kent had handed him the documents from DA Merrick about Connor. As Indy had expected, his story checked out. It had cleared the way for him to come home. Even more, Merrick had informed Connor he was still patiently building a case against the Fitzpatricks. He had found some secondary witnesses willing to testify. Indy shuddered. Fuck, he hoped they'd be safe. And the DA himself, too. Taking on the Fitzpatricks wasn't for the faint of heart.

He'd asked the PI to call the Army JAG Corps. She had

affirmed what he already knew: the appeal had been withdrawn. Beaufort, Moloney, and Winters were going back to jail for another three years. After that, he might have to pay them a little visit to make sure they'd behave. But that was for later. Now, all he wanted was Noah.

The sounds from upstairs were increasing in tempo. Indy smiled. Someone was about to be ecstatic. Hopefully both. He made his way into the living room and spotted Noah, deep asleep on the couch. His head was turned toward Indy, his face peeping out from under a soft blanket.

He kneeled beside him on the floor, studying the face of the man he loved so very much. Noah still looked pale and tired, which sent a fresh wave of guilt though Indy. He should have been there for him.

Indy's heart stuttered, then fell all over again as he watched his man sleep. How had he ever been able to get a man like this to like him, let alone love him? No matter his fears and insecurities, he didn't doubt for a second that Noah loved him. It was too obvious, too clear to miss, even for someone like Indy who had so never encountered love before.

He cocked his head to listen to what Josh and Connor were doing upstairs. It seemed they were gearing up for another round. Perfect. Besides, it wasn't like they would be shocked if they caught him and Noah. Not in this house.

Within seconds, Indy had stripped naked. He lifted the corner of the blanket up and lowered himself on top of Noah, making sure to stay away from his wounds. Almost immediately, Noah's arms came around him, pressed him close. Indy inhaled Noah's scent, reveling in the feel of naked skin on skin.

Half-asleep, Noah's hands trailed his back, then lower to his ass, cupping both cheeks. Indy smiled as he brought his mouth to Noah's and delivered a soft kiss. Noah's lips opened, and Indy teased him with his tongue, sucking and biting until Noah's eyes flew open.

Recognition was instant, and Noah's face lit up. The pure joy he displayed brought tears to Indy's eyes. If he had ever doubted he'd be welcome after running away, here was his answer. Noah's hands came up and tenderly held his face as their kiss deepened.

"I love you," Noah said, his voice broken, after they had kissed for what seemed hours. "I missed you so much. Please, Indy, please, don't ever leave me again. I can't do this without you. I need you by my side."

Indy nodded, his eyes teary at the love he saw in Noah's eyes. "I love you, Noah. I'm so sorry for running off. I fucked up. I'm scared, but I want to be with you more than anything."

Noah's eyes welled up, and he brought their mouths together again for another deep, hot kiss.

"I need you," he said with desperation when they broke off the kiss, almost gasping for breath.

"I'm right here, baby," Indy comforted him.

Noah found his mouth again. His tongue explored every inch of Indy's mouth as if he had to internally map it all over again. Indy's heart softened. His tough man had suffered without him. There was no doubt how much he'd missed Indy.

Indy traced Noah's bottom lip, then nibbled on it. Noah let out cute little sounds, indicating how much he loved it. He kissed Noah's eyelids, still slightly wet from his tears, then proceeded to cover every inch of his beautiful face with little licks, kisses, rubs. Their eyes met, and Noah's hand rose to caress Indy's hair.

"I love you," he said as if he wanted to make sure Indy

knew for certain. How could he not when the love was radiating from those gorgeous green eyes?

Indy found his mouth again and kissed it wet, deep, long. He wanted to keep doing this for hours. It had been too long. But he wanted more than mere kisses. He needed Noah, longed for him to claim him, fill him.

"Can you...?" he asked.

Noah nodded. "If you do most of the work and we're careful with the stump. I need you, Indy."

Indy kissed him again, drowning in his man's mouth. "I need you, too. I need to feel that you're alive, that we're still here."

Lube. He needed lube.

"Stay where you are. I need lube," he whispered to Noah. Noah's face broke into one of those smiles that made Indy go all weak inside. He gave him one last kiss, worked himself off the couch without touching Noah's stump. A quick search in the living room and kitchen revealed no lube. Dammit. He'd have to go upstairs, then.

He ran up the stairs. The sounds were coming from the master bedroom, so he checked the guest bedroom first. There was still a bottle, but it was empty. Indy swore. The guest bathroom yielded nothing. He'd have to barge in on Connor and Josh. Damn, he hated doing this to them, but what choice did he have?

He knocked on the door. "Guys? Sorry to disturb you, but could I have some lube please?"

"Indy!" The joy in Josh's voice was palpable. A wave of love rolled over Indy. God, he'd missed Josh something fierce as well.

"We're indisposed at the moment, but feel free to come in and grab what you need," Connor's strong voice rung out.

Indisposed. Indy grinned. He bet they were.

He opened the door and peeked around the corner. Connor was sitting on one of the sofa chairs, Josh draped across his knee. Josh's ass was bright red, but he turned his head to send Indy a big smile, so Indy assumed he was enjoying himself.

"Glad to see you back safe and sound," Connor said.

Only then did Indy realize he had gone upstairs naked, and it was the first time the cop had seen him like that. Much to his surprise, it didn't bother him. How could it, with what he was witnessing from them?

Indy stepped inside, then spontaneously decided to kneel next to Josh so he could kiss him.

"I'm so glad you're back," Josh said, appearing not in the least embarrassed.

"Me too." Indy rose again. He eyed Connor for a second, who was watching him with kind eyes, then included him as well. He bent over and kissed him on his cheek. "Thanks for taking such good care of Josh."

Connor looked surprised, then composed himself and smiled. "You're more than welcome. Lube's on the nightstand. Take it. We have another bottle in the bathroom."

Indy waved at Josh before he closed the door behind them and made his way downstairs. He threw the bottle to Noah, who caught it with his right hand. He took his spot on the couch again where he watched as Noah lubed his fingers.

They both turned on their sides, Indy with his back toward Noah. He pulled up his leg, resting his foot between Noah's legs so his ass was open. Without preamble, Noah's index finger pushed against his hole. Indy sighed and let him in. Within seconds, Noah had him squirming. Fuck, he was hornier than he had realized. Noah's finger grazed his prostate, and he groaned.

Noah's mouth came close to his ear, and he first licked the sensitive spot behind Indy's ear, then nibbled on his earlobe. It sent delicious trembles through his body.

"You will not believe what happened in the shower this morning," Noah whispered in his ear, his breath tantalizing hot. He added a second finger. Indy closed his eyes, focusing on the whirlwind of sensations in his body. "Connor made Josh suck him off, right in front of me."

Indy's eyes flew open. "For real?" His words transformed into a moan when Noah teased his sweet spot.

"That man has the biggest cock I've ever seen. And fuck, Josh loves every inch of it."

"I'm perfectly happy with your cock."

Noah fucked his ass with three fingers now, slowly pushing in and pulling back. "Not as happy as I am with your ass."

"Noah, please." He was ready, so ready.

Noah pulled out his fingers. Indy pushed back his ass, opening his legs as wide as he could. Noah's tip found his entrance, and he pushed in. Inch by delicious inch, Noah slid in until he was buried to the hilt. Indy laid back his head so it rested against Noah. So perfectly full. A shiver tore through him.

"Make love to me, Noah," Indy whispered. It felt different this time, so much deeper than mere fucking. Their souls were as deeply connected as their bodies.

Noah's arm came around him as he moved his hips to slide in and out. "Indy..." he breathed, "Oh, my sweet Indy..."

Their rhythm was gentle, slowly building up the tension in Indy's body. Noah's arms never left him, holding him close to his body and his heart. Indy didn't touch himself, wanting to last as long as possible. Anything to feel like this. So loved. So precious.

Noah's face was buried in Indy's hair when he came silently. A sob escaped Indy as he came, too, painting his own torso.

"I love you," he said, his voice thick.

"Don't leave me. Please, Indy, please, don't ever leave me."

Indy's heart rested in his chest, his worries gone for now. Still, he couldn't promise him that. He'd give him the words he could. "I love you so much, Noah."

TOGETHER, they went to see the house Connor had proposed. Snow was twirling down, decorating the barren landscape with a fluffy blanket.

"We'll have a white Christmas," Josh commented from the back seat.

Connor didn't care if Christmas was white or not. It could fucking rain for all he cared, as long as they were together. It was the first Christmas as long as he could remember that he was looking forward to.

"I love Christmas," Indy said. "But I didn't get you guys any presents... I'm sorry, but—"

"Don't you dare apologize," Josh interrupted him. "We don't need presents. We'll have a nice, quiet Christmas at home, the four of us. You and I, we'll cook, and we'll all watch Christmas movies."

His voice was dreamy, and Connor smiled. Josh was so happy Indy was back home. Connor hadn't realized how much Josh had missed him until he'd seen the pure joy on his face when Indy stepped into their room.

"We'll also have sex," Noah added. "Lots and lots of sex."

"Noah!" Indy tried to go for indignant but couldn't quite pull it off.

"We're here," Connor announced. He'd contacted the realtor, had asked her to set up an appointment. He'd hinted they were highly motivated to buy and wouldn't haggle over the price. He figured that would help smooth the way and keep other potential buyers at bay. The owners had sold it before, but the sale had fallen through, so they wanted to get rid of it quickly.

"It's gorgeous," Indy commented as they drove up the long driveway. "I love that red color."

Connor parked the car behind another car, which had to belong to the realtor. She got out as she spotted them.

"Mr. O'Connor, nice to meet you in person," she greeted him with a handshake. He didn't introduce the others, figured he'd keep Indy's identity safe. He was dressed like a guy this time, which was exceptional.

The realtor opened the door with a code on a keypad lock. "You indicated you wanted to look around by yourself first, so I'll be in my car waiting. Let me know if you have any questions."

Connor nodded. They didn't need some stranger to watch them, judge them. "Thank you."

He got the foldable wheelchair out of the back of the car while Josh helped Noah get out. He could walk using crutches, but he was still weak and tired, so they'd rented a wheelchair for the first few weeks. Noah lowered himself into the chair, and Connor grabbed the handles. Josh opened the front door, and they all went inside, closing the door behind them.

One of the things Connor had loved about the ranch was that it had an open floor plan. The living room, family room, dining room, and kitchen were all connected, creating a huge open space. Because of the big windows on all sides, light streamed in from every angle.

Josh looked around with a huge smile on his face. "It's so big, Connor," he said.

"Wanna start in the kitchen?"

Josh nodded eagerly. They explored the massive kitchen with the appliances that had Josh oohing and aahing. The kitchen looked out on the backyard, which wasn't much to look at right now, seeing it was winter, but Josh seemed to think it was perfect.

"Look, it's protected against the wind from both sides, you see? And this patch gets sun about half the day, which is ideal for veggies. I could make at least three raised beds here."

Connor smiled, noted Indy and Noah looking at Josh with love.

The first master bedroom was the original one, with an adjoining bathroom with a huge bathtub. "I love the bathtub," Josh said. "We could have so much fun in that."

The shower stall was raised, and Noah's face distorted ever so slightly when he noticed it.

"The other master suite is level," Connor said. "This one would be ours, I think."

Noah nodded, shooting him a grateful look. "Okay."

The newly built master suite was indeed completely level, without any thresholds, even. "Their mother was wheelchair bound, so they had it built wheelchair accessible," Connor explained.

"Look at the windows! It's so big and light," Indy said, a big grin on his face. "I love it."

The bathroom was spacious, too, with handrails already

installed everywhere. "It's perfect for me," Noah admitted, his expression relaxing.

They explored the entire house, Connor watching them all anxiously, but Josh especially. He wanted this to be perfect, so badly. Josh deserved a home where he would feel safe, loved, protected.

They gathered back in the living room. "What do you guys think?" Connor asked.

Josh stepped into his arms and hugged him tightly. "I love everything about it. It's so perfect for us."

He held him tight as he exhaled. He found Noah's eyes over Josh's shoulder. "How about you?"

Noah nodded. "Can't get more perfect than this. How fast could we move in?"

"Fast." Connor kissed Josh on his head, let go of him. "The previous buyers have already done a building inspection, and everything checked out. All we need to do is get the contract drawn up, and we're good to go."

"I can't put up a down payment until we've sold the other house," Noah said.

Connor shrugged. "No biggie. I can manage it. Do we put your and my name on the contract, or Josh's too? Indy needs to stay out of the paperwork, of course."

He looked at Josh, who stuffed his hands into his pockets. "I'm not paying, so I say it's you and Noah."

Noah and Connor had eye contact for a second. "No. We put all our names on it. We'll add yours, Indy, when it's possible. We make this official," Connor decided.

Noah nodded. "I agree. It's not about who pays. We're a unit, a family. All four of us."

Josh and Indy linked hands, both beaming. Connor's heart soared. Noah was right. They were a family. And Connor would do anything to keep them safe.

There had to be a way to keep Indy from harm, to find freedom for him to live. Connor didn't know how and what, but he wouldn't rest until he'd figured it out. He owed Indy for protecting Josh, but it wasn't even because of that. His own guilt over the rumors he'd heard about Duncan and his young boy played a part, because he'd known and not done anything. But mostly it was because he realized how deeply Josh and Indy were connected. If something ever happened to Indy, Josh might not recover from it. And dammit, Connor would do anything and everything to ensure Josh's happiness.

He cleared his throat. "All right, then. Let's buy ourselves a house and make it our home."

(To be continued in No Fear - Start reading now!)

FREEBIES

If you love FREE novellas and bonus chapters, head on over to my website where I offer bonus scenes for several of my books, as well as as two free novellas. Grab them here: http://www.noraphoenix.com/free-bonus-scenes-novellas/

NO FEAR

Don't miss the next installment in the No Shame Series! In No Fear, we'll see how Aaron and Blake find each other:

Confused puppy seeks owner...

Aaron is lost.

 He's lost his parents' approval.

 He's lost his job.

 He's lost his sense of identity.

At least he's out as gay, but all that has brought him is more confusion. He feels like a freak who doesn't fit in anywhere. Even his own brother doesn't want anything to do with him.

Sexy jiu jitsu teacher Blake makes Aaron feel things he's never felt before. Things in his body. Things in his heart. Things he didn't even know he craved, like being cared for, having decisions made for him.

Like being a *puppy*.

But Blake doesn't want a relationship, so how can he want Aaron?

No Fear is a steamy gay romance with mild puppy play elements. It's the third book in the No Shame Series that needs to be read in order. Please note the trigger warnings in the front of the book.

(Turn the page for a sneak peek at No Fear)

SNEAK PEEK OF NO FEAR

The yellow sticky note on the kitchen counter left little room for misinterpretation.

"Aaron: clean your shit up. Now."

Aaron Gordon didn't need a name to know who wrote it. Blake. Aka Professor Kent, the Brazilian-jiujitsu teacher who'd kindly taken Aaron into his home, a home he shared at the moment with two women and an older guy—all victims of domestic abuse. And apparently, Aaron had repaid his kindness by making a mess. Again.

He looked around the well-used kitchen and winced. His stuff was everywhere. He'd left his backpack on the floor, his shoes next to the back door, and his dirty dishes on the counter. He'd even forgotten to throw the carton and plastic from the microwave meal he'd devoured for dinner yesterday in the trash.

A check of the living room revealed the same. The sleeve of the Xbox game he'd played was still on the table, as was the magazine he'd been reading, and the wrapper of his candy bar. He'd even discarded his dirty socks on the floor, right under the coffee table.

The kitchen and living room were common areas, meaning everyone could use them. It also meant you weren't supposed to leave personal stuff lying around. Aaron had his own cabinet in the kitchen where he could store food and china—if he'd had any. His room also had a large closet for his stuff. It wasn't even half-full. All he had left were his clothes. He'd sold his furniture and everything else when he'd lost his job and had to cancel the lease on his apartment in a DC suburb. His clothes and his car were all that remained from the up-and-coming lifestyle he'd once had.

He needed a job. Desperately.

But first, he needed to clean up his stuff. His shit, as Blake had put it, though words like that still did not come easily to Aaron. It was the result of a conservative Christian upbringing, strict parents who did not tolerate that kind of language. He'd never even uttered curse words till a few months ago.

He cleaned up the kitchen first, making the extra effort of wiping down the entire counter after doing his dishes. The living room was little work, which made him feel even guiltier he'd left his stuff there.

It was hard to think of things like that when he'd never had to. His mom had always cleaned up after him, and when he'd lived on his own, nobody else had been around to see. He'd cleaned up maybe once a week, once every other week if he'd been busy. He couldn't do that here, not in a house he shared with others—as Blake had explained to him multiple times in the last couple of weeks. He felt like such a kid when the guy did that, even though they were only ten years apart. And the fact that Aaron had forgotten again, had received this publicly visible reminder from Blake, man, it made him feel like a total loser. A fuck-up, was the better word.

He tasted the foreign, rude word on his tongue. Fuck-up. Yup, that was exactly what he was. An utter and complete fuck-up. And he'd managed to disappoint Blake once again, the man who'd taken him in weeks ago and had asked for nothing in return. Not even rent—which Aaron wouldn't have been able to pay anyway, but that was beside the point. Blake deserved better.

Aaron looked around the living room. It could do with a bit of cleaning, actually. The kitchen too. It wasn't gross, but there was dust, and both the tile floor in the kitchen and the hardwood floors in the living room could use a good mopping. Should he? Yeah, that would make up for his slovenliness.

It took him two hours, but by the time he was done, the kitchen was sparkling and smelling of the lemon-scented cleaner he'd used, and the living room was dust-free. He'd even vacuumed the couch cushions, finding a condom packet when he did. Was it Blake's? He'd never seen the guy with a woman so far, but who knew.

He admired his cleaning work, satisfied he'd done a good job. At least Blake would be happy with him now. He checked his watch. Two o'clock. That late already? Huh, he must have slept in again.

Oh, crap! He was supposed to meet Blake at the jiujitsu studio at two to help him with some stuff. He'd completely forgotten.

He got changed in a hurry and ran out the door. The studio was close, but he still didn't arrive till fifteen minutes past the agreed time.

"You're late," Blake greeted him when Aaron hurried in.

He was dressed in tight gray training pants and a form-fitting black shirt, looking good as always.

Aaron's shoulders slouched. "I'm sorry. I lost track of time. I cleaned the living room and the kitchen?"

Blake's face softened. "I appreciate that, Aaron, but we had an agreement you'd be here at two."

"I know. I'm sorry." He stared at the floor. Even when he wanted to do the right thing, he still messed up. Yup, total fuck-up.

"Look, I know things haven't been easy for you, and I get that you needed some time to figure things out. Time's up. You need to get your shit together, Aaron, because I have no patience for people who don't keep their promises. I need to able to count on you, trust that your word means something, you feel me?"

Much to his embarrassment, Aaron felt hot tears burning in his eyes. Life sucked so very badly at the moment. Would it ever stop? He swallowed, determined to fight back the tears. "You're right. I'm trying, but I don't know where to start. It's all so overwhelming."

"Do you want my help?"

His head jerked up. "Of course, I do!" What kind of question was that?

Blake's expression was kind. "You haven't asked for it, so far."

Aaron frowned. Why would he have to ask for help? Couldn't Blake see he needed it? Why would he make Aaron go through the humiliation of having to explicitly ask for it? "I didn't realize I had to," he said.

"And there is arrogant Aaron again." Blake shook his head. "Boy, you know how to push my buttons, don't you?"

Aaron shoved his hands in the pockets of his jeans,

feeling infinitesimally small. "I don't mean to," he said softly.

"I know, which is the only reason I let you get away with it. What you need more than anything is an attitude adjustment. You have this sense of entitlement that rears its ugly head all the time. Until you get rid of that, you're not gonna get far, boy."

"I'm not a boy. I'm twenty-four." It was all he could say when his soul felt like it had been cut to shreds. He'd never realized how much Blake didn't like him.

Blake's eyes narrowed. "Then fucking act like it. You're entitled to shit, and the sooner you realize that, the better. If you want something, anything, you're gonna have to work hard for it. And you'd better learn how to ask for help, because people aren't lining up to help you."

He would not cry. He clenched his fists, biting back his tears with all he had. "I need help. Please." It didn't come out as nicely as Blake might have wanted, but it was the best Aaron could do right now. He even managed to look Blake in the eye, saw a flicker of something he couldn't identify.

"All right, then. Let's get to work. Since you seem to enjoy cleaning, why don't you start by dusting and vacuuming the entire studio? After that, you can clean the big blue mat with a special cleaning product you'll find in the cupboard below the kitchen faucet. Make sure it's all done and dry before five because that's when the kids' lesson starts."

Aaron's mouth dropped slightly open. When Blake had said he could use Aaron's help, this was not what he had in mind. He'd thought it was a quick job, like hanging up a picture or something. Not hours and hours of cleaning, and especially not after he'd already done the kitchen and living room at home. Besides, he'd asked the guy for help. How did cleaning help him?

"I don't get it. How does this help me?"

Blake sighed. "Remember what I said about you not being entitled to shit? You've lived in my home for almost a month now, without paying rent. Think that's what you're entitled to? Think again. Until you're able to pay rent, you can work it off. Now, get your ass to work, because I have more to do."

FREEBIES

If you love FREE stuff, head on over to my website where I offer bonus scenes for several of my books. Grab them here: https://www.noraphoenix.com/free-stuff/

BOOKS BY NORA PHOENIX

🎧 indicates book is also available as audio book

Forty-seven Series

An emotional daddy kink duology with a younger Daddy and an older boy. Also includes first time gay, loads of hurt/comfort, and best friend's father.

- **Clean Start at Forty-Seven**
- **New Daddy at Forty-Seven**

The Foster Brother Series

They met in foster care. Now they're brothers. Nothing can come between them, not even when they find love...

- **Jilted**
- **Hired**

White House Men

A romantic suspense series set in the White House that

combines romance with suspense, a dash of kink, and all the feels.

- **Press** (rivals fall in love in an impossible love) 🎧
- **Friends** (friends to lovers between an FBI and a Secret Service agent) 🎧
- **Click** (a sexy first-time romance with an age gap and an awkward virgin) 🎧
- **Serve** (a high heat MMM romance with age gap and D/s play) 🎧
- **Care** (the president's son falls for his tutor; age gap and daddy kink) 🎧
- **Puzzle** (a CIA analyst meets his match in a nerdy forensic accountant) 🎧
- **Heal** (can the president find love again with a sunshine man half his age?) 🎧

No Regrets Series

Sexy, kinky, emotional, with a touch of suspense, the No Regrets series is a spin off from the No Shame series that can be read on its own.

- **No Surrender** (bisexual awakening, first time gay, D/s play) 🎧

Perfect Hands Series

Raw, emotional, both sweet and sexy, with a solid dash of kink, that's the Perfect Hands series. All books can be read as standalones.

- **Firm Hand** (daddy care with a younger daddy and an older boy) 🎧
- **Gentle Hand** (sweet daddy care with age play) 🎧

- **Naughty Hand** (a holiday novella to read after Firm Hand and Gentle Hand)
- **Slow Hand** (a Dom who never wanted to be a Daddy takes in two abused boys)
- **Healing Hand** (a broken boy finds the perfect Daddy)

No Shame Series

If you love steamy MM romance with a little twist, you'll love the No Shame series. Sexy, emotional, with a bit of suspense and all the feels. Make sure to read in order, as this is a series with a continuing storyline.

- **No Filter**
- **No Limits**
- **No Fear**
- **No Shame**
- **No Angel**

And for all the fun, grab the **No Shame box set** which includes all five books plus exclusive bonus chapters and deleted scenes.

Irresistible Omegas Series

An mpreg series with all the heat, epic world building, poly romances (the first two books are MMMM and the rest of the series is MMM), a bit of suspense, and characters that will stay with you for a long time. This is a continuing series, so read in order.

- **Alpha's Sacrifice**
- **Alpha's Submission**
- **Beta's Surrender**

- **Alpha's Pride**
- **Beta's Strength**
- **Omega's Protector**
- **Alpha's Obedience**
- **Omega's Power**
- **Beta's Love**
- **Omega's Truth**

Or grab *the first box set*, which contains books 1-3 plus exclusive bonus material and *the second box set*, which has books 4-6 and exclusive extras.

Ballsy Boys Series

Sexy porn stars looking for real love! Expect plenty of steam, but all the feels as well. They can be read as stand-alones, but are more fun when read in order.

- **Ballsy** (free prequel)
- **Rebel**
- **Tank**
- **Heart**
- **Campy**
- **Pixie**

Or grab *the box set*, which contains all five books plus an exclusive bonus novella!

Kinky Boys Series

Super sexy, slightly kinky, with all the feels.

- **Daddy**
- **Ziggy**

Ignite Series

An epic dystopian sci-fi trilogy (one book out, two more to follow) where three men have to not only escape a government that wants to jail them for being gay but aliens as well. Slow burn MMM romance.

- Ignite
- Smolder
- Burn

Now also available in a ***box set***, which includes all three books, bonus chapters, and a bonus novella.

Stand Alones

I also have a few stand alones, so check these out!

- **Professor Daddy** (sexy daddy kink between a college prof and his student. Age gap, no ABDL)
- **Out to Win** (two men meet at a TV singing contest)
- **Captain Silver Fox** (falling for the boss on a cruise ship)
- **Coming Out on Top** (snowed in, age gap, size difference, and a bossy twink)
- **Ranger** (struggling Army vet meets a sunshiney animal trainer - cowritten with K.M. Neuhold)

Books in German

Quite a few of my books have been translated into German, with more to come!

Liebe im Weißen Haus

- **Henleys Liebe** (Press)
- **Seths Freundschaft** (Friends)
- **Calix' Fürsorge** (Click)
- **Denalis Hingabe** (Serve)
- **Kenns Daddy** (Care)

Indys Männer

- **Indys Flucht** No Filter)
- **Josh Wunsch** (No Limits)
- **Aarons Handler** (No Fear)
- **Brads Bedürfnisse** (No Shame)
- **Indys Weihnachten** (No Angel)

Wanders Männer (No Regrets series)

- **Burkes Veränderung** (No Surrender)

Mein Daddy Dom

- **Daddy Rhys** (Firm Hand)
- **Daddy Brendan** (Gentle Hand)
- **Weihnachten mit den Daddys** (Naughty Hand)
- **Daddy Ford** (Slow Hand)
- **Daddy Gale** (Healing Hand)

Das Hayes Rudel

- **Lidons Angebot** (Alpha's Sacrifice)
- **Enars Unterordnung** (Alpha's Submission)
- **Lars' Hingabe** (Beta's Surrender)
- **Brays Stolz** (Alpha's Pride)
- **Keans Stärke** (Beta's Strength)

- **Gias Beschützer** (Omega's Protector)
- **Levs Gehorsam** (Alpha's Obedience)
- **Sivneys Macht** (Omega's Power)
- **Lucans Liebe** (Beta's Love)
- **Sandos Wahrheit** (Omega's Truth)

Standalones

- **Mein Professor Daddy** (Professor Daddy)
- **Eingeschneit mit dem Bären** (Coming Out on Top)
- **Eine Nacht mit dem Kapitän** (Captain Silver Fox)
- **Judahs Dilemma** (Out to Win)
- **Ranger** (Ranger, cowritten with K.M. Neuhold)

Books in Italian

- **L'Occasione Della Vita** (Out to Win)
- **Posizioni Inaspettate** (Coming Out on Top)
- **Baciare il Capitano** (Captain Silver Fox)
- **Professor Daddy** (Professor Daddy)
- **Ranger** (Ranger, cowritten with K.M. Neuhold)
- **L'offerta di Lidon** (Alpha's Sacrifice)
- **La Sottomissione di Enar** (Alpha's Submission)
- **La Resa di Lars** (Beta's Surrender)
- **L'orgoglio di Bray** (Alpha's Pride)
- **La Forza die Kean** (Beta's Strength)

Books in French

- **Le Garçon du Professeur** - Professor Daddy
- **Positions Inattendues** (Coming Out on Top)

- **Une Nuit avec le Capitaine** (Captain Silver Fox)
- **Une Main de Fer** (Firm Hand)
- **Une Main de Velours** (Gentle Hand)
- **Une Main Coquine** (Naughty Hand)
- **Une Main Prudente** (Slow Hand)
- **La Sacrifice de l'Alpha** (Alpha's Sacrifice)
- **La Soumission de l'Alpha** (Alpha's Submission)
- **La Capitulation du Bêta** (Beta's Surrender)
- **Enflammer** (Ignite)
- **Brûler** (Smolder)
- **Ballsy Boys: Rebel** (Rebel)
- **Ballsy Boys: Tank** (Tank)

Books in Spanish

- **Con Mano Firme** - Spanish - Firm Hand

MORE ABOUT NORA PHOENIX

Would you like the long or the short version of my bio?

The short? You got it.

I write steamy gay romance books and I love it. I also love reading books. Books are everything.

How was that?

A little more detail? Gotcha.

I started writing my first stories when I was a teen...on a freaking typewriter. I still have these, and they're adorably romantic. And bad, haha. Fear of failing kept me from following my dream to become a romance author, so you can imagine how proud and ecstatic I am that I finally overcame my fears and self doubt and did it. I adore my genre because I love writing and reading about flawed, strong men who are just a tad broken..but find their happy ever after anyway.

My favorite books to read are pretty much all MM/gay romances as long as it has a happy end. Kink is a plus... Aside from that, I also read a lot of nonfiction and not just books on writing. Popular psychology is a favorite topic of mine and so are self help and sociology.

Hobbies? Ain't nobody got time for that. Just kidding. I love traveling, spending time near the ocean, and hiking. But I love books more.

Come hang out with me in my Facebook Group Nora's Nook where I share previews, sneak peeks, freebies, fun stuff, and much more: https://www.facebook.com/groups/norasnook/

My weekly newsletter not only gives you updates, exclusive content, and all the inside news on what I'm working on, but also lists the best new releases, 99c deals, and freebies in gay romance for that weekend. Load up your Kindle for less money! Sign up here: http://www.noraphoenix.com/newsletter/

You can also stalk me on Twitter: @NoraFromBHR

On Instagram:

https://www.instagram.com/nora.phoenix/

On Bookbub:

https://www.bookbub.com/profile/nora-phoenix

ACKNOWLEDGMENTS

Publishing my first book was a dream come true. Publishing this second book makes me believe in shooting for the stars.

First off, a huge thanks to my readers. You guys sure know how to make a woman feel loved and appreciated. To anyone who has sent me a message about loving the first book in this series: thank you so much. You have honestly no idea how much this means to a writer. We tend to get down after reading critical reviews (Goodreads, sigh...) and appreciative messages like *'I loved your book!'* totally make our day and help us go on.

A massive thank you to my beta readers: Kyleen, Michele, Susi, and Amanda. Your feedback made the book so much better.

Vicki, thanks for the amazing new cover. I love this Connor.

Tanja Ongkiehong, you saved me when my editor/proofreader bailed on me. You, lady, are a rock star. Dank je wel.

Jenni Lea, my roommate-for-one-night, thanks for doing an extra check on the book. I love you hard, woman.

Courtney Bassett, I don't know what I appreciate more about you: your fab smut stash, your awesome book recs, or your spelling/grammar advice. You rock.

To all my new GRL friends: I had such a blast hanging out with you all. I can't wait till next year. I'm not gonna name names, because I'll forget someone, but you know who you are. Thanks for accepting me into your group.

I owe a mountain of gratitude to the members of my FB group Nora's Nook. You guys believed in me before you read one word of No Filter, you pre-ordered this book like crazy, and I cannot tell you how much that meant to me.

My last acknowledgment is to Kyleen Neuhold. Thanks so much for your support. You believed in me before I'd even published the first book, and that gave my self-confidence such a boost. God, woman, I love working with you on our Ballsy Boys books. I can't wait to meet you in real life!